The thudding footfalls of the troll didn't seem to be getting closer. She risked a glance over her shoulder. He was about twenty feet back, farther away than he'd been when she bolted from the bench.

He looked like a giant.

But he wasn't *fast*.

He won't win any track races, Gloria thought. But her terror didn't subside at all. Not a bit of it.

If he gets me, he'll rip me up.

That's absurd, she told herself.

What's the worse that can happen, really?

He rapes and kills me.

A nasty corner of her mind whispered, That isn't the worst.

She glanced back again. Now the troll was even farther behind.

I'm going to make it! If I don't trip. If he doesn't corner me. If there aren't others waiting in the dark places up ahead.

Just ahead, on the right, was the Tilt-a-Whirl. Gloria wondered if she should try for it. What if she had trouble getting over the fence?

No. She didn't dare.

Keep running, she told herself. Widen your lead. *Then* go for a fence.

Once you're on the beach . . .

Light suddenly spilled out of a doorway on the right. It wasn't at boardwalk level, but at the top of a raised platform.

Dunn's place, she realized.

His Oddities place . . .

Other books by Richard Laymon:

FRIDAY NIGHT IN BEAST HOUSE
FLESH
DARK MOUNTAIN
BEWARE
THE WOODS ARE DARK
CUTS
TRIAGE (Anthology)
THE MIDNIGHT TOUR
THE BEAST HOUSE
THE CELLAR
INTO THE FIRE
AFTER MIDNIGHT
THE LAKE
COME OUT TONIGHT
RESURRECTION DREAMS
ENDLESS NIGHT
BODY RIDES
BLOOD GAMES
TO WAKE THE DEAD
NO SANCTUARY
DARKNESS, TELL US
NIGHT IN THE LONESOME OCTOBER
ISLAND
THE MUSEUM OF HORRORS (Anthology)
IN THE DARK
THE TRAVELING VAMPIRE SHOW
AMONG THE MISSING
ONE RAINY NIGHT
BITE

RICHARD LAYMON

Funland

Text copyright © 1990 by Richard Laymon
All rights reserved.
Printed in the United States of America.

Published by 47North
P.O. Box 400818
Las Vegas, NV 89140

ISBN-13: 9781477806289
ISBN-10: 1477806288

This book is dedicated to
Ann Laymon and Kelly Ann Laymon,
my wife and daughter,
my traveling companions,
my best friends . . . with loads of love.

One

He came out of the shadows beside the closed arcade and shambled toward Tanya. He looked like something that had crawled out of a grave in a zombie film—face gray under the moonlight, eyes like holes, head tipped sideways, feet shuffling, ragged clothes flapping in the wind.

Tanya halted. She folded her arms across her breasts. In spite of the chill wind blowing in off the ocean, she was warm enough in her sweatsuit. But now her skin started to crawl as if coming alive and shrinking. A belt seemed to be drawing tight across her forehead. She could *feel* the hair standing upright on the nape of her neck, on her arms.

The man shuffled closer.

Not a zombie, Tanya knew.

Zombies aren't real. Zombies can't mess with you. They don't exist.

This was a troll.

One of the mad, homeless parasites that preyed on anyone—everyone—who ventured near the boardwalk or the beach. More of them all the time. The filthy, degenerate scum of the earth.

This troll, still a few strides from Tanya, reached out his hand.

She took a quick step backward, suddenly suspected that others might be lurching toward her, and snapped her head around. She saw no one else.

She knew they were watching, though. Trolls. Two, or three, or ten of them. Gazing out from the black rags of shadows near the game booths and rides, from around corners, maybe leering up at her through cracks in the flooring of the boardwalk. Watching, but staying out of sight.

"Can y'spare two bits, darlin'?"

She snapped her head toward the troll.

She could see his eyes now. They looked wet and runny in

the moonlight. His teeth were bared in a sly, humble grin. Some in front were missing. The wind wasn't strong enough to blow away the sour stench of him.

"Okay," Tanya said. "Sure." She swung her shoulder bag off her hip. Clutching it to her belly, she opened it and took out her change purse.

"Can y'spare a buck, darlin'?" He bobbed his head, rubbed his whiskery chin. "I ain't had a bite t'eat in free days."

"I'll see what I've got," she said, and snapped open the change purse.

"Whacha doin' out here?" he asked. "Ain't safe, y'know. Lotta *weirdees*, if y'get m'drift."

"I've noticed," Tanya said.

"Purty young fing. Weirdees, they sure like purty young fings."

Instead of coins, Tanya plucked a white card from her purse. She jerked it forward and snapped it across the troll's waiting hand.

"Wha . . . ?" He scowled at it.

"Can you read it?"

"Wha-sis shit?"

"It's a message for you."

He ripped the card and threw it down. The wind flung the pieces aside. "Wanna buck—free, four bucks. C'mon." He jigged his outstretched hand. "C'*mon*!"

Tanya swung the handbag past her hip and behind her, out of the way. She felt its weight against her rump. "What the card said, you illiterate fuck, is 'Dear Troll, Greetings from Great Big Billy Goat Gruff.'"

"Wha-sis shit?"

Tanya lunged at him. Squealing, he staggered backward. She grabbed the crusty front of his coat, hooked a leg behind him, swept his legs forward, and shoved him down. His back hit the boardwalk. His breath whooshed out as she stomped on his belly. He rolled onto his side and curled up, wheezing.

Tanya dug inside the neck of her sweatshirt. She drew out the whistle, turned away from the writhing troll, and blew a quick blast.

They sprang from their hiding place beside the distant

ticket booth and raced toward her: Nate, Samson, Randy, Shiner, Cowboy, Karen, Heather, and Liz.

The team.

Tanya's Trollers.

Watching their charge, she felt a swelling of pride in her chest. She smiled and thrust a fist into the air. All of them pumped fists over their heads. Somebody—had to be Cowboy—let out a whoop.

Tanya turned to the troll. He was crawling, trying to get away. She hurried over to him and pounded down with her shoe, turning his foot, grinding his ankle against the wood. He let out a shriek and flopped. Keeping his foot pinned, she waited. At first she heard only the rush of the wind, the distant heavy sound of combers washing onto the beach. Then came the slap and scuff of the approaching team.

In seconds she and the troll were surrounded.

Nate patted her rump. "How'd it go?"

"No sweat."

The troll disappeared under crouched and kneeling bodies. "Lemme be!" he whimpered. "Le' *go!*"

He gasped and grunted and yelped as blows thumped him.

Turning around, Tanya scanned the boardwalk. She saw nobody. If other trolls were watching, and she was sure they must be—hoped they were—they had no interest in coming to the aid of this one.

"No! Blease!"

Tanya looked down at the troll. Karen had one cuff of his baggy trousers. Heather had the other. They pulled, and the pants shot down his pale, skinny legs.

"Ooocee," Cowboy said. "This ol' boy, he's hung like a mule."

"Sure puts you to shame," Liz remarked.

"My ass 'n your face, bitch."

"Shut up, you two," Nate said. "Come on, let's get him up."

The naked troll, stretched by hands pulling his wrists and ankles, was raised off the boards. He twisted and jerked. He whimpered. He flung his head from side to side. "Lemme be!" he cried. "Lemme be!"

Tanya spread out his coat. Holding her breath, she tossed his shoes and clothing onto it. His shirt and pants felt moist, slick in some places, scabby in others. She gagged once, but went on with her task and wrapped the coat around his other garments. She picked it up. Holding it off to the side, she followed the struggling, spread-eagled troll as he was carried to a lamppost.

Its light—all the lights of Funland—had been extinguished an hour after closing time.

Cowboy slipped a coil of rope off his shoulder. He kept one end. He hurled the rest upward. The coil unwound, rising, and dropped over the wrought-iron arm of the lamppost. The hangman's noose came down. He grabbed it.

"No!" the troll cried as Cowboy dangled the noose over his face. "Blease! I din do nuffin!"

"He din do nuffin," Liz mimicked.

"Let's string him up," Samson said.

"Hang him high," added Karen.

"No!" His head flew from side to side, but Cowboy got the noose around it.

"Gonna stretch your neck," Cowboy said, leaning over him. "Gonna watch you do the air-jig."

"Let's stop wasting time and do it," Tanya said. Dropping the bundle of clothes, she grabbed the loose end of the rope and pulled the slack out. She strained backward, tugging. The troll squealed. The group let go of him. Tanya saw his legs drop. He swung down, his rump off the boardwalk, his feet pedaling as he tried to get them under him. His sudden weight yanked the rope. Inches of it scorched Tanya's hands. Then Samson and Heather and Cowboy joined in.

"Okay, okay," Nate called.

They stopped pulling. "Hold on," Tanya said. She stepped away, leaving the other three to keep the rope anchored.

The naked troll danced on tiptoes, clutching the noose at his throat.

Tanya walked over to him.

"You want to die?" she asked him.

He made sobbing, whining noises. A string of snot hung off his chin, swaying.

"You're disgusting," Tanya said. "You're scum. You're a stinking pile of excrement."

"That means shit," Liz informed him.

"We don't want your kind creeping around, messing with us. You got no business here. We're sick of it. Do you understand?"

He blatted like a terrified baby.

"Hoist him!" Tanya yelled.

The troll went up, clawing at the noose, back arched, legs flying as if he wanted to sprint on the wind.

"That's enough," Nate said.

The troll dropped. His heels bounced off the wood. His rump slapped it. His knees shot up, one of them clipping his chin and knocking his head back. Lying sprawled, he whimpered and tore the noose from his neck.

Nate snatched it from his grip.

Looped it around the troll's right ankle, slid it tight.

"Pull," Nate ordered.

The troll's right leg shot upward.

His body followed.

When his head was a yard above the boardwalk, Cowboy lashed the rope around the base of the post. "That oughta hold the booger," he announced.

They gathered in front of the troll. He was swinging from side to side, twisting and spinning, pawing at the boardwalk. His loose left leg didn't seem to know what to do with itself.

"Now, there's a right pretty sight," Cowboy said.

"It'd be a lot prettier," Tanya said, "if we'd left the rope around his neck." She crouched and glared at the eyes of the dangling troll. "Next time, you motherfucker, we're gonna kill you dead! Understand? So you better get the hell away from here as soon as you're down."

"*Miles* away," Nate added.

With a giggle, Heather lunged in, slapped her hands against the troll's hip, and shoved, sending him high as if he were a kid on a playground swing.

Tanya toed the bundle of clothes toward him. With a small canister of lighter fluid from her handbag, she squirted the coat. She struck a match, cupped its flame from the wind, and touched it to the soaked cloth. The bundle erupted into a ball of flapping fire.

Its glow shimmered on the troll's slimy whiskered face, on his swinging body.

Tanya kicked the bundle.

It tumbled and stopped beneath him. Shrieking, he grabbed his head and jerked as if trying to sit up.

"You nuts!" Nate yelled. Rushing forward, he booted the blazing heap. It rose into the air, falling apart, fiery clothes scattering and flying away on the wind.

The troll clutched the front of Nate's pants. Nate rammed a knee up into his face and staggered backward out of reach. He whirled toward Tanya. "What the *hell* were you trying to . . . ?"

"He looked cold."

"Jesus! Come on, let's get out of here."

They left the troll swinging by his foot above the moonlit promenade, and walked away.

Two

"Oooo, nice gams. Yum yum."

Dave glanced toward the voice, saw that it came from the "mouth" of a green sock on the hand of a beggar woman, and kept walking.

If Joan had heard the remark about her legs, she was ignoring it, just as she usually ignored the appreciative stares, comments, and whistles she regularly drew during patrol of the boardwalk.

"Yummy legs. Where was they? Home in bed, daresay, yes. Snug as a virgin's dug when Enoch bit the weenie."

"She's right," Joan said. "You've got gorgeous legs."

Dave stopped. He looked back at the old woman. She was sitting cross-legged on the bench. Her leathery brown face was turned away as she glared at a young couple strolling by and chattered at them with her sock puppet. The man and woman picked up their pace and didn't look at her.

In spite of the heat, she wore a blanket that covered her head like a hood and draped her shoulders. It hung open, showing the stained front of a T-shirt. There were holes in the T-shirt. A faded skirt was spread across her lap. On the bench beside her was a yellow plastic dish with a few coins in it.

"Go on," Joan said. "Give her a buck. She said nice things about your legs."

"Yours. What was that she said about Enoch?"

"Who's Enoch?"

"I don't know. Something about him biting the weenie?"

"Who knows? Who cares? She's a nut case."

Dave walked back to her. She glanced at him through greasy cords of gray hair hanging over her eyes, then looked down. But the puppet turned to Dave.

"Weee," it said. "Copper legs, here again, gone tomorrow. Copper legs with a Coppertone tan. Fuzzy fuzz legs."

"What did you say about Enoch?" he asked.

The sock seemed to gape up at him as if startled by the question. Its wide mouth was no more than a tuck between the old woman's thumb and fingers. A pretty sorry puppet, he thought. Didn't even have eyes.

The mouth flapped. "Curiosity killed the cop, clap killed the twat."

"He asked you a question, lady," Joan snapped.

The sock shuddered.

"Christ, Dave."

Then flipped over as if dead.

"What happened to Enoch?" Dave asked.

"Gone gone gone," the sock sang. "Mum's the word. Where oh where was the pretty copper then? Home in bed. Nuff said." The sock darted, nibbled Dave's thigh, and scooted toward his crotch.

With a gasp, he lurched back. The sock-mouth caught hold of the edge of his shorts, then lost its grip.

"Dammit, lady!" he snapped.

Joan cracked up.

Dave rushed off without looking back at the crone.

Joan stayed at his side, laughing.

"She tried to *grope* me."

"Going for your gun."

Dave felt a shiver squirm up his back.

"Should we run her in for assaulting an officer?"

"Yuck it up, pal. You'd be laughing out the other side of your face if it was you. Jesus!" He could still feel the damn sock. He rubbed his thigh hard with his hand.

"I'd never get that close," Joan said. "Except maybe to cuff her. And then I'd want to be wearing gloves. And a gas mask. And maybe one of those chemical-warfare outfits if I could lay my hands on one. Those people suck. I had my way, we'd get rid of every last one of them."

"Join up with the trollers."

"Just between you and me, I'd rather join 'em than bust 'em. Not that either's likely to happen. I'm gonna get me a hot dog on a stick. You want one?"

Dave glanced at his hand. It didn't look dirty. But it had rubbed his thigh where the sock had touched him. He was hungry, anyway. They'd been on foot patrol since the fun zone opened at ten, nearly three hours ago. "Grab one for me, okay? I want to wash up."

"Use plenty of soap. It's hard to get those troll-slicks off."

He left his partner in line at the hot-dog booth and headed for the nearest men's room. Funland had two sets of restrooms, one near each end of the promenade. This would be his sixth visit to one or the other.

On park patrol, they made regular stops, Dave looking into the men's, Joan checking out the women's.

"If any shit's going down," Joan liked to say, "that's where we'll find it."

What they often found were loitering bums, folks of various persuasions engaged in sexual activities, and an occasional drug buy. So far today, the only restroom trouble had been a male wino barfing in a toilet of the ladies' room. Joan had escorted him out, looking as if she'd lost the tan off her face.

Dave entered the men's room with his usual caution. It looked deserted except for a kid of about nine or ten at a urinal. The door of one stall was shut. Crouching, Dave glanced under it. Just a single pair of feet, hobbled by jeans. When he stood up, he saw the kid looking over a shoulder at him.

"You having a good time today?" Dave asked, and stepped over to the sink.

"The Bazooka guns are awful neat."

Dave smiled. "I like those myself. They really blast those tennis balls." He tugged a few paper towels out of the dispenser, dampened one under the faucet, and started to rub his leg.

"That a real gun you got?" the boy asked.

"A thirty-eight-caliber Smith & Wesson."

"Are you a policeman?"

"I'd better be, don't you think? Guy wandering around packing heat?"

The boy grinned. He zipped up and flushed and walked toward Dave, staring at him.

"See my badge?" Dave asked. With a wet finger, he pointed at the blue shield printed on the chest of his T-shirt.

"Is that a *uniform*? You wear that all the time?"

"Just on park patrol when it's hot out. Otherwise, we wear blues like normal cops."

"Weird."

Dave was used to such comments. His blue hat looked like a baseball cap. Instead of a major-league insignia, its front was emblazoned with the gold letters BBPD inside the outline of a star. His white T shirt bore a similar emblem. His shorts matched the cap. He wore white socks and blue sneakers. Only the black leather utility belt, laden with holster and gun, nightstick, radio, handcuffs, and half a dozen snap-down cases, marked him obviously as a police officer.

"Kinda neat, though," the kid admitted after a long inspection. Then he ran his hands under water, pulled down a towel, and dried. "I'm gonna be a policeman."

"Good deal. Maybe we'll be partners."

"Naw. I'm from Los Angeles. I'm gonna be LAPD."

"That's a top-notch outfit, mister."

The kid beamed up at him, then said, "Well, see you," and hurried away.

Dave dried his leg. Then he washed his hands, smiling as he recalled Joan's advice to use plenty of soap for the troll-slicks.

His smile slipped off when his mind did a sudden replay of the old woman touching him.

You try to be civil to those people . . .

Gloria's so fond of them . . . I ought to introduce *her* to the puppet witch.

They're human beings, Dave.

Then why don't they act like it?

Great, he thought. I'm arguing with Gloria, and she isn't even here.

If she had about half the smarts of Joan . . .

Forget it.

He dried his hands and hurried out into the sunlight. He found Joan sitting at a small round table at the edge of the boardwalk. She had one hot dog on a stick and a small Coke for herself. Across the table from Joan were two dogs, a paper sack of french fries, and a larger Coke. Dave sat down in front of the meal.

"Trying to fatten me up?" he asked.

"You can't live on bean sprouts and cottage cheese."

"You should've seen what she fed me last night."

"Wanta ruin my appetite?" Joan asked. She used her teeth to rip the corner of a plastic envelope, then squeezed out mustard onto the brown coating over her hot dog.

As Dave watched her, his mouth watered. He pulled the paper wrapper off one of his dogs and took a big bite. The crust of deep-fried cornmeal batter crunched. The skin of the hot dog burst. Warm juice sprayed into his mouth. He sighed as he chewed. "Real food," he said.

"So, what manner of culinary delight did Gloria prepare for you last night?"

"Something in a wok."

"That's a bad sign."

"Stir-fried vegetation."

"Got any clue as to what it was?" Seeming to smile with her eyes, she took a rather dainty bite of her dog. In spite of her care, a yellow dab of mustard found its way onto her upper lip. It stayed there while she chewed.

"I know exactly what it was," Dave said. "Most of it, anyway. Water chestnuts, bamboo shoots, mushrooms, snow peas. The best part was the soy sauce."

"Mushrooms aren't so bad," Joan said. She tongued the mustard off her lip. "Sautéed, they're good with steak."

"Please, don't mention steak."

"Sounds like you're in training to be a rickshaw boy."

"My system is being purified."

"I had a hamburger about yay thick." Joan held up a hand with her thumb and forefinger spread wide. "You mind if I put some catsup on those fries?"

"I thought they were for me."

"They are." She used her teeth on a catsup packet, then smothered half the fries and began to eat some.

"Those'll go straight to your thighs."

"You're the one with the gorgeous gams around here," she said, and poked more fries into her mouth.

Thanks for the reminder, Dave thought. He could *feel* the sock moving up his leg.

"You think the trollers struck again last night?" Joan asked.

"Sounded like that's what the gal was getting at."

"Enoch bit the weenie? Sounds like he was killed. The trollers don't kill them."

"Haven't yet," Dave admitted. "Not that we know about, anyway."

"'Bit the weenie' usually means 'bit the weenie.'"

"Good thinking."

"I don't see them killing someone, do you?" Joan asked. "It's one thing, rousting bums. Murder's a pretty big step from that."

"Not that big. Look how it's been going. When it started out, they were just snatching the bums and giving them a ride out of town. It's gotten a lot meaner."

"Some pretty cruel tricks," Joan said.

"And some rough beatings. They're bound to end up killing someone sooner or later. If they haven't already. And who's to say they haven't? The way these transients come and go, the kids could be nailing them right and left. Nobody'd be the wiser till a body turned up."

"I don't think it's come to that," Joan said, looking down as she stirred her Coke with the straw. "It was just a few nights ago they tied that creep to the Hurricane's tracks. They wouldn't have done that if they're already into killing the trolls and disposing of their bodies. Looks to me like they're still into general humiliation and torment."

"That guy would've been killed the first time the coaster made a run."

"But these've gotta be local kids," Joan pointed out. "They'd know the tracks are walked before the park opens. They just did it to scare the shit out of him."

"Maybe they went too far with this Enoch fellow."

"Or maybe that old bird was just pulling your chain."

"We ought to try asking around."

"Oh, there's a fine idea." She wrinkled her nose. "Spend the afternoon interviewing slugs."

"Some of them must know the guy. Couldn't hurt to ask a few questions."

"We'd need a translator. You know anyone who speaks Bumese?"

A smile broke across Dave's face. "Where's your humanity, partner?"

"I save it for the humans I occasionally meet." She picked up the bag of fries. "You done with these?"

"I haven't had *any* yet."

She waved the bag under his nose. "Go ahead and take one, big guy. They beat the hell out of bamboo shoots."

When the meal was done, Joan gathered up the wrappers and Coke cartons. She carried them to a trash bin. The seat had left red marks across the backs of her legs. If the french fries went to her thighs, Dave thought, they sure hadn't done any damage.

Put her side by side with Gloria, you'd have an advertisement for the health benefits of the very "poisons" that Gloria prided herself on denouncing. Joan was a foot taller than Gloria. She had sleek muscle and flesh where Gloria was bony. She had curves where Gloria was straight and flat. Her skin glowed; Gloria's skin was pallid and dull. Joan radiated confidence and power, while Gloria seemed like a wraith animated by nervous energy.

"You plan to sit there daydreaming?" Joan asked.

"No. Huh-uh. Mind was wandering."

They resumed their patrol.

He felt lousy. Ever since being teamed up with Joan, only

two weeks ago, he'd been comparing the two and growing more dissatisfied.

Sure, there were problems with Gloria. But that came with the territory. You got intimate, you found flaws. The grass was always greener . . . till you got to the other side of the hill and saw it close up. Joan wasn't perfect either. God help anyone who ticked her off.

"Officer?"

One glance, and Dave knew that the four men grinning at Joan were sailors. They were out of uniform, but their bristly heads and boyish faces gave them away. They looked as if they were playing hooky from high school and having a great time of it.

"What can I do for you gentlemen?" Joan asked.

"Can we take your picture? Just one picture, okay? With each of us. You'd really be doing us a favor. What do you say? Okay? No funny stuff, just four pictures. We know you're on duty and all, but we're gonna be shipping out in a couple of days for the Persian Gulf, and . . ."

"Why not," she said.

Dave couldn't believe it.

Seeming neither embarrassed nor annoyed, she let the leader of the group stand beside her. He leaned against her, mugging for the fellow with the camera. And before the picture was snapped, Joan put her arm around him. The kid's face blazed scarlet. When his turn was over, he backed away from Joan, blushing and shaking his head, then whirled around and flopped on the boardwalk. "I've died and gone to heaven, mates," he announced.

The next sailor was a fat kid with pimples. Joan rubbed his brush cut. He rolled his eyes upward. She hugged him to her side and the scrawny kid with the camera caught it.

The third sailor was a grinning black giant. He stood beside Joan as if at attention, ramrod straight, chin tucked down. She leaned against him, reached across his back, and squirmed her fingers into his side. He doubled over, giggling like a woman as the picture was snapped.

Then the first sailor tried to take the camera from the gawky kid in glasses, who'd been taking all the snapshots. "Your turn, Henry. Come on."

"Oh, it's all right." He shook his head. He made a sheepish smile. "We've pestered the lady enough."

"Chicky chick chick."

"Go on, boy, show some hair."

"Henry's scared of women."

"Cut him some slack, guys," Joan said. She looked at Henry. "You're not scared of me. Come here."

The color went out of his face. But he walked toward her. His friends hooted and whistled.

He stood beside Joan. He was only as high as her shoulders. Bending down slightly, she tapped a fingertip against her cheek. The kid looked alarmed and delighted. He leaned in to peck her cheek. She turned her head and kissed him on the mouth, and the camera clicked.

His friends went silent.

When Joan stopped kissing him, Henry wrapped his arms around her and they held each other. Dave could see his face. His glasses were pushed crooked by Joan's cheek. His eyes were shut, his lips pressed tightly together. He nodded, and Dave realized that Joan must be whispering to him. Suddenly a smile spread across his face.

He stepped away from Joan and returned to his friends.

"Lucky son of a bitch," one of them muttered.

The black giant clapped him on the shoulder.

"Have a good tour, guys," Joan said, holding up a hand in farewell.

They backed away in a group, waving, pushing each other, calling out thanks. Henry, silent, lifted an open hand and smiled sadly, as if he were leaving his best friend.

Head down, Joan unsnapped a leather case on her utility belt. She took out her sunglasses and put them on before turning to Dave. "Nice kids," she said.

"You sure made their day," Dave told her.

"Let's move it. We've got peace to keep."

Three

Jeremy Wayne coasted down the hill on his ten-speed Sch-
winn, smiling into the wind, his open shirt flapping behind
him. He felt free and excited.

He was on his way to the Funland boardwalk.

He'd been there last night after a full day of unpacking at
the new house, but that was with his mother. "For a quick
look-see," as she'd put it. And that's all it had amounted to.
They'd strolled the length of the promenade, played no games,
ridden no rides. "There'll be plenty of time for that later," Mom
had said.

Later's now, Jeremy thought.

Whipping around a corner, he left the residential neighborhood behind. He pedaled past the fronts of gawdy motels,
souvenir shops, gas stations, markets and bars and fast-food
joints. The cars on the street mostly seemed packed with
teenagers, radios blaring. The people on the sidewalks wore
swimsuits.

This was too awesome to be believed.

He'd been happy to move away from Bakersfield. The place
sucked, anyway. The way he saw it, just about anyplace would
be an improvement. But this!

This was a vacation place!

And he'd be living here, just a couple of miles from Funland
and the beach.

June wasn't even over yet. The whole summer stretched before him, endless days of doing whatever he pleased—exploring
the boardwalk, lying on the beach, *looking at girls.*

Incredible.

He pedaled alongside the huge parking lot. With no more
buildings in the way, he swept his eyes across the long expanse
of Funland. He saw the arch of the main gate topped by the
grinning face of a clown; the walls that he knew were merely
the backs of the shops, snack stands, sideshow rooms, rides,

funhouses, arcades, and game booths that faced the board-walk; the curving, swooping, ghastly high tracks of the roller coaster; the towering parachute drop; the top of the log ride's slide; the upper reaches of the mammoth, spinning Ferris wheel.

Mom, last night, had said, "It's pretty tacky, isn't it?"

He'd said, "I think it's great."

He knew it was no Disneyland, no Knott's Berry Farm, no Magic Mountain. He'd been to some of the best amusement parks in the country, and Boleta Bay's Funland was small by comparison. Small and primitive and pretty darn tacky.

But his.

And all the more exciting because it wasn't like the other places. It didn't seem commercial, pristine, make-believe, and *safe*.

Roaming its boardwalk last night, he'd felt a tightness in his chest, heat in his groin.

Anything could happen here.

He felt the same excitement as he climbed off his bike at the front of the parking lot. He chained its frame to the bars of the bicycle rack and headed for the main gate.

He bounded up the concrete stairs.

He walked right in.

That was another thing about this place. You didn't have to fork over twenty bucks or more just to get in. Sure, it cost you to *do* things, but you didn't have to shell out a penny to enter.

He would be able to come and go as he pleased—every day.

Though Jeremy had close to thirty dollars in his wallet, he strode past the first ticket booth just for the pleasure of walking in free. On the boardwalk, he knew, there were always booths near at hand for buying tickets. He would just wait until he felt like going on a ride.

He patted his seat pocket, feeling the comfortable bulge of his full wallet. Then he buttoned the pocket flap.

Couldn't be too careful, a place like this. From last night's brief exploration, he knew that there were a lot of sleazy types around.

Heading down the boardwalk, he started seeing sleazy types immediately. A skinny, dirty guy in a straw cowboy hat that looked as if a horse had stepped on it, crushing its crown. A brown cigarette hung off the guy's lip, and he looked as if he hadn't shaved in three or four days. Jeremy saw a fat, bearded biker in saggy jeans. He was shirtless, wore a faded Levi jacket with its arms cut off, and his chest was tattooed with a skull that had a snake crawling out its eyehole. With the guy was a biker woman, skinny and mean-faced. She wore jeans and a fringed leather vest. The vest was loosely laced in front and she didn't wear a bra or anything else underneath it. Jeremy glimpsed the sides of her breasts through the rawhide lacing, but he looked away fast. He didn't want to be caught peeking. And what he saw wasn't all that terrific anyway.

This sure wasn't the kind of crowd you saw at Disneyland.

There were a few clean-cut family types, but he saw a lot of fat, dumb-looking people in drooping old jeans and filthy shirts. Tough guys with sneers and tattoos, many with knives on their belts. Swaggering gals in tube tops and tank shirts. Wild, laughing guys with crew cuts, who pushed each other and whooped and whistled when they spotted a good-looking gal. And bums. This place had more bums than skid row.

Jeremy felt some of his excitement slide into uneasiness.

This *wasn't* Disneyland.

Something could happen.

He began to wish he hadn't come here alone. It had been all right last night, when Mom was with him.

Shit, he thought. I'm not a jerk-off kid who can't go anywhere without his mommy. I'm sixteen.

And nothing's going to happen.

Though a lot of the people looked grubby or rough or wild, there were plenty around who seemed normal enough: nicely dressed couples, families with their kids, scads of teenagers wandering around in pairs and groups.

A lot of nifty babes.

They all seemed to be having a fine time. They seemed oblivious of the creeps.

But they aren't by themselves, Jeremy thought.

"Hey, cutie." The strident voice pushed through the other noises. "You in the blue shorts."

I'm wearing blue shorts.

She doesn't mean me.

Jeremy turned his head.

"Yeah, you," the girl called. She stood inside a game booth, waving for him to approach. Behind her was a platform stacked with pyramids of metal bottles. Both sides of the booth were crowded to the ceiling with brightly colored stuffed animals. "Step right over here," she said. "Come on, lover boy, don't be shy." She tossed a softball from hand to hand. One foot was propped up on the low wall at the front of the booth. Her legs looked sleek. A money apron draped her lap like a towel, hiding whatever shorts she must be wearing. Her breasts, loose under her tank top, swayed from side to side as she tossed and caught the ball. "A dollar buys a throw. Knock the bottles down, you win a prize. You can't win if you don't try."

Blushing, Jeremy shook his head, mumbled, "No, thanks," and hurried away.

Should've tried it, he thought. Shit. Now she'll think I'm a dip.

I could've gotten a better look at her, too. Her face wasn't any great shakes, but the rest of her . . .

"Heya, bud."

Jeremy stopped fast as a bum sidestepped into his path and grinned brown teeth.

"Heya, bud. Gimme a quarter, huh? You're a good kid, huh? Know what I mean?" He reached out a grimy hand. "A quarter ain't gonna bust you, huh? Give a guy a break."

Jeremy felt as if ice had been jammed against his groin. "I don't have a quarter," he said. His voice sounded whiny. "Sorry."

"Gimme a buck, kid." The bum's waiting hand jiggled up and down. "You're a good kid, huh? I ain't had a bite to—"

"Fuck off, dog turd!"

Jeremy flinched and staggered backward as someone lunged past him and whapped the bum in the face with a cowboy hat. "Get outta here! Get! Vamoose."

The bum, ducking and covering his head, rushed away.

The kid—he looked about Jeremy's age or a little older—frowned and brushed off the crown of his hat. "Now I've got his fucking cooties on it," he muttered.

"Sorry," Jeremy said.

"That's how you've gotta treat these scum-suckers." He mashed the hat onto his head and swept his hands along the brim to tighten its curl. Smiling, he held out a hand to Jeremy. "Name's Gibson. George Gibson. My buddies call me Cowboy."

Jeremy shook his hand. The kid gave it a hard squeeze. "I'm Jeremy. Jeremy Wayne."

"Hey, Wayne—like the Duke."

"Yeah. Thanks for getting rid of that creep."

"No sweat, Duke. Mind if I call you Duke? Jeremy's kind of a wimp name, but you already know that, don't you. Just like George. I hate that name George. You with someone?"

Jeremy hesitated. The kid seemed friendly, but maybe he was up to something. Maybe he was even in with the bum, and this was some kind of a trick they pulled to get money out of suckers. Or maybe he wanted to get Jeremy off somewhere and mug him. Or maybe he was a fag.

"Hey, you're here with your squeeze, just say the word. She in the can or something?"

"I'm here by myself," Jeremy admitted.

Cowboy slapped his arm. "Hot damn, so am I. I'll show you around. You look like a guy could use a friend."

"I don't know. I . . ."

"Let's go. Head 'em up, move 'em out."

Cowboy turned away and started walking, his boots clumping on the boardwalk. Jeremy stayed at his side. Why not? he thought. The guy seems okay. If all he really wants is to be friends . . .

"Where you from, Duke?"

"Well, I live here now. We just moved in."

"Yeah? Where?"

"Here in Boleta Bay."

"Yeah? Where?"

Does he want my address? "I don't know," Jeremy lied. "A few blocks from here. Up on a hill."

"I live on Lilac Lane. There's a wimp name for a street, huh? Lilac."

Jeremy knew the street. It was one block north of Poppy. This kid was a neighbor. "Our place is on Poppy."

"Well, I'll be skinned." He slapped Jeremy's arm again. "What grade'll you be going into?"

"I'll be a junior."

"Hey, me too!"

"Small world," Jeremy said. He thought it sounded lame. If he wasn't careful, Cowboy might get the idea he was a dork. He'd lived with that image long enough. Here was a chance to start fresh, to leave the old Jeremy behind, to be accepted as a regular guy. "Shit," he said, "I've been hoping I'd find someone to do my homework for me."

"Haw! Bite my butt. You had one of the waffle cones yet?"

Jeremy shook his head.

"Come on, I'm buying."

At the stand, Cowboy dug a wad of bills out of his jeans, ordered two "Super-Waffles," and paid for them.

Three-fifty each.

"Gosh, thanks a lot," Jeremy said as Cowboy handed over one of the treats—a cone of crisp, sweet waffle at least twice the size of a normal sugar cone, and packed with ice cream that was drenched with chocolate sauce and topped with whipped cream, jimmies, chopped peanuts, and a maraschino cherry.

"Can't travel on an empty stomach, Duke."

"Where to?"

"The dunk tank."

They headed up the boardwalk, eating their Super-Waffles. Though he saw plenty of sleazes, roughnecks, and bums, he no longer felt threatened by them. He had Cowboy with him now. If anyone got funny, he wouldn't have to face it alone.

Cowboy strode along, sometimes calling out to friends he spotted, including a few who were working the game booths. He seemed to know a lot of people—including girls. Plain girls, cute girls, and some who were totally beautiful. And they all acted as if they liked him.

This is great, Jeremy thought. If I can be his buddy, I might meet some of them.

He'd never had a buddy like Cowboy. His best friend in Bakersfield, Ernie, was a skinny, shy kid whose glasses were usually taped together from catching a ball in the face (one

that any normal guy would've caught) or a fist (because something about him just *pissed off* every jock in school), and whose
idea of a good time was raising Anchorage, Alaska, on his ham
radio.

A nice guy, but a real loser.

According to Ernie, all the popular guys in school were
inane assholes, glandular cases, or throwbacks. The good-
looking girls were vapid twits who thought their farts smelled
like roses.

With a best friend like that, you didn't stand a chance. With
a guy like Cowboy, though . . .

"Hey there, gorgeous!" Cowboy suddenly yelled, startling
Jeremy from his thoughts.

A girl smiled at him and waved through the bars of a cage.
She sat on a narrow platform, swinging her legs. Below her
bare feet was a water-filled tank with a glass front.

Even as she waved, a pitched ball struck the bull's-eye,
knocked back the metal arm, and collapsed her perch. She
squealed and dropped, splashing into the deep water. Through
the glass, Jeremy saw her descend in a sudden froth of bubbles.
Like a wind from below, the water pushed her T-shirt up her
belly, lifted her long black hair above her head. She squatted
for a moment at the bottom of the tank, cheeks bulging with
trapped air, shirt and hair slowly drifting down, and shook her
fist at the guy who'd dunked her. Then she stood. Water swirling around her shoulders, she waded to the metal-rung ladder at
the side of the tank. She climbed up.

Her wet legs were shiny. Jeremy saw the outline of her panties
through the clinging seat of her shorts. Her shirt was plastered
to her back, her pink skin showing through the thin fabric.
Her hair hung thick and glossy between her shoulder blades,
almost long enough to reach the cross-strap of her bra.

Leaning away from the ladder, she raised the shelf. Its braces
locked, and she climbed onto it.

"Just a lucky throw, hot stuff!" she yelled.

"Yeah? Watch this!"

"I won't hold my breath."

Hot Stuff threw the ball at the target beside her cage. It
missed and whapped the canvas backstop.

She smirked at him and clapped.

Jeremy thought it was too bad about her face. She was one of those gals who look terrific from behind, slender and shapely, but when you saw her from the front, she was a letdown. As if God had decided he'd blessed her enough from the neck down, so he skimped on her face. She wasn't exactly ugly, but her eyes seemed too close together, her nose small and up-turned and a little piggish, and her mouth too wide. Her front teeth jutted out of her gums like white marble slabs.

Another ball missed the target.

"Nolan Ryan you're not, Bozo!"

The guy flapped a hand at her, put an arm around his girl-friend, and walked away.

"Come on," Cowboy said. He stepped over to the man run-ning the concession and passed his Super-Waffle to Jeremy. "Let me have three of those balls, Jim," he said, handing the man three dollars.

"Couldn't hit the broad side of an outhouse if you were in-side it!" she called.

"Get ready to bite the drink, Lizzie!" He hurled the first ball. It slammed the metal target. Lizzie dropped.

Climbing out, she looked over her shoulder at him. "Nice shot, tenderfoot. Who's your friend?"

Jeremy felt heat rush to his face.

"My pal Duke. New in town. We just met."

"Nice to meet you, Duke."

"Thanks."

She sat on the platform. Cowboy threw. She hit the water again.

Cowboy smiled. "Only way to get her clean. She never takes a bath, filthy scrug."

"Let Duke have a try," she called as she climbed out.

Cowboy offered the last ball to him. "Oh, that's okay," Jer-emy said. "You go on."

"Don't be a woos," Lizzie yelled.

With a sigh, he gave the waffle cones to Cowboy and took the ball.

The beginning of the end, he thought. I'm going to miss by a mile and they'll know I'm a dip.

He wound up and fired the ball.

Right on target!

It struck the bull's-eye and bounced off.

Lizzie's perch didn't collapse.

She cackled and clapped. "Tough luck, Duchess."

Shit!

"You've gotta throw it a little harder than that," Cowboy said, smiling and shaking his head. "Give it another try." He took out his money.

"No, no. That's okay. Some other time. I'm really wasted today. Been moving furniture, unpacking."

"Cowboy!" Lizzie shouted through the bars.

"Yo!"

"Give Tanya a message for me?"

"You bet."

"Tell her about Janet. I want to bring her along tonight. See if it's okay, huh? Give me a call later and let me know."

"You got it. Adios. Don't get your tits wrinkled."

She suddenly looked as if she burned to punch out his lights.

Half a dozen people nearby started laughing. Jeremy was too stunned to laugh.

"Let's move out, Duke."

They hurried away. Jeremy gave a cone back to Cowboy and followed him across the boardwalk. They passed through an open space in the railing and trotted down concrete stairs to the beach.

Four

"Somebody sure knows how to pick a banjo," Dave said. The quick, cheery music was barely audible behind the carnival tunes of the rides, the voices and laughter all around him, the screams of people on the high-swinging Viking Ship, the poomphs of the Bazooka guns.

It seemed to come from somewhere ahead. Dave saw a

circle of spectators in the distance, near the north end of the boardwalk.

"Let's check it out," he said.

"Beats interviewing trolls," Joan said.

Since lunch, they had approached a total of seven indigents. None could be coaxed into admitting knowledge of a man named Enoch. Asked if anything strange had happened last night, one told of being beamed up into a hovering spacecraft from the planet Mogo, where a creature like a man-size lizard stuck a tube down his throat and sucked out the contents of his stomach—which the creature drank as it sucked. One said he'd been grabbed by a pair of albinos who tried to drag him under the boardwalk and feed him to their pet spider. A woman had been visited by the Blessed Virgin, who gave her a rough gray stone and said there was a diamond inside. While the woman told her story, she gnawed the rock as if it were a walnut she figured she could crack open with her teeth. One man ranted incoherently. Another simply glared at them and muttered about assassins. Only one seemed fairly rational, and he claimed to have spent a peaceful night sleeping in the dunes.

Joan had spent a lot of time sighing and rolling her eyes upward. She'd told Dave that it would be a waste of time, questioning the boardwalk's panhandlers.

But it hadn't been a total waste.

After speaking to a few of them, he was half-convinced that Enoch "biting the weenie" had no more basis in reality than the diamond in the rock, the albino attack, or the peculiar feast of the lizard alien.

He heard applause from the banjo-picker's audience. Only a couple of people wandered away from the edges of the circle. Most stayed. Several passersby joined the crowd. A few people moved inward, apparently to contribute money in appreciation of the performance.

As Dave and Joan approached the group, the next number began. "When the Saints Go Marching In." The melody twanged out, strong and lively, with such complex chords and runs in the background that Dave decided there must be at least two banjos. He was listening to a duet, or even a trio of street musicians, banging out a version of "Saints" so fine that those in the audience who'd been clapping along at the start went silent to listen.

Joan stayed at Dave's side while he roamed the perimeter of the group, searching for a gap so he could watch the performance.

A couple of grubby bikers, seeing that they were cops, broke away from the circle and wandered off. Dave and Joan stepped into the opening.

Not a trio. Not a duet.

All that music was coming from the banjo of a lone girl who looked no older than eighteen.

She stood straight-backed as if at attention, her weight on one leg, her other leg forward, heel on the boardwalk, toe tapping as she played. The banjo looked heavy, bigger than some Dave had seen, with thick shiny metal surrounding its tambourinelike body. It hung against her belly by a broad, brightly colored strap. Its neck was tilted upward at a jaunty angle.

The banjo case, open a short distance in front of her, was littered with coins and dollars. Beside the case rested a backpack.

"Saints" ended. Applause exploded from the audience. The girl bowed her head and dropped her arms to her sides. While the clapping went on, several people (mostly kids on behalf of their parents) hurried forward to toss money into the banjo case. Though she kept her head down, Dave heard her murmur thanks to each of those who contributed.

When she raised her head, she stared straight at a kid standing near Dave, wiggled her eyebrows at him, and began playing "Puff, the Magic Dragon."

"Damn good," Joan whispered.

"I'll say."

The girl's left hand flew up and down the banjo's neck, fretting and sliding with astonishing quickness. Her right hand hung nearly motionless while its fingers picked the strings. Except for her tapping foot, her body was rigid and motionless. She gazed straight ahead as she played.

All through the song, the pink tip of her tongue protruded from the right corner of her mouth.

To Dave she seemed very young and very vulnerable.

The backpack showed that she was a wanderer.

He scanned the people gathered around her, trying to spot someone who might be with the girl. Nobody quite seemed to fit the role. That didn't necessarily mean she had no companion, but Dave suspected that she was traveling alone.

Probably hitching rides. Probably sleeping outside.

Sooner or later, a sure victim.

It would be dangerous enough if she were male. The fact that she was female increased the risk tenfold.

From a distance, she might be mistaken for a male. Her blond hair was cut very short. She had a slim body, and her breasts were apparent only because of the way the banjo rested against her shirt, pulling it taut. Her face hardly looked masculine, but it might be the face of a smooth-cheeked, pretty guy who was short in the hormone department.

On second thought, Dave realized, her slender, boyish appearance was a dubious advantage. She might fare worse on the road if the wrong sort took her for a sissy instead of a girl.

She's lucky she made it this far, Dave thought.

Then he wondered what kind of luck that was, making it into Boleta Bay.

She was not a troll. She was a street musician, a roaming minstrel playing for her daily needs.

But the kids might not make such fine distinctions.

And she wasn't exactly dressed for a Rotary banquet.

She wore hiking boots, ankle-high, scuffed and dusty. Her faded blue jeans were frayed at the cuffs, and one leg had a rip that gaped like an open mouth, showing the skin of her thigh. For a belt she wore a brightly colored woven sash that matched her banjo strap. It was knotted at her hip, and the ends of it draped the side of her leg and swayed in the breeze. The sleeves of her old blue shirt had been cut off at the shoulders. The top buttons were undone. A necklace of small white shells hung across her chest. She wore a red bandanna around her head.

The teenagers here in Boleta Bay might very well take it as the costume of a troll.

And act accordingly.

This gal's begging for trouble, he thought as she finished "Puff."

While the audience clapped, he made his way forward along with some others. He took out his wallet and dropped a five-dollar bill into her banjo case. She thanked him. He stepped around the case and stopped in front of her.

She met him with calm, questioning eyes. "Officer?"

"Where'd you learn to play like that?"

"My dad."

"You're great."

"Thank you. Is there some kind of problem?"

"I noticed you've got a backpack. Are you planning to sleep out around here?"

"I thought I might. Is it illegal?"

"We have local ordinances against it, but we generally don't enforce them. Are you with a friend?"

She shook her head slightly from side to side. Her eyes never strayed from Dave's.

"Let her alone," somebody called from behind.

"Goddamn cops," came another voice.

"She's not hurting anyone."

"Why don't you pick on somebody causing trouble!"

The girl held up a hand to silence the protests.

"All I want to say," Dave told her, "is that we've been having trouble with teenagers running around at night attacking people. They've pulled some pretty nasty stunts. They're after winos and bums, actually. But it isn't safe for anyone to camp out in this area. I wouldn't want you getting jumped by these characters. They—"

"Quit hassling her, why don't you!"

"Please," she called, glancing past him at someone in the crowd. "He's not bothering me. I'll play some more in a minute."

"Thanks," Dave said. "There are plenty of motels nearby. I think you'd be wise to check into one of them. Can you afford a motel? Some of them are just around thirty-five, forty dollars a night. And there's a Y over on Clancy Street. I'm sure it's pretty cheap."

"I don't know." She lowered her eyes. "I'll think about it, Officer. I appreciate your . . ."

"Dave. It's Dave."

"I'm Robin."

"Robin." He liked the name. It seemed to fit her. "Why do I get the feeling you're not going to take my advice?"

She shrugged her shoulders.

He took out his wallet again. The bill compartment held three ones and a twenty. He slipped the twenty out and held it toward her. "Take this, okay? Find yourself a room for the night."

Her fingers slipped around the back of his hand and gently pushed it away. "I can't. Thank you, though. Really. That's way too much. You already gave me a five—I saw you. And that's fine. I figure that's for the music. But I don't want to take any handouts. Okay?"

"I don't want you getting jumped by a pack of rabid teenagers."

In the calm of her blue eyes he saw a glint of fear.

"I'll be careful," she said.

My place, he suddenly thought. She could stay at my place. Don't be an idiot. She'll think I just want in her pants.

"It's up to you," he said. "If you won't get yourself a room, at least try to find someplace hidden away. Maybe back in the dunes away from the beach, where nobody'll notice you. And don't come anywhere close to the boardwalk after the fun zone shuts down for the night. That's their favorite place to hit."

"I'll stay away," she told him. "I'll find a good place to hide." Her mouth slipped into a smile. "I always do. My pappy didn't raise no fool."

"All right. Good luck, Robin."

Nodding, she reached out and brushed a hand against his upper arm. "Thanks," she said.

Dave started away. A few people in Robin's audience glared at him as he stepped through the circle.

Behind him, Robin said, "This one's for Officer Dave."

Joan looked at him, her eyebrows high. "What was that all about?"

Before he could answer, the banjo rang alive. He turned around. Her eyes were on him. Her tongue protruded from the corner of her mouth.

Five

"Where are we going?" Jeremy asked.

"Gotta see Tanya," Cowboy said. "What'd you think of Liz?"

"Man, I don't believe what you said to her."

"What was that?"

"You know. About getting wrinkled."

"Oh, that. She likes that kind of stuff. Turns her on."

"You know her pretty well?"

"Are you kidding? She's my squeeze."

"Your girlfriend?"

"You got it, Duke."

He stopped himself before saying "Wow," which would've sounded stupid. Instead he commented, "Not bad. She got a sister?"

"Nope. A cousin, though. Janet. You can meet her tonight, maybe. Her and some of my friends. If you want, I'll check it out with Tanya, see if it's okay with her."

"Great."

They were walking over the sand, winding their way among sunbathers stretched out on towels and blankets. Though Cowboy led the way, his route was the same as Jeremy would've picked if he'd been in the lead. One that took them close to girls. Girls lying on their backs, naked except for skimpy swimsuits, their skin glossy with tanning oil. Others facedown, their backs bare, their untied bikini tops loose beneath their breasts. Some were reading books or magazines, some were talking to friends sprawled beside them, some seemed to be asleep. A few were snuggling with boyfriends as if they thought they were alone on the beach.

Jeremy studied them as he strolled along, working on his Super-Waffle, listening to Cowboy, and sometimes making comments or asking questions. He had a hard time swallowing.

I can come down here every day, he thought.

Man.

Just do nothing but wander around and *look* at them.

Shit, this is *better* than Funland.

Cowboy led him toward a slender young woman lying on a blanket, arms folded beneath her face. Her bikini top was untied. Jeremy could see the pale side of one breast. It bulged as if it were a little bit mashed under her weight. She was bare all the way down to a glossy blue patch of fabric clinging to her rump. The seat of her swimsuit was no more than four inches across at the thin waistband, and tapered to a narrow strip before passing between her legs.

"Hardly enough to cover her crack," Cowboy muttered.

"I sure wouldn't mind trading places with the guy," Jeremy said.

The guy was kneeling beside her, squirting suntan oil onto her back. She shivered as the stream licked her skin. Her smooth buttocks trembled slightly. The guy set the plastic bottle aside and began to spread the oil around. He wasn't just lending a hand, he was caressing her. Jeremy could almost feel her sun-heated skin, smooth and slick under his own hands.

He hated to leave the scene behind, and Cowboy must've felt the same way. After walking past the couple, Cowboy stopped and looked back. Jeremy, grateful, did the same.

The guy was squirting onto one of her buttocks. The oil, glinting silver in the sunlight, streamed down her cheek. He started rubbing it around.

"Kind of wish she'd turn over," Cowboy said.

"Yeah, turn over and forget her top's untied."

Cowboy grinned at him. "Welcome to Boleta Bay."

"I do believe I like it here."

"If you like it now, wait'll you lay your eyes on Tanya." With that, he started walking again.

Jeremy looked one more time, saw the guy sliding a hand down between the backs of her thighs, then turned away and hurried to catch up with Cowboy.

"Who's this Tanya?" he asked.

"Nate's gal. Wait till you see her. Guys've drowned themselves just so she'd pull them out."

"Huh?"

"She's a lifeguard. And head cheerleader at school. You see

her bouncing around the sidelines . . . it's a sight to make a blind man juice his skivvies."

"You got the hots for her?"

"Show me a guy that doesn't, I'll show you a queer. I know *gals* who've got the hots for her."

"But she's Nate's, you said?"

"The rotten dickhead. I reckon I'd lay waste to him so I could free her up, but he's my best bud."

"Liz might not approve, either."

"Well, it ain't about to happen. Nate or no Nate, only way I'd ever stand a chance with Tanya's if maybe I grew six inches and got me a new face."

"Maybe you could drug her."

"Haw! Drug her?" Cowboy swept off his hat and whapped Jeremy across the arm. "Get out of here! You think I'm some kind of pervert? Christ, I don't believe you! Sick! What kind of drug would it take?"

Jeremy walked beside him, beaming. If Cowboy had started suspecting he was a wimp and a dork, the remark about drugging Tanya had put a stop to it. He'd won the guy over, for sure.

"Can't wait to see what she looks like," Jeremy said.

"Don't have to." With the last of his cone, Cowboy pointed at a lifeguard station a short distance ahead. It was a white-painted shack on stilts, wooden stairs leading up to a deck on the ocean side. A girl stood on the deck, leaning forward a bit, hands on the railing.

"Is that her?" Jeremy asked.

"You got it."

They walked closer.

Her head was turned away, so he couldn't see her face. Nevertheless, she looked awesome. Jeremy guessed that she must be nearly six feet tall. Her bare legs, bronze in the sunlight, looked shapely and powerful. She wore red shorts, and a white T-shirt that wasn't tucked in.

Neither the shorts nor the shirt was tight-fitting. Though the shorts were loose, the way they bulged in the seat told of strong round buttocks. The wind rippled her shirt against a flat belly and the high, thrusting mounds of her breasts. Her hair, in a ponytail, shone like gold.

If her face was any match for the rest of her . . .

"Yo! Tanya!" Cowboy called from the foot of the stairs.

Her head turned. She looked down from her high station. She had sunglasses on. They hid her eyes.

But what he could see of her face was even better than Cowboy had led him to suspect. Not just beautiful, magnificent. Hair like a thick curtain of golden threads drifted and shimmered across her high brow. Her cheekbones and jaw were prominent. Her skin was so deeply tanned that her teeth seemed starkly white, almost as if they gave off their own bright light. Her mouth was wide. Her lips, only slightly darker than the skin of her face, were full and luxurious. They looked like the softest part of her. To the magnificent beauty of her face they added something that seemed both slightly vulnerable and powerfully erotic.

"Hi there, Cowboy," she said. Her voice was much as Jeremy might have expected, low and clear.

"Still on for tonight?"

Her head turned slightly toward Jeremy. He felt as if he were melting into warm liquid.

"Don't worry about Duke. He's a straight-shooter. Fact is, he'd like to come along. I told him I'd have to get your okay. And Liz wants to know if her cousin can come."

"No."

Jeremy shrank inside. A lump filled his throat.

Should've known. Everything had been going too good. I fooled Cowboy, but she sees right through me. Knows I'm a reject. Shit. Shit!

Tanya stepped away from the railing. She strode to the top of the stairs and scowled down at Cowboy. A goddess, beautiful but fierce. "It's private business," she said. "No out-of-towners. You and Liz ought to know that."

"Well, Duke lives here. He just moved in."

She took off her sunglasses and looked at Jeremy. The blue of her eyes matched the afternoon sky. They studied Jeremy. His heart slammed. His legs felt weak.

"No wimps," she said.

The words froze his mind.

"Hey!" someone yelled at Tanya.

Me. That was me, Jeremy realized.

"Fuck you!" he shouted.

He still had a handful of sodden Super-Waffle. The remains of the cone had a swamp of melted vanilla ice cream at the bottom.

He hurled it.

Ice cream flew from the tumbling cone. But not all of it. Far from all of it. The cone struck a golden thigh. White glop exploded.

A large portion of it shot straight up a loose leg hole of Tanya's shorts.

Jeremy blinked. He couldn't believe what he had done.

The cone, clinging to Tanya's white-smeared thigh, dropped away as she stormed down the stairs.

"Jesus, Duke," he heard from Cowboy.

He considered running. Instead, he stood stiff with his arms at his sides.

Tanya grabbed the front of his open shirt. She jerked him up on his tiptoes. Glared down into his eyes. One side of her upper lip lifted, baring her gum. "You little rat."

"Fuck you and the horse you rode in on, sister."

He couldn't believe he'd said that.

She's gonna kill me.

Instead, she yanked his shirt back over his shoulders and pulled it off him. She shoved it into his hands. "Clean your mess," she said.

His heart kicked. "Huh?"

"You heard me." Grabbing his shoulders, she shoved him down to his knees.

He stared at the dripping front of her shorts, the white fluid streaming down her thigh. He began at her knee and worked his way up, mopping the ice cream with his wadded shirt. He felt the smooth firmness of her muscles. His mouth was parched. His heart punched the air out of his lungs.

He stopped at the hem of the leg hole, turned the shirt to find a dry area, and patted the front of her shorts. Then he lowered his arms.

"You're not done yet."

"Huh?"

"Do it."

Wearing a tail of his shirt like a glove, he slipped his hand up her leg and inside her shorts. The fabric of the shirt quickly went damp. She felt slick and creamy. Nothing in there felt like panties.

"You're just spreading it around."

He took his hand out, found a dry section of shirt, wrapped it around his hand, and went back to work.

Sick with lust. Cramped, tight, burning.

Wiping at his mess. Feeling her. Her leg, and the shallow slanted valley where her leg joined her torso. If he moved his hand only a couple of inches toward the center . . .

Oh, man. Man! So close!

Don't do it!

Don't. Christ. Don't. No.

He jerked his hand out. Tilting back his head, he looked up at Tanya.

"What do you say?" she asked.

He shrugged.

"What do you say?"

"Thank you very much," Jeremy said.

"Haw!" That came from Cowboy.

"Stand up."

He stood up.

Tanya's lips curled into a smile. "One o'clock tonight. Under the clown."

"Does that mean I can come?"

"Yes, indeed." Her pale blue eyes seemed a little mocking. "Cowboy, fill him in on the rules. And tell Liz to leave her cousin at home, or stay away herself."

Six

Monsters Among Us
By
Gloria Weston

His name is Harrison Bentley. His friends call him Bents. Others among us call him a troll.

A few nights ago he was beaten, stripped of his clothes, and bound with ropes to the steep downhill tracks of Funland's Hurricane roller coaster. A calling card was taped to his forehead. It read, "Greetings from Great Big Billy Goat Gruff."

No, the roller coaster did not race down and crush the life out of Harrison Bentley. No, it was not derailed by the impact and thrown off its tracks, hurtling its luckless riders to their doom. Harrison was discovered in time to prevent such tragedies.

Near death from hypothermia, he was rushed to the hospital emergency room. He had multiple bruises and abrasions. A dislocated shoulder. Two cracked ribs. A broken nose.

The damage to his body will heal, in time. But time is unlikely to mend the deeper wounds—the agony and humiliation of being stripped and brutalized, the terror of being lashed to the Hurricane tracks at a dizzying height above the boardwalk and left there through the long dark hours of the night, knowing that dawn would bring not only the welcome warmth of sunlight but also the roar of the descending Hurricane.

Such wounds may never heal.

Harrison Bentley has been scarred for life.

Why?

We know why, good folks of Boleta Bay. We all know why.

He committed a crime, and he was duly punished for it.

What heinous crime did this man commit?

We all know the answer to that one too.

He was guilty of being homeless.

He was a "troll." And he met rough justice from Great Big Billy Goat Gruff.

He isn't the first victim of the thugs who roam our town, especially our beach and boardwalk, "trolling," visiting mayhem on the downtrodden of our society. He is only the most recent.

Our local authorities have knowledge of at least twenty incidents in which indigents have been beset by roaming bands of teenage vigilantes. The earliest attacks, beginning last summer, were mild in comparison to the brutality apparent in the torture of Harrison Bentley. The victims, then, were bound and gagged and driven out of town. They were left miles away, terrified but unharmed. They were left with warnings never to return to Boleta Bay.

Soon, however, the "bum's rush" ceased to satiate the appetite of the adolescent mob. Instead of a swift ride out of town, transients were beaten senseless and left where they fell—in alleys, on the beach, in the darkness beneath the boardwalk, in the shadows among the rides and game booths of the "fun zone." Always with a calling card proclaiming him—or her—to be yet another victim of Great Big Billy Goat Gruff.

But even beatings, as vicious as they were, proved too tame for the pleasures of the brutes who roam our nights. Though the beatings continued, new and perverse elements have now been added to the repertoire.

Four weeks ago an early-morning jogger found an indigent known only as "Mad Mary" handcuffed to the railing of the boardwalk. Like those before her, Mary had been thrashed. Unlike the others, she had been stripped naked. Every inch of her body had been sprayed with green paint.

Biff, the next victim, was painted with red and yellow stripes.

Lucy's buttocks were glued to a boardwalk bench. The plastic bowl she used for collecting a few paltry coins from passersby was glued to her face.

James was placed on a carousel horse, hands tied behind his back, a hangman's noose around his neck. Had he fallen during the night or early-morning hours . . .

Harrison was tied to the Hurricane's tracks.

It won't stop with him. Our own local band of barbarians will strike again, commit more atrocities, fall with ever-increasing cruelty and ferocity on the homeless of our town.

And we are to blame.

We are their accomplices.

We fear the "bums, winos, and crazies," who seem to be everywhere, always with a hand out, begging for change. We treat them like carriers of a dread disease, spreading contagion by their mere presence.

They do spread a disease.

The disease they spread, my friends, is guilt.

We *have.* We have homes, families, food, clothes, and countless luxuries. They do not.

We hate them for reminding us of that fact.

And we want them gone.

The trollers want them gone too. The trollers, our children, react to the "bums" as the adults do—with fear and loathing. They have seen the revulsion on our faces. They have heard our muttered curses, or derisive laughter. And some of them, perhaps only a handful, chose to do us all the favor of cleaning up the town, getting rid of these hated nuisances. They invented the sport of "trolling."

From the beginning, of course, our authorities denounced their activities.

But so many of us were pleased.

At last something was being done about our "bum problem." Stickers began to appear on car bumpers and store windows: "Troll Buster" stickers; others that read, "One Troll Can Ruin Your Whole Day" and "Billy Goat Gruff for President." Jokes abounded. "What bait do you use for trolling in Boleta Bay? . . . Cat food." And, "How can you tell if a troll's dead? . . . He doesn't ask for two bits when you step on him."

We did not condemn the acts of violence perpetrated against the "trolls," we made sport of them. We applauded them. And with our cynical attitudes, with our approval, we acted as a local booster club for Great Big Billy Goat Gruff.

Will we celebrate, I wonder, when an indigent lies dead on the boardwalk, murdered by our children?

I doubt it.

We'll have the opportunity, though. Tomorrow, next week, or next month, they *will* kill.

For us.

The moment is rushing toward us with the momentum of the Hurricane thundering down its tracks.

A troll will die.

A bum, a wino, a crazy. A beggar who talks gibberish, dresses in rags, and smells of garbage. And some of us may think that the world is a better place with that troll dead.

But the murderers will be you and me.

And the victim, let us not kid ourselves, will not be a troll.

Not a troll, but a human being—a man or a woman who ran out of luck somewhere along the way, who was condemned from birth by a cosmic roll of the dice, or who was trampled beneath the merciless boots of substance addiction. A person, not a troll.

A person. A child, once, who was loved by a mother and father. A child who fought to stay awake on Christmas Eve in hopes of spying Santa Claus. A girl who skipped rope and sped along on roller skates. A boy who beamed when he was given his first bicycle, who cried when his balloon popped, who popped bubble gum and ate ice-cream cones.

A child who would've loved Funland with its hot dogs and cotton candy, with its arcades and game booths and thrilling rides.

This is our troll.

This is our victim.

This is who will die on the moonlit boardwalk, one night soon, with a card taped to his body: "Greetings from Great Big Billy Goat Gruff."

Let me suggest a revision in the card's message.

Let it read: "Greetings from Great Big Billy Goat Gruff and the Citizens of Boleta Bay."

Dave folded the *Evening Standard* and tossed it onto the coffee table. He lifted his beer mug. He took a drink.

"So, what do you think?" Gloria asked. She was sitting beside him on the sofa, one leg tucked beneath her, an arm resting on the back cushion. She looked at Dave with one eyebrow cocked high, daring him to strike out at her editorial, eager to defend it.

"Nice job," he said.

"You don't mean that."

"It sure ought to stir things up."

"That was the idea. It's a disgrace, what's happening in this town. Something has to be done about it."

"I agree." Dave finished his beer and set the mug down. "Why don't we head on over to the Wharf Rat?"

"You're trying to change the subject."

"I'm getting hungry."

"What do you really think about my article?"

Dave sighed. Why not go ahead and get it over with? Tell her what she's waiting so eagerly to hear. "Wouldn't you rather fight on a full stomach?" he asked.

With kids waiting for Santa Claus, roller-skating, and popping gum so fresh in his mind, Dave thought that Gloria looked like one who'd just felt a tug on her fishing line.

"I knew it," she said. "You're pissed off."

"Do you have to use that kind of language?"

Now she looked *really* pleased. "Oh? And Joan doesn't?"

"That's different."

"In what way?"

"I thought you wanted to argue about bums."

"We'll get back to them. Tell me, why is Joan permitted to use that kind of language, and I'm not? This ought to be good. Is it because she's 'one of the guys'? She obviously is not one of the guys. Or hadn't you noticed?"

"You're certainly feeling your oats tonight. Or your bamboo shoots."

"Joan was talking like a sailor at the barbecue last week. You never once said boo about that."

"I don't criticize my guests."

"But it's all right for her to talk that way."

"Doesn't bother me."

"But I'm not allowed to say 'pissed off'?"

"Coming from you, it sounds incredibly phony and childish. You sound like a second-grader trying to shock her parents."

Her face went red. Her mouth dropped open.

"You bastard," she muttered.

Dave knew that he'd gone too far. She had been spoiling for a fight—for a chance to pit her superior social conscience against the cynical cop—but she hadn't expected it to get up close and personal. She hadn't counted on being humiliated.

"I'm sorry," Dave said. He put his hand on her arm.

She jerked it away from him.

"You asked," he pointed out.

"Go to hell. Oh, pardon me. Phony, childish me." She pushed herself off the couch and walked toward the front door.

"Gloria."

She opened the door.

"Come on, let's forget about it and go to the Wharf Rat."

She looked back at him.

Her eyes were red.

Good Christ.

"Hey," he said, "I didn't mean anything."

"No. Of course not. Enjoy your dinner." She left and shut the door hard.

Joan slid the zipper up the front of her white denim dress and checked herself in the bedroom mirror. A lot of leg showed. This was her first new dress since minis had come back into fashion. She supposed it would take some getting used to.

"Neat outfit," Debbie said from the doorway.

Joan looked at her sister. "Do you think it's too short?"

"Looks great," Debbie said, wandering into the room. "Can I borrow it sometime?"

"Sure, I guess so." The girl lacked Joan's height and figure, but the dress would probably fit her. Hard to believe that she had grown so much recently. And a little sad.

"What's wrong?"

"I don't want any of your boyfriends drooling on it."

"Get real."

"Your boyfriends don't drool?"

"You ought to know. You see as much of them as I do."

"Somebody has to watch out for you."

"Somebody ought to watch out for *you*."

"What's that supposed to mean?"

"Are you going out with *him* again?" Debbie's upper lip lifted slightly as she spoke.

"He'll be here any minute."

"It's your life."

"That's right, it is. There's nothing wrong with Harold."

"No. Huh-uh. He's perfect. Why don't you marry him?"

"He hasn't asked," Joan said.

Debbie's eyes widened. "You wouldn't, would you? I mean, if he asked, you'd tell him to screw off, right?"

"I think I'd be more diplomatic about it."

"But you wouldn't marry him?"

"I doubt it."

"Well, at least you're not totally bonkers."

"Thanks."

"'Cause he's sure no prize. If you ask me, I don't know why you go out with him at all."

"Did you hear me ask?"

"What do you see in him, anyway?"

"Harold's a nice guy."

"You could do a lot better."

"Yeah? Who appointed you Mother?"

The smug smile fell off Debbie's face.

"I'm sorry," Joan said.

The girl shrugged, but her face had gone pale and for just a moment her eyes looked frantic. She quickly turned her head away. "Where's Mr. Wonderful taking you?"

"A movie. You know, that Summer Film Festival at the university."

"What a thrill."

"We might go someplace afterward. I'll be home by midnight, or I'll call."

"Don't tear yourself away from him on my account."

Still regretting the "Mother" comment, Joan said, "How would you like to come with us?"

"Oh, that'd be rich."

"I'm sure Harold wouldn't mind."

"And I could pick up a few pointers on erogenous zones."

"I doubt that very much," Joan said.

"Yeah, he might wilt in front of a spectator."

"You kidding? He keeps his hands to himself. Spectators or not."

"Bullshit." She stared at Joan, eyes narrow. "He's putting it to you."

"That's news to me."

"You're lying."

"Right. I'm a world-class liar."

"But that's . . . too weird. You don't let him, or what?"

"Is this any of your business?"

"I'm just curious, that's all. I mean, you've been going with this guy for a month. What's the story?"

"I don't know." She felt herself starting to blush.

"So it's him, huh? Is he a homo or something?"

Joan shrugged. "Let's just drop it, okay? I don't know what's wrong, and I don't want to talk about it."

"Why the hell do you go out with him?"

"I told you, he's a nice guy. So, do you want to come with us or not?"

"What do you do when you're out with him? Nothing?"

"Come along and find out."

"Not a chance. Jeez. I knew something was wrong with that guy."

The doorbell rang.

"See you later," Joan said. "Midnight."

"Yeah. Have a ball."

Joan grabbed her handbag off the bed and hurried down the hall. She opened the front door. Harold stood on the porch, a few strides back. He glanced at her face as if to confirm who she was, then focused on her chest, as usual. Not that he found her chest special. He just seemed unable to look at her face for any period of time. "How's my favorite copper?"

"Feeling brassy," she said.

He smiled and nodded. "Well, ready to go?"

"Yep." She pulled the door shut, stepped up to him, and took his hand. He squeezed it slightly.

"I think you'll enjoy tonight's film," he said as they walked toward his Volvo.

"Does that mean it doesn't have subtitles?"

"It's Polanski's *Macbeth*."

"Really? I thought Shakespeare was the brains behind that one."

"You're awful."

"I'm not awful, I'm a wag."

"Terrible."

He opened the passenger door for Joan. As she climbed into the car, she watched him. He stood there and never once glanced at her legs.

Typical. But she'd thought that the new dress might spark some interest.

Could've saved my money, she thought as he shut the door.

She looked down. If the dress were any shorter, her panties would be showing. She felt the seat's upholstery against the back of her thighs.

Harold slid in behind the wheel.

"What do you think of my new dress?" Joan asked.

"It's very becoming," he said, and started the car.

"Why don't we skip the movie?"

"But it's a classic." He pulled away from the curb.

"I've seen it. It can't hold a candle to the Orson Wells version. The height of its innovation is having some gals parade around bare-assed. Is *that* why you're so eager to see it?"

"Don't be silly."

"Let's go to the boardwalk."

He looked at her. He looked aghast.

"Have you ever been there?"

"Once. And I assure you, once was enough."

"I'd like to go. It'll be fun."

"Joan. You *patrol* the boardwalk. You're there every day. Have you lost your senses?"

"What do you think I do while I'm on duty, ride the Ferris wheel and carousel? You know what I did today? I checked out the rest rooms about a dozen times and listened to a bunch of lunatics rant about flying saucers and visits from the Virgin Mary."

"It's a disgraceful place. And dangerous."

"'Danger knows full well that I am more dangerous than she. We are two lions, whelped by the same—'"

"And dirty. That park is filthy, and you're wearing a brand-new dress—a *white* dress. You'll ruin it the minute you sit down on something. It's madness. Sheer madness."

"I've seen enough artsy-fart films the past three weeks to choke Renoir. So how about it? Come on, let's go to Funland. Please? I'll buy you a cotton candy."

"I can't stand the stuff."

"Party pooper. Okay, never mind. Let's see *Macbeth*. I'll go to the boardwalk some night when you've got a class. Maybe meet a nice sailor."

Harold drove to Funland.

Seven

The age guesser said, "Twenty-three." Joan showed her driver's license to prove she was twenty-seven, and he gave her a pencil eraser shaped like a dinosaur.

She tried to get Harold to have his age guessed. He said, "That'd be pressing our luck."

The way his hairline was receding and his somewhat paunchy stomach held the front of his sport coat open, she figured he stood a good chance of winning. The guy would probably suspect he was closer to forty than thirty-four. Harold, self-conscious about his looks, no doubt preferred to avoid the embarrassment.

They wandered up the boardwalk.

Joan hadn't been here at night since last summer. It seemed so much more festive after dark: the game booths were brightly lighted; the names of rides and attractions blazed with neon; everywhere she looked, she saw strings of multicolored bulbs. The familiar aromas of cotton candy, popcorn, hot dogs, french fries, machine oil, perfumes and after-shave, and the ocean all smelled more fragrant and alluring than during the day. The crowd was larger. She felt an aura of mystery and anticipation.

It's like this every night, she thought, and I've been missing it.

If Harold would just get into the spirit of the thing . . .

"What do *you* want to do?" she asked.

"I suppose it's too late for *Macbeth*."

"There must be something here that you'd enjoy. How about the Tilt-a-Whirl?" she asked, stopping to watch people climb out of the hooded cars. Girls laughing. Couples holding each other and staggering. "Come on," she said. "There's no line. We can get right on."

"You go ahead. I'll stay here and watch."

"Oh, that would be loads of fun."

"No, do it. I insist. I don't want to be responsible for spoiling your fun."

Joan shrugged. "Maybe later. Come on." She took his arm and led him away. "We'll find something you like."

"Approximately in the year that hell freezes over."

She spotted the hag with the sock puppet. The old crone hadn't moved all day. Her sock was darting out, "talking" to people unlucky enough to be passing near her. Joan was tempted to steer Harold in her direction.

After all, he was hot to see *Macbeth* tonight, and this gal was certainly a weird sister.

But that would be cruel.

She remembered how the puppet had gone for Dave's leg, and laughed.

"What?" Harold asked.

"One of my favorite bums." She nodded toward the woman.

Harold looked. "I don't see anything especially amusing about her."

"Her puppet nibbled Dave's leg today."

"Did you read Gloria's piece on trolling?"

"She laid it on pretty thick."

"I thought she did an admirable job."

"She ought to get off her high horse. Accomplices, my ass. Typical bleeding-heart bullshit. We're *all* guilty?" She flung an arm up, pointing at the high, down-sweeping tracks of the Hurricane's steepest drop. "Dave and I, we risked our butts climbing that damn thing to rescue that derelict she was rhapsodizing about. Either of us had slipped, we would've been dead meat. Don't tell me about accomplices. She knew we did that, too. But did she put it in her sermon? No way. Her whole point was to make the town—and the cops—look like we're all in favor of trolling. Called us a booster club, no less. I don't know how she could look Dave in the face after writing that crap."

Releasing Harold's hand, she strode over to the Bazooka Guns. She paid the man behind the counter. He loaded the feed trough with five tennis balls. Joan jacked one into the chamber, sighted down the wide barrel, and fired. The first ball poomphed out, rocketed forty feet, and whacked the suspended dummy. The ball caught it in its belly. Its legs flew up and it twirled on the end of its rope.

She glanced at Harold. He looked as if he regretted mentioning Gloria's article.

She blasted another tennis ball at the dummy. This one knocked its stuffed head backward.

"We might be able to *apprehend* the goddamn Billy Goat Gruff if we got a tiny little bit of cooperation from the victims. They give us nothing. Nothing. Do you know what we've found out so far?"

She shot a ball into the dummy's chest.

"It's teenagers. We've been told they're all girls. We've been told they're all guys. There are anywhere from three to fifty of them, depending on which victim you listen to. The leader is Satan replete with horns and tail, a gorgeous blonde, Mayor Donaldson, a giant black guy, Charles Manson's twin brother, Zarch from the Sixth Dimension . . ."

"I get the point," Harold said.

Joan missed the dummy.

"Ignorant, self-righteous bitch."

Her last ball struck the dummy in the face.

Harold put a hand on her shoulder. "I didn't mean to upset you."

"Who's upset?"

"Gloria's only doing her job."

"And we're doing ours, but she conveniently forgets to point that out."

They wandered into the stream of the moving crowd.

"Want to try the bumper cars?" she asked.

"In your mood, you'd probably hurt someone."

"My mood's fine," she muttered.

"Step right in, folks!"

She glanced at Jasper Dunn. The cadaverous old man leered at her. She quickened her pace.

"Don't rush off, Miss Cop. Step right in, you and your handsome beau, and see the amazing, astonishing wonders of Jasper's Oddities. Lead her this way, fellow. Right this way. Don't miss out. See the two-headed baby, the hairless orangutan of Borneo, the mummy Ram Cho-tep, and other rare and mysterious wonders. She'll quiver and shake at the sights. She'll swoon in your arms."

She kept walking.

"I take it," said Harold, "you're not interested in Jasper's Oddities?"

"That guy's swamp scum."

"Has he done something to you?"

"Just with his eyes. Every time I walk by . . . Fortunately, he spends most of his time inside with his Oddities. Sometimes I go a whole shift without seeing him. He likes to go in and watch the reactions. And ogle the females."

"Enjoys watching them quiver and shake," Harold said. "Have you ever gone in?"

"Just once. Some gal had fainted."

"Those Oddities must be something to see."

"I think it was the heat. She was on the floor and her skirt was hiked up around her waist and Dunn was on his knees. I'm not saying he fooled with her or anything, but he sure looked startled when the boyfriend towed us in there."

She stopped and looked back. A couple of teenage guys with their dates were climbing the stairs, giving tickets to Dunn. One of the girls was husky, but the other was slender and wore a halter top and white shorts. "Watch," Joan said. "He'll follow them in. Goddamn lech."

Dunn followed them through the doorway.

"I wish the creep would dry up and blow away. He's the guy that owns the Funhouse, you know." Joan nodded toward the two-story building that stood adjacent to the Oddities. The dark neon sign above its front door, visible in the glow of nearby lights, read, "Jasper's Funhouse." All the windows were boarded with sheets of plywood. "I've heard he had a grating in one of its corridors. On the floor. And he used to hide under there and look up the skirts of the women when they walked across it."

"Charming fellow. Is that why it's closed?"

Joan shook her head. "A couple of his freaks got loose in it one night. He used to have a freak show. In there with his Oddities. Some pretty hideous . . . people. That's what I hear. A couple of them got into the Funhouse. This was five or six years ago, I guess. I was still at Stanford. Dave told me about it. He said they jumped a little girl and her grandmother."

"Terrible," Harold muttered.

"The old woman keeled over with a heart attack."

"What about the girl?"

"She wasn't hurt. Some sailors came to the rescue. But the grandmother died. Dunn was forced to shut down his freak show. Then he couldn't afford the liability insurance to keep his Funhouse going, so he closed it. He still owns it, though. Nobody can get him to tear it down."

"Maybe he wants to reopen it someday."

"I wouldn't be surprised. He doesn't have a *grate* on the floor of the Oddities place."

Harold looked at the abandoned Funhouse and shook his head. "I might've enjoyed that," he said.

"Right. That's a real shame. The one attraction on the entire boardwalk that you might've enjoyed, and it isn't open."

"No, I mean it. When I was a kid, I used to go to Riverview in Chicago. I guess Riverview's long gone now. But they had a funhouse called Aladdin's Castle. Or was it Palace? I don't recall. But I used to love it."

"Gee, there is hope for you." She took hold of his arm, and they strolled on. "So, you used to enjoy amusement parks. In your callow youth."

"Before I became a stick-in-the-mud."

Joan smiled. "Tell me more about your prestick days."

"I was always too timid for my own good."

She squeezed his arm, said, "Just a minute," then smiled and raised her other hand in greeting. "Hiya, Jim, Beth."

The two officers walked over to them. Jim looked at her legs.

"Don't you see enough of this place during the day?" Beth asked.

"Dave won't let me ride the Hurricane."

"Just lets you climb on it," Jim said.

She introduced them to Harold. He shook hands with them.

"Be careful with her, Harry," Jim said.

"Is she fragile?"

"She's got a black belt."

"And I'm not above hitting people with it," Joan said.

"Don't let her cuff you to the bed. Once she's got you help-less, out comes the belt."

"Are you speaking from personal experience?" Harold asked him.

"In his dreams," Joan said.

Beth nudged Jim with her elbow. "Come on, Casanova. Nice meeting you, Harold."

"Yeah," Jim said. He slapped Harold's arm. "Got one word of advice for you, Harry. Go for it."

Harold grinned and nodded.

"That was three words, dipstick," Joan said.

"But who's counting?"

He and Beth ambled away. Before they vanished into the crowd, Joan saw them look at each other and start talking. No doubt discussing her boyfriend. Jim, for one, would not be voic-ing approval.

"Interesting fellow," Harold said.

"Rarely."

At least Jim goes for it, Joan thought. You may not *want* him to go for it, you may have to inflict some pain to stop him, but he's interested enough to make the try.

"Is it true that you have a black belt?"

"I have a black garter belt."

"Would you like some cotton candy?"

"Sure. That'd be great."

What does it take to get a rise out of him? she wondered.

He bought a cotton candy for Joan, nothing for himself. She tore off a puffy wad with her teeth, drew it into her mouth, and felt it dissolve before she had much chance to chew it.

"So at that Riverview place," she said, "what did you like besides Aladdin's Castle? The roller coaster?"

"They couldn't drag me onto the Bobs. Or the parachute drop. As I said, I was timid."

"How about the Ferris wheel?"

"I wouldn't go near it."

"How about the Ferris wheel right now?"

"Oh, I don't think so."

"I do." The sign by its gate showed that five tickets were needed. She headed for a nearby ticket booth, Harold hurrying after her.

"Joan, I'm not going on that thing."

She stepped into line. "Hold this," she said, and handed the cotton candy to him. "Try it, you'll like it." He looked warily at the confection. He shook his head. Joan took the wallet out of her shoulder bag and removed a ten-dollar bill.

"If you think you're going to get me onto that death-trap contraption . . ."

"My friend, everyone is afraid of heights."

"This from the lady who scaled the Hurricane."

"I was scared shitless. But I did it anyway, because it had to be done. And you're going to ride the Ferris wheel for the same reason."

"It does not have to be done."

"Oh, yes it does." She bought ten tickets and received five dollars in change.

Harold followed her to the line for the Ferris wheel. He had a nervous smile on his face as he handed the cotton candy to her. "You don't honestly expect me to go through with this?"

"You'll like it. I promise."

"I won't like it, because I won't do it."

"I've already bought the tickets."

"You may ride it twice. I'll stay right here, safe on the ground, and wait patiently."

She looked him in the eye. "I want you to go on it with me, Harold. Just the Ferris wheel. I won't ask you to try the Hurricane or the parachute drop or anything else. Just this one ride. It won't kill you."

"That's because I won't be on it."

"Harold, please."

Now the nervous smile was gone. Replaced by a frown of annoyance. "I don't understand why you insist on being so adamant about this. For heaven's sake, it's just a carnival ride. It's hardly worth bickering about. It won't make one whit of difference, in the scheme of things, whether or not I go on the stupid thing."

"It makes a big difference to me," Joan said.

"Oh, I have to prove I'm a man, is that it? Is this some kind of a test?"

"It didn't start out that way," Joan told him.

"I'll ride the damn thing if it'll make you happy."

"Good," she muttered. She turned away from him. She took a bite of the cotton candy and it melted away in her mouth and she felt like crying.

The Ferris wheel was still going full speed, its lighted spokes spinning, cars rocking, riders squealing as they were swept down from the staggering height. Some of them, she saw, were embracing. She tossed her cotton candy into a trash bin.

"I said I'll do it." He sounded petulant.

"I heard you."

"So what are you pouting about?" he asked.

"This was supposed to be fun."

"I'm sorry." He didn't sound sorry at all. "I guess I'm just not a very fun guy. Maybe you should've come here with one of your macho cop friends. I'm sure *Dave* would be delighted to ride the goddamn Ferris wheel."

"He wouldn't whine about it."

"Now I'm a whiner. Isn't that wonderful."

"Not especially."

"Christ."

"You've never touched me, Harold."

His mouth fell open.

"Joan, for Christsake." He glanced around as if fearful that someone might be listening. But the others waiting in line were talking among themselves. The air was thick with laughter and screams, the spiels of pitchmen, the crackle of gunfire from the shooting gallery, hurdy-gurdy music from the Ferris wheel.

He didn't need to worry about eavesdroppers.

"Is it me?" Joan asked. "Is something wrong with *me*?"

"No, of course not."

"Then what is it? We've been going together for weeks. We hold hands and kiss good night—*I* kiss *you* good night. And that's it."

"I thought you preferred it that way."

"Then you don't know much about—"

"Move it along, folks."

Harold stiffened.

Joan saw that the line had moved forward, that their turn had come to board the Ferris wheel.

"We don't have to do it," she said.

But he shook his head and went through the gate. The man took the tickets from Joan. They stepped onto a platform and climbed into the waiting gondola of the Ferris wheel. It rocked gently as they sat down. The man swung a metal safety bar across the front and latched it secure.

With a jerk that made the basket tip, the wheel carried them upward. It stopped, and the next passengers boarded.

Harold was clutching the safety bar with both hands.

Joan put a hand on his thigh. He looked at her. He gasped as they were suddenly lifted higher.

"There's nothing to be afraid of," Joan said. "The Ferris wheel's safe. So am I."

"Sure," he muttered.

The wheel abruptly lifted them once more. Harold squeezed his eyes shut. He sat there gripping the bar, feet planted on the floor panel, back rigid, eyes tightly shut, teeth gritted.

Joan patted his thigh. "Loosen up, would you? You're making *me* nervous."

"I'm sorry." He managed to say it without moving his jaw.

"Hey, you're not going to capsize us if you open your mouth."

He sucked in a quick breath as the wheel moved again. When it stopped, they were near the top.

They were damn high.

Joan felt as if her insides had been left at the previous level. "Jesus," she muttered.

The boardwalk was *way* down there.

If this damn thing tips over . . .

"I'm not the kind of man," Harold said, "who *has* a woman like you."

"Self-fulfilling prof . . . Uh!" She grabbed the safety bar with both hands.

When the wheel stopped, they were at the very top. Their gondola swayed back and forth.

She realized that this position, though higher than the previous one, was considerably less unnerving.

Because, at the pinnacle of the Ferris wheel, the ground was out of sight. She could see the distant wooded hills of the coastline range, and the headlights of cars on the highway, but nothing of the boardwalk.

Nothing directly below.

Nothing of what she would land on if the contraption fell apart or tipped over.

Not without leaning forward or sideways and peering down.

They started down and she could see the boardwalk again. To avoid the view, she turned her head and looked at Harold. He still sat rigid with his eyes shut.

The man, she thought, is a coward.

I'm scared too, she reminded herself.

But not like that.

And she realized that she had learned nothing new here tonight. She had confirmed her suspicions, nothing more. Maybe that was why she had brought him here—to take him out of his safe academic world and . . . put him on trial. Not a conscious plan, certainly. But maybe in the back of her mind that was why she'd insisted they skip the film and come to Funland.

The Ferris wheel moved, dropping them lower. This time it didn't stop after a few feet. It swept them down close to the ground and lifted them toward the heights, and Joan's fear slipped away. They flew over the crest and swung downward.

This is all right, she thought. Just takes some getting used to.

I just take some getting used to.

Get him into bed just once, he'll be fine.

Right. Fine. That little piece of him will be fine, the little piece that's scared of me. But what about the rest of him?

She knew that she would never be able to count on him, lean on him, be comforted by his strength. She would have to be the strong one, the leader.

More like his mother than his lover.

I don't need that.

Soon the Ferris wheel stopped. They were gradually lowered toward the ground. Not until the attendant stepped up to their gondola did Harold release his grip on the safety bar. They climbed down.

On the boardwalk, Joan said, "You can take me home now."

"You're upset with me," he said.

"No. It's all right."

"I rode the damn ride."

"I know. That was very brave."

"About the other thing . . ."

"That's all right," Joan said. "I understand."

She took his hand. They walked out of Funland and into the parking lot, and he opened the door of his car for her. She leaned across the seat and unlocked the driver's door. He climbed in without looking at her.

He drove out of the parking lot.

"I knew we should've gone to *Macbeth*," he said.

Joan said nothing.

"Would you like to stop someplace for a nightcap?"

"No, thanks. I don't think so. I'm not feeling very well. Just take me home."

"We really should discuss . . ."

"Some other time, okay?"

"Fine."

When he reached her house, he swung to the curb and killed the engine and turned to her. "I'll go in with you," he said. In the dim light from the streetlamps, she saw a nervous smile on his face.

"Not tonight," she said. "I really don't feel very well."

"Joan, please."

"I'll give you a call." She patted his knee, sensed that he was about to reach for her wrist, and quickly pulled her hand back. She swung the door open.

"Don't be this way. Please."

"It's all right," she told him. "I'll give you a call."

She climbed from the car, shut the door, and hurried up the walkway to her house.

Eight

Robin woke up, and couldn't believe that the movie was over. She had come into the theater a little late and missed the start of the new James Bond, so after watching the film, she had waited through the intermission and looked at the opening. She'd planned to leave when it came to a familiar scene.

So much for plans.

Apparently she'd drifted off and slept through the rest of the showing. Now the auditorium lights were on and people were leaving their seats.

She was glad nobody had ripped her off.

One arm was still hooked through the shoulder strap of her pack, a precaution she must've taken before dropping off. The banjo case still stood on the floor, propped up between her legs.

She moved the case aside, stood up, and swung the pack onto her back. Lifting the case, she sidestepped across the deserted row to the aisle.

On her way out, she stopped in the rest room. Nobody was around when she left the toilet stall. She took a few minutes to wash her face and brush her teeth.

The lobby was deserted except for a few workers in the process of closing for the night. Teenagers. As she headed for the door, she heard one of the girl's behind the refreshment counter say, "And he goes, 'It won't kill you,' and I go, 'No way, Jose.'" A different girl said, "I should hope not. Total gross-out."

Robin shouldered open the glass door and stepped outside.

The wind was chilly on her bare arms and slipped in through the front of her shirt. Shivering, she hurried up the sidewalk until she came to the recessed entryway of a dark shop. There she opened her pack. She took out a lightweight nylon parka. She put it on and snapped the front. From a side pocket of her pack she removed a sheathed knife. She slid it into a seat pocket of her jeans.

Then she shouldered her pack, picked up her banjo case, and walked into the street. She stopped in the middle. No cars were coming. Only a few remained parked at the curbs. Down near the corner, a man was walking his dog. Otherwise she saw no one. The lights of the theater marquee were dark. All the shops and restaurants appeared to be closed for the night.

She crossed to the other side of the street and headed south toward the boardwalk.

This was obviously a town that rolled up its sidewalks after dark.

It's a lot later than "after dark," she told herself.

Still, she thought it strange that a place as touristy as Boleta Bay would be shut down so completely at this hour.

What hour are we talking about here? she wondered. Must be after midnight.

Which means that Funland's closed too.

She felt a small tug of fear, and didn't know why. Then she remembered the policeman's warning about a gang of teenagers.

They try to mess with me, she thought, they'll bite the knife.

With each stride, she felt its broad flat blade press against her buttock.

It was her father's hunting knife.

It had saved her many times. Usually, just pulling it was enough to stop trouble.

She'd cut someone only once. That was at the bus depot in San Francisco. A guy came into the rest room while she was washing up, sometime before dawn, and slammed her against the wall and ripped her shirt open and was trying to get her jeans down, and she shoved the knife between his ribs. He said, "Look what you done to me!" and fell to his knees.

Though the parka kept her warm, Robin felt cold and tight inside from remembering that night.

She crossed another street, leaving behind the self-consciously quaint section of downtown. Here the road wasn't lined with trees. Instead of imitation gaslights, the area was lighted with sodium lamps on metal poles. Gone were the boutiques, tea shops, restaurants, bakeries, and bookstores. A Woolworth's took up half the block. On the other side of the street stood a gas station, an auto-parts store, and the café where Robin had eaten a cheeseburger, then sipped coffee and worked on song lyrics until she decided to call it quits and go to the movie. All were closed now. Dim lights glowed inside. The auto-parts store had a steel gate across its front.

On the next block, she started seeing bums. One was stretched out on the bench of a bus shelter. Another was curled up inside the dark entryway of a television-repair shop.

Robin switched the banjo case to her left hand, freeing her right hand to go for the knife if they made trouble.

Neither of the bums spoke or moved as she hurried by.

Before reaching the intersection, she heard a tinny rattle and knew it came from a shopping cart. It still sounded distant. She quickened her pace. Hurrying past the corner of a closed liquor store, she glanced to the right and spotted a hunched old woman pushing the cart toward her. The cart's wire basket was stacked high with junk. Quickly Robin looked away.

"C'mere, princess!"

She rushed into the street.

"C'mere! Got a sticky treat for ya! Don' go off!"

Robin didn't look back.

"Blood on ya, then! Blood on ya!"

She bounded onto the other curb. Glancing over her shoulder, she saw the cart woman stop beside a trash container and lean into it.

She was breathing fast and her heart was pounding.

They're so *creepy*, she thought.

Some of them, like that old woman, hardly seemed human at all. More like . . . creatures from another planet or something. Lurking in the dark, babbling nonsense, ready to *get* you if you let your guard down.

Shouldn't let them spook me, she told herself. They're just people.

She spotted another one. Even though he was on the opposite side of the street, she felt a chill squirm up her back. He stood straight and motionless, his back to the dimly lighted display window of a thrift shop, his arms at his sides. He wore a dark coat that covered him to the knees. His legs below the edge of the coat were bare and pale. So was his hairless head. And he seemed to be *staring* at Robin.

That's ridiculous, she told herself. I can't even see his eyes. Just dark holes.

But she could feel his fierce gaze, and it made her shiver. She imagined him suddenly swooping across the street, grabbing her, and carrying her away to some secret foul place.

Man, she thought. I'm sure spooked tonight.

She walked a little farther, and turned her head to keep an eye on him.

So damn many of them.

The town seemed *infested*.

No wonder the kids are causing trouble. They're scared. So they band together and go after some of these spooks. Who can blame them?

If this place is crawling with bums, she thought, what about the beach?

Maybe she ought to take Dave's advice and check into a motel.

But it might be all right over there. If the kids had been hitting the boardwalk and beach, maybe the bums had scattered. Maybe that's why so many were over here—driven from their lairs, refugees from the danger zone.

At the corner, Robin waited while a lone car approached from the right. It had a rack of lights on top. A police car. It slowed down.

She looked back. The bum was there, halfway down the block, standing rigid, staring at her.

But no longer in front of the thrift shop.

Closer now.

The patrol car stopped.

"Like to speak to you," a man's voice called from the driver's window.

She stepped off the curb and walked to the middle of the street. She bent over slightly and peered into the car. There were two uniformed policemen inside. They didn't look much older than Robin. They both had mustaches. The one in the passenger seat had a cardboard cup in his hand. He took a sip from it.

Real people.

But cops. Cops could mean trouble.

Dave had been nice, though.

"Officers?" Robin said.

"It's late to be wandering the streets," the driver said.

"I just got out of the movies."

"You see the Bond?" asked the other cop. "Bitchin' flick, huh?"

"The guy's no Sean Connery," Robin said.

"Yeah, but who is?"

"Where are you heading?" the driver asked.

"The beach."

"Not a great idea."

"I know. I've been warned about the troubles. You know a policeman named Dave?"

"Carson? Sure. He told you about the trolling?"

Robin nodded.

"Climb in, we'll give you a lift."

"Thanks." Though her heart was slamming, she opened the back door, tossed her backpack onto the seat, and climbed in. She rested the banjo case across her lap and pulled the door shut.

They seemed nice enough, but who could tell? In the car with them, she was at their mercy. But you don't argue with cops, you do as they say. That was a lesson she'd learned early, and never ignored.

At least they were taking her away from that creep.

The car turned the corner.

"I really appreciate it," she said. "All those bums were making me pretty nervous."

"Most of them are too spaced-out to give you any real trouble," the driver said.

The other cop twisted around and looked at her. "It's the kids you've gotta worry about," he said.

"I've had bums attack me a few times," she told him.

"You been on the road a lot?"

"A couple of years."

"No way to live," he said.

"It suits me fine. I figure I've got a whole life ahead for settling down."

"Some bastard doesn't snuff it out for you."

"You a runaway?" asked the driver.

"I'm over eighteen, so I guess it doesn't matter, does it?"

"Your folks know where you are?"

"My father's dead. My mother's too busy to care."

"Shame," the other cop said.

Robin shrugged.

"So you're what?" he asked. "A street musician?"

"A boardwalk banjo picker. This week."

"You're planning to stick around a week?" the driver asked.

"It's nice out at the beach. I don't know. Depends."

Maybe I'll just hit the road tomorrow, she thought. Put some distance between me and this damned army of bums.

"You've gotta watch out for those trollers," said the one who was watching her.

"If I run into them, I'll play them a ditty and warm their hearts."

"Little fucks haven't *got* hearts," the driver said. Then he added, "Pardon the language. Not that I've got any use for the indigents, but . . ."

"They make good doorstops," the other said.

"They have a right to be left in peace."

"Yeah, there's no excuse . . ." He suddenly turned to the front. Robin realized that something must've come over the radio. It had been crackling, sputtering nasal tinny words while the men talked. "Fourteen," the passenger cop said. "We're on it."

The car swerved to the curb.

"Sorry, we've gotta leave you off."

Robin threw open the door. "Thanks for the ride," she said, grabbing her pack and scurrying out.

"Be careful."

She threw the door shut. The rack on the roof blazed with flashing lights and the car sped away.

On the corner nearby was Traveler's Haven, a motel with a blue neon vacancy sign, a few cars parked in front of its numbered doors. Across the street stood a mini-market that was open and looked busy. A car was leaving its lot. A man entered the store. Half a dozen teenagers were clustered around a pickup truck at the edge of the parking area, sitting on its hood and bumper, standing in front of it, smoking and laughing and drinking from cardboard cups while music blared from the pickup's radio.

Robin wondered why they were out at this hour.

She wondered if they were trollers.

But she didn't feel afraid.

The part of town she'd left behind had been empty and silent, a cemetery haunted by the shuffling lost. Here the streets were bright and noisy. Places were open. There were real people. Cars were passing.

She stepped around the corner. Ahead, only two blocks away, stood the dim archway entrance of Funland. Moonlight glowed on the face of the clown.

She walked toward it, passing motels that lined both sides of the street, all-night diners, bars, liquor stores with people coming and going.

When she saw a whiskered bum sitting on the sidewalk with his back to the wall of a closed souvenir shop, she felt no fear. He lowered his bag-wrapped bottle as she approached. "Spare a quarter for a cuppa coffee?"

She dug a dollar bill out of her jeans and gave it to him, but withdrew her hand quickly, fearing his touch.

"G'bless you," he mumbled.

Robin hurried away.

What was that for? she wondered. A payoff to ease the guilt of fleeing the others, of fearing them, of letting herself toy with the idea that they were aliens on the hunt?

She looked back. He was still sitting against the wall. In the distance, the kids were still gathered at the pickup truck. The music of its radio was faint.

She crossed a street and walked alongside the Funland parking lot. Its ticket booths were closed. A few cars remained on the asphalt field. One had a flat rear tire. She wondered if the others were victims of dead batteries. Or had people abandoned them for other reasons? Or *were* they abandoned?

The windows of a Chevy near the sidewalk were fogged. She looked away quickly, afraid that someone might suddenly rise and press his face to the glass and peer out at her.

Maybe I should go back, she thought. Check into one of those motels. Just for tonight.

That'd be chicken.

I can take care of myself.

She strode across the street, across the walkway, and up the concrete stairs. The moonlit face of the clown greeted her with a smile.

Nine

Earlier that night, Jeremy was still at home, sprawled on his bed.

He reached out and lifted his pillow off the alarm clock. Twenty till one. The alarm was set to go off in five minutes. He fingered the stem in, shutting it off.

He hadn't slept at all. He'd tossed and turned, his mind whirling with memories of Cowboy and the boardwalk and the beach and Tanya, with curiosity and hope about tonight, with fantasies about Tanya that made him yearn and ache. He'd trembled. He'd sweated. He'd rolled and squirmed so much that, a few times, his pajamas had become twisted around him, binding him tightly, seams digging into his armpits and crotch. After a while he'd taken them off. But being naked had pitched him into a worse frenzy of excitement, so he'd put them on again.

Two hours had never been so long or so delicious.

At last the waiting was over.

He eased out of bed. He arranged his two pillows length-wise and covered them with the blanket so that his mother would at least see more than an empty bed if she should wake up and glance in, maybe on her way to the bathroom.

He took off his damp pajamas, balled them up, and stuffed them in with the pillows.

Shivering, he sank to his knees. He reached beneath the bed and pulled out the roll of clothing he'd prepared for to-night's adventure. Cowboy had instructed him to wear some-thing dark, warned him that it would be "colder than a wet butt in a blizzard," and suggested that he bring a knife along just in case of trouble.

The comment about the knife had prompted Jeremy to ask, "What'll we be doing, anyway?"

"Just having a hoot. But that time of night, you never know. You wanta be ready for anything."

It was pretty clear that the kids were up to no good. You didn't sneak out of your house and meet at Funland at one A.M. just to stand around and talk. He'd wanted to ask more, but feared that Cowboy might think he was worried. Besides, it didn't really matter what they'd be doing. He wanted to be with them.

One of them.

Whatever it was, he planned to join in.

Jeremy slipped into his underwear and dark blue corduroy pants. He patted the front pocket to make sure his keys and knife were still there. He put on his shirt and tucked it in. He put on his blue windbreaker. He carried his socks and sneakers.

At the bedroom door he peered down the dark hallway to-ward his mother's room.

In the other house, when he'd crept out at night sometimes to wander the neighborhood and look in windows, he'd had to sneak right past her door. In this house, her bedroom was at the end of the hall. A much better arrangement.

Jeremy made his way slowly to the front of the house. He slipped the guard chain off the door. It rattled a little, but not much. The door opened without a sound because he'd oiled the hinges before supper while his mother was taking a bath.

This house had a screened-in porch, another thing that made it better than the last house. His bicycle stood in a corner, ready to go. At the old place, he'd had to keep it in the garage, so he'd never bothered to use it on his prowls.

Leaning against the door frame, he put on his socks and shoes. Then he lifted his bike, carried it to the screen door, pushed open the door with his back, and hurried down the three porch stairs to the walkway.

The neighborhood was lighted by streetlamps and the moon. Deep patches of darkness hung under the trees. A few of the nearby homes had porch lights on, but most of the windows were dark. He saw no one.

The wind felt chilly on his face and hands. It had a wet fresh smell that made him uneasy with its hints of lonely distances. A feeling of gloom began to smother his excitement, and for just a moment he wished he were still in bed.

I'll be with the kids pretty soon, he told himself. It'll be great.

Shivering, he set his bicycle in the street, pushed it along with one foot on a pedal until it was gliding fast, then swung himself onto the seat. As he coasted down the lane, he checked his wristwatch. Ten till one.

Soon Jeremy found himself on Ocean Front Drive, pedaling alongside Funland. He spotted a wino sprawled between bushes in front of the wall, but farther up, near the entrance, there was nobody.

Maybe I'm the first one here, he thought.

Or maybe they're gathered on the boardwalk, out of sight.

He glided to the bicycle rack, hopped down, slid his bike between the bars, and chained it there. He walked toward the archway. He trotted up the stairs. Standing beneath the face of the clown, he scanned the darkness ahead. He saw the ticket booth and the boardwalk beyond it, but nobody was there.

He checked his wristwatch. Two minutes after one.

He strode forward into the shadowed tunnel of the entry-way, past the ticket booth, past the salt-water-taffy shop on his right and the souvenir shop on his left. Standing in the middle of the boardwalk, he looked from side to side. He had a clear

view of Funland from one end to the other—except where
shadows tore out patches of blackness—and he saw no one.

Where are they?

Not here, that's for sure. Unless they're hiding, planning to
sneak up and scare me.

Jeremy waited. Nobody appeared.

What if it's a trick? he thought. Suppose they never planned
to show up, and this was just a rotten trick to stick it to the
wimp?

He leaned back against the main ticket booth. Off in the
distance, a sea gull squealed. Combers, pale in the moonlight,
tumbled onto the beach. He felt cold and small and alone.

Should've known it was too good to be true, he thought.

Probably Tanya's idea to stand me up like this.

Tanya.

Jeremy sank down and hugged his knees to his chest.

Big joke. Set up the nerd. All the time, they were laughing
at me behind my back.

Maybe they're only late, he thought.

Sure thing.

He slid up the cuff of his jacket and pressed a button to
illuminate the numerals on his wristwatch. Twelve minutes
after one.

They *might* be late, he told himself. I'll give it till one-thirty.

He suddenly heard quick, quiet footfalls.

They're here!

His gloom vanished. He sprang up and stepped around the
side of the ticket booth, smiling and raising a hand to greet
them.

The girl, a few strides away, let out a startled gasp. She
lurched to a stop.

She wore a backpack and carried an instrument case that
looked as if it might hold a banjo.

Her face was a faint blur in the darkness. But she didn't
look short and skinny enough to be Liz, or large enough to be
Tanya.

"Sorry if I scared you," Jeremy said.

Her head turned. She looked to the sides, then glanced behind her.

"The others aren't here yet."

She faced Jeremy. "So you're one of *them?*"

Not, *So you're one of us?*

He felt like a fool. The backpack and banjo should've tipped him off. She wasn't a town kid. She was a camper or drifter or something.

"Depends who you mean by 'them,'" Jeremy said, wondering what she knew.

"The trollers."

He shrugged. "I don't know. What're trollers?"

Again the girl looked over her shoulder. Then she walked straight toward Jeremy. "Get out of my way, kid." It was no timid request. It was a command. Jeremy sidestepped out of her path.

She walked past him. She looked to the right and left, but not back at him, and made her way straight across the boardwalk to the open place between the railings. She trotted down the stairs to the beach.

When she reached the sand, only the top of her head showed. Moments later, her shoulders and backpack came into view. She turned around, and Jeremy felt a quick tug of fear. But she didn't come toward him. She walked backward several paces, then swung around again and strode away in the direction of the shore.

"Bitch," Jeremy muttered.

Get out of my way, kid. What was her problem, talking like that?

I should've stood my ground and said: Yeah? Who's gonna make me?

And she smiles—oh, she's a tough one—and sets down her banjo and swings the pack off her shoulders and takes off her coat. She's wearing a T-shirt. And she pulls that over her head because that's just how she likes to fight, in nothing but her jeans.

Jeremy imagined her, bare to the waist, her skin creamy in the moonlight, her nipples dark. She came for him slowly. Hunched over like a wrestler. Arms out. Circling him, looking for an opening.

Don't force me to hurt you, he warns.

You and what army? she asks.

Yeah, that'd be something. Wrestling with her, throwing her down. It could get really interesting then.

Better, though, if she were Tanya.

How about that, wrestling with Tanya?

She'd cream me.

It'd be worth it, though.

Where is she!

A hand clapped Jeremy on the shoulder, and he flinched and whirled around.

"Snuck up on you Indian-style," Cowboy said.

"Jeez, you scared the shit out of me."

"Lucky it was just me. You gotta be on your guard, you're out here alone. The fuckers'll have you for breakfast."

"Where're the others?"

"Home in bed, I reckon."

"What's going on?"

"They called it off for tonight."

I was right! Jeremy thought. They don't hate me. It wasn't a setup.

He had a tightness in his throat and a tingling hollow ache between his eyes, as if he were very close to crying, but he didn't know whether it was relief or disappointment that made him feel so strange.

"How come?" he asked.

"Damn story in the *Standard.* Did you see it?"

Jeremy shook his head.

"Some goat-twat reporter did a number on us. Read the dag-blamed riot act. Nate figured the heat might be too much to-night. You seen any cops around here?"

"No." He thought about mentioning the girl, but decided against it.

"Well, I didn't reckon it'd be a problem. Nate, though, he likes to play it careful. He was afraid they might have the place staked out tonight or something. Make a big play to grab us. So he got on the horn to Tanya and talked her out of tonight's little hoot."

"I didn't know," Jeremy said.

"Why do you think I'm here, Duke? Couldn't have you wait-ing out here all night, the party called off."

"Well, thanks."

"Would've been here sooner, but you know how it goes."

"Sure," Jeremy said. "Better late than never."

"Hope you didn't think we forgot about you."

"Naw. I figured it was something like this."

"Come on, let's get out of here before *we* get jumped."

Jeremy followed him toward the archway. "Jumped by who?" he asked.

"The trolls, man."

He remembered that the girl had asked if he was a troller. "What's all this troll stuff?" he asked.

"You know, *trolls.*"

"Like monsters that live under bridges?"

"You got it, Duke. Under bridges, under *boardwalks*, on the beach, everywhere. They're like cockroaches. They hide in all the dark places, then they come out and get you."

"That's fairy-tale stuff."

"You calling me a fairy?" Cowboy elbowed him and laughed.

They trotted down the concrete stairs and Jeremy nodded toward his chained bike.

"We're not talking fairy-tale trolls," Cowboy told him. "We're talking bums, winos, space cadets, like the buttwipe tried to hit you up for change before I came to your rescue."

"He was a troll?"

"Durn tootin'."

Jeremy stopped beside his bike and dug into his corduroys for the key case. There was no other bicycle in the rack. "How'd you get here?" he asked.

"Walked. You oughta walk too, next time."

Next time!

"When'll that be?" he asked, trying to control his excitement and sound nonchalant.

"Who knows? Tanya, she'd be at it every night if Nate didn't keep her in line. So she'll be rarin' to go by tomorrow, I reckon."

"Count me in, okay?"

"You betcha, Duke."

Smiling, Jeremy crouched to open the padlock.

"But lose the bike," Cowboy told him. "Never know when we might have to vamoose fast. You don't want to be tied to something like that, you might have to leave it behind."

"I'll walk, next time." He pulled the chain free, wrapped it around the seat post, and locked its ends together. Then he rolled his bike backward out of the rack. "Maybe we can meet and come down together."

"Sorry, man. You're okay, but you ain't no Liz."

"Hey, that's all right. No problem."

They started off side by side, Jeremy rolling his bike.

"What is it that you do, anyway?" he asked. "You know, when you meet over here?"

"Have us some fun."

"Are you . . . trollers?"

"You got it, Duke. They're the trolls, we're the trollers."

Jeremy nodded. All his guesses, he realized, had been wrong. Even the crazy ones.

"So what you do," he said, "you go hunting for them?"

"Fishing's more like it. Trolling, get it? We just put out the bait. We worm the hook. Tanya makes a right fine worm. One of them comes along and bites, we reel him in. Then we have us some fun with him. Or her."

"You beat them up or something?"

"Or something." Cowboy turned his face toward Jeremy. The brim of his hat hid his eyes, but his mouth was a tight line. "You got a problem with that?"

"Me? No. Fuck 'em."

The mouth tipped into a grin. "Figured you'd see it that way, Duke. I can always tell. I saw the look on your face when that scum on the boardwalk went sucking up to you. You damn near crapped your skivvies."

"Hey, I wasn't—"

"Yeah, man, you were scared brown. But that wasn't all. You looked like you wanted to rip his heart out and shove it up his Rio Grande."

Jeremy smiled. "Really?"

"You know it, man. And that's how the rest of us feel. Those maggots, they make your skin crawl, and they got no right messing with you. They oughta do us all a favor and crawl in a hole and die."

"But they don't," Jeremy said.

"Shit, no. What they do, they crawl right up out of their

holes and get in your face. 'Got a quarter, friend?'" Cowboy mimicked in a withered, whiny voice. "'Poor me, I ain't had a bite to eat in a week. Can y'spare two-bits?' And you just know the creep's gonna *touch* you if you don't come across with the coins."

That's just how it is, Jeremy thought. That's *exactly* how it is.

"Know what I say?" Cowboy asked.

"Fuck 'em."

"I say, 'No quarter, troll.' Do you know what that means, 'no quarter'?"

"He isn't going to get any money off you."

"More than that, Duke. More than that. No quarter."

Ten

"Baxter."

"Huh? Whuh?"

"Wake up."

Moaning, he opened his eyes. The motel room was dark. He was lying on his side, Kim's warm body curled against his back. "What is it?" he mumbled.

"Let's get up," she whispered, her breath tickling the nape of his neck.

"Huh? It's . . . middle of the night."

"It's a little after three," she said.

"Jesus."

"Let's get up and go out, okay?"

"Go *out*?"

"Down to the beach. We'll have it all to ourselves."

"You're out of your mind."

"It'll be neat."

"Neat. Forget it."

"Please?" She brushed her lips against his neck. Her hand roamed down his chest and belly, caressing him. "It'll be so romantic. We'll watch the sun come up."

"Wrong coast," he muttered.

"It'll still come up. Okay? It'll be something we'll always remember, you know? Watching the sun come up, our first morning together."

"This isn't the first."

"The first as man and wife. I want it to be special."

"We'd freeze our cans."

"We'll take a blanket. Okay? Please?" Her hand moved lower and gently pulled him. "I'll make it worth your while, big fella."

"Yeah?"

"Yeah," Kim said. "So how about it?"

"We must be out of our minds."

"You'll love it, just wait and see."

The mattress rocked Baxter as she rolled away from him and bounded off the bed. Light hit his eyes, stinging them like soapy water. He squeezed them shut. And felt the covers fly off, leaving him naked and chilled.

"Aw, jeez."

"Up up up," Kim chirped, grabbing his ankles and dragging his legs toward the bedside.

He squinted at her. She was bent over, gazing at him through a soft sway of bangs, a rosy suck mark on her shoulder. When she let go of his legs, he sat up.

"Last one dressed is a rotten egg," she said.

"Consider me a rotten egg." He sat there and watched Kim prance over to her open suitcase. Her rump jiggled slightly. It had the same golden tan as her back and legs except for a stark white triangle down the middle.

It'll be cold out there, he told himself. But it will be neat. She's right about that. Something to remember.

Kim stepped into baggy gray sweatpants. She hunched over a little as she knotted the drawstring at her waist. Then she lifted a matching sweatshirt out of her suitcase and turned around. "You just going to sit there?"

"Admiring the view."

He watched her breasts rise as her arms went up to pull the sweatshirt over her head. They swayed slightly as she searched for the sleeves. Her hands appeared and plucked the front down. "View all gone," she said.

"Shucks."

She took her hairbrush off the dresser and went into the bathroom. While she was gone, Baxter put on his own sweatsuit. It was the same as Kim's, but not as old. He'd bought it as a replacement after Kim had moved into his condo and started wearing his sweats on chilly mornings. He was tying his shoes by the time she came out of the bathroom.

He went in and brushed his teeth. On the counter beside the sink was the plastic bottle of suntan oil. After rinsing his mouth, he picked up the bottle and slipped it into the pouch-like pocket of his sweatshirt.

Kim was folding the bed's blanket when he returned. He saw that her shoes were on.

At the dresser he picked up the room key by its big plastic tag printed with the name and address of the motel. He dropped it into his pocket with the suntan oil.

She raised her eyebrows. "What've you got in there?"

He took out the bottle and showed her.

"Well, now. I see you're getting into the spirit of things."

"Might as well make the best of it."

He opened the door and they stepped out onto the balcony. The street in front of the motel was well-lighted, but no cars were going by and he saw no one wandering about. The parking lot of the all-night market across the street was deserted.

"Neat, huh?" Kim asked. She put an arm around his back and snuggled against his side. "It's like we're the only people in the world."

"They're all snug in bed."

"We'll be snug on the beach."

They walked to the end of the balcony and down the flight of stairs and across the motel's parking lot. Though Baxter felt her warmth where her body pressed his, the wind seemed to be seeping through his sweatclothes. He began to shiver, and he gritted his teeth to stop their clicking.

"Poor boy," Kim said. Stopping at the corner, she shook open the blanket. They draped it across their shoulders and pulled it closed in front. That was a lot better. Kim slipped her hand inside the rear of his pants, and that was better still.

They walked past a bum sleeping huddled against a store wall. Kim's hand stopped roaming.

"Guess we're *not* the only people in the world," Baxter said.

"Poor man."

"Yeah. He doesn't have you."

"We're so lucky. It makes you realize how lucky we are, doesn't it? I mean, wouldn't it be awful to live like that? With nobody who loves you, and no place to go at night?"

"We could offer him the use of our room while we're gone."

She gently slapped his rump. "It's nothing to make fun of. I think it's awful. I wish we could do something for him."

"I didn't bring my wallet. The blanket doesn't belong to us. You might give him the clothes off your back. I'd like that."

"Horny toad," she said, and gave him another slap.

They crossed the street and walked alongside the Funland parking lot. A few cars were still there. Baxter wondered if kids might be inside some of them, screwing around. This late? Not likely. Even in his heyday of humping in the backseat of his car, he'd never been out past about two.

Nobody's out at three-thirty.

Just us. And some snoozing bums. Maybe a few patrolling cops.

Cute if we got stopped by the cops.

We're not breaking any laws, he told himself. It only *feels* like it, wandering around at this hour.

"Trespassing on the wrong side of midnight," he said.

"Huh?"

"Just thinking," he explained. "It feels illegal, doing this."

They hurried across Ocean Front Drive, climbed the stairs, and entered the shadows beneath the Funland archway. In spite of the blanket, in spite of Kim's hand, Baxter began shivering again as they stepped into the moonlight. He looked up and down the boardwalk.

"What's wrong?" Kim asked.

"I just hope it's safe around here."

She squeezed his rump. "Don't be a worrywart."

They stopped at the edge of boardwalk. "Isn't this great?" she asked.

It didn't look great to Baxter. The familiar beach where he'd lazed in the sun, slicked Kim with oil, and gazed out at the warm blue Pacific was gone. The beach looked cold and desolate, like a wasteland at the border of an alien ocean.

He didn't want to go down there.

"I'm not so sure about this anymore," he said.

"Oh, really?" Kim slipped her hand out of his pants and turned to him. She swept the blanket open. Holding it at her shoulder, she raised her sweatshirt above her breasts and eased against him. She lifted his sweatshirt. He felt the warm smoothness of her skin. Her hand crept down into the front of his pants and stroked him.

"Why don't we go back to the motel?" he whispered.

"Why don't we not?"

"I don't like it here."

"*Feels* like you like it."

He squirmed.

While she caressed him, he stared past the side of her head. The planks of the boardwalk were moon-bleached bone. The black shadows weren't empty. They were hiding places.

I'm really getting paranoid, he told himself.

And felt his pants drop down around his ankles. The wind wrapped his bare skin.

"Woops," Kim said.

He bent over. As he grabbed the top of his pants, Kim tugged the blanket off him and whirled away with it and trotted down the stairs to the beach.

"Dammit, Kim!"

She danced on the sand, spinning and swinging the blanket overhead like a giant flag.

Baxter pulled his drawstring tight and knotted it. He descended the stairs. Not rushing. Watching Kim cavort.

He stepped off the last stair. The sand was soft and silent under his shoes. It pushed this way and that as he walked toward her. He wanted to run at her and grab her and carry her to safety. But if he made quick moves, she would flee, laughing.

He stopped. "Come here," he said.

She smiled. She draped the blanket over her shoulders. "What'll you give me?"

"A kiss."

"What else?"

"Kim, come on. I mean it. This place gives me the creeps."

"I think it's neat."

He made a dash for her.

Kim lurched aside. He grabbed a handful of the blanket, but she got away. Laughing, just as he'd guessed. She ran along the beach, kicking up plumes of sand, angling gradually closer to the dark shadow cast by the boardwalk. Baxter, in pursuit, couldn't rush full speed because of the blanket. He gathered it in as he chased her. Once it was wadded and pinned under his left arm, he began to catch up. But Kim was already far ahead of him.

She looked over her shoulder. In a singsong voice she called, "Slowpoke, slowpoke, you're so slow it ain't no joke."

Doesn't she realize?

Realize what? We're alone out here. She's having a good time. *I'm* the one with the problem.

But Baxter didn't like the way she was getting closer to the boardwalk, closer to its long shadow and the dark land of pilings below the fun zone.

She glanced back at him again. "Catch!" she called, and pulled the sweatshirt over her head and tossed it high. The wind snagged the shirt and tossed it toward the shadow. Baxter almost caught a sleeve as it tumbled away. He dodged to the left and snatched it off the sand at the edge of the darkness. He ran a few more strides, then had an idea. He stopped.

"So long, Kim. Have fun walking back to the motel."

She slowed. She halted. She turned around and put her hands on her hips. Her chest was heaving as she tried to catch her breath. Her breasts rose and fell. The rest of her skin was dusky. Her breasts looked as if they'd been dipped in cream. And the cream had been licked off the nipples, leaving them dark.

Baxter stared at her. She stared back.

"I don't think you're going anywhere," she said.

The beach seemed no less forbidding than before, and Baxter felt as if eyes were watching from the black area under the boardwalk, but Kim was right. He no longer had the urge to escape from this place.

Kim was bare to the waist, exposed and vulnerable.

Baxter wanted her.

He wanted her right here, right now.

Hands still on her hips, Kim ambled toward him.

He glanced into the dark forest of pilings, and shivered, and knew he wouldn't run.

His fear, moments ago crying out warnings to flee, now felt like icy fingers caressing him, tickling and stroking him, the fingers of a phantom whore sick with lust and aching for the party to start.

Kim halted a few paces in front of him.

"You must be freezing," he said.

"I'm not. Feels good."

He supposed the running had warmed her up. He no longer felt the cold himself. The shivers that still shook his body had little to do with the chilly wind.

"Take off the rest," he said.

In the moonlight he saw her smile. "Does this mean you aren't spooked anymore?" she asked.

"Just makes it better."

Balancing on one foot, she pulled off a shoe and sock. "I feel so *daring*, don't you?"

Baxter nodded. He glanced into the darkness. The icy fingers of his fear probed him and squeezed.

Kim hopped, her breasts jiggling as she removed the shoe and sock from her other foot. "You just gonna stand there?" she asked, untying the knot at her waist.

"Yes," he said.

Her sweatpants fell. She stepped on them to free her feet from the elastic around the cuffs. Then she came to Baxter, but instead of embracing him, she took the blanket. She carried it into the boardwalk's shadow. As the darkness closed over her, the fear squeezed Baxter hard, too hard suddenly, no longer a lusting slut but a cruel hag hurting him.

Kim shook the blanket open.

"Not over there," he said. "Let's put it here in the moonlight."

"What if somebody comes along?" Kim asked. "This is a lot more private."

"I want to be able to see you."

"Ah-hah." She came out, and Baxter's fear eased its clutch. Kim turned her back to the ocean wind. She unfurled the blanket. Squatting, she lowered it to the sand. As she pinned down two of the corners with her shoes, Baxter caught the other end and held it down. He took his shoes off and used them as weights.

Kim crawled onto the blanket. She lay down. She rolled onto her back and folded her hands beneath her head. "This is really great," she said.

"Is it too cold for the oil?" Baxter asked, his voice shaking.

"I want it," Kim said.

He found the plastic bottle in his pocket. He tossed it onto the blanket at her feet, then took off his socks and sweatsuit. He knelt in front of her.

She lay straight, legs tight together, and where her skin was tanned it was almost the same shade as the sand alongside the dark blanket, but bright compared to the shadow just beyond her head. Her hands were still pressed beneath her head, her elbows out to the sides. She squirmed slightly, as if relishing the feel of the blanket or impatient for the touch of his hands.

Baxter popped open the bottle's squirt top. He squeezed a line of oil up Kim's right leg. She flinched and arched her back when the stream crossed her groin, and seemed to relax again as it drew a silver trail down her left leg. Baxter closed the bottle and dropped it. He slid his hands up her skin, spreading the slick film. Its sweet coconut aroma reminded him of cotton candy, smelled good enough to eat, made him want to lick it off her.

Kim's shaved shins were a little bristly, but her thighs felt like silk.

She opened her legs. She moaned and writhed as he rubbed her.

Baxter, leaning forward, roamed her with slippery hands. The look and feel of her were almost too much to bear, and so was the wind. It stroked the backs of his legs, swept between his legs and licked his groin, stole the heat from the cleft of his buttocks, scurried up his back, ruffled his hair.

Hoping to calm himself before it was too late, he rested his hands on Kim's hips and lowered his head and shut his eyes.

She had said it would be neat.

What an understatement.

They'd already made love twice in the motel room before going to sleep. And countless times during the previous months. But it had never been like this.

And they were only beginning. She hadn't even touched him yet.

Should've started with her back, he thought.

He felt Kim's hands. They covered his hands and slid them down between her legs.

He lifted his head. "Eager beaver," he said.

She smiled and squirmed and stretched her arms out straight overhead.

He stroked her with his thumbs.

She gasped.

That couldn't have hurt her, he thought, and then she scooted away, thighs sliding under his hands, and he thought: How's she doing that?

"Bax!" she shrieked.

He looked up.

The shadow of the boardwalk was eating her, sucking her in.

No, not the shadow.

Two vague, hunched shapes dragged Kim by her wrists.

"No!" he yelled.

She was already gone to the waist. Her moonlit lap bucked and tossed. Her legs kicked.

Baxter caught one flailing ankle. He clutched it with both hands. In spite of the oil, he held on to it. But he didn't stop her. He was dragged along with her, his knees rucking up the blanket and pushing ruts in the sand.

"Stop!" he shouted. "What're you . . . ?"

His voice froze in his throat.

Beyond the two attackers, in the darkness under the boardwalk, were others. They scurried out from behind the pilings—bent, ragged shapes. Eight of them? Ten?

Baxter released Kim's foot.

The moonlight lost her.

"Don't leave me!" she squealed.

Baxter staggered to his feet.

He stood motionless, knowing he had time to flee. Then, with a growl of fierce despair he rushed into the dark. He hurled himself at the pair dragging Kim. He tore them down. On top of them, he yelled for Kim to run. Bony arms hooked around him. Fingers clawed his skin. Teeth clamped on his arm and thigh. He cried out with pain and punched and tried to push himself up, but the savage things clutched him, bit him. He gagged on their stench.

"Get up! Bax! Quick!"

"Run!" he yelled. Damn her, why hadn't she run? Didn't she see all those others?

Where *are* the others? he wondered. They should've been on him by now.

He pounded a fist into one of the foul shapes beneath him. This time, he did some damage. The guy wheezed and jerked and released him. He drove an elbow down into the midsection of the other.

Suddenly he was free. On hands and knees, he scurried off their twisting bodies. He looked up and saw Kim.

She had found a club of driftwood. She stood tall in the dark of the shadow, between Baxter and the hideous pack, swinging the wood as if she were Davy Crockett defending a wall of the Alamo with an empty musket. None in the pack seemed brave enough to attack and risk a blow.

Baxter stared at Kim—astonished and proud and afraid.

He struggled to his feet.

And glimpsed a smudge of motion high to his left. He turned his head in time to see a crone leap from the top of the board-walk's railing. She sailed down, arms out like the wings of a giant bat, black rags flapping. Kim saw her. Tried to leap back. But the hag folded over her, smashed her to the sand.

The silent pack rushed in.

Baxter rushed the pack.

Eleven

Mag and Charlie shambled out from beneath the boardwalk and made their way toward the stairs.

"No fair," Charlie said. "No fair no fair."

"Clam up," said Mag.

"Gonna *miss out!*" he whined.

Mag cuffed his arm.

He grabbed the hurt and stumbled out of reach. "Gonna miss out!"

"We was picked," Mag said. " 'Sides, we're gonna have us some fun." She waved the motel key at him and grinned.

"I wanna be in on it."

"Well, you ain't."

"No fair."

They climbed the stairs. As they scuffed across the boardwalk, Charlie heard a faint, muffled scream. He knew it came from the Funhouse. Without him. Moaning, he punched the side of his head.

"Hey."

He scowled at Mag. She dug into a pocket of her coat, pulled out a pint bottle, and offered it to him. He snatched it from her hand. A couple of hits, and he felt a little better.

Still wasn't fair, though.

He took another tug at the bottle, then reached it back toward Mag.

She waved it away. "G'on, keep it," she said. "I got more."

Whenever he saw Mag around, she seemed to be equipped with a fresh bottle. And it was usually good Scotch, not cheap wine. He didn't know what her story was, but figured maybe she got disability pay. She didn't seem crippled up, but she might've pulled a cheat on the state. That would explain her riches. Disability was a lot more than general relief, maybe three times as much. On the other hand, maybe she had some money put away. Or she might just be better at begging. He'd seen her at it, now and again, and she never outright asked for money. All she did was look her marks in the eye and say, "God bless you," and more often than not they'd fork over some change.

Charlie kept the bottle and worked on it, and it was good stuff. It heated him up. It gave him a buzz. By the time he finished the bottle, he was following Mag up the stairway to the motel's balcony.

She unlocked the door of room 210, and they stepped inside. Charlie shut the door. Mag flicked a wall switch, and a lamp came on beside the bed.

"Land," she said, "ain't this the berries, though?"

Charlie stood by the door and watched while she wandered the room. She seemed awfully chipper about being here. She found a wine bottle in the wastebasket and upended it, dribbling the last few drops into her mouth. On the dresser was a pack of Salems. She shook a cigarette out, stuck it between her lips, and fired it with a match. She ran her hands over the bed. Plucking the cigarette from her mouth, she picked up a pillow and rubbed her face with it. She stopped at each of the open suitcases and inspected what was inside. Then she went into the bathroom.

From where he stood, Charlie couldn't see what she was doing in there. Maybe she'd found something good. He hobbled forward and stopped when he spied her through the doorway.

Mag's coat was a heap on the floor. She stood behind it, unbuttoning the front of her sweater. The cigarette hung from a corner of her lips, its ribbon of smoke curling into one eye and making her squint. She got the sweater off, dropped it onto her coat, and started fumbling with the buttons of her old plaid shirt.

"What're y'doing?" Charlie asked.

"Mind yer own beezwax."

"I wanta go."

"Tough toenails."

"I'm gonna miss out."

"You already missed out. Stop your bellyaching."

He guessed she was right. Even if they left right now, it would all be over by the time they got back. "No fair," he muttered.

"This here's your first clean-up," Mag said. "You oughta be happy you ducked it this long."

"Poop," Charlie said.

Mag scowled at him, and pulled her shirt off. She wore a gray sweatshirt. She started lifting that, and Charlie caught a glimpse of gray skin blotchy with sores and scabs. He turned away fast.

Mag giggled. "Oooo, Charlie's shy."

"Ain't neither," he said. But he didn't look again. He crawled onto the bed and flopped. The sheet felt smooth and good against his face. It smelled nice too. He supposed it smelled from the woman they got. Oh, she was sure something, and he was missing all the fun.

He heard water start to splash, heard the skidding clink of a shower curtain.

He closed his eyes.

"Hey! Looky here."

He woke up, rolled over, and saw Mag in front of the dresser, facing him. She wore a low-cut white nightie that he could see right through and wished he couldn't. A string of pearls hung against her bony, mottled chest. There were rings on her fingers, bracelets on her wrists, and a pearl earring on each ear. The lobes of her ears dripped blood onto her shoulders. Her lips were red and glossy. She was grinning at Charlie with brown stubs of teeth as she drew a brush through her long black hair.

"Ain't I the purty one?" she asked.

"Like a whore that's three weeks dead," he told her.

Her eyes bugged out. She hurled the brush. It clopped Charlie over the left eye. As he dropped onto the bed, she rushed at him, squealing. He rolled away and curled up, hugging his head. The mattress rocked him as she leapt onto it.

"No-count cockless bag of shit!" she cried out.

Charlie yelped and whimpered as she pranced on the mattress, kicking and stomping him, as she sat on him and yanked his hair and rapped his head with sharp knuckles. Finally she left him alone. But he didn't move.

When he heard her weeping, he sat up.

Mag was sprawled on the carpet, hands tight against her face.

He got up and went to her.

He kicked her in the ribs.

"Even-Steven," he muttered.

She just stayed there sobbing while Charlie gathered up the man's clothes and toiletries and took them to the suitcase.

In a pants pocket, he found a wallet with almost three hundred dollars tucked inside the bill compartment. He didn't dare take any of the twenties. He'd be in trouble, sure, if he tried that. A few months back, Edgar'd been on clean-up and the next day Nasty Nancy spied him paying for a quart of bourbon with a ten-dollar bill. When you went on clean-up, it was okay to keep clothes. But nothing else.

Edgar claimed he found his ten on the beach. Nobody bought the story, though, and they'd made him "walk the house."

Charlie fingered through the money again. Along with the twenties and a few tens in the man's wallet, there were eight one-dollar bills. Charlie thought he might take a chance on some of those. Who was to say he didn't get them from some generous marks?

He glanced over his shoulder at Mag. She had rolled onto her side, and her head was turned away from him.

Nobody'd ever know.

But suddenly his last sight of Edgar filled his head and Charlie shuddered, legs going weak and shaky, scrotum shrinking tight, ice in his stomach, gooseflesh crawling up his spine.

With trembling hands he closed the wallet and slipped it into the pocket of the man's pants. In a front pocket he found a key case. He kept that, and put the pants inside the suitcase.

As he shut the suitcase, Mag came up beside him. He cringed and raised his arms to protect himself, but she didn't strike.

"Let me in there," she said. Charlie stepped back. She brushed past him and stepped to the corner near the wall. There, she opened the woman's suitcase. She peeled the nightie off. Charlie squeezed his eyes shut. "Damn fool," she muttered. When he opened them again, she had on shiny pink panties and was stepping into a pair of green slacks. She fastened the slacks. Grinning at Charlie, she lifted a black bra out of the suitcase

and draped it over his face. Then she lifted out a green pullover sweater. She put it on. Sighing, she rubbed it against her
belly and hanging breasts. "Nice," she said. "You get yourself
some nice duds, Charlie."

"I like what I got," he told her.

"Damn fool." She unclasped the pearl necklace and dropped
it into the suitcase. She tossed in the rings. She took the earrings from her bloody lobes. Charlie saw that the earrings
were for pierced ears, and hers weren't pierced. At least they
hadn't been.

She took white socks and tennis shoes from the suitcase,
put them on, then went to the closet and came out wearing the
woman's nylon windbreaker. She retrieved her clothes from
the bathroom and stuffed them into the suitcase. After that,
she wandered around gathering the rest of the woman's things.

"You got the keys?" she asked.

Charlie held up the key case. She plucked it from his
hand.

They latched the luggage, and Mag went to the door. Charlie lifted both suitcases off their stands. He followed her outside.

In the east, the sky was pale. But the sun wouldn't be up for
a while yet. From the balcony's height, he had a good view. He
saw no one. The street in front of the motel was deserted.
There were about ten cars in the parking lot.

Mag hurried ahead of him. He struggled along with the heavy
suitcases. By the time he came to the bottom of the stairs, Mag
had already found the car to match her key. It was a blue
BMW. She opened the trunk while Charlie hurried across the
parking lot.

He swung the suitcases into the trunk.

Mag, in the driver's seat, leaned over and unlocked the passenger door for him. He climbed inside. The car smelled new.

Its engine thundered to life. Mag backed it up, then swung
it toward the exit.

"How 'bout a ride?" Mag asked, gunning it onto the street.

"I wanna get back," Charlie said.

"Yer too late for the fun."

Maybe not, he thought. "I don' care," he told her.

She muttered something that Charlie couldn't make out. But she took him toward Funland, the car weaving a little as she raced it up the middle of the street and sped through the blinking red traffic light. She stopped it with a hard lurch that flung him at the dashboard.

"You take the stuff," she told him.

She gave him the keys. He opened the trunk and removed the suitcases. Then he stepped to her window and handed back the keys.

"What're y'gonna do?" he asked.

Mag grinned at him. "Take her for a spin. Don't ya fret, fool, I'll leave the thing a good ways off."

The car squealed, laying rubber, and shot away, heading north.

Charlie picked up the suitcases.

He lugged them up the stairs to the boardwalk.

He wondered how long they'd been gone. Too long, probably. The fun was sure to be over by now.

Never knew, though.

Sometimes it lasted pretty long.

He quickened his pace.

Twelve

Robin crawled out of her sleeping bag. The morning was gray with fog. Shivering, she sat on the nylon bag. She searched her pack, took out fresh underwear and socks, her blue jeans and sleeveless shirt. She swept her eyes over the tops of the dunes surrounding her encampment. She saw nobody, and the sand was piled high enough to conceal her from anyone who might be nearby.

Quickly she slipped the folded money out of the front of the underpants she was wearing. She tucked the bills into the front pocket of her jeans. Then she took off the T-shirt and panties she'd slept in and put on the clothes from her pack.

She had used her rolled windbreaker for a pillow. She picked it up, uncovering the sheathed knife that lay on her ground cloth. Once she had the windbreaker on, her shivers subsided.

She slipped the knife into a side pocket of her pack.

Then she put on her hiking boots. The chill of them seeped through her socks, but her body heat quickly warmed them.

She stood up and climbed the sand slope. From the top she had a clear view of the rolling grass-tufted dunes and the flat beach stretching out to the ocean. Gulls whirled and swooped through the gray air. A man was running along the shore, his black Lab trotting at his side. Far down the beach, in the area near Funland, a man was hunting for treasure with the help of a metal detector. Even farther away, surfers stood around in their wet suits and others were on the water—some riding in on combers, but most of them either paddling out, belly-down on their boards, or already way out on the rolling slate of the sea, legs dangling, roosting there as if content to sit.

Her attention strayed from the surfers as she noticed some-one descending the main stairs from the boardwalk. A woman in a white sweatshirt and red shorts, a satchel swinging at her side. She was a long way off.

Those were the stairs that Robin had gone down last night, and she was amazed that she had walked so far.

The kid by the ticket booth had really spooked her. The kid, and his friends who hadn't shown up yet. They had to be troll-ers. Why else would they be meeting there at that hour?

Robin looked the other way.

She had put just about as much distance as possible between herself and the kid. No more than forty or fifty feet ahead, a chain-link fence marked the end of the public beach. Beyond it, set far back from the shore, stood somebody's house.

The tide was in now, waves washing past the end of the fence. Last night she could've stepped around that post without get-ting her feet wet, and taken refuge beyond the barrier. But she'd been reluctant to trespass.

Her place in the dunes, she thought, had been fine.

The kids hadn't found her there.

She wondered if they'd tried.

"Now, there's as fair a maiden as ever claimed a heart."

Robin whirled around. The man stood on the crest of the dune behind her campsite. A bum. Fat and old and wearing soiled clothes, a knobby staff in one hand. She felt squirmy inside as she wondered how long he'd been watching her. Had he been hiding, spying on her while she dressed?

"Professor E. A. Poppinsack," he said, doffing his hat. The hat was a faded brown bowler. Red feathers, tucked into the band on each side, stuck up like wings. He was bald, but he had a thick mustache with ends that curled up in points. He wore a dirty buckskin jacket, fringe swinging in the breeze, and plaid pants that looked more suited to a golfer roaming the links than a bum on the beach. "Top of the morning to you, dear. Have a spot of tea?"

Robin shook her head. "Sorry," she told him. "I don't have any."

"Ah, but I have. Join me, won't you? Let us sit upon the ground and tell sad tales of the deaths of kings." Without waiting for a reply, the man turned away and descended the slope. He held his staff high. Its tip twirled a bit when he was out of sight.

Odd bird, Robin thought. But she'd liked the merry twinkle in his eyes, and he'd seemed harmless enough. His outfit made him look, somehow, like a medicine man—the kind of fellow who might have wandered into frontier towns, hawking elixir from the back of his wagon.

Curious, she followed him over the dunes. His encampment was directly behind hers, forty or fifty feet further inland, in a depression surrounded by high drifts of sand.

"Welcome to my estate," said Poppinsack. He gestured to his rolled sleeping bag. Robin sat down on it. The old man crouched over the pot of boiling water on his propane stove, and added more water from a canteen.

"All the comforts of home," Robin said.

"Indeed, unemcumbered by the nuisances of mortgage, tax, insurance, and utilities. God provides, Poppinsack abides." He fetched tea bags from the bulging pocket of his buckskin coat, turned off the flame beneath the pot of roiling water, and plopped in the two bags—along with their strings and paper tabs. "Shall we allow that to steep for a bit?" he asked.

He lowered himself onto a nearby slope. "Are you a Puck or a Pip?"

"A Robin."

"Ah, Cock Robin. Cockless, as the case may be."

The remark unsettled her. Maybe this man wasn't just a harmless eccentric.

"Born to be hanged, mayhap, but not hung. Words. Words are Poppinsack's passion. The music of the mind. Twenty-six letters, infinite realms."

"I write some poetry myself," Robin told him, relaxing somewhat. "Songs."

His eyes lit up. "A bard?" He slapped his knees, and dust popped from the faded plaid of his pants. "We're kinsmen, then. Sing me a song."

Smiling, Robin shrugged. "I don't have my banjo."

"Fetch it, then, and sing for your tea."

"Why not?" She got up and hurried off. Descending the sand bank to her camp, she was struck by the close proximity of the two sleeping places. She wondered whether Poppinsack had been aware, all night, of her presence. If so, he hadn't tried anything. She realized that she felt more comforted than troubled by knowing he'd been nearby.

She hadn't been completely alone, after all.

If the trollers had found her, would Poppinsack have come blustering to her rescue, brandishing his staff?

Banjo case in hand, she returned to his "estate." She took out the instrument and sat on his bedroll.

"Was it you I heard yesterday?" Poppinsack asked.

"It might've been. I was playing on the boardwalk."

"While I played words on the strand."

"Played words?" she asked.

"*Beowulf*, Tennessee Williams, Mickey Spillane. Smiting Grendyl, flying with the bird that never lands, plugging a dame in the guts. 'It was easy.' And you, my dear, performed the background score. It's a pleasure to make your acquaintance. Now, sing me a song."

"There's a new one I've been working on. I'll test it out on you."

Smiling, Poppinsack closed his eyes, folded his hands on the lap of his buckskin coat, and leaned back against the sand.

Robin's fingers flew over the banjo strings, lifting out a quick, spangled tune. After running once through the melody, she started to sing:

Darling, I've been here and I've been there
And I've been next to nowhere.
I've been upside down, and inside out,
Topsy-turvy and tossed about.
I've been flying high, and crashing low.
I laugh and cry wherever I go—
And it's all from looking for you,
And it's all from looking for you.

You ain't got a face and you ain't got a name,
But I'm gonna find you just the same.
I'll know you by your swaggering walk
And the way I tremble when you talk.
You're the guy with the sunlight in your eyes,
With the laugh that makes my goose bumps rise—
And I'll keep looking for you,
And I'll keep looking for you.

You're the moon and stars and the sunlit sea,
And yabba-dabba doo and diddly dee,
I ain't writ more so I gots to stop.
Boppity hoppity dibbidy dop.

Nodding and grinning, Poppinsack applauded. "Minstrel girl," he said. "The Robin is a bardling sure. 'Laugh that makes my goose bumps rise'—oh, dear."

"You think that line sucks?" she asked.

"Fetching. *You're* fetching. And I shall fetch the tea." He pushed himself off the sand, went to his duffel bag, and searched inside it. After a few moments he came up with a glove and two plastic mugs. Wearing the glove on his hand, he poured steaming tea into one of the mugs and brought it to Robin. He smelled as if he'd doused himself with cologne, but under its sweet aroma lurked a dark musty odor. Purple capillaries webbed his cheeks. His veiny, bulbous nose was so pitted that it reminded Robin of a huge strawberry decomposing. Trapped in the hairs of his mustache were bits of old meals.

Poppinsack, she decided, looked better at a distance.

"Care for cream?" he asked.

"You have cream?"

"Not a drop. Care for a dollop of rum?" he asked, and pulled a plastic flask from a pocket of his coat.

"Thanks, anyway."

He filled a mug for himself, splashed some rum in, and returned to his seat on the dune's slope.

Robin inspected her tea. She was glad to find nothing afloat in it. She took a sip. "Good," she said.

Poppinsack drank from his mug, sighed, and smacked his lips. "Tell me, minstrel girl, what curse has brought you to this blighted beach?"

"I'm just wandering, seeing the world."

"Fleeing from what, and whom?"

She shook her head. "What makes you think I'm fleeing from something?"

"Your hurt and haunted eyes."

"You're nuts."

"I've seen all things in the heaven and in the earth. I've seen many things in hell. How, then, am I nuts?"

"Poe, right?"

"Mercifully butchered. And what tale has your heart to tell?"

She saw no reason to keep the truth from Poppinsack. "My father died. My mother had a fiancé more interested in me. I hit the road. End of story."

"And how have you fared on the road?"

"I'm still kicking," Robin said. "What's your story?"

"To outmatch the wit of your brevity, I am a book bum."

"Are you really a professor?"

"I have ceased to profess. 'Tis far more pleasurable indeed to hoard pearls than to cast them before swine."

"So you gave up teaching and now you read all the time?"

He nodded and drank his spiked tea.

"How long have you been here in Boleta Bay?"

"Forever and a day."

"Aren't you afraid of the trollers?"

He gazed at Robin and lifted his thick gray eyebrows. "Are you not afraid of the *trolls?*"

"We're trolls, aren't we? I mean, I guess the kids might think so."

"Thar be trolls and thar be trolls," Poppinsack said, sounding a lot like Robert Newton playing Long John Silver. "Thar be them that's harmless, and thar be them that ain't. Poppinsack could tell such tales of madness as would turn a wench's blood cold and freeze the chambers of her heart."

Robin wrinkled her face at him. "You trying to scare me, or what?"

"You're a roving bard and minstrel," he said, dropping the pirate growl. "You're a smart dame, and long on moxie. But under it all, you're a kid and you don't know the score."

"Maybe I know more than you think. I've been around some."

"And have you been God's spy in the court of the damned?"

"Whatever that means," she muttered.

"Hie thee away from here. Take a powder, hit the road, ride your thumb to Frisco or L.A., hop on a bus to Palookaville." And in a voice suddenly void of borrowed rhetoric, he said, "Get the hell out of town, Robin. If you stick around, you might just disappear."

She stared at him.

"Everybody knew Cock Robin. Nobody knows where she's gone."

"You really are scaring me."

"The robin that flies today won't be a dead duck tomorrow."

"If it's so dangerous around here," she asked, "why do you stay?"

"Why, indeed? Perhaps because the mermaids sing to me." Poppinsack finished his tea. "Farewell," he said.

Robin nodded. "My cue to exit?" she asked.

"Your company has been much appreciated. Heed my warning and flee."

"I think I will," she told him. "This place gives me the creeps anyway, and you're about the fourth person to warn me so far." She drank the last of her tea, set the mug down on the ground, and closed her banjo case. "Thanks for the tea," she said, standing up.

"And I thank you for the song."

With a wave, she turned away and climbed the dune out of Poppinsack's encampment.

In a coffee shop two blocks east of the boardwalk, Robin ate a breakfast of fried eggs, sausage links, hash browns, and toast. While she worked on the meal, her mind kept straying back to the strange old man and his warnings.

Evil trolls. Disappearances. The court of the damned.

Weird stuff. But he might've made it up, just wanting to scare her away. Maybe he felt that she had invaded his territory or something. Perhaps he simply enjoyed scaring people.

But he'd seemed a little spooked himself.

Maybe he believed what he'd told her, but none of it had any basis in reality. After all, he was a boozer.

Whether or not the stuff was true, Robin's experiences with trolls last night had been unnerving, and the kids were an actual threat.

Reason enough to blow this town.

When she finished eating, she picked up the tab. Breakfast had cost four-eighty. She pulled the pack of money from her jeans pocket and folded it open.

She spread the bills.

Her mouth fell open. Her stomach sank.

She looked through the stack again and again.

Every bill was a one.

Yesterday, after she left the downtown bank, six of them had been twenties, one a ten.

Between last night at the movie theater and right now in the coffee shop, somebody had taken her money, substituted singles for twenties, and returned it to her.

And there was only one possible time when it could've been done.

While she slept.

In spite of the restaurant's warmth, chills crawled up Robin's back. She squeezed her legs together.

She saw Poppinsack kneeling beside her in the dark, sliding open the zipper of her sleeping bag, maybe after already searching her boots and pack and guessing that whatever money she might have was kept on her body. She imagined his hands roaming over her while she slept, not just seeking the money but feeling her up, finally slipping a hand inside her panties and taking out the bills and touching her there too.

Cockless Robin.

The dirty bastard.

And he gave me tea and I sang for him, and all the time he had my money and *he knew what he'd done to me.*

Robin's face burned. Her heart pounded. She trembled.

He robbed me and groped me while I slept, and then he pretended to be my friend.

So much for his warnings to leave town.

Hoping I'll be gone before I find out what he did.

She left her tip on the table, shouldered her pack and picked up her banjo case, and went to the front counter. After paying the cashier, she had only seven dollars.

She stepped outside.

Wouldn't dare leave town now, she thought, even if I wanted to.

Seven dollars was as good as nothing. That short, she'd be too vulnerable on the road.

Feverish with humiliation and outrage, she strode toward the boardwalk.

Funland hadn't opened yet, but workers were there getting ready for the crowd. Down on the beach, clean-up crews were dumping trash barrels and raking debris out of the sand. A few bums were also going through yesterday's litter. But not Poppinsack.

Several joggers were out, running along the shore. A man in leotards was doing a peculiar routine that looked like slow-motion ballet. A little kid was on her knees, parents watching, father snapping photos while she dug in the sand. There were no sunbathers; there was no sun. The surfers were gone. No one was in the water. The lifeguard was at her station anyway. She wore red shorts and a white sweatshirt.

Robin trudged on. She left them all behind. Finally, forty or fifty feet from the chain-link fence marking the boundary of the public beach, she turned away from the ocean. She climbed up and down the dunes.

In a sheltered depression, she set her banjo case on the sand and slung the pack off her back. She took her knife from the pack and slipped it into a rear pocket of her jeans.

He'll deny it, she thought. What're you going to do, cut him up?

We'll see.

Dammit, nobody messes with me!

She found the place where she had slept, where Poppinsack had crept up on her in the night and . . . *handled* her.

From there, she knew where to find him.

She rushed over the dunes. Charging up the last slope, she jerked the knife from its sheath.

And then she reached the top.

He was gone. All that remained were two sodden brown tea bags lying in the sand.

Thirteen

Jeremy climbed down the stairs to the beach. The sun had broken through, back around noon, and a lot of gals were sprawled out, sunbathing. But they held no interest for him. His eyes swung toward the lifeguard station.

She was there.

Tanya.

Even at this distance he recognized Tanya by her size and curves, her tanned legs and golden hair.

The sight of her made him ache.

He wished he could go to her, take her in his arms, kiss her, feel her body pressed against his.

I can at least go over and say hi, he told himself.

But he didn't move. He couldn't force himself to take even one step closer.

He gritted his teeth hard.

Such a goddamn chicken.

He climbed back up the stairs to the boardwalk. Cowboy had said to meet him here this afternoon, but hadn't been specific about the time. Jeremy turned in a circle, trying to spot his friend.

He suspected that Cowboy was somewhere along the south end of the boardwalk. The good rides and attractions, including Liz's dunk tank, were in that direction. But Jeremy hadn't seen much of the north end. He had all afternoon to find Cowboy, so he headed that way.

The people passing near him looked much the same as those he'd seen yesterday: many were sleazy; plenty were slobs; there were tough guys and rowdies; he saw wild groups of teenagers; there were a few, but only a few, people who looked harmless and well-groomed and nicely dressed. Those were mostly couples and families. Probably on vacation.

Yesterday, before meeting Cowboy, he'd felt intimidated by the assortment of unsavory characters. But not today. Though he was alone, he didn't *feel* alone. He knew that he had friends nearby. Not just Cowboy, but Liz in the dunk tank, Tanya out on the beach, even teenagers who were strangers to him but probably were friends of Cowboy or the others, and therefore almost like Jeremy's own friends, though they didn't know him.

He felt as if he belonged.

And then he heard the distant tinny strains of banjo music. The music came from somewhere ahead, past the pavilion.

Did it come, he wondered, from the bitch who'd snapped at him last night?

He kept walking, and the music grew strong.

Ahead, up near the end of the boardwalk, an audience was clustered around the musician. Or musicians—it sounded like more than one. Did she have friends? Where had they been last night?

What if she recognizes me and sics them on me?

I didn't do anything to her.

Her friends won't dare try anything, he told himself. There are too many people around.

Jeremy reached the outer edge of the audience. He side-stepped until he found a gap.

She was playing alone.

"Battle Hymn of the Republic"? At first, it seemed to be. Then it turned into "Dixie." Then "When Johnny Comes Marching Home" worked its way in, and the three songs seemed to flow into each other, blending into a tune that was a mix of all three.

The bitch was good.

And good to look at. Kind of boyish, but feminine too. Her arms were bare, and her faded blue shirt was unbuttoned partway down, showing a narrow strip of her chest.

A final flourish, and the song ended. People clapped and yelled. Some stepped forward to toss money into her banjo case. Jeremy was ready to duck if she should look in his direction, but she kept her head down, her eyes low.

When she raised her head, he slipped behind a tall man.

"Here's a piece I composed myself," she said. "You might call it an antiwar song . . . or you might not."

She started playing. Jeremy eased over and peered at her. She was gazing straight ahead, off to his right, at about the same spot where she'd kept her eyes during the last number.

She began to sing along with the quick pounding music of the banjo.

It's the greatest weenie roast
That the world has ever seen—
We got fires coast to coast,
In our hair and in our jeans.
We got hot lemonade,
And we sure got fries.
Though we ain't got shade,
We got crisp cherry pies.
We got steamy watermelon
And marshmallows too—
If you're willin',
There's plenty to drink and chew.

So grab yourself a weenie and join in the fun
And for Godsake don't burn your buns.

Sick, Jeremy thought. But some of the people in the audience laughed and hooted as if they thought it was funny.

Though the song went on, he had heard enough. He moved away from the crowd and hurried back down the boardwalk.

She was a bitch, all right. Making fun of nuclear war. He wished he'd stood up to her last night. Slugged her in the face and thrown her down.

Ripped her shirt open.

Not so tough now, are you, honey?

How do you like *this* weenie?

Maybe she'd write a song about how much fun it is getting the shit kicked out of you and raped.

Almost as if reading his mind—or maybe just troubled by the look on his face—a female cop fixed her eyes on Jeremy. She was coming toward him. A man was with her. They both wore white T-shirts, blue caps, and shorts. Except for their gunbelts, he wouldn't have guessed they were cops.

She nodded as the guy talked to her, but she didn't take her eyes off Jeremy.

What is she, psychic?

Trying to be casual about it, he turned his head away.

She's going to stop me, he thought.

His face felt hot. His heart pounded. He felt shaky inside.

I didn't *do* anything!

She walked right past him.

He sighed.

He gave her a few seconds, then looked over his shoulder. Her face was turned toward the other cop.

Stupid bitch, he thought. Why'd she want to stare at me like that?

Good-looking, though, for a cop. He realized that she looked a lot like Tanya. The hair hanging below her cap had the same golden color. Her back was just as broad, her legs as tanned and strong.

She could almost be Tanya's older sister. Or her mother.

Her mother. Fat chance.

Besides, the cop was too young for that.

He saw the straps of her bra through the T-shirt. Lowering his eyes, he watched the way her buttocks moved inside the blue shorts.

Someone wandered in behind her, blocking Jeremy's view. He sidestepped, trying to see her again, but it was no use.

"Hey, amigo."

He swung around and grinned. "Hey, man, you're always sneaking up on me."

"Scoping out the local fuzz?"

"She's got a nice ass," Jeremy said, and started following Cowboy down the boardwalk.

"A nice everything, Duker."

"You know her?"

"Officer Delaney. Seems okay. She's just been on the board-walk a couple weeks."

"Is she actual police," he asked, "or just some kind of rent-a-cop?"

"The real McCoy. This here's a public park. Patrolled by the BBPD, not some rinky-dink private security outfit."

"Not even a night watchman or anything?"

"Nope. Just the local fuzz. Matter of fact, makes it easy for us. All we do is post a lookout and scram if a patrol car shows up. Which ain't all that often. The cops on graveyard, seems like they spend most of their time at the doughnut shop."

"So they've never caught any of you?"

"Never come close," Cowboy said. "Hey, check it out." He stopped walking and nodded to the right, where people were leaving the fenced area in front of the Tilt-a-Whirl. Through the gate staggered a slim girl clinging to the arm of her boyfriend as if she were too dizzy to stand on her own. Jeremy guessed they were both about twenty years old. She wore blue-jean shorts, cut off so high they had no legs at all. The side that he could see had a slit running up to her belt. Her T-shirt had been chopped off halfway down. It was long enough to cover her breasts, but not by much, and the ragged edge hung inches away from her body.

She looked hard, though. Her hair, bleached white, stuck out in all directions. Her earrings were red feathers. Her lip-stick was silver. She snapped gum.

Her boyfriend looked twice as hard. He wore motorcycle boots and faded jeans. He had a knife case on his belt. He was shirtless, tanned and muscular. A dagger wrapped by a snake was tattooed on his chest. From his earlobe dangled something that looked like a miniature set of handcuffs.

Outside the Tilt-a-Whirl's gate, those two turned around and waited for another couple.

The next guy looked wiry and mean. He had a Mohawk haircut, dyed purple. He wore a brass band around his neck, another on his upper arm, and a brass earring. He was bare to the waist and wore black leather pants. He had no tattoo that Jeremy could see, but he wore a knife case just like his friend.

The girl at his side had a shaved head. Her thin black eyebrows, curving upward, reminded Jeremy of Ming the Merciless. He could see her nipples through her tank top. They were big dark disks. The fabric jutted out as if being poked by fingertips. Her breasts seemed much too large for her small frame. The front of her shirt swayed and bobbed as she walked. It was tucked into a black leather miniskirt. She wore black boots that reached nearly to her knees.

"Now, there's a couple of gals I wouldn't kick outta the bunk bed," Cowboy said, and started following the group down the boardwalk.

"I bet they bite."

"Yeah, bite me, babes. Oooo." Cowboy walked fast, staying close behind them. "How about the bald one?"

Jeremy wanted to warn him to keep his voice down.

"Chrome-dome."

"They're gonna hear you."

"Check out those butts. Swish swish swish."

The group angled to the left, and Cowboy hurried after them. They stopped in front of a sideshow called Jasper's Oddities. A bony old man standing on a platform by the entrance swept the top hat off his head and leered down at them.

"Step right in, folks. See the amazing, astonishing wonders of Jasper's Oddities. Right this way, folks. Don't miss out. See the two-headed baby, the hairless orangutan of Borneo, the mummy Ram Cho-tep, and other rare and mysterious wonders. Yes, sirs, step right in. Bring in the ladies. They'll quiver and shake at the sights. They'll swoon in your arms. Step right in, folks. Three tickets is all it takes. You couldn't ride the Hurricane for that. Three tickets each, cheap at any price. See the Oddities, collected by yours truly, Jasper Dunn, world explorer and renowned connoisseur of the truly bizarre. Never before on the continent of North America has such a collection been offered under one roof. Offered for your perusal and delight. Step right in, folks."

"Bet it's a rip-off," Mohawk said to his friends in a voice loud enough for Jasper to hear. The old man grinned. He was missing a front tooth. "Me, I went in a freak show one time, all it had was fucking *pictures* of the dudes."

"I assure you," Jasper said, "my exhibits are genuine. And in days gone by, when yours truly had a freak show, each and every specimen was present in the flesh, remarkable and hideous beyond your wildest fantasies. They, alas, are no more. The honorable folks of this fine town prevailed, and the freaks were cast out like the spoiled garbage of yesterday's meal. However, their memory is preserved in the Gallery of the Weird, a truly astounding collection of photographs which you may see when you enter Jasper's Oddities."

Mohawk's head bobbed up and down. "What'd I tell you, fucking *pictures.*"

"You are in error, young man. The only photographs are those you'll see in the Gallery of the Weird. Each and every oddity is authentic, there for you to gaze upon—and touch, if you dare."

"Let's go for it," said the tattooed guy. "What d'you say?" he asked his girlfriend.

She shrugged. Her half-shirt rose with her shoulders, a frail curtain that lifted briefly and gave Jeremy a glimpse of the pale underside of a breast. "I'm kinda hungry," she said. Her voice sounded low and husky.

"Yeah," said the hairless one. "Let's get some fries."

Jasper raised a hand. "Did I mention that today is Ladies' Day? The young women enter for absolutely no charge, no charge whatsoever, absolutely free with the paid admissions of their escorts. So step right up. See the Oddities. Right this way." He swept his top hat toward the open door behind him.

"Yeah, I'm doing it," said the tattooed guy. He dug some tickets out of his pocket. "Come on, Jingles." He grabbed the girl's arm and pulled her toward the stairs.

Mohawk took out some tickets too.

"And how about *you?*" Jasper asked, his watery eyes turning to Jeremy and Cowboy.

"We're in," Cowboy called.

Jeremy's stomach went cold. "I don't know," he muttered.

"Chicken?"

I'm not a chicken, he told himself. "I haven't got any tickets," he said.

"That's okay," Cowboy said. "I got plenty."

He'd wanted to watch Jingles, in the half-shirt, climb the stairs, but she was already at the top by the time he looked. He saw only her back as she followed her boyfriend through the doorway. The girl in the leather skirt was still climbing the stairs, but Mohawk blocked the view and he missed his chance to see up her skirt.

Jeremy realized that he didn't really care. He wouldn't have enjoyed the peeks anyway. Not now. Not knowing that he had to enter Jasper's Oddities.

Jasper gave him the creeps.

He didn't want to see the weird stuff inside.

Even though the girls wore such scanty clothes and so much showed, he didn't want to be in a confined place with those four weirdos.

But he couldn't let Cowboy think he was chicken.

He went up the stairs behind Cowboy, who handed a strip of tickets to the skeletal old man.

Fourteen

Oh, just great, Jeremy thought. Bad enough, being in here with those four geeks, but Jasper had followed him through the doorway. The old fart probably wanted to make sure nobody screwed around with his collection.

The door swung shut, cutting off the light from outside.

Jeremy had expected the interior of Jasper's Oddities to resemble a small room in a museum. Instead, he found himself in a corridor. The only light came from a shaded bulb placed below each of the framed photographs that lined the walls.

The Gallery of the Weird.

Jingles and her friends had stopped in front of the first photo. From where Jeremy stood, he couldn't see what it showed.

Jingles giggled.

"He could get ya coming and going," said the tattooed guy.

"Gimme a break," Mohawk said. "He ain't real. It's trick photography."

Jeremy flinched as hands clasped his shoulders. Gooseflesh spread up his back. "Pardon me, young man," Jasper said, and let go and stepped past him. Cowboy lurched out of the way. For all his bravado, he must've been nervous too.

Jasper hurried on. He stopped at the far side of the picture. "Behold Jim and Tim, the Siamese twins."

"We can read," the hairless girl said.

"Let's get to the real stuff," Mohawk said. "Who gives a hot fuck about a buncha stupid pictures?"

"These are photographs of the most unusual, bizarre—"

"Does he *have* to breathe down our necks?" Jingles blurted.

"Yeah, man. Get outta our face."

"As you wish," Jasper said, and slinked away down the corridor. He didn't disappear, though. He stopped at the corner and stood there waiting in the darkness.

"Good going," Cowboy said, taking off his hat and brushing it against Mohawk's shoulder. "That's tellin' the old sack of fart gas."

"Screw off," Mohawk said.

"Well, pardon my ass, Chingachgook."

Jeremy groaned.

"You lookin' to get busted up, boy?"

Cowboy opened his mouth. Jeremy elbowed him.

The hairless gal put an arm around Mohawk and said, "Come on, Woody. Don't fool with them scrotes." They turned away, and Jeremy held on to Cowboy's arm.

"Let's give them some room," he whispered.

"You hear what she called us?"

"Those guys'd clean our clocks."

"They don't scare me."

Jeremy saw that the others had wandered farther down the corridor. They weren't stopping to inspect the photos. Apparently they felt the same way as Woody and wanted to get to the real stuff.

Jeremy stopped at the photo of Jim and Tim, the Siamese twins. The two young men were joined at the hip. They shared something that looked like a double-pouched G-string. The sight of them made Jeremy feel queasy, but he stayed in front of the picture and stared at it.

"They're getting away from us," Cowboy said.

"I want to see this stuff," Jeremy lied.

"Well, shoot. Stay, then." Cowboy went on ahead.

Jeremy hurried after him. He gave the photographs only quick glances as he passed by them, and was rather glad he didn't have a chance to look more closely. What he glimpsed as he rushed along wasn't pleasant: a man with an extra arm, a small, withered thing that grew out of his chest; a furry woman in a bikini who had a face with a canine snout; a man with his tongue sticking out, a tongue that looked eight or ten inches long; a legless man doing a handstand; a woman with two heads; a woman with three breasts in a row, bare except for sparkling pasties with tassels; a giant man standing beside a midget who came up to his knees; and a man with arms so long that his hands almost touched the floor.

The photograph of the long-armed man was the last in the corridor. Jasper no longer stood in the corner. He must've followed the punkers.

Jeremy took a deep breath. He felt shaky and a little nauseous. The close, stifling air didn't help. It smelled like an old house, abandoned and sealed tight for years. Lifting the front of his shirt, he wiped the sweat off his face. Then he followed Cowboy around the corner.

They stepped past the wall. A second corridor, similar to the one they'd just left, stretched toward the front of the building. The four jerks were gathered at the first display. Jasper stood beyond them, almost invisible except for his pale face.

"Let's wait," Jeremy whispered.

"Don't be a woos," Cowboy told him, and walked toward the group. But not quickly.

"It winked at you," said the tattooed guy. His hand was on Jingles' back, up under her T-shirt.

"Did not," she said. She sounded worried, though.

"Which head?" Woody asked, and laughed.

They moved on toward the next exhibit, and Jeremy saw that they'd been looking at a human fetus in a jar. "Farout," Cowboy said. He stopped in front of the platform and leaned close to the lighted bottle. Jeremy stayed beside him, but didn't bend down. He could see just fine from where he stood.

The fluid in the bottle was yellowish and murky. The skin of the suspended fetus looked yellow too. The thing had two heads. Its eyes were open.

Jeremy wondered if the thing might've come from the two-headed woman whose photo he'd seen in the Gallery of the Weird.

Cowboy stuck his face so close to the jar that his nose nearly touched it. "Looks just like a little old man," he said.

Jeremy swallowed hard and turned away. The group was clustered near the next oddity. Hairless and Woody stood together, arms across each other's backs. Tattoo was standing partly behind Jingles, his hand moving slowly up and down her side.

"Check it out," Cowboy said.

Jeremy looked at him.

Cowboy clutched the jar in both hands and gave it a quick shake. The fetus tilted, swayed, turned. Bits and flecks of something swirled in the fluid.

Jeremy gagged. He clutched his mouth. Praying he wouldn't vomit, he whirled away. He blinked tears from his eyes and saw Jasper standing motionless in the dark. The old man must've seen what Cowboy did. But he raised no protest. Apparently he didn't care.

By the time Cowboy lost interest in the fetus, Jingles and the others had moved on. A mummy remained—brightly illuminated by a spotlight at its feet.

"That ain't Karloff," Cowboy commented, heading for it.

It looked like no mummy Jeremy had ever seen in horror movies or museums.

It wasn't wrapped.

It was a dried-up, brown cadaver, held into a standing position by a harness of leather straps nailed to the wall.

It had no eyes. Its jaw hung open. Its right arm was gone.

"Looks like he's made outta beef jerky," Cowboy said.

For the sake of decency, a rag had been tied around its pelvic girdle. Jeremy supposed the old man had done that.

When Cowboy crouched and lifted the rag, Jeremy shut his eyes.

"Ooooph," Cowboy said. "Who let the air out? Come here and check this out."

Jeremy opened his eyes, but averted them from the mummy. There were two more exhibits in this corridor. The four geeks had finished looking at both, and were turning the corner.

"The gals are getting away," he warned.

"Well, shoot." Cowboy stood up and hurried forward. Approaching the next display, he slowed his pace. He angled toward it, but turned his head toward the end of the corridor as if he were torn between inspecting the oddity and catching up to the girls.

The oddity won.

Jeremy had caught a glimpse of it, so he stayed as far away as he could. "Haven't you ever been in here before?" he asked.

"Never had the urge before. Can't stand that crud, Jasper. Jesus, look at this sucker."

This sucker was a black spider nearly three feet in height. Jeremy took another quick look at it, and kept walking.

He supposed it must be dead, stuffed.

If it weren't, it would be in a cage, not standing there on its display platform with nothing between it and the customers.

He hurried toward three shrunken heads on pedestals. He was glad to see them. Their monkeylike faces with stitched eyelids and lips seemed almost friendly compared to the other things he'd seen.

From behind him came Cowboy's voice. "'Jasper's Giganticus.'" He sounded as if he were reading. Probably from one of the hand-lettered cards tacked up close to each exhibit.

"'Discovered by Jasper Dunn in the jungles of New Zealand, April 10, 1951.' Poor critter," he added in his regular voice. "Reckon its mother whacked it with an ugly stick."

"Some shrunken heads over here," Jeremy said, wishing Cowboy would come away from the damn spider.

"Yeah? Anyone we know?"

He heard Cowboy's footsteps. They came up behind him. "Yeah. Hmm. Let's go." Cowboy didn't stop for a close look at the heads, but kept walking.

Jeremy went after him. Before turning the corner, he glanced back at the spider. It was still on its pedestal. Of course, he told himself. What did you expect?

He stepped around the wall, and halted abruptly. He'd thought the punkers would be halfway down the corridor by now, but they were still gathered in front of the first exhibit.

This oddity *was* in a cage. More of a display case, actually. Jeremy had a good view of it through the glass or clear plastic side. It didn't seem to be alive.

Like the mummy, it was held upright by leather straps.

"That ain't no hairless orangutan of Borneo," Tattoo said.

"Why, you seen one before?" Jingles asked.

"I seen orangutans at the zoo, and that ain't one."

It didn't look like an orangutan to Jeremy either. More like what you'd get, he thought, if you took the Creature from the Black Lagoon and gave it claws instead of flippers and changed its lizardy skin to flesh that was white and smooth. Though it looked more than six feet tall and powerfully muscled, something about the texture of its flesh made it seem soft and a little sluglike.

It wore nothing except a G-string. The garment's black pouch was enormous.

"What is this thing, really?" Tattoo asked, turning his head toward Jasper, who was standing some distance off.

"I was requested to remain 'out of your faces,'" Jasper replied, "such as they are."

"It's nothing but a rubber suit," Woody said. "The worldwide explorer picked it up at a rummage sale in Hollywood."

"Yeah," his girlfriend agreed. "I seen it in a flick."

"I assure you," Jasper said, "the creature before you is authentic, as are all my Oddities. Less than a decade ago, it lived and breathed. It rampaged, committing murder and rape."

"Gimme a break," Woody muttered.

"I think it's your old man, Chingachgook."

Jeremy's stomach dropped.

Woody whirled around. His eyes seemed to be bulging from their sockets. His mouth hung open. He was breathing hard. Except for the quick rise and fall of his chest, he didn't move.

Then his hand moved to the knife case on his belt. He unsnapped the flap and drew out a folding knife. He started to pry the blade from the handle.

"Uh-oh," Cowboy said. He grinned, tipped his hat, then spun around and lunged around the corner.

Jeremy raced after him.

"Let's get 'em!" he heard Woody yell.

Cowboy blasted open the door. Sunlight struck Jeremy's eyes. Squinting, he saw Cowboy vault the wooden railing and drop to the boardwalk. He did the same. His feet hit the planking. His legs folded and his knees pounded the wood. Wincing, he scurried forward and tried to stand.

Someone landed on his back, smashing him down.

"Gonna trash you, fuckhead." Woody's voice.

He felt his hair being grabbed. His head was yanked up, scalp burning with pain, and he *knew* Woody was about to slash his throat. Instead, the guy jerked his hair downward, bouncing his forehead on the boardwalk.

"Hey, creepo," Jeremy heard. "He didn't do nothing."

Cowboy's voice.

Woody crawled off his back, making sure to dig in with his knees before leaving.

"Come 'n get it, jack-off," Woody said.

Jeremy got to his hands and knees. Lifting his head, he saw all four of the creeps in front of him. They had Cowboy surrounded. Cowboy wasn't even trying to run away. He just stood there, turning around slowly, grinning at each of them.

Woody and Tattoo both had their knives out. They were grinning back at him.

Spectators had formed a semicircle around the group. They looked excited, eager to see what might happen next. Did they think this was some kind of *performance?*

"Last time I saw turds like you," Cowboy said, turning from Jingles to Woody, "was just before I flushed."

You idiot! Jeremy thought.

Tattoo darted in from the side. Cowboy danced out of the way, but the knife jumped at him and sliced his forearm.

"Hey, now, ratface . . ."

Woody charged at him from the rear.

Jeremy threw himself forward. Diving, he caught one of Woody's ankles. As the guy flopped flat, Jingles rushed over and stomped Jeremy's forearm. He cried out. She raised her boot to stomp again, and he pulled his arm in quickly and started to roll away from her. Jingles pranced after him. She stopped his roll when Jeremy was on his back—by ramming her boot down on his belly.

For an instant, as the foot descended, he realized he had a wonderful view right up the front of her chopped-off T-shirt. He saw the round undersides of her breasts, even the bottom parts of her nipples. Just the sort of view he'd been hoping for.

Great, he thought.

Then his body seemed to explode with pain and his breath blasted out.

Fifteen

Up ahead, a bum swatted at the woman standing in front of him. The miniature cassette recorder flew from her hand. It tumbled, nearly striking a passerby in the face. As the woman whirled away from the bum to go after the recorder, Dave got a side view and saw that it was Gloria.

"Ace reporter in action," Joan said.

"Christ," Dave muttered.

Joan drew her nightstick from the ring on her belt and headed for the bum. Dave strode toward Gloria. She scooped the recorder off the boardwalk and shook it near her ear as if to find out whether it had developed a rattle.

"Gloria."

Her head snapped toward him. For an instant she looked startled and disoriented. Then she smiled. "Oh, it's you."

"Yes, it's me." He couldn't keep the annoyance out of his voice. "What the hell are you doing?"

"I was trying to conduct an interview, but—"

"No please, no please!"

"Shut up." Joan prodded the bum closer to Gloria. His watery eyes looked terrified.

Sighing, Gloria shook her head. "Don't hurt him. Leave him alone. He didn't do anything. I . . . intruded on his territory." She met his eyes. "I'm awfully sorry. I didn't mean to get you in trouble."

"Let him go," Dave said.

"Take a hike, mister," Joan told the bum, and slipped the nightstick into her belt.

He wandered away, muttering to himself.

"I'm sorry, you two," Gloria said.

Joan shrugged, smiled, and said, "No problem. Are you all right?"

"Fine. I didn't mean to cause any trouble. I've been trying to get *their* side of the trolling story . . . and meeting with a good deal of resistance. They just don't trust me."

"They're all paranoid," Joan told her.

"Why don't you find yourself a different story?" Dave said. "You're never going to get any straight answers from—"

"*Cops!*"

Dave pivoted away from Gloria. A kid ten or eleven years old was racing through the crowd. He turned and pointed behind him. "*Cops!*" he yelled again. "A fight! Knives!" He slowed down as he got close to them. "Somebody gonna get killed! Fronta the Funhouse!"

Dave yanked the radio from his belt. He thumbed the speak button. "Officers need assistance. Funland. In front of Dunn's." For good measure he added, "Send ambulance." He jammed the radio back onto his belt, and took off after Joan.

She had already sprinted past the huffing boy. Dave put on

the steam, but couldn't catch up to her. He didn't like the idea of Joan being first—not heading into a situation they knew so little about. The kid had said there were knives. Plural. At least two knives, but how many? Dave wished he'd taken a second to get more information.

Find out soon enough, he thought.

"Wait up!" he called to Joan.

She didn't wait up.

"Dammit," he muttered.

Worried and frustrated as he felt, Dave had to admire her moves. God, she was fast! And the way she darted and dodged around the people in her way reminded him of O. J. Simpson in the old days, going for a touchdown.

Her moves were too damn good.

Dave had a last glimpse of her blue shorts; then the milling crowd blocked her from his view.

The group of spectators Joan saw in front of Jasper's Oddities reminded her of the banjo girl's audience. Except there were more here. And some were rushing away. And the rest weren't standing still, listening; instead, they jumped and shouted.

She stopped running and worked her way into the crowd, squeezing between the onlookers, snapping, "Out of my way! Police. Move aside. Out of the way. Police. Move it!" Some refused to budge. They didn't want the show stopped. She fought her urge to knock them out of the way. She stepped around them.

People elbowed her.

Someone yanked the seat of her shorts, and she felt them slip down a bit before she batted the hand away.

Then she broke through the front of the crowd.

Like entering an arena.

"Police!" she shouted, rushing forward and trying to make sense of what she was seeing. "Break it up!"

A teenage male with a bloody face was bent over, driving a knee up into the stomach of a female. The female was naked except for cut-off jeans. The blow from the kid's knee lifted her feet off the boardwalk.

A second female, this one in a leather skirt and torn tank

top, pushed herself off the wood and charged the boy. She knocked the boy off his feet, and all three tumbled into a heap.

Drawing her nightstick, Joan turned her attention to the other group of fighters.

She wished she'd seen them first.

She rushed at them.

"Police!" she yelled.

The one on top, a freak with a purple Mohawk, leapt off the body and turned on Joan. He had a knife in his right hand, a severed ear in his left.

Behind him, a kid was sprawled on the boardwalk, clutching the side of his head. Another guy, under him, apparently an accomplice of the one with the Mohawk, thrust the victim aside and started to get up.

"Both of you freeze!" she shouted.

She glimpsed movement out of the corner of her eye, looked to the left, and saw the two females fleeing. Joan had thought they were victims, but she quickly changed her mind. The crowd parted to make way for them. The kid stayed put, sitting on the boardwalk and wiping the blood off his face with a white T-shirt.

Joan snapped her eyes back to the pair of shirtless males. They both had knives. They glanced at each other.

"Drop your weapons!"

The one who'd been under the victim shook his head. The one holding the ear shook his head.

Joan considered going for her sidearm.

Right, she thought. And blow away a few spectators.

"Drop 'em right now!" That was Dave's voice. It came from just behind her.

The grinning jerk with the Mohawk haircut popped the severed ear into his mouth. He started to chew, and Joan thought: They could've sewn it back on, you fuck-head!

The ear flew out of his mouth and slapped gently against Joan's right breast an instant after her shoe drove into his solar plexus. It clung to her T-shirt. She cupped her free hand over it at the same moment the toe of her shoe caught the guy under the chin. Blood and bits of broken teeth exploded from his mouth. His knife sailed into the crowd at his back. Then he slammed the boardwalk and lay motionless.

His friend spun around. One of the spectators didn't get out of his way fast enough. He jammed his knife into the man's stomach, shoved the squealing guy backward, and rushed through the quickly parting crowd.

"I've got him," Dave said.

As Dave went after him, Joan crouched by the kid squirming on the boardwalk. "I've got your ear," she said. "They'll put it back on. You'll be good as new." She hoped so. He appeared to have several other wounds.

She heard sirens.

"An ambulance'll be here in a minute. Hang on."

"Reckon I ain't got much choice," the kid muttered.

She hurried forward, and knelt beside the man who'd been knifed in the stomach. He was conscious, clutching his wound, whimpering and trying to dig his heels into the boardwalk.

She placed her empty hand on his hands and gently squeezed them. "You'll be all right. Keep that pressure on the wound. Ambulance is on the way."

Then she left him, deciding her best immediate course of action was to check out the wounds of the kid whose ear had been taken off, administer whatever first aid she could before the ambulance arrived.

Dave hurled himself over the railing and dropped to the beach. When his feet hit the sand, he let himself tumble forward. He rolled on his shoulder, came up facing the ocean, couldn't spot the kid running away, and pivoted in time to see the kid dashing at him from under the boardwalk.

Not in time to avoid the thrusting knife.

As the blade sped toward him, he twisted sideways. Instead of plunging into his chest, it ripped across him. He didn't feel pain, but he heard a tearing sound and felt a streak of warmth along his ribs.

He grabbed the attacker's wrist. With his other hand he smashed the back of the elbow. He heard a pop, felt the joint go. The guy cried out and dropped the knife.

Dave threw him down on the sand. Kneeling, he yanked the

broken arm up behind his back. The kid screamed, but didn't resist. In seconds, Dave had him cuffed.

Jingles sat with her back against a piling, deep in the shadows beneath the boardwalk. Her stomach ached from catching that jerk-off's knee. It seemed to help, sitting curled up this way, hugging her legs to her breasts.

"How long's it been?" Lorna asked.

"Who knows? An hour?" Maybe even longer, Jingles thought. It seemed like ages ago that she'd heard the sirens. She'd peed herself when the kid smashed her, and her damp shorts hadn't been uncomfortable at first. After a while, though, they'd started making her skin feel hot and itchy. It seemed as if she'd been living with that forever. "Maybe a couple hours," she added.

"I bet the cops've cleared out by now," Lorna said.

"So what?"

"Maybe we oughta get going."

"Oh, right. I'm sure. Case you hadn't noticed, I'm missing something. That rotten dickhead."

"What're we gonna do?"

"I don't know." Jingles stood up, and let go of her belly long enough to pluck the damp seat of her cut-offs away from her rump. Turning around, she peered through the dark forest of pilings. She saw segments of bright, sunlit beach. A few people were wandering by. "How about you go out and find me a top?" she suggested.

"What, like grab a bikini off someone?"

"Or a towel."

"Just like that, huh? Then the cops nail me and you're still under here with your tits in the breeze."

Jingles stepped back behind the post and met Lorna's eyes. "You got any money?"

"I left my purse in the car."

"Yeah, me too. Shit. Those shops up there, they're loaded with stuff. How about going up and lifting me something?"

"Get real. Look at me." She plucked at the front of her clinging tank top. "Where'm I gonna stash you a blouse or whatever, huh?"

Jingles shook her head. She could see right through the thin fabric of her friend's top. Nothing could be hidden under the skirt either. It was way too short.

"You don't gotta stash it anywhere," Jingles explained. "*Wear* it. Grab a blouse, put it on, they'll think it's yours."

"Forget it. Look at me. You think I can waltz into some shop and get away with *anything?*"

"Guess not," Jingles admitted. Lorna was right. Eyes would be on her the whole time because of her shaved head and clothes that revealed so much of her body. People had stared at her *before* the fight. Now her lower lip was split and puffy. Now a strap of her top was broken, leaving her right shoulder bare, the strap hanging down so that her breast was partly uncovered. Everybody would watch her. For one reason or another.

"One look at me," Lorna said, "a damn shopkeeper'd send for the cops."

"Not if it's a guy," Jingles said.

"No way. Forget it."

"Then how about going to the car?" she asked.

"Woody locked it."

"So break a window."

"He'd kill me."

"He ain't gonna kill nobody. He's probably behind bars. So you smash a window and get the purses and buy me—"

"You think I'm nuts? Break into the car in broad daylight?"

"I'd do it for you."

"Easy for you to say, since you ain't."

"Gimme your shirt, I'll go out and grab something."

"Yeah, no thanks. Leave me here alone? You get picked up, and I'm stuck. Huh-uh. I can just see me trying to hitch a ride back to Three Corners, my . . ." Her eyes went wary. "Don't even think about it. I can take you."

"Maybe, maybe not."

"Come on, we're pals. I'm gonna stick with you. We'll figure something."

Even if she could manage to get Lorna's shirt, there'd be hell to pay later on. Lorna wouldn't rest until she got even. Woody'd be in on the payback too.

"Look," Lorna said. "How about we wait till dark? Then we

jump whoever comes by, and get you something to wear. Good idea?"

"That's *hours*."

"You got any better ideas?"

Jingles shook her head. "Guess not."

They sat and waited, several feet apart, each with her back against a piling. After a while Lorna stretched out on the sand.

Jingles listened to the waves washing in against the shore, footsteps passing overhead, distant sounds of calliope music, the faint, far-off roar of the Hurricane.

There was nothing much to look at: the sand in front of her; some discarded bottles, bags, and rags probably left behind by winos; pilings as thick as telephone poles; the foundations of some buildings.

Not many foundations. She supposed that most of the buildings just rested on pilings. Where there were no foundations, the area under the boardwalk stretched into almost total darkness.

She didn't like staring into the dark area.

She turned her eyes to the nearby foundation. She guessed it belonged to the Funhouse, since it was right next to the Oddities place and it was two stories high. That big, it probably needed a foundation.

The cinder-block wall rose all the way up to the planking of the boardwalk. The gray blocks were decorated with crude artwork, the kind of stuff Jingles had seen, and sometimes drawn, on the walls of bathroom stalls. Among the sketches of sex organs were cartoonlike drawings of skulls, spiders, snakes, mutilated bodies. Words scribbled around and over the pictures mostly referred to sex acts, but others were more disturbing. She read such phrases as "Suk my blood" and "Rip her up," "Beware!" and "Satan Rules."

One phrase, "Inter my parler," was scrawled on the wall above a patch of crisscrossed boards near the middle of the foundation.

Jingles supposed that the planks covered a hole in the cinder blocks. Some of the winos had probably broken through the foundation, hoping to take shelter inside the abandoned Funhouse, and the boards had been put up to keep them out.

After dark, she thought, this place is probably crawling with bums.

We'll be gone by then. Soon as the sun goes down, we're out of here.

But before the sun went down, the fog came in. The area of darkness in front of Jingles spread closer. She found that she could no longer see the artwork and slogans on the cinder-block wall—which was just as well, since much of the graffiti made her nervous. But the afternoon's heat was stolen away.

Shivering, Jingles eased away from the post. On hands and knees, she looked toward the beach. Out beyond the board-walk, the air looked gray and misty.

A few people walked by. She could see them all right.

The fog was heavy enough to block out the sun, but not so thick that it would offer cover for their escape.

The sand seemed a lot warmer than the air, so Jingles crawled to her place behind the piling and lay down. She crossed her arms under her face for a pillow. That was better. The chilly air still crept over her back, but her front felt good, nestled in the sand.

She looked to the right. Lorna was still sprawled there, sleeping. She turned her head the other way.

She squinted through the faint light at the patch of boards on the Funhouse's foundation.

If she could pry some of those boards away . . .

Nice and warm inside.

She gritted her teeth to stop their clicking.

Wait in there till dark. Safe and cozy.

Jingles pushed herself up. On her knees, she brushed the sand off her skin. Then she crawled over to Lorna and shook the girl awake.

Lorna rolled onto her side, curled up, and hugged herself. "God, it's freezing!"

"Come on."

"What?"

"You'll see."

Lorna followed Jingles to the boarded area of the foundation. "What're we doing?"

"I think we can get in."

"Oh, shit."

"You rather freeze?"

Jingles dug her fingers under the end of a plank and pulled. She expected resistance.

Figured the boards were nailed into the cinder blocks.

But the entire patch of crisscrossed wood swung toward her like a door.

It *is* a door!

Christ.

Through the opening in front of her was total darkness. But she felt heat swelling out.

"I don't like this," Lorna muttered.

I don't either, Jingles thought. An actual door. A secret door. She didn't like it at all.

But the heat felt wonderful.

"It's warm," she said. "Come on."

Jingles stepped into the darkness. Lorna entered after her.

Jingles pulled the door shut.

"Yeah," she said. The warmth seemed to seep into her skin. Her shivering stopped. She sighed. "This is great, huh?"

Then she felt hands all over her.

Sixteen

After taking a shower, Dave removed the sodden bandage that had been applied at the emergency room. The cut, about two inches below his right nipple and nearly four inches long, was cross-hatched with stitches so it resembled a zipper. Though the blade had sliced through his skin, it hadn't penetrated to the muscle tissue.

If he'd been a little slower turning aside . . .

You really lucked out, he told himself.

He put together a fresh bandage of gauze and tape and pressed it over the wound.

In his bedroom, he combed his hair and got into a robe. He went into the kitchen for a beer. As he opened the refrigerator, the doorbell rang.

He hadn't really expected Gloria to come by. He'd seen the look on her face when Joan got into the ambulance with him. She hadn't bothered to show up at the emergency room. But she must've decided to come by, after all, and offer her sympathy or congratulations—or interview him for the *Standard*.

Maybe she's not here for that, he thought as he approached the door. Maybe she wants to comfort me. I could go for some comforting of the right kind.

He opened the door.

"Hey there, tiger."

He felt a smile break out. "My own Chuck Norris."

"I brought you some medicine," Joan said, and lifted a bottle of champagne from the paper bag she was bracing against her chest. Dave saw the foil-wrapped top of another bottle inside the bag.

"Come on in," he said.

She shrugged with one shoulder. "I just wanted to drop these off for you. I'm not in the habit of barging in on people."

"So break the habit." He waved her inside and shut the door. "Sit down, make yourself comfortable. I'll put some clothes on."

He hurried to his bedroom. There he shed his robe and stepped into underwear and corduroy pants. He put on a plaid shirt, slipped his feet into moccasins, and rushed back into the living room.

Joan was bending over the coffee table, setting the twin bottles of champagne on top of the flattened bag. She smiled at him, straightened up, and rubbed her hands on the sides of her skirt.

The skirt was very short. It was part of a white denim dress that had a zipper up the front. The zipper wasn't pulled to the neck. The opening showed a narrow V of skin. Joan's sleeves were rolled halfway up her forearms.

"I like your outfit," Dave said. "You seeing Harold later?"

"I doubt it. Threw this on figuring it might perk you up."

"Consider me perked."

She went with him into the kitchen.

"So, how are you feeling?" she asked. "That was a nasty gash he gave you."

"It's not so bad." As if calling his bluff, the wound burned him with pain when he reached into a high cupboard for wineglasses. He grimaced.

Joan put a hand on his shoulder. "You'd better take it easy, pal."

"I wonder how the others are doing."

"I just stopped by at the hospital." Joan took the glasses from him and headed for the living room. "It was touch and go with Willis for a while, but he's going to make it. They think they saved the kid's ear. It's a bit mangled, but it's back on his head."

"Thanks to your lightning foot," Dave said, not even trying to keep his admiration out of his voice. "You *destroyed* that guy."

Joan looked around at him. A corner of her mouth was tipped crooked. "That's what the doctors think too."

"Are you kidding?"

"He still hasn't regained consciousness."

"Is he going to?"

"They don't know."

"Oh, Jesus."

"Hey, it's his tough luck. Come on, let's drink. Sit down."

Dave lowered himself carefully onto the sofa. Leaning back against its soft cushion, he watched Joan peel the foil off one of the bottles. "The cork isn't plastic," he said. "Must be good stuff."

"Safeway's best." She removed the wire hood and dropped it onto the table. Clamping the bottle against her side, she began to twist the cork out. "Any heirloom pottery you'd like me to target?"

"Just don't hit me."

With a loud *pwomp*, the cork shot across the room and landed in a rocking chair. A wisp of white vapor curled out of the bottle's mouth, but foam didn't gush out.

"Nice job," Dave said.

Joan filled the glasses. She handed one to Dave, took one for herself, and sat down beside him. "Here's to quick reflexes and narrow escapes," she toasted.

"I'll drink to that."

They clinked the rims of their glasses and drank. "Real good," Dave said.

"I nearly picked up a six-pack instead, but I figured, what the hey. Isn't every day we get a chance to subdue a pair of knife-wielding bad-ass cruds. Calls for a celebration."

"That it does. How's my guy?"

"His arm'll be good as new by the time he leaves prison. That's maybe ten years down the road—assuming Willis doesn't succumb."

"He's not a juvie?"

Joan wiggled her eyebrows. "Nineteen."

"Great. How old's his buddy?"

Her cheery look slipped a bit. "Same. Not that it matters much. I don't see a trial in his future."

"He'll be all right."

Joan shrugged, forced a smile, and took another sip of champagne. "His name's Woodrow. Would you believe it? Woodrow Abernathy. A name like that, he's trotting around with a purple broom on his head like some kind of a freak out of *Mad Max*. Did you see him stick that kid's ear in his mouth?"

Dave nodded. He watched Joan's eyes. Her eyes usually seemed confident, somewhat amused. Now they looked a little frantic. He saw confusion in them, and pain and fear.

"I mean, if Woodrow was hungry, he could've had a hot dog."

"You did the right thing," Dave said. He patted her thigh, meaning only to comfort her, but the smooth feel of her skin sent a sudden surge of heat through him. He brought his hand back quickly and rested it on his own leg. "The creep knew what he was doing."

"My first kick did the job."

"He was still armed."

"I could've taken the knife away. I didn't have to demolish him." She finished the champagne in her glass, filled the glass again, and topped off Dave's. "I shouldn't have done it," she muttered.

"He'll probably be all right. If he's not, you can figure you saved somebody down the road. His next victim . . . victims."

"Yeah. I've been telling myself that. Shit."

"Is this the first time you've ever hurt someone?"

"Broke a guy's collarbone last year. Stopped him for speeding and he threw a punch at me. Hardly in the same category as scrambling a kid's brains."

"Comes with the territory," Dave said. "I killed a guy once. Back when I was LAPD. A drug bust. The guy sprayed a Mac 10 in my direction."

"Jesus."

"Wonderful thing about those weapons, you have 'em on full auto and they spit themselves empty in about two seconds. The bastard really filled the air with lead, but he ran clean out of ammo about the time he'd worked the spray in my direction. While he tried to change magazines, I put four rounds in his chest."

"Jesus," she said again.

"It was a pretty clear case of him-or-me, don't you think?"

"I'd say so."

"The guy was scum. He'd spent half his life behind bars: a few years here for assault with a deadly weapon . . . a few years there for rape . . . a few more for armed robbery. At age eighteen he was out long enough to blow away a creep who stiffed him in a coke deal, but the search warrant didn't hold up, so the charges were dropped."

"Not a nice guy," Joan said, looking and sounding more like her usual self.

"Not nice at all. And then he tries to mow me down with a goddamn submachine gun. And I drop the hammer on him, and the guilt turns me into a basket case. I was messed up for *months*. Makes no sense at all."

"Makes sense to me. Now."

"That's how I ended up here. Small town, I figured it'd be *peaceful*, you know? And it generally is. It's no L.A. What brought you here?"

"A family move. Mom married a poet who'd been out here for a writers' convention and couldn't wait to get back. You know how artsy this place is."

"The town's schizophrenic," Dave said.

"You noticed, huh? Downtown thinks it's Carmel, and the south end's a mecca for rednecks."

"And you throw in the military for some extra color." He remembered the way she'd acted with the sailors yesterday. "Were you in the Navy or something?"

"My dad was. We lost him in Vietnam. The Mekong Delta. He was a gunner on a patrol boat." She took another drink of champagne. "Anyway, so Mom had this thing with the poet, and she moved us out here. That was three years ago. I got started on a master's program in library science at the university . . ."

"You, a librarian?"

With the back of her wrist, she knocked him gently in the arm. "You got a problem with that, tough guy?"

"Hard to picture you. How did a future librarian end up a cop?"

"Mom and her poet pulled a disappearing act. I needed a job, and I met some cops during the investigation. Beth Lanier and I hit it off pretty well. She's the one who put the idea into my head. The rest is history."

"How come I didn't know about all this?" Dave asked.

"Never asked." Smiling, Joan took his empty glass, set it on the table with hers, and drained the bottle into them. She started to open the second bottle.

"I was here when you joined the force," Dave said. "Nobody ever said anything about your mother disappearing."

"Lone Wolf Carson? There's probably a lot of stuff you never heard about. Everybody but you musta knew." She laughed softly. "Known," she corrected herself.

She aimed the cork at the rocking chair where the first had landed, and shot it. This time, foam began to gush from the bottle. "Whoa shit!" she gasped. The white froth tumbled into the glasses, filling them both too fast, and kept rolling out, so she swung the overflowing bottle up to her mouth and gulped the suds.

"Don't choke yourself," Dave warned, laughing. He leaned forward and watched her throat work, watched champagne trickle down her chin and neck, down her wrist and forearm, watched the bottom of the bottle drip onto her leg and dress.

It was no longer erupting when she lowered it and sighed.

She made a silent burp. Her face went red and she looked downward. "Gosh, I'm sorry."

"No sweat."

She rubbed her wet thigh and spread her legs and peered down at the upholstery. "Don't think I got any on your couch," she muttered.

Dave joined her in looking, but didn't notice the upholstery. He saw only her smooth inner thighs and glimpsed her pink panties and felt a sudden swell of desire and turned his head away.

"Don't worry about the couch," he said, his voice coming out a little shaky. "I'll get you some paper towels."

"Thanks. I'm sorry."

"Don't worry." He pushed himself up, wincing slightly as a burning sensation reminded him of his wound, then hurried into the kitchen and pulled a yard of paper towels off the roll beside the sink.

When he came back into the room, Joan was standing. She looked up at him, a self-disgusted smirk on her face. The front of her white dress was blotchy with wet spots that gave the fabric a slightly gray coloring.

She shook her head as she took the towels from him. Instead of using them on herself, she wadded them into a huge ball and picked up the champagne bottle and dried it, then got down on her knees and lifted the glasses out of the puddle and wiped their bases and moved them to a dry spot and mopped the table's surface.

Dave almost told her not to bother. It was an old table and the champagne wouldn't hurt it anyway. But he kept his mouth shut and watched her.

This was a Joan with all her toughness gone.

She stood up, the wad of towels in her hand. "Want to point me to a wastebasket?" she asked.

Dave stepped around the table and took the wet clump from her. He tossed it onto the table. He put his hands on her shoulders. He looked into her eyes.

She shook her head. "I'd better go."

He said nothing. He eased her forward, and Joan wrapped her arms around him. Her smooth cheek slid against the side of his face. He felt the tickle of her breath on his ear, and he whispered, "You're *taller* than me," and he felt her laugh—gusts of warm air on his ear, her back shaking just a bit under his hands, her belly pulsing against his, her breasts moving slightly with her laughter, rubbing his chest.

She squeezed him hard, and he winced. "Ouch," she gasped. "I'm sorry."

He pushed a hand up into her thick hair and turned her head, turned her mouth toward his, pressed his mouth to her open lips, felt their softness and wetness, felt her breath enter him.

The doorbell rang and Joan lurched back and looked at Dave, her eyes wide and questioning.

He shook his head.

Joan ran a forearm across her slick mouth.

The bell rang again.

"Gloria?" she whispered.

"I don't know."

"You got a back door?"

"Forget it. Sit down and have a drink."

"God, Dave."

"I won't have you sneaking out."

"I shouldn't be here."

"Yes you should. Sit down, relax."

Grimacing, she bent over the table and picked up her glass. She took it to the rocking chair. She flinched as the doorbell rang again. Quickly she grabbed the two corks off the cushion, straightened her dress, and sat down.

Dave went to the door and opened it.

He forced himself to smile.

"How are you feeling?" Gloria asked, glancing at his chest, then gazing up into his eyes.

"Not bad."

She stepped into the doorway, leaned against him, wrapped her arms around his back, and tipped her face up for a kiss.

Dave didn't want to kiss her. He didn't like the way she clung to him. She felt small and bony and tense, and she was hugging him too hard.

He wondered if Joan was watching.

Probably not, he thought. She was probably sitting in that rocker with her eyes turned in the other direction and wishing she were anywhere else.

He kissed Gloria on the mouth. Her lips were cool and stiff, but they parted and she thrust her tongue into his mouth with a nervous urgency that chilled him.

He backed away. Her eyes looked stunned, annoyed. "What's gotten into . . . ?"

"Joan's here," he said, and watched Gloria's mouth snap shut. "Come on in."

"Oh. Oh?" She made a tight, curled smile and stepped past him.

Joan rose from the chair. "I just dropped by for a minute to bring our conquering hero some medication." A smile on her face (a smile that, to Dave, seemed sick with guilt), she raised her nearly empty glass for Gloria to see that the medication was champagne.

"That was very thoughtful of you," Gloria said.

Dave saw that Joan had raised the zipper of her dress a few inches higher. The moist spots on the fabric hadn't quite gone away. They were faint, though.

"I'll get another glass," Dave said.

"Are you sure I'm not interrupting?" Gloria asked.

Joan shook her head.

Dave rushed into the kitchen. He reached into the cupboard with his left hand this time, and managed not to awaken his pain as he took down a wineglass.

When he returned to the living room, Gloria was seated on the couch. Where Joan had been sitting.

Could she feel Joan's warmth on the cushion?

So what if she can? Dave told himself.

She sat stiffly, hands folded on her lap, eyes darting from Joan to Dave.

He didn't want to think about what she must be feeling right now.

He took the glass to the table and lifted the champagne bottle. "Just a dab," Gloria said. "Besides, I see there's not much left."

"We've been knocking it back pretty good," Dave said, hoping to lighten the situation. Gloria arched an eyebrow. He filled her glass halfway to the top before she stopped him.

He turned toward Joan with the bottle. She shook her head. "No more for me, thanks. I really should be getting home."

"Oh, don't rush off on my account," Gloria said.

"Debbie and I usually eat about now." She stood up. "Are you going to take tomorrow off, Dave?"

"No, I'll be in."

"Can't keep a good man down," Gloria said.

Dave set down the bottle and walked Joan to the door. "Thanks for coming by," he said. "The medication helped." He stepped onto the porch with her, but left the door open for Gloria's sake.

"Sorry if I made trouble for you," Joan whispered.

"You didn't."

"Don't bet on it."

He wanted to hold her. He kept his hands at his sides. "Take it easy, huh?"

"You too."

He watched her walk to her car. Then, with a sigh, he entered the house and closed the door.

"You two must've had quite a party," Gloria said.

"We had a tough day. Both of us."

"Did you enjoy consoling one another?"

He leaned over the table and filled his glass with champagne. He took it to the rocker.

"Oh, that's nice. Keep your distance."

"You're in a lousy mood."

"Oh, and I should be delighted to walk in and find Joan here, half-smashed?"

A few choice disclaimers ran through Dave's mind: it's not what you think; nothing happened; there's no reason to be jealous.

Lies.

"What was I supposed to do?" he asked. "Send her away?"

"And miss out on the sheer pleasure of her company? I hardly think so."

"She doesn't come in and start giving me a hard time."

"Oh, I suspect she gave you a very hard time. I saw that cute

little dress she was wearing. I saw the guilt on her face . . . and
yours. What were you doing before I put in my untimely appearance? More than drinking, I should imagine."

"Don't push it, Gloria."

"Oh, I touched a nerve?"

"I got stabbed today. I'm really not in any mood for one of
your scenes."

"Didn't she kiss it and make it all better?"

"What's happened to you?"

"To me?" Her eyebrows darted high.

"You've turned into a real bitch. All of a sudden, the past
couple of weeks, you've been acting like your chief goal in life
is to give me grief. If it isn't my eating habits, it's my politics. If
it isn't that, you're giving me shit about Joan. I'm sick of it."

"And I'm sick of her. Has that occurred to you as a possibility? It's not enough you spend eight hours a day with your
golden girl, you insist upon inflicting her on me *all the time*. It's
Joan did this, Joan said that. We even had her to a goddamn
barbecue so you wouldn't be deprived of her presence on your
day off."

"Calm down."

"Do you know how many times we've *fucked* since she came
into the picture?"

Dave didn't answer. He took a drink of champagne.

"Not once. Not once!"

"Well . . ."

"You've been putting it to her all along, haven't you? Haven't
you!"

"I think you should leave now."

"You and that slut have been—"

"Shut up!" He lurched to his feet and pointed at the door.
"Get out. I've had enough."

Gloria sprang up, glaring at him, shaking her head. "Oh, this
is cute. This is very cute." Back rigid, she walked toward the
door. "So long, Gloria," she said, not looking back. Her voice was
a quiet, lilting singsong. "Ta-ta. I had my fun with you, time to
throw you away. You're no match for the golden Amazon bitch.
Ta-ta. Fuck off, now, there's a good girl."

"Wait," Dave said.

He didn't want her to wait; he wanted her gone, but not like this. It shouldn't end this way, Gloria jabbering about being discarded like trash, sounding like a madwoman.

She opened the door.

"Gloria."

She stopped. She turned around and raised her eyebrows. "Did the pig speak? Is it sorry? Is it feeling guilty? And what does the pig have to say?"

Forget it, he thought. What he said was, "Oink."

Seventeen

Instead of calling it quits at six, as she had done yesterday, Robin took a short break. She ate a hot dog, then stationed herself above the main stairs to the beach and resumed playing and singing.

It hardly seemed worth the effort.

Few people had remained at Funland after the fog rolled in, and even fewer seemed willing to stand around and listen to her music. She was cold herself. Though the windbreaker kept her top warm, the chill, moist air seemed to soak through her jeans. She couldn't play with gloves on. Between songs, she tucked her hands into the warmth under her armpits.

As she stood there in the cold, playing for two or three people and sometimes gaining a quarter for her efforts, her mind wandered to all the places she would rather be. Warm places. A café, the movie theater, her sleeping bag. She even imagined herself checking into a motel and settling into a bathtub full of hot, hot water.

But she had to be here instead. Thanks to Poppinsack.

Working for a few coins to build up her stake. So she could afford warm places, so tomorrow or the day after, she could afford to hit the road out of this nest of bums, thieves, and trollers.

All day she'd been keeping a lookout for the fat old man in the buckskin jacket and feathered derby.

He must've made himself scarce, just in case she had ignored his advice to flee town.

While her hands were busy playing a Stephen Foster medley (though she realized she had no audience at the moment),
her mind replayed the scene she had already imagined so
many times.

She is crouched out of sight and Poppinsack comes staggering over the crest of the moon-washed dune. He sees her and
doffs his hat. "Ah-ha, we meet again. How do you fare, Cockless Robin?" Pretending he's glad to see her. And coming down
the slope.

She stands and pulls her knife on him. "You've got something that belongs to me, you thieving rat."

"Nonsense. Balderdash."

"Turn your pockets out," she snaps.

"You do me wrong, lassie. 'Twas't Poppinsack dipped into
your dainties and snatched the treasure."

"Don't try it!" she suddenly shouted, clamping her hands over
the banjo strings as a wino lurched in from the side, crouched
beside her case, and clawed out a folded dollar bill. "Hey!" She
took a step toward him, but he lurched away, spun around, and
ran, his long coat flapping behind him.

Robin stood there watching him flee, wanting to go after
him. If she left her things here . . .

The bum tried to run past a man coming down the boardwalk. The man swung an arm up. The bum's face hit it. He
flopped onto his back. The man stepped on his wrist, bent
down, and took the bill. When he lifted his foot off the wrist,
the bum scurried toward the side of the boardwalk, rolled under the railing, and dropped out of sight.

The man came toward her, holding up the dollar and smiling. Robin saw that he wasn't very old, maybe eighteen. He
wore jeans and a plaid shirt, and his hair was short. He looked
athletic and clean-cut, the kind of guy you might find wearing
a varsity letter sweater in the halls of a high school.

"Here you go," he said, and gave the dollar to her.

"Thanks." Robin stuffed it into a pocket of her windbreaker.
"You didn't have to go to all that trouble."

"No trouble. It's always a pleasure to clothesline a guy who'll stoop to stealing from a woman."

"Name's Robin," she said, and held her hand out.

"Nate," he told her, shaking it.

His hand felt warm and strong.

"How's business?" he asked.

"Booming," Robin said, and swept an arm toward her huge invisible audience.

"That's how it is, usually, when the fog's in. I went ahead and closed up early."

"You work here?"

"Sure." He gestured behind himself with a thumb. "Have you checked out the arcade?"

"Huh-uh."

"Well, if you had, I'm the guy who would've given you change."

"I'm the gal who wouldn't have needed any. I've got quarters up the . . . I get a lot of quarters."

"The way you sing and play, you oughta be on a stage getting twenty bucks a head."

"Well, thanks."

"I've been listening from the arcade. Couldn't make out the lyrics too well, but you sure play a mean banjo. I've never heard anything like it."

Robin smiled and shrugged.

"Matter of fact, it isn't right for me to enjoy it that much and not shell out." He reached to his rear pocket and took a wallet out.

"No. Please. You nailed that bum for me . . ."

"I insist." He took out a twenty-dollar bill.

"No. Don't be ridiculous."

"I don't want to force it on you."

"Then put it away. Please."

"I tell you what. Suppose you sing a song for me, and I'll throw a buck or something into your case."

"I guess that's fair enough."

She took a couple of steps backward and began to play for her audience of one. As she picked the quick, bouncy lead-in, she saw a smile spread across his face. His head bobbed with the rhythm, and Robin began to sing:

Kelly and Katie took off one day
For the Land of Purr where the kitty-cats play.
They packed their pockets with nacho chips,
Bubble gum, jelly, and chocolate lips,
Then hit the road for the Land of Purr
So fast on their skates they were just a blur.

Along about noon they stopped for a snack
Under the shade of a bamboo shack—
Where who should they meet but a cat named Clew
Who said, "I'm Clew! So who are you?"

"We're Kelly and Katie and we're on our way
To the Land of Purr where the kitty-cats stay."

"May I come too?" asked the cat named Clew.
"I'm hungry here since the birdies flew—
And I have no ears, as you can see,
So I can't hear the mice when they're close to me.

"It's been three weeks since I've munched a bird
And a mouse hasn't passed these lips, my word!—
Since the awful day that the Dog of Toff
A year ago chewed my ears right off!"

"Oh, dear! Poor Clew!" said Kate and Kelly.
"Please eat some nacho chips and jelly.
After you've cleaned it off your fur
You can come with us to the Land of Purr."

So Clew ate a snack, and when she was through
Each girl gave a skate, so Clew had two—
And they all set out. What a happy crew!
They hit the road and away they flew.

Kelly, Katie, and little gray Clew
Were off for the land where the grass was blue
And the sky was green and the kitty-cats grew
Soft and beautiful and

Sometimes
Often
Uh-oh!
A little weird, too.

Smiling at Nate, she did a quick shuffling dance as she finished the tune.

He clapped and shook his head. "Hey, that was great!"

"A little silly, maybe . . ."

"It's *your* song?"

"Yeah, I write a lot of them. That one's meant for kids, actually, in case you hadn't guessed. It goes on and on."

"Really? They run into that Dog of Toff?"

"Sure do."

"I've got to get a move on, but I'd sure like to hear the rest of it sometime."

"I guess I'll still be around tomorrow."

"Good. Don't rush off." Bending over, he dropped a folded bill into the banjo case.

"Thanks," she said.

"It was really nice meeting you, Robin. See you tomorrow, huh?"

She nodded. "See you. And thanks for the help."

"Anytime." He started backing away. "So long."

"'Bye."

He raised a hand in farewell, then turned around and strode toward the main gate.

Poppinsack peered at the clock behind the bar. "Today," he said, "has tumbled into tomorrow and become yesterday. And a fine day it was, indeed."

He hoisted his glass of Scotch toward the clock, winked, and gulped it empty.

He climbed off the bar stool and tucked his half-read paperback into the duffel bag. It went in on top of his other new books and bottles. He clipped the bag shut and hefted it. "Ah, 'tis a weighty matter. Santa's own bag, itself, was never packed with such delights. Yuletide in summer."

Singing "Deck the Halls," he lumbered to the tavern door and stepped outside.

He sucked the fresh night air into his nostrils, and sighed. "Delicious," he proclaimed. "The elixir of the gods, best savored with a belly full of hooch."

He adjusted the canvas strap of the duffel bag on his shoulder, tipped back his hat with the knobby handle of his cane, and continued on his way.

Fog hung heavily over the street, so he couldn't see Funland. He knew it was straight ahead, though. And he knew it was already closed for the night.

He felt a little quiver of fear.

Normally, he would've been safely tucked away in the dunes long before Funland shut down.

"Poppinsack has spreed too late," he said. "But one must sail when the tide goes out, and spree when the purse is full. And full of gratitude is he to her who provided so generously for the night's entertainment. I thank thee, Robin red-breast. And have you flown the coop? Or do you wait in ambuscade to retrieve your filched funds? There's a hearty, foolish lass. A dame that's long on moxie and short on brains, doomed to be brained."

He chopped the air with his cane. "Felled, poleaxed, dropped like a sack of tomatoes. And a ripe tomato she is, my lovely songbird, minstrel, bard, my Robin red-breast of the smooth hot breasts, my cockless Robin of the saucy quiff. Shall we meet in mortal combat on the strand this night? Prepare yourself to taste my staff, and then my staff."

But as he lumbered past the Lighthouse Bar, a man came out.

Poppinsack stopped and turned toward the door. In the few seconds before it swung shut, he saw the dim lights inside, the smoky air, the colorful array of bottles along the far wall. He heard laughter, talking, the song of a woman from the jukebox, the soft click of pool balls, the tinkle of glass. He felt the warmth of the bar's air. Best of all, he *smelled* it. He sucked into his nostrils the familiar, cozy aromas of sawdust, stale smoke from cigarettes and cigars, and the heady mix of sweat, urine, and booze.

"Bless the gods," he said. "Poppinsack feels a fresh thirst coming on."

With that, he entered the bar.

Robin sat on the soft roll of her sleeping bag, waiting for Poppinsack at the bottom of the sand slope where he had camped last night.

He's probably too smart to come back, she told herself again.

But I told him I was getting out of town. He'll think I'm long gone. And even if he knows I stuck around, he'll never think I have the guts to jump him.

What if he *doesn't* come?

How long do I wait?

Though she was huddled down, hugging her knees to her chest, the cold kept her shivering. She longed to be warm inside her sleeping bag. But what if she got into the bag, and even fell asleep, and then he showed up? She would be at his mercy.

Robin rose to her feet, as she'd done every so often since settling here, and climbed the sand slope. At the top, she scanned the area. Though she heard the surf rushing in, the fog was so thick that she couldn't see the ocean. The pale, blowing vapors allowed her to see only twenty or thirty feet in any direction, and nothing was visible except the deserted dunes.

She supposed that she might've missed Poppinsack while she was sitting at the bottom. He could've found himself a nearby place to camp. Maybe he'd even returned to his old spot, peered down and spied her, and crept off, planning to keep away from her—or sneak in after she fell asleep.

She knew she ought to scout around for him.

But the fogbound, desolate landscape made her nervous. She didn't even like to be standing up here, exposed. It didn't feel safe. She wanted to be at the bottom, hunched low and out of sight.

Come on, if you're coming, she thought.

As she looked around, she began to fear that someone *would* come wandering out of the fog. Maybe not Poppinsack. Maybe two or three mad, jibbering trolls. Right now, they were just out of sight. If she stayed up here a moment longer, they would shamble into view and spot her.

Robin whirled around, rushed to the bottom of the slope, and sank onto her rolled sleeping bag.

This is ridiculous, she told herself. I'm just spooking myself. Nobody's out there.

Anyone could be out there.

And if she got into her bag and went to sleep, anyone could creep up on her.

What the hell am I doing here? she wondered.

Nothing good can come of this. If Poppinsack shows up right now, maybe I get some of my money back and maybe I don't. One of us is bound to get hurt. At best, it's him and not me. Then I'll have that on my conscience. Instead of just the guy I stabbed at the bus depot, I'll have two guys I'll wish I hadn't hurt.

Even if I get *all* my money back, it won't be worth the guilt.

With the guy at the bus station, at least I didn't have a choice. He attacked me. This would be my choice.

Forget it, she decided.

And felt, at once, as if an awful burden had been cast aside.

She strapped the sleeping bag to her pack frame, shouldered the pack, lifted her banjo case, and climbed again to the top of the dune. Though she checked around to make sure nobody was approaching, her imagination conjured no phantoms. She no longer felt so exposed and vulnerable.

She trudged northward over the mounds of sand. Soon she came to the chain-link fence marking the boundary of the public beach. She followed it toward the sound of the combers. The sand became smooth and hard-packed under her boots. The black ocean came into view.

The tide was out, so she didn't get wet when she stepped around the end of the fence.

On private property now, Robin felt as if she'd crossed into a territory that was beyond the reach of the trolls—and the trollers, though they were the least of her worries. The trollers, after all, were rational humans, not crazies.

She walked in the direction of the house, and soon it appeared through the fog. Its windows were dark.

The house stood on pilings.

Ducking down beside the porch stairs, she gazed into the black area among the posts. It looked like a cozy place to spend the night.

A real intrusion, though, to sneak in there right under someone's home. And she might be spotted coming out in the morning.

Robin realized she didn't care.

All that mattered was finding a secluded place where she might sleep in safety.

She dropped to her knees and began crawling into the darkness, dragging her banjo beside her.

Eighteen

Jeremy stopped beneath the dim, grinning face of the clown. He saw no one ahead—only the deep darkness under the roof of Funland's entryway, the lesser darkness of the boardwalk beyond, and fog like a pale curtain suspended at the far side of the railing.

He lighted the numerals of his wristwatch: 12:58.

He was two minutes early.

He supposed that Cowboy was still in the hospital. Though he felt nervous about meeting the others without Cowboy present for moral support, the urge to be with Tanya had been so strong that he'd decided to come anyway.

Maybe they won't even meet tonight, he thought with a mixture of hope and dismay.

As he stepped past the ticket booth, a hand clamped his shoulder and spun him around. A huge guy grabbed the front of his jacket, jerked him up onto tiptoes.

"It's all right." Tanya's voice.

The guy set him down.

A girl came in from the side, followed by a cluster of teenagers. She wore a dark sweatsuit and her face was blurred by shadow, but Jeremy knew from her size and pale hair that she was Tanya.

"I didn't think you'd show up," she said.

"I didn't know if I should," he told her, and wished his voice didn't sound so weak. "But I came last night, and . . . Do you know about the fight? Me and Cowboy—"

"We heard about it."

"I saw him tonight," Liz said, stepping up beside Tanya.

"Is he okay?"

"They put his ear on. He might be out of the hospital tomorrow."

"Great."

"He said you showed hair."

"Yeah, good going," said a girl he didn't recognize.

Jeremy felt himself blush. "Well, I tried to help."

"Wish I'd been there," said the big guy. "I would've killed the fuckers."

"One of the cops damn near did." That came from the girl he didn't know. She took a stride forward, pressing between Tanya and Liz, and offered her hand. "Nice to meet you, Jeremy. I'm Shiner."

"Nice to meet you," he said, shaking her hand. She looked slim in her windbreaker and jeans. She had light-colored hair. Though he couldn't see her well in the darkness, he got the impression that she was pretty, and maybe younger than Tanya.

She stepped back, and a guy standing on the other side of Tanya extended his hand. "I'm Nate," he said.

"Hello." Jeremy shook the hand. It felt strong, but it didn't try to crush him. He remembered Cowboy telling him that Nate was Tanya's boyfriend. "Welcome aboard," Nate said.

I don't stand a chance, he thought. The guy looked like a jock—a handsome jock, at that.

"I'm Samuel," said the big guy who'd grabbed Jeremy from behind the booth. He wore a letter jacket with an enormous B on its chest. A varsity letter, probably for football. Or for sumo wrestling, Jeremy thought.

Samuel shook his hand. And squeezed it hard.

"You can call me Samson."

"You can all call me Duke if you want," Jeremy said, pulling his hand free and flexing the fingers. They still worked. "Cowboy came up with that."

A small, skinny kid wearing glasses came in from the side. "Greetings and salutations. I'm Randy. You may call me Randy." He smiled.

"Or Sandy," Liz said.

"You'll have to excuse Elizabeth, Duke. She resents anyone whose I.Q. exceeds her own, which is roughly equal to that of an oyster."

She swatted the back of his head.

Tanya shoved her. "Cut it out."

"He's such a toenail."

"Save it for the trolls," Tanya said.

"Let me in," came a whiny female voice. "I wanta meet him too." She pushed her way in from behind the others. She had a pudgy face. Her dark hair enclosed her head like a football helmet. She wore a tight jumpsuit of stretchy fabric that hugged all her bulges. "I'm Heather," she said, pumping his hand.

"Hi," Jeremy said.

She moved in close. Her breasts and stomach pushed against him. Her breath smelled of onions. "Hey, you're kinda cute."

He managed to smile and thank her.

"That's everyone except Karen," Tanya said, and looked over her shoulder. "Come in here and meet Duke."

"Yeah, yeah."

Tanya sidestepped, and a brunette moved in from the rear. A beret was tilted atop her head. Around her neck was a silken scarf, one end draping her shoulder, the other slanting downward to her right breast. She wore a jumpsuit similar to Heather's, but the body it hugged looked slender and compact and somehow hard.

"Hi," Jeremy said.

"God, I can't *tell* you what a thrill it is to meet you."

Her sarcasm gave Jeremy a sinking sensation.

"It's nothing personal," Randy explained. "Karen lavishes her disdain on every creature of the male gender."

"Which includes you out," Liz remarked.

"Another clever retort from the cretin."

"So now you've met everyone," Tanya said. "I suppose Cowboy's told you what we do here?"

"Go after trolls?"

"You got any problem with that?" Karen asked.

"No. Hell, I think they're a pain in the ass."

"What have they done to you?" Nate asked.

Jeremy shrugged. "Nothing much, I guess."

"Then why do you want to help us trash them?"

He knew better than to reveal the truth: that he had no special grudge against the trolls, that he simply wanted to be part of the group and close to Tanya. He didn't care what they did out here at night, so long as he could be with them.

But he couldn't say that, so he thought about his first afternoon on the boardwalk when the bum jumped in front of him and started begging. He remembered the man's wild eyes and brown teeth and sour stench. He remembered his own confusion and disgust. Most of all, he remembered his fear—the fear that had made him feel small and helpless and shameful.

He heard anger in his voice as he said, "I hate them. They hang around and bother everybody. They bug you for money. They're dirty and they stink. They act crazy. They're creeps. I think they ought to be tossed out with the garbage. They *are* garbage. They ask me for a quarter, I want to give them a knee in the nuts."

"My man," Samson said, and clapped him on the shoulder.

"Right on," Liz said.

"They're disgusting and creepy," the girl called Shiner said, "but it's more than that. They're *evil*. That's why we come out here night after night. They *do* things. They attack people. They make people *disappear*."

Some of the others nodded. Nobody disagreed.

Jeremy felt himself going shaky inside. "They make people disappear?" he asked, trying to keep his voice steady, but not succeeding.

"We haven't, like, seen it happen," Heather said.

"It's conjecture on our part," Randy explained, "that the trolls are responsible."

"It's them, all right," Shiner said. "They got my sister. She went for a walk on the beach one night, and . . . just vanished. They got her."

"We don't know that for sure," Nate said. "We don't know

what happened to Shiner's sister, or any of the others. But
people do disappear without a trace. I guess that happens
everywhere, but it happens here a lot."

"Happens to our own trolls," Samson added. "The ones we
nail? Most of 'em, we never see again."

"We used to think we were scaring them out of town," Nate
said. "But we're not so sure of that anymore."

"They get got," Liz said, and giggled.

"We suspect," Nate went on, "that other trolls come along
after we've left."

"And mop up for us," Liz said.

"Christ," Jeremy muttered.

Samson's head bobbed. "If we don't handcuff 'em to something or glue 'em down or stick 'em someplace where nobody
can get at 'em, they're gone with the wind. Most often, anyhow.
Some get through, but most don't."

"What . . . what do the trolls *do* with them?"

"Gobble 'em up," Liz said, and giggled again.

"We don't know," Nate said.

Jeremy groaned.

"You don't have to get involved," Nate told him.

"Nothing to be scared of," Heather said. "They've never got
any of us."

"We're the getters," Liz added.

"But you need to know the score," Nate said. "This is heavy
stuff we're doing. If you're with us, you'll be an accomplice in
the eyes of the law. Whatever any one of us does to a troll,
we're all equally guilty just by the fact of our presence. Do you
understand that?"

"Sure," Jeremy said.

"So far, we haven't been touched by the cops. But that could
change. Our luck might run out. Sooner or later, some of us
might get busted. Could be you."

"If you rat on us," Liz said, "we get you."

"I wouldn't rat."

"You still want to join up?" Nate asked.

"Yeah, sure I do."

"Okay," Tanya said. "Let's get on with the initiation. Tonight
you're the bait. We wait here, and you wander up and down

the boardwalk till a troll hits on you." She dug into the pouch-like pocket at the belly of her sweatshirt and drew out a card. She handed it to Jeremy. "Give him this."

"Or her," Randy added, "in the event that the troll is of the female gender."

Jeremy held the card close to his eyes. The hand-printed message was large and dark enough for him to read it. "DEAR TROLL, GREETINGS FROM GREAT BIG BILLY GOAT GRUFF."

He felt a grin stretch his mouth. "Neat," he said.

"It's our calling card," Tanya told him.

"Most of them maggots can't read," Samson said. "We think it's a cool touch anyhow."

"Yeah. I like it." He slipped the card into a pocket of his jacket. "So, I give it to the troll, and then what?"

"You signal us." Tanya drew a shiny whistle from inside her sweatshirt, slipped its chain over her head, and passed it to Jeremy. "Just give it a short blow."

He closed his hand around the whistle. It felt warm. It held the warmth of Tanya. It had been under her sweatshirt, resting against her skin, and now it was in his hand. He imagined the whistle down there, swaying on its chain as she walked, brushing the sides of her smooth bare breasts.

"Then all you do," Tanya said, "is keep the troll from getting away until we show up."

He nodded, hearing her but paying little attention as he dropped the chain over his head and tucked the whistle inside his shirt. Now it was against *his* bare skin.

"Any questions?"

"Huh?"

"Are you ready?"

"Which way do I go?"

"Take your pick."

He turned toward the south end of Funland, since that was the area he knew best. A hand clapped his shoulder. A hand patted his rump (and he liked that and wondered who had done it, but he didn't look back). A few voices quietly wished him good luck.

Then he was striding down the boardwalk alone.

He raised a hand to the front of his jacket and pressed the

whistle against his chest. He thought again about where it had been. Then he realized that it had touched more than her breasts. She not only wore the whistle but also *used* it—maybe today on lifeguard duty, maybe a few nights ago to summon the trollers. It had been in her mouth, clamped between her lips, filled by her warm breath, wet by her spittle, touched by her tongue.

Jeremy lifted the whistle out of his shirt. He put it into his mouth. Could he taste her? The whistle seemed to have no more taste than an empty spoon. Still, to know that it had been against her skin and in her mouth . . .

The low, forlorn moan of a foghorn rolled through the night, intruding like the blare of an alarm clock stunning him out of a sweet dream. The magic of the whistle vanished. He was suddenly aware that he was alone on the boardwalk, bait for a troll.

He went cold inside. He felt his scrotum shrivel up tight, his penis lose its stiffness and pull itself in as if to hide.

Looking over his shoulder, he saw only a few yards of dark boardwalk, the iron railing on one side, a game booth on the other side. The booth was a faint, indistinct shape through the fog. There was no sign of the group.

He stopped walking and listened. The night seemed strangely quiet, as if the fog not only blinded him but also muffled sound. He wished he could hear the others talking back there.

He started walking again. He squinted, straining to see more deeply into the fog. The planks of the boardwalk looked wet. To the right was a bench. Empty, thank God. Beyond it he saw the ghostly, hooded cars of the Tilt-a-Whirl.

He wondered if *those* were empty.

The whistle felt glued to his lips. He peeled it off, let it hang against his jacket, and licked his lips.

He quickened his pace.

He tried to stay in the middle of the boardwalk. The places off to the sides were where the trolls might lurk—in among the rides or booths. If he stayed in the middle, he wasn't so likely to be taken by surprise.

Then he saw, off to his left, the wooden stairway, platform, and entrance to Jasper's Oddities.

Right here is where we had the fight, he thought. He *liked* thinking about the fight. In his mind, he had relived it over and over again. The pounding he took had been worth it. He'd helped Cowboy ("You showed hair"), and he'd trounced those girls and felt them up and even ripped the shirt off one and got a good look at her tits. Whenever he remembered it, he felt excited and proud and got a hard-on.

Now he tried to call up those feelings, but couldn't.

His mind refused to replay the fight.

Instead it focused on the displays inside Jasper's Oddities. The Gallery of the Weird with its grotesque photographs. Worse, the *real* stuff. The eyeless mummy hanging by straps, an old rag hiding its groin. The giant spider. The hairless orangutan of Borneo—or whatever it *actually* was. The disgusting two-headed yellow fetus in its jar of murky fluid.

All that stuff was just inside the building, there. Just beyond its closed door.

Jeremy felt sick and frightened, knowing he was so close to such a collection of horrors.

He walked faster.

The way the Oddities building was joined to the Funhouse forced him to remember the photo of Jim and Tim, the Siamese twins connected at the hip.

At least the Funhouse had been closed down. He was glad of that, glad that he'd had no opportunity to try *it* out.

He wished he'd stayed away from the Oddities.

I'll be lucky if I don't get nightmares from that shit, he thought.

But if he hadn't gone into Jasper's Oddities, the fight wouldn't have happened.

You've got to pay for the good stuff.

Pay with the bad stuff. Like this right now. This is the cost of joining up with the trollers and getting to be with Tanya. Just like looking at the damn Oddities was the cost of the neat fight.

Why doesn't a troll just *come* so I can get it over with?

Suppose one doesn't come? he wondered. Do I have to wander back and forth all night?

Do I pass the initiation if I don't get one?

His heart gave a sickening thump as he heard footsteps rushing toward him. From behind? He whirled around. Eyes searching the fog, he jammed the whistle between his dry lips. His other hand slapped the pocket of his corduroys and felt the lump of his folding knife. He wondered if he should dig it out. Then he remembered the card in his jacket.

He reached for it.

A dim shape, darker than the fog, came running at him. Suddenly it stopped. It was still obscure, as if standing behind pale gauzy veils.

"Is that you, Jeremy?" a voice asked.

A girl's voice.

"Yeah. Who's that?"

"Shiner," she said.

She stepped toward him. He saw her blowing hair, the blur of her face, her dark windbreaker and jeans. He took a deep breath and let it out slowly.

She squeezed his arm. "Come on back," she told him. "One's coming in the front way."

"A troll?"

"Yeah. Quick. We're going to nail him."

Nineteen

They stopped running, and Jeremy let Shiner lead him by the hand. They pressed their backs against the wall of a shop. As he tried to catch his breath, he saw Samson crouching behind the ticket booth. Heather stood at his rear. Nate and Liz were against the wall at the other side of the entryway.

Where were the others?

Where was Tanya?

A movement caught his eye, and he realized someone was waiting on the flat roof of the ticket booth. All he could see was a faint curve of back, but he figured it must be Tanya. The others were in sight except for Randy and that bitchy girl,

Karen. It had to be Tanya. The booth was seven or eight feet high. Samson, he guessed, must've helped her get up there.

As he gazed at her, he heard a man's low slurred voice.

The troll?

From the sound of it, he must be nearby.

"Who killed Cock Robin?" he intoned. "Who laid her low? ''Twas me,' says I, 'whom you shall know by the name of . . . Poppinsack, me.' Bug-fuck. In this kingdom by the sea. And all the clouds did lower o'er her tomb."

Shiner, still holding Jeremy's hand, inched sideways along the wall. Jeremy stayed with her. Leaning forward, he looked past her and saw the man staggering toward the darkness beneath the archway.

A fat old guy in a weird feathered hat and a jacket with blowing fringe. He carried a walking stick in one hand, a duffel bag on his back.

"To pee, to piss, perchance to take a whizz," the man proclaimed, turning to a wall.

He sounded to Jeremy like a drunken actor, one with a rich voice like Richard Burton in the *Hamlet* movie he'd seen in English class last year.

Jeremy heard a splashing sound.

The guy was taking a leak right there in the entrance, no more than three yards from where Nate and Liz stood waiting.

At least the dirty old fart's back is toward us, Jeremy thought. But he could feel himself blushing. He wished Shiner weren't here to witness this.

"And in that whizz, perchance to flood the very marrow of the land and soak the roots of Satan's beard. 'Tis a fine thing. 'Tis mete that we should meet, this night, in the warm bosom of . . .'tis meat, indeed." He chuckled. "And shall the cockless Robin meet this meat? This staff of life?"

The splashing stopped.

Shiner turned her head. She smiled at Jeremy. He made a disgusted face, but wasn't sure how well she could see it.

The old troll turned away from the wall.

Jeremy was glad to see nothing hanging out.

He wasn't so glad to see the troll start staggering at an angle across the entryway—a route that was bringing him toward the place where Jeremy stood with Shiner.

"What ho! What ho! 'Tis a brave night to be abroad. A broad, a chick, a dame, a quiff. A rose by any other name. Arise, my rose, or be forever fallen!"

He weaved, flung up a hand, and caught himself against the side of the ticket booth.

"Steady as she goes! I am an ancient mariner. Not a cross, but an albatross. I plugged it with my gat. It falls on me to tell my tale to every tail will hear it. And every piece that hears my piece will have no call to fear it. And every—"

Tanya leapt from the roof of the ticket booth.

She dropped. Feetfirst. Crouching slightly. Arms out. Sweatsuit flapping. Pale hair swept up by the wind of her descent.

Jeremy heard the quiet slap of her soles striking the leather shoulders of the troll's jacket. He heard a grunt of pain and surprise.

The old man's knees folded and he crumpled forward. Tanya hopped off his shoulders as if he were a diving board. She cleared his back. She landed on her feet and stumbled away for a few steps before finding her balance. By the time she turned around, the troll was sprawled facedown.

"Let's get him," Shiner whispered. She tugged Jeremy's hand, pulling him away from the wall. Staying beside her, he rushed toward the fallen bum.

Shiner got two kicks in. Jeremy went ahead and gave him a good one in the side. Then the others arrived. Samson hurled the duffel bag out of the way, and they rolled him over. He seemed too stunned to struggle. Hands grabbed his arms and ankles, stretched him out. Heather stomped on his belly. Randy, who'd found the troll's walking stick, whacked him across the chest with it, barely missing Liz's head.

Wheezing, the troll jerked a hand free of Shiner's grip. His closed fist struck her in the chest and she tumbled backward off her knees. Jeremy caught the troll's wrist. The hand flew open. Jeremy clutched the middle finger and yanked it back until it snapped and the troll yelped in agony. That's for hurting Shiner, he thought, but he felt a little sick.

Liz drove an elbow into his chest, just below the throat.

Karen kicked him in the groin, and Jeremy winced.

The troll's head jerked up. Samson pounded him between the eyes and his head shot down and bounced off the wood.

He went limp.

"Okay," Tanya said. "That's enough. Let's get him up."

Jeremy helped. The old man seemed to weigh a ton. But when they raised him off the boardwalk, Samson drove a shoulder into his midsection and hefted him.

"You got him all right?" Nate asked.

"No sweat," Samson answered, but his voice sounded squeezed, as if the load was almost too much for him. "Where do we want him?"

"Follow me," Tanya said.

Nate lifted the duffel bag. "What's he got in here, bricks?"

Tanya led the way, Nate on one side, Karen on the other. Samson strode along behind her, the fat troll folded over his shoulder, limp arms swinging against his back. Jeremy saw that the broken finger was sticking out at a right angle from the rest of the hand.

God, how could I do that to someone?

Shiner came up beside him. "Are you okay?" he asked.

"Fine."

"He sure clobbered you. But I busted his finger for him."

"Good going."

They turned left and headed down the boardwalk.

Randy hurried to the front, holding the knobby cane high, the feathered derby perched on top.

Like a severed head on a pike, Jeremy thought, though he wasn't sure where the image came from. A movie? A drawing in a history book?

Somebody patted his rump. He looked back, and saw Heather behind him. "How you like it so far?" she asked.

He shrugged. He didn't know what to say. He felt a little sick with guilt, but also very excited. His heart was pounding, his mouth was dry, and his throat felt tight. All he said was, "Neat."

"A blast," Heather said. "But it's gonna get better."

"What happens next?" he asked.

"It's up to Tanya," Shiner said.

Heather added, "You can bet it'll be cool," and put an arm

around his back. He felt her big soft breast against his upper arm, and wanted to pull away.

Of all the girls here, why did *she* have to be the one snuggling up to him?

Tanya was too much to hope for, of course, but he liked Shiner and she didn't seem to have a boyfriend here. Even though the darkness had made it impossible, so far, to get a good look at her face, she seemed pretty. She certainly wasn't a fat slob with stinky breath.

Just what I need, he thought. This one hanging all over me.

Shiner, walking on the other side of Jeremy, quickened her pace and moved ahead, leaving him with Heather.

Who slid a hand into a rear pocket of his corduroys and rubbed his rump. "Good and warm," she said.

"Too bad Cowboy's missing out on the fun," he told her.

"He's an asshole."

The word, coming from her, sounded especially gross.

"He's my best friend," Jeremy said.

He hoped she might back off, hearing that. Instead, she gave his butt a playful squeeze and kissed his ear.

Jeremy turned his head away.

And saw Jasper's Oddities through the fog. An image filled his mind: Heather inside—an exhibit—her bloated, naked body suspended in a harness of leather straps. She looked as if she were made of white bread dough that hadn't gone into the oven yet. The straps sank into her flab so far they were almost out of sight. Her tongue lolled out. Her dead eyes were rolled upward so he could see only their whites. The picture made him go hot with shame.

She's just being nice to me, he told himself. She's probably lonely. It's not a crime.

The troll suddenly began to struggle. With his good hand he pounded Samson's back.

Samson bent at the waist and hurled him down. The troll crashed against the boardwalk. Before he could move, he was surrounded.

Jeremy, free of Heather, sighed with relief and stepped on the man's wrist.

"Don't hurt him," Tanya ordered. "Just bring him along."

"I've got him," Samson said. He grabbed one side of the troll's thick handlebar mustache and started pulling.

With a lot of gasps and whimpers and groans, the old guy got to his feet.

Samson walked beside him, leading him by the mustache.

"Over here." Tanya hurried on ahead, Randy rushing after her with the derby wobbling high above him. They both melted into the fog. Then Karen and Nate vanished too.

Jeremy heard the squeak of a gate swinging open.

"Where'd you go?" Samson called.

"The Ferris wheel," Tanya answered.

"Oh wow." That came from Heather. Close behind him.

Jeremy hurried forward and caught up with Shiner. "What's going on?" he asked.

"We're about to find out," she said.

Samson and the troll, with Liz walking close behind the troll as if to grab him if he should somehow free himself, angled across the boardwalk toward one of the low fences that enclosed each of the rides. They passed through the open gate.

The Ferris wheel stood beyond the gate, mostly hidden by the fog. Jeremy could see only the front of it: a few of the gondolas, some distinct and others vague in the grayness; the curves of the wheels connecting them; spokes running inward toward the axle, but fading, and vanishing entirely before they reached it.

More came into view as he walked with Shiner through the gate. He saw the elevated platform. The lowest gondola was there, where it had been stopped at the end of the last ride of the night to let its passengers out. Dim shapes stood near it. He saw Samson leading the troll up the few stairs, Liz hurrying after them.

"Ooo, this is gonna be good," Heather said. Instead of latching on to Jeremy again, she hurried past him and bounded to the top of the stairs.

Shiner stayed at Jeremy's side while they climbed the platform.

"Everybody here?" Tanya asked.

"Anyone who's not here," Randy said, "speak up."

"You're as funny as crotch rot," Liz told him.

"Okay," Tanya said. "Let's air this bastard out."

Samson, standing in front of the troll, kept him on tiptoes by dragging upward on his mustache. Liz, Karen, Heather, and Shiner began to undress him. He danced and whimpered a little as they did it, but offered no real resistance. Tanya watched like a foreman, arms folded across her chest, nodding with approval.

Soon they had the troll down to his long johns.

Jeremy was surprised. He'd thought nobody wore long johns— just actors in cowboy movies. But this old fart wore them, all right.

Heather and Liz peeled them off him.

Jeremy couldn't believe it. He felt shocked, and his skin burned with his embarrassment.

The guy was as hairy as an ape. The mound of his sagging belly was in the way, so Jeremy couldn't see his privates and was glad to be spared the sight. But Liz and Heather were on their knees, having drawn the long johns down his legs, and they stayed there, inspecting him, whispering to each other, giggling. The guy obviously wanted to cover himself, but Karen and Shiner had his arms. So he just whimpered.

Heather reached up.

The troll's eyes widened and his mouth dropped open.

"What're you, desperate?" Liz muttered.

"I just wanta see if—"

"That's enough," Nate snapped.

"Let's get on with it," Tanya said. "We didn't post a guard, so we'd better finish up and get out of here." She reached out toward Randy. He dug into a pocket, took out something that clicked and rattled, and gave it to her.

Jeremy saw that it was a pair of handcuffs.

"I'll get the thing going," Nate said, and ducked away.

The troll was guided to the Ferris wheel and forced down. The gondola started to swing backward when his rump hit the footrest, but the platform stopped it.

As if he suddenly realized that the pain of the beating and the humiliation of being stripped were mere preliminaries to the main event, the troll shrieked and went wild. He kicked, squirmed, flung his arms at the kids trying to hold him down.

Tanya kicked him in the belly. His breath blasted out and he slumped against the front edge of the gondola's seat, whinnying as he struggled for air.

She swung the metal safety bar down and clamped it.

A motor rumbled to life. Jeremy felt the platform begin to vibrate under his shoes.

Astonished, he muttered, "It'll *go?*"

"Nate's folks own the thing," Liz said.

Tanya finished with the troll and stepped aside. He was still sitting on the footrest, sprawled backward against the seat, fat hairy legs sticking out.

His hands hung beneath the safety bar, suspended there by the chain of the cuffs.

"Watch it," Tanya warned. Jeremy and the others stepped out of the way. "Okay, Nate," she said.

Nate, over at the side, worked a lever forward.

The Ferris wheel lurched, and slowly started to turn. As the gondola moved backward, rising, it rocked away beneath the weight of the troll. He slipped off the footrest and cried out as the bracelets tugged at his wrists.

"No!" he yelled. "Please!"

A second later, he was hanging straight down—all his weight borne by the handcuffs, by the connecting links, by the safety bar.

The Ferris wheel lifted him higher, then squeaked and stopped with a slight jerk that made him yelp. He swayed up there, six or eight feet above the ground.

"Take him higher," Tanya said.

"That's high enough," Nate told her. "He's an awfully big guy. Something could give out."

"Let me down. Please? I'll get out of town. I'll do anything. *Please!*"

"Give him one spin over the top," Tanya said.

"Christ, yeah!" Heather blurted.

"Make him *ride* it!" Liz said.

"I don't think we—"

"Shit!" Tanya snapped. "Give it to him! He's a fucking *troll!*"

Nate shook his head.

He kept shaking it as Tanya strode toward him. *"I'll* do it, then—shit."

"Tanya . . ." he said. But he didn't try to stop her.

She rammed the long lever forward. With a quick lurch that dragged a shriek out of the troll, the wheel started turning.

The naked, kicking troll flew upward as if being sucked into the fog. He screamed all the way up. He kept on screaming after Jeremy couldn't see him anymore.

Tanya tugged the lever backward.

The Ferris wheel stopped.

The screams of the troll came down through the fog.

"God," Shiner muttered, "he must be right near the top."

"A good place for him to spend the night," Tanya said.

"Let's bring him down," Nate told her. "I'll take care of it."

"Fine," Tanya said. "In the morning. Go ahead and shut it off."

"We can't . . ."

The troll had never stopped screaming, but the pitch suddenly jagged high. It made Jeremy's teeth ache. Goose bumps prickled his skin.

He heard a thump.

The screaming stopped.

Another thump.

"Oh, Jesus," Nate murmured.

And down through the fog came the troll, striking spokes and braces, bouncing off them, cartwheeling, flipping, tumbling like a mad acrobat.

Twenty

The platform shook when he crashed against it.

Nobody said a word. There was silence except for the rumble of the Ferris wheel's motor.

Jeremy stared at the body. It lay only a couple of yards from him, faceup on the floor between two of the gondolas. The shadows weren't dark enough to shroud it. The face looked black with what was surely blood. The nose was mashed flat. One leg stuck out sideways, as if it had been wrenched from its socket. The other stood straight up from the knee. The hands, still cuffed, rested on the hill of the troll's belly. A spike of bone protruded from the left forearm.

Jeremy turned his eyes away from the corpse and looked around the group. Everyone else was motionless, gazing at it.

Liz raised a hand to her mouth. He wondered if she was about to vomit. *He* felt a little like throwing up. But she began to make strange muffled noises, and he realized she was giggling. A moment later she said, "Woops."

Shiner said, "Oh, God. Now we've done it."

"He fall down go boom," Heather said.

Nate broke away from the group and shut down the motor.

"Everybody stay cool," Tanya said.

"What *happened?*" Randy muttered.

"Obviously," Tanya said, "the safety bar wasn't strong enough to support him."

"We killed him," Randy said.

"Brilliant deduction, dickhead." From Liz.

"Look," Tanya said, "the main thing now is not to panic. We've got to get rid of him and clean up. Nobody ever has to know this happened. Liz, Karen, Heather, I want you to clean up the blood. Go get a bucket and mop. Jeremy, get the guy's stuff together and throw it under the boardwalk. Shiner, help him. Samson, you give me a hand with the body. Nate, go get your surfboard. We'll float him out and dump him."

"What about me?" Randy asked.

"Do us a favor and stick your head up your ass," Liz said.

"You can stay with me," Tanya told him. She pushed the sleeves of her sweatshirt up her forearms, ducked beneath the outer rim of the Ferris wheel, and crouched by the body. Samson followed.

Nobody else moved.

Tanya lifted the sideways leg by its ankle and swung it inward. As she lowered the other leg—the one bent upward from the knee—Randy spun around, gagging. He threw himself against the platform's railing and vomited.

"Good going," Liz said. "I'm not cleaning *that* up."

Somebody squeezed Jeremy's arm. He looked, and saw that it was Shiner. "Let's take care of his junk," she said.

He turned away from the grisly sight of Tanya and Samson struggling with the body, and started to pick up the troll's clothes.

Nate brushed past him and hurried down the stairs. Then Liz, Karen, and Heather left.

"I'll help you guys," Randy said. He still had the cane in one hand, the derby hanging on its top. The derby fell off when he bent down to pick up the long johns. It rolled under the Ferris wheel, and he scrambled to retrieve it.

Jeremy saw that Tanya and Samson had the body out from under the wheel. Tanya was holding the legs up while Samson dragged the body by its arms. They were moving it toward the rear of the platform.

"I never thought something like this would happen," Shiner whispered.

"It's pretty gross," Jeremy told her.

"God."

He picked up the shoes and socks. And looked up in time to see Samson and Tanya lift the troll over the railing behind the Ferris wheel. They dropped him toward the beach.

On the way back, Samson grabbed the duffel bag. He lifted it and followed Tanya down the stairs.

"I guess we've got it all," Shiner said.

With Randy in the lead—but no longer holding the derby high on the staff like a trophy—they climbed down from the platform. They walked through the open gate. Tanya and Samson were off to the left, climbing over the boardwalk's railing. Samson must've already tossed the duffel bag down. He and Tanya jumped, and vanished from sight.

When Jeremy reached the railing, he saw them striding across the beach. They took only a few steps before the fog devoured them.

The duffel bag lay in the sand straight below him. He emptied his arms over the railing. The troll's shoes dropped fast, but the socks and pants fluttered down. So did the shirt released by Shiner. It sailed down, billowing, sleeves out. The wadded leather jacket plummeted, and hit the sand before the shirt. Randy hurled the cane. It stabbed the sand and stood upright like a spear. He kept the derby in his hand while he ducked between the bars of the railing.

Standing there, he hesitated. With the stiff brim of the derby, he nudged his glasses more firmly against his face.

"You don't have to jump," Shiner told him.

"I'm not afraid."

"Liz isn't here to razz you."

"Tanya jumped, I can jump." And he did. His feet hit the sand, his knees folded, and he seemed to dive forward. After getting up, he watched Shiner and Jeremy climb over the railing.

Hanging on to the outside of the bars, Jeremy could see why the smaller kid had been reluctant to leap from such a height. But the others had done it. He didn't want to look like a chicken by turning around and trying to lower himself off the boardwalk so the drop wouldn't be as great.

Shiner leapt.

As she fell, Jeremy stepped into space. He didn't want to think about the troll, but suddenly he imagined himself as the old man plummeting from the top of the Ferris wheel, knowing he was as good as dead. For just an instant, terror seized him.

Then his feet struck the sand. The impact collapsed his knees. His rump was pounded, and a knee clipped him on the chin, jarring his teeth together. He flopped onto his back. As he sat up, Shiner reached down to give him a hand. He took hold of it. She pulled, helping him to rise.

"Are you okay?" she asked.

Nodding, he ran his tongue across the edges of his teeth. He half-expected to find some chipped, but they seemed all right.

"You should've rolled," she told him.

"Yeah, I guess so."

"If you two don't require my assistance," Randy said, "I'll catch up with Tanya."

"Sure," Shiner said.

The boy rushed off into the fog.

Jeremy and Shiner wandered around, bending over and gathering the troll's scattered clothes.

"I kind of feel sorry for Randy," she said. "He's a pretty sensitive kid. This was rough tonight."

"That's for sure."

"He's not . . . into this like some of us. He's only here because he's got some kind of crush on Tanya."

"Really?"

Shiner stepped up close to a piling and tossed the troll's jacket and pants into the darkness.

"Shouldn't we take the stuff in under there? Maybe like scatter it around some?"

"No. Just throw it. There's probably trolls."

"Jesus."

"Yeah. We'd better not hang around too long."

Jeremy hurled the shoes, socks, and shirt, then backed away. "You think anybody saw what happened?"

"You mean trolls? Some might've. They're always hidden around. I bet they know everything that goes on." She picked up the long johns, pulled the cane out of the sand, and retrieved the feathered derby.

Jeremy lifted the duffel bag. It was awfully heavy. "Will they tell?" he asked.

"Not a chance."

They stopped just under the edge of the boardwalk, and Shiner threw the troll's things into the darkness.

"I'd better carry this in a little ways," Jeremy said.

"No, don't. Just toss it under. It'll be picked clean by morning anyway."

Holding the canvas bag by its strap, he swung it forward and let go. It vanished. A second later, it landed with a soft thump and a clinking of glass, as if bottles were knocking together.

"Some trolls'll be glad to find that," he said.

"Tha's a fack." The dry, withered voice came out of the blackness in front of him.

He flinched rigid. Shiner grabbed his arm. He wanted to spin around and run, but she held on to him and walked slowly backward. He heard her breathing hard.

"Aren't you glad you didn't go under there?" she asked after several strides.

"God."

"I have all kinds of nightmares about getting caught by them. That's about the worst thing I can imagine, you know?"

She let go of his arm and turned around.

Jeremy turned around too. Then he looked back over his shoulder. The black space beneath the boardwalk was a vague blur through the fog. He tried to spot the Ferris wheel, but it was out of sight.

"I bet you never thought you'd get into anything like this," Shiner said.

"That guy biting it." He shook his head.

"Bad. Real bad. Makes me feel kind of sick, you know? I mean, he was a troll, but still . . ." She leaned against his side, and Jeremy put an arm across her back. "It was pretty terrible, anyway."

"Yeah."

They kept walking. He could see nothing in front of him except sand and the fog.

"I hope he doesn't wash in sometime," Shiner said. "That'd be awful if people are on the beach and he comes in, you know?"

From the sound of the surf, Jeremy guessed they must be getting close to the shore. But he still couldn't see the water, or Tanya and the others.

"Nate's going to take him out on a surfboard?" he asked.

"I guess so."

"Does he have to go all the way home to get it?"

"No. Shouldn't take him very long. He keeps it in a store-room in the arcade. He surfs in the morning sometimes before the place opens."

"He's Tanya's boyfriend, huh?"

"Yeah."

Jeremy noticed that his feet no longer pushed into the sand. The beach felt solid. It slanted downward slightly. Here and there, it was littered with dark clumps of kelp that looked less like seaweed than like strange tentacled creatures dead on the shore.

A ragged fringe of white foam spread toward him. Shiner stopped walking. A couple of yards before reaching their feet, the foam settled and faded away. Jeremy heard the water receding, a fresh wave washing in.

"The others must be over there," he said, nodding to the left.
Shiner turned her head that way. Then she looked forward
again. Her hand tightened against his side, so Jeremy pressed
her a little bit closer.

"I guess we should go over there," she said.

"Yeah."

But she didn't move, so neither did Jeremy. He realized his
heart was beating more rapidly than before.

This is fine, just standing here, he told himself.

He wondered what she was thinking about.

"You'd think we could hear them," Shiner said.

"Should we try to find them?"

"Do you want to?" she asked.

He shrugged. He wanted to stay right here. And *that* was
weird too. Tanya was the one he was crazy about, not Shiner.
He could be with Tanya right now—looking at her, hearing
her voice.

But I wouldn't be holding her like this, he thought. She's
Nate's girl. I don't stand a chance with her.

"I think I might quit trolling," Shiner said.

"Really?"

"I don't know. Killing a guy like that. I hate the trolls, but
killing them . . ."

"If you quit, when'll I see you?" The words were out before
he had a chance to think about them and back off.

She turned her face toward Jeremy.

"Why don't you give me your number?" she said.

His heart felt like a drumming fist.

"I . . . we just got our phone. I don't know the number. If you
give me yours . . ."

"I can't," she said. "I'd like to, but I'm not allowed to get calls
from boys."

"Huh?"

"My mother, she's . . . a little peculiar. She thinks I'm too
young to have a boyfriend."

"How old are you?"

"Sixteen."

"Same here."

"Maybe we could meet somewhere," she suggested.

"Sure." He felt as if he could barely breathe. "Yeah. That'd be great."

"How about here at the beach tomorrow afternoon? The fog'll probably burn off by noon. How about one o'clock? We could meet over by the lifeguard station."

"Great."

Shiner squeezed him against her side.

Then someone came striding along the beach in front of them, and they both flinched.

Nate. Barefoot and wearing a wet suit. Carrying a surfboard under one arm.

He turned and came toward them. A few strides away, he stopped. His head swiveled from side to side. "Where are the rest of them?" he asked.

"Over there someplace," Shiner said. She raised her left arm and pointed.

He started away. "You coming?"

"Yeah, I guess."

Shiner let go of Jeremy, and they both started walking along behind Nate. Jeremy's side felt cold where she had been pressed against it.

"Tanya?" Nate called.

"Over here." Tanya's voice sounded far away, but straight ahead.

Shiner took hold of Jeremy's hand. Her warmth seemed to flow up his arm and fill him.

He found himself thinking about tomorrow. It would be like having a real date with her. He hoped she was as pretty in the sunlight as she seemed in the darkness. She would probably be wearing a swimsuit—maybe some kind of a bikini. And they'd be meeting near the lifeguard station, so Tanya would be there. He could look at both of them.

It'll be great, he thought.

Then he saw three faint dark figures standing in the fog ahead of Nate. The naked body of the troll lay at their feet. The cuffs had been removed.

Shiner didn't let go of his hand when they joined the group. Jeremy was glad. In a way, it seemed as if she were showing him off, saying, "Look what I've got."

He felt as if the two of them had suddenly become a "couple."

"Anybody see you?" Tanya asked Nate as he set his surfboard down beside the corpse.

"Nope. Maybe some trolls, but I didn't spot any."

"This is one troll they won't be getting their hands on," Samson said.

He and Nate crouched at the other side of the body. They rolled it over onto the surfboard. Jeremy's stomach clutched a little when he saw the broken legs flop loosely. But he was relieved that the troll was facedown now, penis out of sight. There was a dark splotch on one of the buttocks. A birthmark?

"He's going to slide right off there if we don't strap him down," Nate said. "I couldn't find any rope. Any of you wearing belts?"

"Yeah," Samson said. "Won't go around him *and* the board, though."

"We'll need a couple, at least."

"I've got one," Jeremy said.

Shiner said, "Me too."

"Sorry," said Randy, and lifted his jacket as if he felt the need to prove he had no belt.

While Jeremy removed his belt, he watched Shiner raise her windbreaker above her waist, open her belt, and slide it through the loops of her jeans. She wore a plaid shirt. The side of it was untucked and bunched up. A small pale patch of skin showed near her hip. Once the belt was off, she tugged the windbreaker down again.

"Are you going to bring them back?" she asked Nate as she gave it to him.

"I'll sure try."

"It was a present from my sister," she added.

Her sister. The one who had vanished. The one the trolls got. When Jeremy had heard about it earlier, Shiner had been a stranger. Now she was special to him and he felt a tug of sorrow for her loss.

Nate buckled Jeremy's belt to Samson's. While Samson held an end of the surfboard off the sand, Nate slipped the joined belts underneath it. Samson lowered the board. Nate straddled the body, brought up the ends of the belts, and fastened them in the middle of the troll's back. He used Shiner's belt to strap the troll's ankles against the surfboard's tail.

"Okay," he said. "All set."

"Not quite," Tanya said. She stepped around the body and approached Jeremy. "Let me have the card," she told him.

He was confused. What card? Didn't she mean the whistle? Then he remembered. He dug into his pocket, found the Billy Goat Gruff calling card, and handed it to her.

She smiled at him.

"Here," he said. "You can have your whistle back." He took it off and dropped it into her hand.

"I guess you didn't need it," she said, and slipped the chain over her head. A finger of the hand that held the card hooked the neck of her sweatshirt out, and she dropped the whistle down her front. "Let's just say you got initiated," she told him.

"We *all* got initiated," Nate said.

Tanya stepped to the front of the surfboard and squatted down. Reaching between her knees, she turned the troll's face toward her. She pulled the chin. The mouth opened. She stuffed the card inside, then clapped the mouth shut.

"I'm not sure that's such a good idea," Nate said.

She left it there, and stood up. "The guy's fish bait," she said. "Besides, nobody'll be able to read it anyway by the time he's been in the water a few minutes."

Nate shrugged. He muttered, "What the hell."

Then he and Samson lifted the surfboard off the sand. They carried it like a stretcher down the beach.

The others followed. Jeremy saw the thin, foamy edge of the water sliding toward him, but he kept going. Cold wetness soaked through his shoes and socks.

He saw the ocean. Black waves, crested with white, rolled toward him out of the fog.

He imagined the troll sinking out there, all alone in the cold dark water, and felt himself go frozen inside.

It's not like the guy's alive, he told himself. He's dead. He won't feel a thing. He won't *know.*

But the awful frigid feeling stayed.

They all halted except Samson and Nate. Randy moved over close to Tanya. Shiner curled her fingers around Jeremy's hand.

The two boys waded out with their cargo. They set the surf-board down in knee-deep water. As Samson hurried back, Nate pushed the board farther out.

A wave broke over the head and back of the dead man.

After it washed by, Jeremy saw Nate behind the surfboard, pushing it in front of him.

Shiner turned Jeremy toward her and held him tightly against her body and pressed her face to the side of his neck.

When he looked again toward the ocean, he saw only the surf and the fog.

Twenty-one

After roll call, Dave sat at his desk to prepare his report on yesterday's incident at Funland. He relived it all in his mind as he pecked the typewriter keys. When he wrote of Joan's deci-sive moves against the knife-wielding perpetrator, his thoughts drifted away to the other, vulnerable Joan in her anguish over demolishing the kid. He lingered on the way she'd felt in his arms, and how it had been, kissing her.

Joan's desk was off to the side. He looked at her. She was leaning back in her swivel chair, phone at her ear, legs stretched out. Like Dave, she wore her bright blue BBPD jacket over her beach uniform. The jacket wasn't fastened. It hung open in a way that showed her right breast stretching the fabric of her T-shirt.

As he stared at her, she sat toward and cradled the phone. She swiveled toward him and raised her eyebrows. "Woodrow Abernathy regained consciousness two hours ago," she said.

"Glad to hear it." He was glad for Joan, not for Woodrow. Other people would probably suffer in years to come because the creep had pulled through, but Joan wouldn't have to live with the guilt of knowing she'd destroyed him.

Smiling slightly, she shook her head. She took a huge breath that swelled her chest, let it out, and slumped forward as if the air in her lungs had been all that was holding her up. Her forearms dropped against her thighs. Then she just sat there, hunched over and gazing at the floor.

Dave typed more of his report, but his eyes kept straying over to Joan. He wished he could go to her. They weren't alone, though.

Finally she sat up straight. She met his eyes. Her head tipped a bit to one side. She smiled and slapped her open hands against her knees. "About ready to go, partner?"

"I'm almost done here."

"I'll hit the john and meet you in the car."

He watched Joan stride away. Without the distraction of her presence, he quickly finished the report, signed it, and took it to the chief's In basket.

By the time he reached the patrol unit, Joan was already sitting behind the steering wheel. He climbed in. She drove out of the parking lot and headed for Funland.

"You must be pretty relieved," he said.

She nodded. "How are you doing? How's the chest?"

"A little stiff and tender. Not bad. Thanks for the medication."

Joan grimaced. "I'm really sorry about all that."

"About what?"

"Guh . . . what could I *possibly* be sorry about? All I did was make a goddamn spectacle of myself, get soused, spill the goddamn champagne, throw myself at you, mess you up with Gloria. Shit. Nothing much."

"It was a disgusting display," Dave said.

She didn't look at him. He saw her lips press together in a tight line. Her head nodded once in sharp agreement.

"The worst damn part of the whole thing," Dave continued, "was when we kissed."

Her head jerked toward him. For a moment her eyes were wide with shock. Then they narrowed. A corner of her mouth tilted upward. "Liar," she said.

"Ah, you caught me."

"I thought I'd made that kid into a vegetable. And you'd been stabbed. But it was like some kind of a victory too—we'd stomped those scrotes. So I just thought it'd be nice to *be* with you, you know? We're partners. It seemed like the right thing to do, commiserate and hoist a few—"

"There was nothing wrong with it."

She glanced at him. "I'm your partner, but I'm not a guy. That's what screwed it up. Would've been the right thing except for that little detail."

Dave reached over and patted her shoulder. "Don't fret. I *think of you* as a guy."

"Yeah. Right."

"A guy who's *taller* than me," he added, hoping she would remember he'd first made that observation yesterday while he was embracing her.

The way her face softened, he knew she remembered.

"My only regret about yesterday," he said, "is that Gloria showed up and I had to stop kissing you."

Joan swung the patrol car into Funland's parking lot. She stopped it, shut off the engine, and looked into Dave's eyes. Her hand curled over his thigh.

"What about Gloria?" she asked.

"She's out of it now."

"Aw, geez." Joan lowered her eyes. She seemed to be staring at her hand as it began to move slowly up and down his leg.

"Don't worry about her," Dave said.

"No, of course not. All I did was steal her guy out from under her."

"I was never really hers."

Joan's hand stopped moving. She peered into his eyes, frowning. "Maybe you'll say the same thing about me someday. 'Don't worry about Joan. I was never really hers.'"

"I've been yours since our first patrol together," Dave said. "You just didn't notice."

Her eyebrows darted up. Her lips curled into a wise-guy smirk. She slapped his leg and said, "Bullshit."

"What about you and Harold?"

"I was never really his."

Dave grinned. "You were head-over-heels for me since our first patrol?"

"Don't flatter yourself."

He tried to look shocked. "You mean you weren't?"

"I just knew I liked your legs."

*   *   *

Robin saw a few familiar faces in her audience. Not Nate's, though. Where was Nate?

He'd said he would see her today.

She'd been watching for him all morning. It was nearly noon now.

She wondered if she should take a break and visit his arcade. That might seem pushy, though.

He'll show up, she told herself.

He has to.

It worried her, though. She'd half-expected to find him waiting when she came back from breakfast and took up her usual position at the north end of the boardwalk.

Maybe he's just too busy at the arcade to get away.

He'll show up.

As she played and wondered about Nate, she noticed that Dave and the female cop had joined her audience. They had been stopping briefly each time their foot patrol brought them to this end of the boardwalk. Dave hadn't given her a talk since the first day, but he always nodded and smiled when he showed up.

Yesterday, she'd been tempted to tell him about Poppinsack. Each time she saw him listening to her music, she'd thought about it. He seemed like a good guy. He'd probably go out of his way to help her. But he would have to ask how the theft happened. That would be just too embarrassing. Besides, yesterday she'd still hoped to confront Poppinsack herself, and if the old creep ended up stabbed or something, she didn't want any cops knowing she had a problem with him.

She could tell Dave now, since she no longer planned to nail the guy. But that still left the problem of telling him that the money had been stolen out of her panties.

I might tell his partner, she thought. It wouldn't be so bad, talking to a woman about something like that. Robin liked her, even though they'd never spoken. She had a terrific smile, and her eyes looked friendly.

Robin considered it while she played. She wondered if there was any point. By now Poppinsack had probably spent most of the money. Besides, he was nowhere around.

When she finished the number, Dave came up, nodded to

her, and tossed a folded bill into her banjo case. She thanked him. He smiled, gave her a little wave, then headed away with the woman.

"Let's hear 'Weenie Roast,'" called a heavyset guy who'd been in her audience several times during the past three days.

"You got it," she said, and started in on the song.

As usual, people shook their heads and laughed or groaned.

She was just finishing when she spotted Nate at the rear of the small group. A quick rush of excitement made her forget the lyrics for a moment. She got back on the track, and ended with a flourish.

She waited for the clapping and hoots to die down, then announced that she would be taking a short break. People moved forward to drop money into her case, and wandered off.

Nate stayed.

He stepped up closer to her. Over his T-shirt he wore a money apron with bulging pockets that jangled as he moved. His arms looked muscular. He had a deep tan that she hadn't noticed last night.

A real hunk, she thought, and smiled at herself. A stupid term, "hunk." But appropriate.

"That's a nasty little song," he said.

"I'm a nasty little woman."

He shook his head and smiled. The smile seemed a little strained.

"Hey," she said. "About last night. You went ahead and gave me the twenty. You weren't supposed to do that, you know."

"I had nothing better to do with it."

"Well, you've got to let me buy you lunch."

"I have to get back to the arcade," he said. "I left Hector in charge, and he's a doufuss."

It sounded to Robin like an excuse.

"That's okay," she said, and shrugged and hoped he couldn't see her disappointment.

"I just wanted to come by and say hi, see how you're doing."

She tried to smile. "I thought maybe you wanted to hear more of 'The Land of Purr.'"

"Some other time, maybe," he said.

"Whenever."

"I've gotta get back."

He just stood there looking at her. He seemed so different from the energetic, cheerful guy Robin had met last night. Weary, *deflated.*

Concern for him pushed aside her disappointment. "Are you all right?" she asked.

"Sure."

"Maybe you're coming down with something." She took a step forward and pressed an open hand against his forehead. The skin of his brow felt smooth, moist, and hot. "I think you've got a little fever," Robin said, lowering her hand.

He made a tired smile. "What are you, a nurse?"

"Just a gal." *Cockless Robin.* Damn you, Poppinsack. "We've all got built-in thermometers on our hands. You'd better go home, take a couple of aspirin, and get plenty of rest."

His smile perked up slightly. "I guess I could use the rest, anyway. I didn't get much sleep last night."

"Neither did I," Robin said, remembering her restless hours under the beachhouse.

"Where did you sleep?" Nate asked.

"On the beach."

Frowning, he shook his head. "You shouldn't do that."

"I know. The trolls, the trollers."

His frown deepened. "It isn't safe."

"I've noticed."

"Has someone bothered you?"

"I was robbed in my sleep two nights ago. And, of course, you know about that creep last night. Thanks again."

"You oughta stay off the beach, Robin."

"I like the fresh air."

"That twenty I gave you, you could've stayed in a motel."

She shrugged. "I'm saving up for a BMW."

"It's nothing to joke about."

"I can eat good breakfasts for a week on twenty bucks. I'd rather have that than a roof over my head."

"I don't want you getting hurt."

"I can take care of myself."

"That's a stupid-fuck thing to say."

Robin flinched.

Nate shook his head, squeezing his eyes shut. "I'm sorry. Jesus." He rubbed his face. "I shouldn't have . . . I'm sorry."

"It's all right."

"I've gotta go. See you around." He hurried away.

Robin watched him until he disappeared in the crowd. She wondered what was wrong with him, really. Though his brow had felt slightly feverish, she didn't think he was sick—he seemed depressed or upset, not ill.

Could it have anything to do with her?

That didn't seem likely.

But he'd sure been in a hurry to get away.

Robin thought that they'd made some kind of connection last night, that he was eager to see her again. She'd tried not to read too much into it, but he had been on her mind a lot ever since their meeting. Especially once she had given up the idea of trying to jump Poppinsack.

Lying in the dark space beneath the house last night, she'd slept fitfully. She'd flinched awake, time and again, certain that someone was crawling toward her or that she'd been discovered by those who lived in the house. Huddled there, feeling small and frightened, she had comforted herself with thoughts of Nate.

It all seemed a little stupid now.

He was just being nice last night, and you blew it all out of proportion.

A feeling of sadness hollowed her out. She had been on the road a long, long time—drifting, savoring the freedom, not minding much that she was alone, and looking forward to each new day. It had started with running away, but it had soon become an adventure, a quest.

It had led her here.

And she realized, now, that she had allowed herself to hope it was over.

Nate could've been what she'd been looking for.

Could've been.

But wasn't.

She stood there with a loneliness inside that felt as vast and cold as the ocean.

*   *   *

"I'm getting a case of the hungries," Joan said.

"What do you feel like?"

During her two weeks of patrolling the boardwalk with Dave, she'd sampled food from most of the shops. She ran the list of possibilities through her mind: hamburgers, cheeseburgers, hot dogs, chili dogs, submarines, fish and chips, fried clams, Mexican food and Chinese and Greek.

"What were those gizmos in the pita bread with the lamb stuff and sour cream?" she asked.

"Gyros?"

"Yeah. Does that sound good to you?"

"They're kind of messy," Dave said. "I wouldn't want you to embarrass yourself by slobbing."

"Screw you," she said, and bumped into him.

"Anytime."

"Don't hold your breath, partner." She saw that they were passing the main entrance. "Why don't I ditch our jackets?" she suggested. "You can go ahead and order, I'll meet you there."

"What do you want to drink?"

"Beer, but I'll settle for Coke or Pepsi."

"You want onions?" he asked, taking off his jacket.

"Just ice."

He handed the jacket to her. "I am having onions on my gyro," he said, speaking with slow precision. "Would you care for onions on your gyro?"

"I promise I'll care for them," she said, smiling as she watched Dave roll his eyes upward. "I'll feed them, take them for walks, clean up after them."

"I'll take that as a yes."

"I wouldn't want you to be the only one with stinky breath."

"Won't matter," he said. "I'll be holding it."

Smiling, Joan turned away from him. She pulled her jacket off as she walked past the ticket booth. She glanced back and saw that he was watching her. Nice.

It had been a terrific morning once their talk in the car was out of the way and she knew where they both stood. She still felt a little guilty about Gloria, but she figured she could live with that burden. Gloria hadn't been right for him anyway.

And I am? she asked herself as she trotted down the stairs.

Damn straight I am.

It felt so good.

Joan arrived at the patrol unit. She tossed their jackets into the trunk, slammed the trunk shut, and hurried back through the parking lot.

She breathed deeply, savoring the fresh smell of the ocean. The sun warmed her, and the breeze caressed her. She felt light and compact and strong and vibrant. She liked how the breeze ruffled her T-shirt and shorts against her skin. She liked the weight of the utility belt around her hips, and the way the leather creaked. She liked the feel of her muscles sliding under her skin. She liked the feel of her breasts moving inside her bra and how the fabric felt against her nipples. And the subtle tightness of her panties. And the soft springy feel of the soles of her shoes. She even liked the hungry feeling in her stomach.

Then she saw two bums sitting on the concrete stairs. Two female bums. And she stopped feeling good.

Her breath snagged. Her heart raced. Her stomach felt cold and numb. The muscles of her legs seemed to go soft and shaky.

One of the bums was Gloria.

My God, she thought. Losing Dave might've hit the woman hard, but to disintegrate this much so fast . . .

She suddenly realized it was a disguise.

The shock started to wear off.

Gloria hadn't fallen apart, after all. She'd done that piece about trolling a couple of days ago, and yesterday she'd been trying to interview bums on the boardwalk. Now she had taken it one step further—one major step—and made herself up to look like one.

She'd done a good job of it too. Her hair, normally black and well-groomed, was a tangled mop streaked with gray. Her face looked dirty. She wore a dingy gray sweatshirt that gaped with holes—probably made by scissors, Joan thought. An undershirt showed through the holes. Her faded skirt, a purple thing with a flower pattern, looked like a reject from a thrift shop. She wore red tights under the skirt. One knee of the tights was slit open. Instead of shoes, or over her shoes, she wore brown paper grocery sacks tied at the ankles with twine. On the stair beside her rested a grocery bag intended to represent the receptacle for all her worldly goods.

Either that, Joan thought, or it's a spare shoe.

So far, Gloria hadn't noticed Joan. Her head was turned toward the subject of her interview—a fat older woman wearing a knit cap and overcoat. The woman's pasty white knees were bare below the edge of the coat. Her calves looked as if they were being choked by the bands of her knee-high brown nylons. She wore big scuffed army boots.

As she talked, she waved her hands around, scrunched up her face, and rolled her eyes. Gloria nodded. The way she nodded in response to the woman's babbling was enough to blow her cover, Joan thought. It showed she was alert, focused. Not that the troll was likely to pick up on such a clue.

Joan took a step toward the women.

Then turned away and trotted up the stairs.

I'm not going to interfere, she told herself. The hell with it. Gloria's a big girl.

But she knew she would have to tell Dave.

Twenty-two

Jeremy left the bathroom and rushed into the kitchen. His mother was on her knees, applying Contact paper to the bottom of a cupboard. He looked at the clock. Ten minutes till one. He should've been on his way by now.

His mother pulled her head out of the cupboard and frowned at him. "Are you all right, honey? You've been running to the toilet every five minutes."

That was an exaggeration, but he *had* gone three times during the past hour. "Must be something I ate," he said.

"If you've been eating junk at Funland . . ."

Cramps hit him again. Gritting his teeth, he hurried back to the bathroom. He tugged his swimsuit down and dropped onto the toilet seat just in time.

Jeez, he thought, now I'm *really* going to be late.

He was sure his problem had nothing to do with what he'd been eating. He suspected it had to do with a dead troll, or maybe it had to do with Shiner. As if his bowels wanted to stop him from returning to the scene of the death, or prevent his date with the girl. Or both.

He finished, and rushed back into the kitchen. The clock now showed two minutes till one.

"Would it be okay if I take the car?" he asked.

"I have a hair appointment at two," his mother said. "I'll drive you to the beach, if you'd like. But I'm not sure you should be going anywhere in your condition."

"I have to. I'm meeting someone. I'm going to be late if I have to take my bike."

"All right. Go on out to the car. I'll be along in a minute."

"Thanks," he said.

He waited in the car. As he sat in the passenger seat, the tightness came back. Goose bumps scurried over his skin.

It's just nerves, he told himself. I *can't* have to go again. It'll stop once I'm there.

His mother arrived and climbed in behind the wheel. She backed the car out of the driveway. "Are you sure you're okay?" she asked.

"Yeah." He wondered if she could see the goose bumps on his face.

"Maybe it isn't something you ate," she said. "It might very well be that you're upset about going back there after what happened yesterday."

He knew she was referring to the fight with the four creeps, and nothing else.

"I guess I am a little nervous about that," he said.

"You have to be more careful, honey. There seem to be a lot of unsavory characters who hang around that area. As you found out."

"Yeah."

"And I'm not so sure that Cowboy is a good influence."

"You've never even met him."

"Do you think the fight would've happened if you'd been alone?"

"Probably," he lied. "Anyway, I'm not seeing Cowboy today. I think he's still in the hospital."

"Then who are you meeting?"

"A girl."

She turned her head toward him, smiled, and raised her eyebrows, looking both pleased and surprised. "I wasn't aware you'd met any girls."

"She's a friend of Cowboy's. She's really nice," he added quickly, wondering if he'd made a mistake in linking her to Cowboy. "You'd like her."

"What's her name?"

"Shiner."

"Doesn't she have a real name?"

"I only met her yesterday." He realized that his cramps had subsided. Explaining things to Mom was a distraction that must help.

"Is she your age?"

"Yeah, I think so."

They reached the boulevard at the foot of the hill, and she stopped for a traffic light. "Is she pretty?"

He almost said that he'd seen her only in the dark, but caught himself. "Yeah, kind of."

"Well, I think that's grand. It's about time you met a nice girl. I'd like to meet her sometime. Maybe you should ask her over for dinner one of these nights."

"Mom, I hardly even know her yet."

The light went green. She drove forward and turned left toward Funland.

"If you're afraid I might not approve of her . . ."

"It isn't that. *Jeez!*"

She gave him a sharp glance. "If you're so ashamed of this girl that you won't let your mother meet her, then something is very definitely wrong and you'd better think twice before you get involved with her. We've been in this town only a few days, and you've already managed to get into trouble. I'm not at all sure your new friends are the sort of people you should be associating with."

"They're just normal kids."

"With odd nicknames. You're not involved with some kind of a gang, are you?"

"No. That's ridiculous."

"I'd like to meet this Shiner."

"Okay, okay."

"I'd like to meet her today." The car slowed as it approached the parking-lot entrance.

"You can just drop me off in front," Jeremy said.

"I think I'll go with you and meet this girl."

"You mean *now?*"

Nodding, she swung the car into the parking lot and took a ticket from the man beside the booth.

"Mom, no! Jesus! You'll ruin everything!"

"You're only sixteen years old. I won't have you getting involved with some kind of tramp or criminal—"

"She's not! Dammit, Mom!"

"Don't use that language with me, young man." She jolted the car to a stop in a parking space. "Let's go."

Jeremy shook his head. "You can't come with me."

"Don't tell me what I can't do."

"Then I'm not getting out of the car."

"That's fine with me. I'll drive you home."

"Mom, please!"

She stared at him. The hardness seemed to melt out of her face. "I only want what's best for you, honey."

"There's nothing wrong with Shiner," he said, his voice shaking. He felt as if he might start to cry.

"I'd like to meet her and see for myself. I've been a teacher so long I can tell a good kid from a rotten one in about a second."

"I'll ask her to come over. Okay? But you can't go out on the beach with me. Please. It'd ruin everything. These kids here, they like me. They don't think I'm a wimp or a fag or a mama's boy. If you walk me out there like I'm a four-year-old, I'd never live it down. I'd be screwed in this town, just like I was in Bakersfield. I might as well stick my head in the oven."

"Don't you ever say that."

"I'm sorry," he muttered. "But I hated it, the way things were before. I've got a chance here. Don't mess it up for me."

"I just want to make sure you don't get hurt."

"I know. Trust me, though, okay?"

"Have a good time. Ask the girl to have dinner with us to-night."

"I will. Thanks, Mom." He leaned across the seat and kissed her.

Then he climbed from the car. He walked around its rear. His mother looked at him through the driver's window. He waved. She drove away.

God, he thought, she'd nearly blown everything.

He never should've mentioned Shiner. He never should've asked for a ride. He should've just taken his bike.

Well, you learned a lesson. From now on, keep your mouth shut.

He saw a couple of trolls sitting on the steps. They were busy talking to each other. He rushed toward the top, taking the stairs two at a time, hoping to get out of range before either of the trolls decided to hit him up for money.

When he crossed the boardwalk, he glanced to the left and saw the distant towering structure of the Ferris wheel. It looked so *high*. He saw the old man falling through the fog.

He rushed the rest of the way across the boardwalk and trotted down the stairs to the beach. He headed for the life-guard station. It was too far away for him to recognize Shiner among those sprawled on the sand around it.

Would he recognize her, he wondered, if he could see her?

Only a portion of the platform in front of the lifeguard shack was visible from this angle, and no one seemed to be there.

Though he kept walking, his head swung around and he gazed back at the Ferris wheel. He didn't want to look at it, but couldn't help himself. The gondolas of the spinning wheel were bright red against the pale sky.

Again he saw the old troll falling.

He felt cold and tight in his stomach.

It wasn't my fault, he told himself.

He wondered if Funland was ruined forever now. What if he could never come here again without being tormented by the memories of last night?

Some of it was good, though. Being part of the group—the first time in his life he wasn't an outsider. The way he'd felt when Tanya gave him the whistle. And afterward on the beach with Shiner. Holding her.

It was like you thought before, he reminded himself. You've got to go through it all. The bad stuff's part of the good stuff. It's all mixed together and one thing leads to another and you wouldn't be meeting Shiner here today, probably, if the old coot hadn't fallen. That's what brought you together.

It's worth it.

It has to be worth it.

As if those thoughts had released him from the need for further punishment, he found that he was able to look away from the Ferris wheel.

He was a lot closer to the lifeguard station now.

He spotted someone on its platform. Not Tanya. A male in red swimming trunks.

Disappointment tugged at Jeremy.

I didn't come here to see Tanya, he told himself.

But he realized that wasn't true. He'd come here to be with Shiner, but he'd expected Tanya to be at her post. Even if he didn't go to her, he would've been able to watch her. Gaze at her standing there golden in the sunlight, her hair and T-shirt and red shorts fluttering in the breeze, her legs long and powerful and bare.

He remembered hurling the remains of his waffle cone at her, day before yesterday.

What a dumb-ass thing to do. What a great thing to do. That's what proved I'm not a wimp. If I hadn't done that, maybe she wouldn't have let me meet the trollers.

He thought about how she had forced him to clean the ice cream off her leg. His mind lingered on that, savoring the memory of the slickness and the way she'd made him go up inside the leg hole of her shorts.

Shiner might be nice and even pretty, Jeremy told himself, but she's no Tanya. She's a girl; Tanya's a . . . A what? Something more. A force? A . . .

"Jeremy?" The call came from a girl kneeling on a blanket,

waving an arm at him. Her blanket was spread out several yards this side of the lifeguard station.

Would've had a good view of Tanya, he thought as he raised a hand in greeting and walked closer. He was surprised to realize that he suddenly felt no more than a mild sense of regret over Tanya's absence.

Shiner bore only a vague resemblance to the girl last night. In the dark, he hadn't been able to see the shine of her yellow hair. Maybe that's where she got the nickname, he thought. The dark had also hidden the deep blue of her eyes, the soft tan of her skin. Her teeth had been gray; now they were brilliant white. The features of her face had been smudged with shadows; now he could see the shapes of her eyes and nose, her lips, her delicate chin.

She was beautiful. But cute too. The cuteness came from her smile. It was a wide stretch of a smile that seemed too big for her face. It creased her cheeks. It crinkled the skin around her eyes. If *filled* her eyes with a look of happiness and maybe a touch of mischief.

It's the smile, he thought. The smile is why she's Shiner.

The smile slipped sideways a trifle. "What's wrong?" she asked.

He realized that he had stopped walking. He was standing there gazing at her like a dope from seven or eight feet away. Embarrassed, he shook his head and stepped to the edge of her blanket.

"Sit down and stay awhile," she said.

He dropped to his knees. His heart was slamming. He could hardly believe that this was the girl from last night—the same girl who'd been at his side when they threw the troll's junk under the boardwalk, who'd leaned against him as they walked the beach, who'd held him tightly there at the end as the body was being floated out. If he'd known she looked like this . . . Good thing you didn't, he thought. You would've been a wreck.

"What's *wrong?*" she demanded, her smile gone and worry in her eyes.

"You're . . . so beautiful."

The smile returned, this time sheepish, as her face went red.

"I'm not so hot," she said. "But thanks." She patted the blanket in front of her. "Come on, sit down." She moved backward on her knees to make more room for him, then sat and crossed her legs.

Jeremy sat down facing her.

"I thought you weren't going to show up," she said.

"I'm sorry. I had trouble getting away from home."

"No problem. I've only been here a few minutes myself." A corner of her lip lifted slightly. "It wasn't easy, coming back after what happened."

"I know what you mean."

"Aren't you awfully warm in that shirt?" she asked.

"Yeah." He took his sunglasses from a pocket and put them on. Then he took off his shirt. He rolled it into a bundle, being careful not to let his wallet and keys fall out, and dropped it onto the blanket. "That's better," he said.

With the sunglasses on, he allowed himself to look at the rest of the Shiner.

"Does it bother you?" she asked.

She wore a one-piece suit, not a bikini.

"What?"

It wasn't low-cut. Its neck was as high as the top of a T-shirt, and straps went over her shoulders.

"The guy."

But it was black, and the thin, glossy fabric was skintight.

"Yeah," he said. "It bothers me a lot."

It hugged her breasts, which were somewhat cone-shaped and pointed.

"Me too. I keep seeing him . . . everything."

It clung to her rib cage and slanted down against her flat belly.

"It's like a nightmare," she continued. "But it really happened, didn't it?"

It swept inward, leaving her hips bare, and was very narrow where it passed between her legs.

"Nothing we can do will change it," Jeremy said.

The way she sat, he could see the bare hollows where her legs joined her groin. He didn't see any pubic hair.

"I guess," he added, "it'll get easier as time goes by."

The inner sides of her thighs, turned upward, glimmered with suntan oil.

"I sure hope so."

Jeremy raised his eyes to her face. "I'm sorry the guy got killed," he said, "but I'm awfully glad I met you."

A corner of her mouth lifted. "I'm glad we met too." Leaning forward, she reached out and put a hand on his knee. It rested there for a moment, then rubbed him, then patted him and went back to her own knee. "You want some of my suntan oil?"

"Yeah, okay."

She uncrossed her legs, swung them away from Jeremy, and stretched out on her side. Bracing herself up on one elbow, she reached into the side pocket of a denim bag. She pulled out a plastic bottle of oil and gave it to him.

Head resting on her hand, she watched him spread the oil over his skin. He was glad he'd spent some time in the sun so he wasn't white. He knew his body wasn't great, but he'd worked out enough to develop his muscles so he no longer looked so much like a skinny weakling.

When he finished, he gave the bottle back to Shiner. He rubbed his slick hands on his swimsuit. Then he lay down on his side, facing her.

"Do you need the sunglasses?" she asked. "I like it better when I can see your eyes."

Jeremy felt a flutter of alarm. Had she noticed the way he'd inspected her?

He took the glasses off.

She smiled. "You've got neat eyes."

"Thanks. So do you."

For a long time they stared into each other's eyes. Hers were so blue that even their whites seemed to be tinted with the color. Her face was so close to him that apparently she couldn't focus on both his eyes at once. Her gaze flicked slightly from side to side. He supposed that his did too.

It felt very strange to be staring at each other this way. It felt good, but strange. Nothing like this had ever happened to Jeremy before. It made him feel shaky inside.

It was as if she were looking into him.

And I'm looking into her, he thought.

He found it hard to believe that this was the same girl who had kicked the troll last night. The toughness didn't seem to be there now. He saw only softness, and a bewildering mixture of joy and sorrow, knowledge and curiosity and hope.

He wished he knew what she was thinking.

Maybe she's wondering what *I'm* thinking.

Maybe she's waiting for me to kiss her.

"I wish all these people weren't around," Shiner said.

"Yeah," Jeremy said. "Me too."

"Why?" Shiner asked.

He smiled. "Hey, that's no fair. You're the one who said you wished we were alone."

"But you agreed."

"Well, sure."

"What would you do if nobody else was around?"

"What would *you* do?"

Shiner reached out and stroked the side of his face. "I think I might want to kiss you," she said. "Is that what you were thinking too?"

"Yeah."

She twisted onto her stomach, held herself up on her elbows, and looked around at him. "Not with other people around, though. That's why I wished we were alone. It's supposed to be a private thing, you know? Don't you think so?"

"Yeah."

"I think it's disgusting when I see people making out on the beach in broad daylight in front of everyone. It just shows they don't have any self-control."

"Or self-respect," Jeremy added, staring at Shiner's back.

Which was bare except for two straps that crossed between her shoulder blades, and a triangle of shiny black fabric that started just below her waist and looked as if it were glued to her buttocks. Her skin was about the same shade as a marshmallow after it has been heated over a fire to a mellow golden tan.

He wondered is she would ask him to put suntan oil on her back.

"Where did you move here from?" she asked.

"Bakersfield."

"Did you have a girlfriend?"

"Not exactly."

"What does that mean, 'not exactly'?"

"There was nobody I actually went out with. Just some girls in school who were okay."

"They don't have any boys in my school."

"Really?"

"I go to St. Anne's. It's all girls."

"So you haven't had any boyfriends?"

She smiled and shrugged one shoulder a little. "I've had some. Nobody I really cared much about, though. And I never got to see much of them, not with my mother the way she is. She has a way of scaring them off."

"Sounds like my mother."

Shiner rolled over and folded her hands under her head.

There went my chance to oil her back, Jeremy thought.

"They're so protective," she said, one eye shut against the sun, the other squinting at him.

"Yeah, that's for sure. I got the third degree when I told my mom I was meeting a girl here."

"Probably shouldn't have told."

"I know. What a goof. Now she wants to meet you."

"She does, huh? She afraid I'll corrupt you?"

"Yeah."

Shiner raised a hand to shield her eyes from the sunlight, and stared at Jeremy. "Maybe she's right."

"I hope so."

She laughed. "If you want to get corrupted, you'll have better luck with someone else. Like Heather."

"Give me a break."

She put the hand down again and shut her eyes.

Her elbow was near Jeremy's eye. The underside of her arm, though turned upward, had almost no tan at all. The hollow of her armpit looked smooth and white and soft.

"I'll meet your mother if you want me to," she said, keeping her eyes shut.

"You don't have to."

"No, it's all right. If it'll make things easier for you."

"Okay. I'll meet yours too."

"When hell freezes over. Forget about mine. That'd be the last I'd ever see of you."

"She can't be that bad."

"Believe it." Shiner rolled onto her side. "How about tonight?"

"Hey, you really don't—"

"We're getting together at Tanya's house at eight. You're invited."

"No kidding?"

"This is her day off. She asked me to tell you about it. All of us are supposed to be there. Trollers only."

"Like a meeting or something?"

"I don't know. This is a first. It must have something to do with what happened last night."

"Man."

"Should be interesting, huh?"

"Yeah, I'll say."

"Anyway, I'll be driving myself over, so why don't I give you a ride? That way, I can meet your mother when I come to pick you up. Put her mind at ease."

"That'd be great!"

"You think she'll let you come?"

"Sure. Once she's met you, she'll . . . she'll like you. Hell, she'll be overjoyed. But what about *your* mom?"

"No sweat. I'll make up a story, tell her a friend from school's having a party. She'll buy it. She believes whatever I tell her. She's so strict it drives me crazy, but she trusts me. I can get away with just about anything."

Shiner went silent. Jeremy lay down beside her. He folded his hands under his head. His elbow brushed against her elbow. She didn't move it out of the way. He kept his elbow there, touching hers, and shut his eyes.

The heat of the sun pressed down on him. He felt the mild breeze roaming over his skin.

Everything's going so great, he thought.

She would kiss me if nobody was around. Tonight we'll be alone in her car.

He wondered what would happen at Tanya's house. It made him excited and nervous to think about that.

But he felt even more excited, more nervous, about being in the car with Shiner. Maybe she wouldn't take him straight home after the meeting. Maybe she would park someplace dark and deserted. Maybe they would do more than kiss.

Robin couldn't shake the cold, hollow feeling that had settled into her after Nate left. She played her banjo and she sang, but she ached inside.

It felt like homesickness.

It'll pass, she told herself.

She'd gone through a heavy period of *real* homesickness after running away two years ago. It hadn't come at once. In the beginning there had been only rage against Paul, anger against her mother for taking up with him, fear that she would be caught and sent back to them, and fear for her own safety on the road. The homesickness didn't hit until she'd been gone for more than a week. When it came, it was crushing.

She'd been walking through a small town just after dark. It was October. A chilly wind tumbled leaves past her. She smelled wood smoke from chimneys. On both sides of the street, warm light glowed from the windows of homes.

It hit her then. The loss. The sudden understanding that she was outside, alone, unloved, with no hope of ever returning to the home that had once been so cozy and safe and full of happiness.

She fell apart, but she kept on walking, striding into a wind that filled her gaping mouth and blew her tears across her cheeks.

She hadn't been able to stop crying until sometime later that night when she decided to return home. She would find a way to deal with Paul. Maybe even go to the police.

The next morning she started hitching her way back.

A man named George picked her up. He was about forty, cheerful and talkative. It went fine for a while. Then he stopped the car on a deserted stretch of road with nothing but cornfields all around. He turned to Robin. She saw the look in his eyes, and she knew what was coming.

It was the same dazed, feverish look she'd seen so many times in Paul's eyes.

"Don't try it," she said.

"Aw, now, don't be that way. I've been nice enough to give you a lift."

She wanted to leap from the car. But her pack and banjo were in the backseat. She couldn't escape from George without risking the loss of them.

Her knife was in the side pocket of her pack.

She unfastened her safety harness and faced him. "Just let me get my things and leave, okay?"

He unfastened the top button of her shirt.

Voice shaking, she said, "You don't want to do this. I've got syphilis."

He smiled and opened more buttons. "Imagine that. So do I." With both hands, he spread her shirt open.

Her fist crashed into his nose. Blood gushed from his nostrils. Hurling herself at him, Robin clutched his throat and slammed his head against the driver's window. His eyes rolled in their sockets. She shook him by the neck, bouncing his head off the window until he sagged. Then she tore the key from the ignition. Hanging on to it, she left him behind the wheel, hurried from the car, and unloaded her pack and banjo.

She tossed the key case onto the floor between his feet, gathered her things from the roadside, and ran into the cornfield. Hiding there she got out her knife.

She waited for George to come looking.

While she waited, she thought about how foolish she'd been, wanting to go home. She had no home. Paul was there, and Paul was worse than George.

Before long, she heard the car drive away. She waited a few more minutes, then walked out to the road. It stretched straight in both directions. George's car was out of sight. She turned west, and started walking.

That was the end of her homesickness.

But this felt like homesickness—this empty, longing ache that Nate had brought to her.

She took a break. After her audience had scattered, she gathered the money out of her banjo case, latched her banjo inside, and carried her case and backpack to a nearby bench.

She piled all her money onto her lap and counted.

She had a total of $63.75.

She took a cotton sock from her pack and filled it with loose change. She folded the paper money and tucked it into a pocket of her jeans.

Though she didn't have a wristwatch, she suspected that she still had time to reach one of the banks in town and exchange her coins for bills. From there she could go to the bus terminal and buy a ticket out of this place.

No reason to stay, she told herself. She had enough money to hold her for a while, even if she spent half of it for a bus ticket. Nate was certainly no reason to stay. And it would be good to get away from this nest of bums and thieves and trollers before she ran into real trouble.

Leaning forward, she stuffed the sock full of change into the side pocket of her pack.

Someone sat down on the bench. Robin looked up to see who it was.

Nate.

He smiled at her. He didn't look haggard or troubled anymore. "How's it going?" he asked.

"Okay."

"Sorry about before. I shouldn't have talked to you that way."

"It's all right," Robin said. Her heart was pounding hard.

"I was worried about you. That's why I blew up. See, I know what can happen to people around this place. I don't want you getting hurt. And sleeping on the beach . . . you're just asking for it."

You don't have to worry anymore, she thought. I'll be out of Boleta Bay by dark. Gone forever.

And I'll never see you again.

Frowning, he stared into her eyes. He pressed his lips into a tight line and shook his head. "I don't want you to get the wrong idea," he said.

"About what?"

"I want you to take this." He dug into a front pocket of his pants and brought out a key attached to a big oval of green plastic. He put it into Robin's hand.

She turned the tab over. On raised white-painted letters

were the words "Wayfarer's Inn" and an address. The key had a room number on it.

"No argument," Nate said. "The room's already paid for. I knew it wouldn't do any good just to give you the money and ask you to use it on a motel." He shrugged. "You'd just save the money for breakfasts."

Robin's throat felt tight. Her heart felt like a fist punching inside her chest.

"You don't have to worry," he told her. "I'm not going to show up there and try to put moves on you. Hell, I don't even know the room number. I just want you to stay safe."

She took hold of his hand and squeezed it. "That's . . . awfully nice of you," she said. Her voice was shaking. "You shouldn't have done it, but . . ."

"You will use it, won't you? The room?"

"Okay. But let me pay you for it."

"No way."

"Really. I've got some money to spare now." She heard herself laugh. Her eyes were suddenly wet. "I was going to buy a bus ticket this afternoon, but now I guess I'll stay."

"You were going to leave?" He looked stunned, and she felt his hand tighten.

"Well, yeah, but . . . Can't leave now, can I? Not with a motel room waiting."

"You were just going to go away? I thought you'd be sticking around here."

She sniffed. She shrugged.

"I have to get back to the arcade," Nate said. "But you promise you'll use the room?"

"I promise."

"Great."

"But you've got to let me pay for it. You can't be spending so much money on me. Geez, you're busting your hump working for peanuts at that arcade . . ."

"My family owns it," he said, smiling. "The arcade, the Hurricane, the Ferris wheel, and the Tilt-a-Whirl. We're pretty well-off. In fact, we're filthy rich. I drive a Trans Am, for God-sake, and live in a twelve-room house with a swimming pool and tennis court. So I can afford a motel room for you, don't worry."

"You convinced me," Robin said, staring down at the key. "I accept the gift. Thank you."

"My pleasure." He pulled his hand away and rose from the bench. "So I'll see you tomorrow, okay?"

"If not sooner?"

"This isn't some kind of a trick, Robin. I told you, I didn't even look at the room number."

"I believe you."

"Hope you enjoy it," he said, and turned away.

"It's two-forty," she called. "Room two-forty."

Nate looked over his shoulder. He gazed at her with wide eyes. His mouth hung open slightly.

"Just in case you want to check up on me," Robin said, "see if I'm really there."

"I don't know. I don't know." Shaking his head, he hurried away.

"You'd better wake up and turn over, or you'll burn."

Jeremy opened his eyes. Shiner was on her elbow, smiling down at him.

"I can't believe I fell asleep," he said. He felt hot and heavy, as if weighted down by the sun.

"You were zonked. Didn't you get any sleep last night?"

"Loads," he said.

Shiner laughed. "Roll over," she said. "I'll put stuff on your back."

When he heard that, the weight seemed to vanish. He quickly turned onto his stomach and rested his chin on his crossed arms.

"What time did you get home?" she asked.

"About three."

"Me too."

He squirmed as a warm stream of oil zigzagged his back. Then he felt Shiner's hands. They slid over his skin, spreading the fluid.

There was nothing *romantic* about the way she touched

him. She swept the oil around as if this was an ordinary task, and Jeremy wondered if maybe she was trying hard not to let it seem like anything more. But the smooth rubbing felt wonderful to him.

"How long do you suppose Nate was out there?" she asked.

"I don't know."

"I was starting to think he'd drowned or something. God, it was so spooky, waiting for him."

"That's for sure." Jeremy remembered being so spooked that when he finally saw Nate coming back, he'd thought for a moment that it was the troll surfing toward him through the fog.

Shiner's hands glided down his sides.

"I'm sure glad you were there," she said. "I would've really freaked out, I think. It almost made it okay, hugging you like that."

"That part was nice," Jeremy said.

He felt oil dribble onto the backs of his legs. When her hands began sliding, he squirmed and turned slightly to ease the pressure on his penis. She rubbed the tops of his legs, and the outer sides. She rubbed the inner sides of his calves. Higher up, though—above his knees—she left the inner sides untouched. The very fact that she stayed away from that area confirmed Jeremy's suspicion that she knew this was a sex thing and didn't want it to seem that way.

Her hands went away. "All through," she said. "Would you mind doing my back?"

"No. Sure."

She lay down and Jeremy knelt beside her, bending at the waist in an attempt to hide his bulge.

She unfastened the straps at her shoulders and flipped them out of the way.

Something like a strip-tease, but innocent too. She wasn't *really* stripping, just getting the straps out of the way so they wouldn't leave pale marks on her tan. Girls almost always did that when they sunbathed. It meant nothing.

But Jeremy knew that she knew what she was doing.

She stroked her hair, parting it away from the nape of her

neck. She was smooth and bare all the way down to the glossy seat of her suimsuit.

Jeremy squirted curly trails of oil onto her back, stood the bottle between his knees, and began to spread the oil with both hands. Her skin was warm and slippery.

I've gotta not think about it, he warned himself, horribly aware of his aroused condition.

This was a lot like wiping the ice cream off Tanya.

Don't think about that!

He quickly finished her back, leaving her sides unoiled because—God!—that'd be getting awfully close to her breasts and that might be too much to stand. He wondered if he dared to do her legs. But he couldn't *not* do them.

"Did you walk home alone?" he asked, trying to take his mind off the situation as he moved sideways past her rump and knelt by her legs.

"Yeah," she said. "It's not very far."

He squirted the fluid onto the backs of her legs. It started to trickle down between them. He thought, *Oh, no!* and quickly rubbed away the dribbles, trying not to think about where his hands were. "I wish you would've let me walk you home," he said, his voice shaking.

"Then you'd know where I live."

"What's wrong with that?" He quickly spread the oil down her calves.

"I don't let any of the trollers know where I live," Shiner said. "Or my real name, for that matter."

Jeremy stopped.

Done. Thank God.

He capped the bottle. He flopped onto his back and brought his knees up. "Why don't you want anyone to know?"

"It's in case something goes wrong. One of us might get caught by the cops. It hasn't happened yet, but it could. I don't care what anyone says about promising not to talk. Maybe some of them wouldn't, but it'd only take one. The cops or D.A. or somebody would promise a lighter sentence for naming names, and that'd be pretty tempting. Next thing you know, they've rounded up everyone. Except me."

"So none of the trollers know who you really are?"

"Or where I live. So I can't get fingered. I tell you what, too—after what happened last night, I'm really glad I've kept it that way."

"Yeah," Jeremy said. He felt a little let-down that she didn't trust *him*, but he could see the wisdom of keeping her identity a secret. "I wish I'd done the same thing," he said.

"Does anyone know who you are?"

"I told Cowboy my last name. Where I live, too."

"Well, don't worry about it. It wouldn't have worked for you. The only reason I get away with it is that I go to a different school. None of the other trollers go to St. Anne's. They all attend the public school, and that's where you'll be going in September, isn't it?"

"Yeah."

"So they'd find out who you are when school starts. You couldn't have stayed anonymous, no matter what."

"Man, that's the pits."

"You shouldn't lose any sleep over it. Nobody's been caught so far, and I have a feeling that the trolling is over."

"Really?"

"I'll bet that's what the meeting tonight is all about. I mean, nobody ever counted on someone getting killed. That changes everything. I think Nate has probably talked Tanya into breaking up the group."

Jeremy felt a sudden sense of loss, as if he'd just been told that all his friends were moving out of town.

"I know I'm finished with it," Shiner said.

"But we'll still see each other, won't we?"

"I hope so. I don't know any reason why not, do you?"

"No. Jeez, I'd like to see you all the time." Speaking those words, he felt a warm rush of guilt. As if he were betraying someone. But who? Tanya? Cowboy? The whole group of trollers? Or Shiner herself?

Twenty-three

Straddling the padded bench of her weight machine, Joan adjusted her grip on the bar handles. The pulley squeaked as she drew the bar down to her chin and let it up, lifting and lowering the 110 pounds on the cable behind her back.

Maybe she would give Dave a call as soon as she finished her workout, and see how things had gone with Gloria. It was after seven now. He ought to be done.

She pulled the bar down again.

How many was that, six?

Her heart was pounding with quick solid thumps, she was breathing hard, and her sweatshirt felt sticky inside.

Six more, she thought, and you're through.

She had already spent half an hour working out. After some simple warm-up exercises, she'd started to run through her karate moves. The karate depressed her, though. She kept seeing her foot smash into Woodrow Abernathy's chin. She'd been feeling great until those memories started up, so she knocked off the karate and moved on to the weight machine. She'd worked on each muscle group until she ached, and this was the last.

She drew the bar down one more time, let it up, and released the grips. She fluttered the shirt. Air buffeted her hot, moist skin. Then she lifted the shirt and wiped her dripping face.

She felt fine except for a touch of guilt about skipping the karate. Strength was all well and good, but the karate kept her quick, and kept her balance and agility finely tuned. Still, she was reluctant to try it again.

An idea came that cheered her up a lot. She went to the old stereo in the corner of her exercise room, selected an album from the cabinet, and placed the record on the turntable. She carefully lowered the arm onto the band she remembered so well, then stepped to the corner of the mat.

John Denver's high, clear voice began singing "Calypso."

She danced onto the mat in time with the music and did three handsprings to the opposite corner. Her timing was off just slightly. She staggered off the mat. There goes your ten, she thought. But she whirled around and continued her routine, dancing, kicking, leaping, spinning, doing cartwheels and somersaults, and finishing with a triple back flip that used to bring down the house but tonight landed Joan on her butt.

Clapping came from the doorway.

She saw Debbie standing there, a smirk on her face. "How'd a klutz like you ever make the state finals?"

"I wasn't five-eleven then."

"I'd show you how it's supposed to be done, but I've got to get going."

"Don't let me stop you."

"Do I look all right?"

She wore white jeans. The blue of her shiny blouse brought out the blue in her eyes. Her face had a faint reddish glow from her afternoon at the beach. Her blond hair curled softly around her face.

"You look great," Joan said. "You'll knock the fellows dead."

"If any are there." Debbie wrinkled her nose. "You know Jessica. She's such a goody-two-shoes, I'll be lucky if there's a guy within miles."

"Well, have fun anyway. And be home by twelve."

"If it's too much of a drag, I might be home a lot earlier. You going to see Dave tonight?"

"I don't know."

"Maybe you could have him over and show him your floor exercise. I'm sure he'd go ape—especially the way you nearly lose your sweatshirt on the cartwheels."

"Aren't you going to be late or something?"

Debbie laughed. "When do I get to meet him?"

"What do you want? I haven't even gone out with him yet."

"I'd like to see what he looks like."

"If you're all that eager, come over to the boardwalk while we're on duty tomorrow."

"Yeah. Thanks, but no thanks."

"What've you suddenly got against Funland? You used to go there all the time."

"That was before Big Sister started walking the beat."

Joan grinned. "I cramp your style?"

"Might, if I went there and tried to have fun."

"Well, sorry about that. But a job's a job."

"When'll you get reassigned?"

"Who knows? But don't worry, I won't be there forever."

"Just all summer, my luck."

"If you miss the place so much, go on my days off. Or some night, as long as you go with friends."

"Anyway," Debbie said, "I'd better get out of here or I'll be late. So long. Don't do anything I wouldn't."

"Haw haw."

Debbie raised a hand in farewell, then stepped out of the doorway.

Joan sat on the floor and did some stretching exercises until she heard the car drive away. Then she went to her bedroom. Her stomach fluttered as she sat on the edge of her bed and lifted the telephone onto her lap.

Silly to be jumpy about calling Dave, she told herself.

She gazed at the phone.

Christ, I'm not a damn teenager.

She took a deep breath, lifted the handset, and dialed.

His telephone rang eight times before she hung up.

Okay. So he's not home. Big deal.

That doesn't mean he's still at Gloria's. And even if he is, so what? Afraid they'll make up?

No chance.

What makes you so sure? Hell, they were going together hot and heavy till a few days ago. And he obviously still cares about her, or he wouldn't have been so upset when I told him about the bitch playing dress-up.

He was upset for the same reason as me—because he felt responsible.

Joan wished they'd skipped lunch and rushed right over to find her. But Dave hadn't wanted to. "The hell if I'm going to ruin my meal chasing after her. She wants to pull a dumb stunt like that, it's her problem."

Lunch was ruined anyway. Joan had been too upset about Gloria to enjoy the gyro, and she suspected that Dave's appetite had also suffered a trouncing. Worry and anger had a way of turning food tasteless.

When they finished eating, they headed for the Funland entrance. Joan waited by the ticket booth while Dave went down the steps. But he came back in about a minute and explained that Gloria was no longer there. They resumed their patrol, expecting to run into her along the boardwalk. During the afternoon they spotted eight or ten derelicts. No Gloria, though.

At the end of their tour, Dave had said he would drop by Gloria's house and try to warn her off. He hadn't seemed eager about it, but they'd both known it was something that needed to be done.

She'd been jilted and gone off the deep end.

It was their fault.

It would be their fault if her stupid "undercover work" got her pounded or raped or worse.

Somebody had to talk some sense into her, and Dave was it.

Joan gazed at the phone, wondering if she should try calling again. Maybe Dave had been in the shower.

Maybe *I'll* take a shower, and try him when I'm done.

She wished she'd gone along with him. But Dave hadn't asked, and she hadn't offered. The less Gloria saw of her, the better.

That was obvious.

She lifted the telephone onto the nightstand, stood up, and went down the hallway to the bathroom. She shut the door and locked it.

Big tough cop locking the door, she thought.

She *always* locked it before taking a shower or bath. Always, when she was alone in the house.

Something creepy about it. Something to do with being cut off from the rest of the house and water running so you couldn't hear what might be going on out there. Something to do with a movie called *Psycho.*

The air felt humid from Debbie's bath. And the aroma of her cologne was almost overpowering. What had she done, spilled the stuff?

Joan slid the window open a few inches. She pulled off her

shoes and socks, hung her sweatsuit on the knob, and stepped to the tub. The bathmat still showed Debbie's footprints. It felt soggy where the girl had stood.

Leaning over the edge of the tub, Joan reached for the hot-water faucet and flinched when the doorbell rang. Gooseflesh swarmed up her body.

The bell rang again, a faint chiming sound.

She grimaced and straightened up.

Great timing, she thought. Here I am, bare-assed.

She rushed to the bathroom door, leapt into her sweatpants (which were just as moist and clammy as she'd feared), hooked her sweatshirt off the knob, and pulled it down over her head as she hurried to the front door.

She peered through the peephole.

Harold.

Shit!

She opened the door and twisted her face into a smile.

He glanced at her face for an instant before lowering his eyes in typical Harold fashion. "I'm sorry," he said. "Did I catch you at a bad time?"

"No. Huh-uh. I'd just finished my workout. Come on in." She stepped aside.

He entered and shut the door. "I suppose I should've phoned first, but . . ." He shrugged.

"That's okay. Could I get you a drink or something?"

"Some white wine would be nice, if you have any."

"Sure. Come on." She headed for the kitchen, Harold following. Her heart was beating fast. She felt a little tight and sick inside.

He wasn't supposed to show up.

Didn't he understand? Hadn't she made it clear enough the other night?

Obviously not.

She'd been about as clear as possible without coming right out and saying she didn't want to go out with him anymore.

Squatting down, she took a bottle of chablis from the cupboard. "I'm afraid it isn't chilled," she said. "You want ice cubes?"

"Just one. Don't want to water it down too much," he added,

and gave out a tiny coughlike chuckle that sounded miserably nervous.

Oh, he got the message, all right.

But he's here anyway.

Joan gave the bottle to him. He went to the drawer where she kept the corkscrew. He'd been here for dinner three times, so he knew right where to find it.

Good old Debbie. Sharp kid. After the *first* dinner, she'd said, "Harold's a dingus. Why are you wasting your time with him? Dump him and find a *guy*. You're a cop, you must know *guys*."

Joan set a pair of wineglasses onto the counter. She dropped an ice cube into one, and left the other empty. Harold was having trouble with the cork. Bending over, he clamped the bottle between his legs, gripped its neck, and tugged the handle of the corkscrew.

As Joan watched, she remembered popping open the champagne at Dave's house yesterday.

If only I were there right now, she thought.

He isn't there.

He's dealing with Gloria, and I've got to deal with Harold. We each have our own messes keeping us apart.

Harold popped the cork. He filled the glasses and handed the one without ice to Joan.

"I hope you don't mind me dropping by like this," he said as they walked into the living room.

"No, that's fine. I'm kind of a mess, is all."

"You look terrific. As always."

"Thanks," she muttered.

Harold sat on the sofa. Joan sat down beside him.

"I was planning to call you," she said.

Harold nodded. He took a sip of wine, then gazed at his glass. "I understand that. And I can well imagine what you would've had to say. I wasn't especially eager to hear it. Each time the phone rang, I thought it was you and . . . This is not at all easy for me, Joan. To come here like this. I've felt . . . physically ill . . . all day."

"I'm sorry," she murmured.

He held up one hand as if to ward off her apology. "It's not your fault. It's me." He looked at her, smiled bleakly, and returned his gaze to the glass. "I was actually twenty-five before I had my first sexual encounter. And that was a case of the girl seducing me. I had no interest in her. She was . . . not attractive. In fact, she was distinctly unappealing. As was every female I've ever dared to approach."

"Thanks a heap," Joan said, hoping to cheer him up.

"If you remember correctly, you approached me."

"I did, yes."

"And I was . . . instantly smitten. I could hardly believe that I was in the company of a woman who was not only exceedingly attractive but also intelligent and well-read and witty. That sort of thing had never happened to me before. I found it incomprehensible that you would even speak to me, much less . . ."

"I like you, Harold. I really do. I've enjoyed our times together."

"Enjoy." He made a small huff through his nose. "Such a pallid word. To me, the times we spent together were . . . like glimpses of paradise. Which is why I never dared to risk it all, why I never . . ." He shook his head.

"Put moves on me?"

"I wanted to," he admitted, frowning at his wineglass. "You've no idea how much I've wanted to kiss you, embrace you. I've dreamed of—"

The jangle of the telephone stopped his voice.

Joan's heart lurched.

Dave? It had to be Dave.

The phone rang again, again.

"Aren't you going to answer it?" Harold asked.

"No," she said, and rested a hand gently on his knee. The phone rang seven more times.

The silence when it stopped felt heavy and dark.

Harold began to weep. He reached out and set the wineglass on the table, then turned his face away from Joan. She rubbed his back. She could feel it hitching under her hand as he struggled to stifle his sobs.

"I know it's over," he said in a choked voice. "You were looking for a . . . a Rhett Butler, and I'm . . . not even an Ashley. A Prufrock, that's what I am, nothing but a Prufrock."

"Hey, come on. Everything's going to be okay."

"No. No, I don't think so."

"We'll still see each other, Harold. We'll still be friends. And really, it was never more than that. Maybe we both wanted it to be more, but it never was. So we'll leave it that way and stop trying to make it something else."

He sniffed. He shook his head. He wiped his eyes.

"We'll go to the movies next week."

"No. I couldn't. God, I don't want your pity."

"Well, then, the hell with you."

His head jerked around. His eyes were wet and red. His cheeks were shiny with tears. He looked at her eyes. He looked at her smirk. And a laugh sputtered out of him.

"Take my pity or take a leap, Gonzo."

He laughed again.

The telephone began to ring. "This time, I'm going to get it. Take the opportunity to pull yourself together."

He stayed on the sofa. Joan rushed into the kitchen and grabbed the telephone. "Hello?"

"Hi there. It's me."

"Hiya, Me," she said, and felt a warmth come into her. "How'd it go?"

"It didn't. I went over to her place and she wasn't home. In fact, I went over twice. Once before supper, once after."

"You think she's still out playing games?"

"Wouldn't surprise me. I'm going to drive down to the boardwalk and search around, but that'll take a while. I just wanted to talk to you first, let you know what's going on."

"I was starting to get worried. Hey, how about letting me go with you?"

"I think it'd just make matters worse if we're together, and . . ."

"I know. I know that. Shit."

"Are you all right?"

"Yeah. It's just that I miss you."

"You miss me?"

"No, I'm sick of your face. Of course I miss you. I thought we might see each other tonight. I called you a while ago."

"I called you too."

"Yeah, I thought it was you. I couldn't answer it. If you really think Gloria will freak out or something if we're together . . ."

"Aah, let her. I'll come by and get you. How about ten minutes?"

"How about half an hour? I need to take a shower."

"Can't it wait till I get there?"

"Haw haw. In your ear, Davy boy."

"I'll have to think about that."

"See you later." She hung up and went back to the living room. She stopped at the edge of the table. Harold was sitting up straight. He was no longer crying. "You all right?" she asked.

"As well as can be expected, I suppose."

"You'll pick me up for the film next week?"

He made a limp smile. "Ah, my cue to evacuate the premises."

"Afraid so. I have to get cleaned up and leave. That was Dave. We've got a little bit of an emergency we need to take care of."

Nodding, Harold drank the last of his wine.

He stood up. Joan took hold of his hand, and they walked toward the door. "The film?" she asked.

"I don't know."

"Let's give it a try and see how it goes. Unless, of course, you dump me between now and then for someone even more beautiful and charming than *moi.*"

"The dumping, my dear, has already been done. Not by me, of course."

The words wrenched her. She'd thought she had healed his wound. All she'd done, she realized, was slap a bandage across it. The gash was too big for such a flimsy patch. She could almost see the tide of blood.

Harold opened the door.

Joan clutched his arm to stop him from leaving. She turned him to face her. He didn't look tormented now. He looked resigned, defeated, a little dazed and hollow in the eyes.

"I wish I could make it all right," she said.

"You get an E for effort." He eased his arm out of her grip and walked out into the dusk.

Joan closed the door and leaned back against it. She let out a deep sigh.

She felt awful. She was glad that he was gone. She was glad that it was over.

It *was* over. He'd lost, and he wasn't about to accept the consolation prize of friendship.

And she was *glad*.

And it was not too different from kicking Woodrow Abernathy in the chin. A feeling of relief and joy because she'd taken care of business, finished the matter, brought a bad situation to a quick end. But guilt was like gray rain in her soul.

Twenty-four

"It was very nice to meet you, Mrs. Wayne."

"Well, it was nice to meet you too, Shiner."

"I have to be home before midnight, so I'll get Jeremy back here around eleven-thirty. Is that all right?"

"Fine, fine. Have a good time, kids."

Jeremy opened the door for Shiner. As she walked out, he smiled at his mother. She made a face at him—eyebrows rising, eyes rolling upward, lips pursing—a face that said, "I can't believe it. How did you possibly manage to latch on to a girl like *this*?"

Once the door was shut, he took hold of Shiner's hand. "You wowed her!"

"But of course."

"She was all set to hate your guts."

"She's nice. I like her."

They reached the curb. Shiner unlocked the passenger door for Jeremy, then walked around the front of the car.

"You sure look nice tonight," he said as she slipped in behind the steering wheel.

"Thanks. You too."

He wished she were wearing a dress, but she looked awfully good in the white jeans. And he liked the way her blouse seemed so light and clingy. If he held her, it would feel slick and he would be able to slide it on her skin.

She had an aroma that made him think of the way the air might smell in a forest after a spring rain.

She started the car and pulled away from the curb. "I've been thinking," she said, "and there's no law says we *have* to go to this thing at Tanya's. It's going to be a bummer, you know. A lot of talk about that guy who kicked it. We could do something else. Go to the movies or fool around at Funland or something."

"Don't you *want* to go?" Jeremy asked.

"If you do. I'm just saying we don't have to."

The idea of going to a movie or to Funland with Shiner excited him. On the other hand, he hated to miss Tanya's party.

"I'm pretty curious about it," he said.

"Okay. We'll go, then. No problem."

"Are you sure?"

"It was just a thought. And, I mean, we *should* go. Tanya wants everyone to be there. I've just got cold feet, I guess."

"You're scared?"

"No, not scared. A little nervous, maybe. I don't know, I have this feeling I'm going to wish we'd stayed away."

"Maybe we'd better not go, then," he said, being gallant and self-sacrificing and feeling dismal about it.

"No. Hey, you don't want to miss the thing. And I'm not sure whether I do or not. Maybe it'll be terrific."

"Let's just go for a while," Jeremy suggested. "Just put in an appearance and see what's going on. Then, if we feel like it, we'll split."

"Sounds good to me," Shiner said.

He settled back into the car's bucket seat.

The rest of the trip was wonderful. Jeremy felt nervous, but excited too. He was alone in the car with Shiner, his girlfriend, his actual girlfriend who wasn't a dog, who was—as Letterman would put it—"a fabulous babe." She was beautiful and his. And they were on their way to a party. At Tanya's. Where anything might happen but where one thing would happen for sure: he would be in Tanya's presence. And she wasn't a fabulous babe, she was a Force of Nature.

It's really happening, he assurred himself. Right now. To me.

When Jeremy came out of his reverie, he saw that they were on a residential street that he'd never seen before. "Where are we?"

"You might call it 'the other side of the tracks.'"

"Huh?"

"We're heading into the north end. Where the rich folk live."

"Tanya lives over here?"

"Sure. She's loaded. Her father's a chiropractor and her stepmother's a lawyer."

"If they're so rich, why does she have to work?"

Shiner steered the car into a narrow lane that slanted up a wooded hillside. "Well, she obviously doesn't have to. She likes it. Look what she does. She's a lifeguard. Stands around on the beach all day, looking fabulous, the center of attention for every guy within eyeball distance—and now and again she gets to play hero."

Shiner sounded a little amused, and maybe as if she were above such things herself.

"You kind of sound like you don't like her," Jeremy said.

"No, I like her fine. I just don't *adore* her the way everyone else does."

Is she including me? Jeremy wondered. Does she know? How could she?

Shiner stopped at a Y in the road. She took a sheet of paper from the blouse pocket over her left breast and unfolded it. In the faint, bluish light of dusk, Jeremy saw that it was a rough map drawn with a ball-point. Shiner frowned at it for a while. Then she swung to the left and drove slowly up the road.

Jeremy could see no houses. Just woods and sometimes a driveway entrance with a mailbox beside it. The houses, he guessed, were hidden in the trees far above the winding road and far below it.

"How did you meet Tanya?" he asked, wanting to get away from the subject of adoration. "You don't go to the same school, and she lives . . . Do you live up here too?"

"Hell, no. I'm over on . . . in your neighborhood. I met her by hunting out the trollers. Everybody in town was talking about them—and Great Big Billy Goat Gruff. I started sneaking out late at night, and pretty soon I found them. I just explained that I wanted to join up, and why."

"Because of your sister?"

"Right. And they put me through the initiation. I've been with them ever since."

"Was it always the same kids?"

She nodded. "Mostly. A couple of them moved away, and Randy wasn't with them yet. He got involved after Tanya pulled him out of the drink. She did mouth-to-mouth, and he woke up and figured he'd died and gone to heaven. He's been one of her worshipers ever since."

Shiner stopped. She peered through the windshield at the road sign, then checked the map again. "Okay, that's Avion," she said, nodding to the right. "Her place should be the third driveway." She drove forward.

The third driveway was on the left side of the road, and slanted upward with a steep grade. Shiner shifted to first gear, turned onto the driveway, and started to climb it slowly, the engine racing. Jeremy wasn't sure what he expected to find at the top. A cabin or cottage would've seemed about right. But when the road leveled off and the forest opened, he saw something that looked very much like a southern plantation house—complete with a veranda and white columns. He supposed it was smaller than the real thing, but it seemed awfully big to be sitting up here above Boleta Bay.

The whole top of the hill must've been lopped off to make room for the house, its three-car garage, and grounds. The driveway looped around the front lawn and led to a broad paved area to the right of the garage. There, five other cars were already parked.

Shiner parked beside a Jeep that had a Confederate flag on its radio antenna.

She took hold of Jeremy's hand as they walked toward the veranda. Her hand felt moist.

She really *is* nervous about this, Jeremy realized. Why? What does she think might happen?

At the top of the stairs they stopped in front of twin oak doors. Jeremy pushed the doorbell button. From inside came the sound of chimes playing a few bars of "My Old Kentucky Home."

"Are they southerners?" Jeremy asked.

"Who knows? Tanya isn't. She grew up here."

The door on the right swung open.

"Howdy there, Duke, Shiner." Cowboy clapped him on the shoulder. "Long time no see, pardner." The whole right side of his head looked like one huge bandage with a big hump where his ear must be. He wore his old battered Stetson. There were a few bandages on his arms, and Jeremy could see others through the thin white fabric of his T-shirt.

"Come on in, folks. Join the party." As they followed him across the foyer, he said, "I hear you aced a troll last night. Fuckin'-A, and I missed it."

"How are you feeling?" Shiner asked him.

"Like the old lady that bit the hatchet."

He led them down a staircase into a huge carpeted room with furniture along the paneled walls, a pool table, and a bar at the far end. All the trollers were there.

Jeremy's eyes sought out Tanya. He spotted her bending over the pool table, lining up a shot. She was barefoot, wearing white shorts and an oversize shirt with tails so long that they almost covered the shorts. The shirt was a plaid of bright blue and yellow. The way she was bent over, its loose front probably didn't even touch her body.

Karen, standing beside Nate at the other side of the table, looked as if she might be trying for peeks.

Tanya banked the eight ball into a corner pocket and punched her fist into the air. Nate shook his head. Apparently the shot had just won the game for Tanya.

Randy, at a corner of the table, waved a greeting toward Jeremy and Shiner.

Tanya set her cue stick on the table, turned around, and smiled. "Glad you made it," she said, coming forward. Jeremy saw the way her shirt moved, and quickly raised his eyes to her face.

Someone patted his rump. He looked over his shoulder and tried to keep his smile as he met Heather's tiny piglike eyes.

"How's it hanging, Duke?" she asked.

He shrugged.

Samson, behind her, winked and hoisted a glass full of red liquid.

Liz, off to the side, held a glass with the same stuff in it.

The three of them—Heather, Samson, and Liz—had all been at the bar a minute ago when Jeremy first scanned the room.

Heather bumped soft bulges against Jeremy's side. "Why don't you get some punch and join the party?" she said.

"What's the occasion?" Shiner asked, slipping an arm around Jeremy's back as if to let Heather know he wasn't available.

"Let's just call it a wake," Tanya said. "A tribute to the 'good troll.'"

"Only good troll's a dead one," Cowboy added. "Shit, I should've been there."

"And I thought *I* was good at the high dive," Liz said, hooting out a laugh. "That guy did the best damn triple-back-somersault . . ."

"He lost points on his entry, though," Samson said.

"Yeah. I'd only give him an eight."

Some of them laughed. Shiner didn't. Neither did Nate.

"I propose we all get drinks," Tanya said, "and hoist one to the memory of the good troll."

She led the way to the bar, stepped behind it, and uncapped a liter bottle of rum.

"Yo ho ho," Heather said.

Tanya dumped half the bottle's contents into the cut glass punch bowl. The liquor slurped into the red juice with soft plopping sounds. Setting the bottle aside, she stirred with a glass dipper.

When everyone held a glass full of the spiked punch, she raised her own glass. "To the one who took the big dive," she toasted, "and shall be known henceforth as Fish Food."

"I'm not going to drink to that," Nate muttered.

"Lighten up, would you?" Tanya said. "He was a fucking *troll.*"

"He was a human being, and we killed him."

"We didn't kill him. It was an accident."

"A lucky accident," Liz added.

"And I missed it," Cowboy said.

"We murdered him," Nate said.

Tanya stared at him. She looked annoyed, frustrated. "It was an accident. He would've been okay if he hadn't been a fat slob. He would've been okay if *your* Ferris wheel had safety bars worth a shit."

Nate's face went slack. "You think I don't know that?" he asked, his voice little more than a whisper.

"Okay," Tanya said. "We went out to nail a troll and we nailed one. He happened to die. All the moaning and whining in the world isn't going to bring him back to life."

"Who'd *want* to?" Liz said.

"So let's just have a good time, huh? I didn't ask everybody over here to bellyache about it. The whole idea's to loosen up, have some drinks, fool around, and put the whole thing behind us. We all know what happened out there. None of us is happy about it."

"Speak for yourself," Liz said. "Me, I think it's great. One less troll in our faces. We oughta do it to all of 'em."

Grinning, Cowboy rubbed her hair. She smiled and put an arm around him.

"I'm with Liz," Samson said. "Fuck 'em all. The deader the bedder."

Nate gave him a betrayed look, then turned his eyes to Tanya. "It has to stop. We should've stopped it a long time ago. It's just been getting more and more out of hand. Something like this was bound to happen . . ."

"You sound like that shit editorial in the paper."

"That shit editorial was right! We proved it right last night, didn't we? And don't give me this crap about not being happy about it. You were *delighted* that the old guy fell. You've been itching to . . . You tried to set the one on fire Tuesday night!"

"Could've had us a weenie roast," Cowboy said.

"Are you all crazy?"

"It's war, man," Samson said.

"What'd they ever do to you?"

"They piss me off."

"Oh, isn't that wonderful. They piss you off, so you kill them?"

"You dumb fuck, that was an accident and you know it."

"You're in this because of me," Nate said. "Same with you, Cowboy. Remember? I wanted you to help me kick ass because of what they did to Tanya. You never had anything much against the trolls. *I* talked you into it. And it's time to stop. We kicked ass. We paid them back a hundred times over. For Tanya *and* for Shiner's sister."

Nate's fierce eyes moved across the faces of the trollers and stopped on Randy. "What've you got against them? Nothing, that's what. You just have this thing about Tanya. Is it worth killing for? Same with you, Karen."

Smirking, Karen gave him the finger.

"What'd they do to you, Heather? You're just in it for the company. And great company we are! Lose some weight and join the world."

Heather pressed her lips together and blinked at him.

Nate's eyes met Jeremy's. "I don't know what your story is. Do you hate the trolls? Do you want to kill them? Or is this just some kind of a social club like it is for Heather?"

Jeremy, face hot, didn't dare speak.

"Some goddamn war," Nate said, glancing at Samson.

"You've had your say," Tanya told him. Her voice sounded calm but hard. "Now, get out of my house."

"Call it off," he said. "You're the only one who can. You tell them it's over, and it's over."

"All that's over is you and me."

"You're right about that."

For just a moment she looked stunned. As if she'd expected him to be staggered, maybe to relent or ask for forgiveness. Jeremy got the feeling that she didn't *want* to lose him. Her upper lip made a tiny twitch. "Go on," she said. "Get the fuck out of here."

"You're obsessed, Tanya. Don't drag them all down with you."

"*Get out!*"

He set his glass on the bar counter. "I'm leaving. Anybody else? Samson? Cowboy?"

"Not me," Samson said. "Sorry, pal. I'm with Tanya on this one. We gotta clean the place up. I'll quit my trolling when I can walk around all day without some slime bag asking me for two bits."

"Same here," Cowboy said. "Far as I can see, nothing's changed. I hate to lose you for a friend, and I hope it don't come to that, but we got us a job to do here."

Nate kept shaking his head while he listened to Samson and Cowboy. When they finished, he glanced around at everyone. "You're all making a big mistake," he said. "She's turning you into a gang of thugs."

Alone, he walked toward the stairs.

"Don't even think about going to the cops," Tanya warned.

He stopped and looked back. "I'm not trolling anymore," he said. "But that doesn't make me an asshole who'd snitch on his friends." Then he started up the stairs and disappeared.

"Chickenshit bastard," Tanya muttered. "Who needs him, anyway?" With a trembling hand she lifted her glass high. "No trolls," she toasted.

"No quarter," said Cowboy.

They all gathered in close around Tanya and clinked their glasses together.

Twenty-five

Robin sat on the bed in the motel room, propped up with two pillows behind her back, and stared at the television while she waited for Nate.

There was a chance, she knew, that he might not come at all. Giving her the key, Nate had assured her that he wouldn't make a visit. She had believed him, too. But telling him the room number had been a clear invitation.

He'd seemed surprised and confused.

For all Robin knew, he might have a regular girl. Maybe he was with her right now. Or maybe he was still working at the arcade.

He owns it, she reminded herself. He could get someone else to run the place, or he could even shut down early. He shut it early last night.

Come *on*, Nate. Where are you?

From the time Robin had arrived at the motel, she'd been expecting him to show up at any moment.

While she waited, she took the opportunity to use the laundry room downstairs. Wearing a T-shirt and gym shorts, she stuffed all her dirty clothes into the washer, started it up, then hurried back to her room for a shower. She wanted to be clean for him. But she took the shower fast, fearing that Nate might knock and she would miss him.

Maybe that's just what happened, she thought now as she waited on the bed. Maybe he came, knocked, and left.

If that's how it went, he'll come back and try again. Won't he?

Except for the time in the shower, she couldn't have missed him.

She'd waited in the room while her clothes were drying. When she went to dinner, the balcony in front of her room was always in sight. She'd taken a booth at the window of the café across the street and watched for him.

Back in her room after dinner, she ached for a long, hot bath. While the tub filled, she stayed out of the bathroom so the noise of the rushing water wouldn't prevent her from hearing Nate's arrival. She arranged clothes on the bed so she could get into them fast: panties, a bra, and a pale blue dress she'd bought at a souvenir shop that afternoon before leaving the boardwalk.

With the water off and the bathroom door open, she didn't need to worry about missing him. She settled down, sighing as the hot water wrapped her body. A bath was a rare luxury.

Most of the time, she kept herself clean by washing in rest rooms. Coffee shops and gas stations often had doors that locked, so she could strip down and do a good quick job of it. Occasionally she used shower rooms at public swimming pools and Y's. Many beaches had outside showers for getting the sand and salt water off before heading home, and she took advantage of them when she could, though she had to keep her swimsuit on. Often she bathed in streams and lakes, which were always cold.

Only when she checked into motels did she get to take a hot bath in a tub. Usually once a month. If she could afford it.

Then she would take marathon baths. Often fall asleep in the tub. Wake up with the water cool and her skin pruned. And take another the next morning before checkout time.

Tonight she didn't fall asleep. Though the caressing heat seemed to steal away all her strength, she wouldn't allow herself to drift off. If she slept, she might not hear Nate's knocking.

When the drowsiness threatened to overpower her, she left the tub. She dried herself with a threadbare towel. It was a tiny thing. She wrapped it around her waist. Though the corners met, there wasn't enough for a tuck. She hung the towel on a bar and left the bathroom. She returned with her toothpaste and brush. She cleaned her teeth.

She took a fresh towel from its clamp on the wall. Sitting on the bed, she rubbed her hair dry. Her skin was hot and moist from the bath. A breeze came in through the open window, lifting the curtain, cooling her. When she felt dry enough so her clothes wouldn't stick, she put them on.

Then she brushed her hair in front of the big mirror over the bureau.

She was pleased with the way the dress looked. It was a short-sleeved pullover. It hung almost to her knees.

A dark blue emblem above her left breast showed a silhouette of the Ferris wheel with the Hurricane roller coaster in the background. Both owned by Nate's family, she thought, smiling. It read "Funland" above the illustration, "Boleta Bay, California" below it.

The dress was soft and clingy. In the shop, she'd been concerned that it might be a nightshirt until she noticed that one of the clerks wore an identical garment.

It does look like a nightshirt, she thought as she studied her reflection.

She went to her pack and took out her freshly laundered belt. The belt was woven of bright reds and blues to match her banjo strap. She tied it loosely around her hips, its ends hanging down the side of her left leg. Now the dress looked like a dress.

She put on her necklace of white shells. The V neck of the dress was wide and low enough to let the necklace show. In the mirror, the shells resting against her tanned skin looked as white as her teeth.

Slowly she turned around, watching her reflection.

She looked like Robin the tourist or Robin the coed. Certainly not like Robin the street musician.

Cockless Robin.

Poppinsack.

Her skin went hot.

The bastard.

Don't ruin it thinking about him.

Hope you rot, you . . .

Forget him.

Nate, where *are* you?

Robin saw that a new program was starting on the television, and realized a full hour had passed since she'd finished dressing. She climbed from the bed. At the window she parted the curtains and looked outside. Night had fallen. Must be nine, she thought.

He'll come, she told herself.

And no more than a yard away, he walked past the window and did a double-take when he saw her, and Robin wondered if her mind were playing tricks. Nate stepped up close to the screen. A smile tugged a corner of his mouth. "I guess you're here, all right."

"I guess so." She hurried over to the door and opened it.

He stood on the balcony, staring in at her. "You look . . . very nice."

"Thanks. Come on in."

His eyes shifted and he glanced into the room behind her. "Maybe we should . . . would you rather take a little walk? It's nice out tonight."

She felt an odd mixture of disappointment and relief. "Okay. Sure. Just a minute."

He waited while she put on white socks and tennis shoes.

"How's the room?" he asked.

"Great. I love it. Especially the bathtub."

She snatched the motel key off the dresser, stepped onto the balcony, pulled the door shut, and tested the knob. Then she turned to him. "I don't have a pocket," she said.

Nodding, he took the key from her and slipped it into a pocket of the chamois shirt he wore like a jacket over his T-shirt.

"Now, don't lose it."

He smiled. "I'll try not to."

They began walking side by side along the balcony. There was no fog, but the night was cool and breezy. Nate probably felt just right in his heavy long-sleeved shirt and jeans. Robin, in her thin dress, shivered.

She thought about going back to the room for something warm to wear. But she didn't want to ruin the way she looked by putting on her windbreaker or sweatshirt. The chill wasn't that bad.

They trotted down the stairs and crossed the motel's parking lot.

"Where are we going?" she asked.

"Anyplace but Funland," Nate said.

"Good choice."

At the sidewalk, they turned their backs to the distant amusement park. The street was brightly lighted and noisy with passing cars. People were all around, entering and leaving stores, walking by.

"Did you close the arcade early?" Robin asked.

"No. My brother-in-law's working it. Where would you like to go? Are you hungry?"

"Not right now."

"How about a movie?"

"It's fine with me if we just walk. Maybe we could get off the main drag, though, and find someplace a little more peaceful."

"Good thinking."

They were in the middle of a block when a troll staggered around the corner. He started toward them, shambling along with short, unsteady steps, scowling and shaking his fists, blurting gibberish in an angry voice.

"Why don't we cross here," Nate said.

"Good thinking."

He smiled and took Robin's hand. They waited for a break in the traffic, then hurried to the other side of the road. When they got there, he didn't let go of her hand.

"I'm getting a little tired of those people," Robin said.

"Everyone's tired of them."

"Maybe the trollers have the right idea."

Nate said nothing. At the corner, he led her to the right. The street ahead sloped upward, but it didn't look steep. A lone car was approaching. All the other cars in sight were parked at the curbs or in driveways. The houses were small and close together. The only person in sight was a woman walking her dog.

"This is a lot better," Robin said.

"It's a nice town. Mostly. It has a lot going for it."

"The downtown section is pretty ritzy."

"A lot of artists and poets and things. And people with money who like the atmosphere." He looked at Robin. "You're a poet."

"Not *that* kind."

"Yeah, your stuff makes sense. At least from what I've heard. But this is still a good place for . . . creative people. A lot of bookstores, and the university. Coffee shops where you can sit all day and write. I think Funland is great. I see too much of it, but I get a kick out of the place. It's wild and picturesque and trashy."

"You like trashy, do you?"

"In its place. But there are a lot of different sides to Boleta Bay. You can't judge it all by a couple of bad experiences on the boardwalk."

"You with the Chamber of Commerce?"

"It's just that Funland is its own thing. The whole town isn't . . . seedy. It has a lot that's nice about it."

"Are you saying I shouldn't be in such a hurry to leave?"

"Yeah."

Robin felt a quick spread of warmth in the pit of her stomach. She squeezed his hand.

"Are you going anywhere?" he asked. "I mean, are you on your way to Hollywood or something?"

She laughed. "Hardly. I'm just a roving minstrel girl."

Cockless Robin.

The echo of Poppinsack's voice, this time, seemed faint. Being with Nate, she supposed, had robbed it of the power to upset her.

"If you don't have any real destination," he said, "why don't you stay around for a while?"

"I guess I could."

They crossed a deserted road. Nate led her onto a walkway that traversed a park. The park was dark except for a few lamps along the walk. In the spray of glow beneath each lamp was a bench.

From here she could see several of the benches.

Each was empty.

"Where are all the trolls?" she asked.

"There's a neighborhood patrol. They've discouraged the riffraff."

"Sort of like a grown-up version of the trollers?"

"Not much. They're good citizens. From what I've heard, the trollers aren't much better than thugs. That's why I don't want you sleeping down near the shore. That's where they hunt. The boardwalk, the beach. I know you're not a troll—"

"Well, thanks."

Nate halted and faced her. He took her other hand in his. Holding both, he stared into her eyes. He was frowning. "It's nothing to joke about. They *hurt* people, and they might hurt you if they catch you around there at night."

"What am I supposed to do?" Robin asked. She wished her heart would slow down. But it kept racing. Because she knew what was going on here. Nate planned to fix it so she could stay. Because he wanted her to be with him.

Jesus!

Trying to keep her voice steady, she said, "You're asking me not to leave town. At the same time, you're saying I might get attacked by the trollers if I stay. And I already know the bums are dangerous. So I'm risking my butt if I sleep on the beach. You can't put me up in a motel every night."

"We'll find you a place to stay."

"That would take money. I'm in short supply of it. And I'm not going to let you pay."

"I'll give you a job. We'll put you on the payroll."

"I don't know, Nate. I . . . My music's important to me. It's *me*, you know? If I had a real job . . ."

"A job doing what you do now. But not down at the end of the boardwalk. In front of my family's concessions. The arcade, sometimes." He smiled. "So I can hear you. And see you. But mostly over by the Hurricane and Ferris wheel. The lines can get awfully long for those rides. You'd be entertainment for the people while they wait. We'll pay you an hourly rate. Start you off, say, at seven bucks an hour. You still go ahead and collect from them—wouldn't want to cheat your audience out of the joy of showing their appreciation."

"And I'd keep the tips?" she asked.

Smiling, he said, "What do you think this is, a charity?"

"I hope not. I can't see paying someone just to help your customers pass the time of day."

"At quitting time, you turn over a percentage of your take. Forty percent. And you keep sixty, over and above whatever we pay you."

"It's awfully generous, Nate."

"Hell, it's good P.R. Once word gets around, I wouldn't be at all surprised if people don't start coming to Funland *just* to hear you."

"I'm not that good."

"Don't bet on it. We'll see how it goes. Maybe down the line, we'll even set up some actual concerts."

Grinning, Robin shook her head. "You've got some pretty big ideas, fella."

"You just don't know how good you are. And it isn't just your music. Your music's great, but it's more than that. It's you. I've watched your audiences. Those people . . . they fall in love with you."

His words excited her. Robin knew she had magic. She'd noticed that many of those who watched her play seemed enthralled, that often the same people appeared in her audiences day after day. But to hear Nate speak of it was thrilling and a little embarrassing.

They fall in love with you.

She suddenly wondered if Nate meant that *he* had fallen in love with her.

"Is it a deal?" he asked.

Though she hadn't felt cold since about the time they rushed across the street to avoid the troll, she was shivering again. "Couldn't hurt to give it a try," she said.

He squeezed her hands and shook them up and down. "Great," he said. "Great."

"Don't break my hands off, kiss me."

A familiar look of surprise and confusion came to his face. It was the same expression Robin had seen that afternoon when she told him the room number.

He let go of her hands. He raised his arms. She stepped into them and pressed herself against him. He felt warm and solid. He felt like a home.

Don't count your chickens, Robin started to warn herself.

Then his mouth was there and she seemed to be melting into him.

Twenty-six

"There it is," Dave said when he spotted Gloria's Volkswagen.

Driving up and down the lanes of the parking lot, they'd passed at least twelve other VW Bugs. But this one was hers. Dave recognized the license plate. And he recognized the bumper stickers: "No Vietnam in Nicaragua" and "One Nuclear Bomb Can Ruin Your Whole Day."

"Guess she's here, all right," Joan said.

Dave found an empty space nearby, and parked. Before leaving the car, he took his flashlight out from under the seat.

"Do we start with the boardwalk?" Joan asked.

"I suppose. Great way to spend our time off."

Dave slipped an arm beneath the back of her open jacket. As they walked toward the front of the lot, he moved his hand slowly up and down her side. He felt her warmth and smoothness through the blouse. Each time his hand drifted down close to her hip, his knuckles brushed the walnut grip of the off-duty .38 clipped to her belt.

"What do we tell Jim and Beth?" she asked.

"Ohhh, boy."

"We're bound to run into them, you know. Beth's no problem. But Jim isn't likely to let it alone. If he gets the idea we're going together, it'll be all over the department. The brass gets wind of it, and one of us'll be reassigned."

"We'll just have to play innocent."

Smiling, Joan patted his rump. "Think you can keep your hands to yourself?"

"Sure. No sweat."

She peeled his hand off her side. "Better start practicing."

They crossed to the walkway. Dave looked both ways, scanning the pavement and the grassy slope in front of Funland. A few other couples were nearby, heading for the entrance. And he spotted someone lying on the grass near the wall of the old pavilion at the far north end. From this distance, the person looked like a pile of clothes. The heap next to the form was probably a pack.

"Over there," Dave said.

Joan nodded. "Let's check it out."

As they approached the sprawled figure, Dave saw that the face was bearded.

Joan must've noticed it too. "Unless Gloria's hormones flipped out," she said, "that ain't her."

"Let's go around this end anyway. If we go back to the main entrance, we'll have to waste time doubling back."

"I hope he's asleep."

He wasn't. He got up and stumbled down the slope in time to block their way. The nearby lamp provided plenty of light for Dave to see the glare in the man's eyes—a wild, mad look that reminded him of Charles Manson. "Help a fella down on his luck." It wasn't a plea. It was a demand.

Dave said, "We're looking for—"

Joan grabbed his arm and tugged him off the curb.

"Lookin' for *God*?" the man blurted. "Tha's me! Gimme a buck."

"Get lost!" Joan called over her shoulder as she dragged Dave along beside her.

"Ge' fucked, cunt! Huh? Wha'sa matter witcha, cunt?"

Dave jerked his arm free. He whirled toward the man. "*I'll give you something, you filthy . . . !*"

"Gimme a buck! Gimme a buck 'r I'll put the cursa squirmy death on ya!"

"Dave!"

His left arm was suddenly grabbed from behind. He realized it was cocked back, ready to swing. In the hand was his sixteen-inch metal flashlight.

"Dave!" Joan snapped again. "Don't! Come on! Let's go!"

He let Joan guide him backward off the curb. As she pulled him along, he sidestepped, keeping his eyes on the derelict.

In a leaping frenzy, the guy yelled, "Fuck ya!" He jammed the middle fingers of both hands together in front of his snarling mouth and blurted, "Cursa squirmy death, cursa squirmy death! Whammy whammy presto fuck ya!"

He kept on leaping, waving his arms, and shouting. Once they rounded the corner of the pavilion, they couldn't hear him anymore.

Joan leaned back against the wall. She seemed to sag against it. She shook her head.

"Are you okay?" Dave asked.

"Me? You were gonna *brain* him."

"Yeah. I lost it for a second there."

"That's for sure. Jeez." She pushed herself off the wall. She rested her wrists on his shoulders and caressed the back of his head. "I appreciate the gallantry, pal, but you don't have to defend my honor. I don't give a rat's ass what a troll calls me."

"I do."

"Macho pig."

"That's me."

The way she massaged his scalp and neck soothed his tension, made him feel a little drowsy.

"Now you got us whammied with the curse of squirmy death."

"Bummer," he murmured. "Should I go back and pay him a buck to take it off?"

"Give him five. Can't be too careful."

Dave started to move back, but she clamped his neck.

"Where do you think you're going?"

"Oh." He realized she'd been joking about the five. Of course. Pay the guy to remove some ridiculous curse? But it *had* seemed like a good idea there for a second.

Joan's grip on his neck relaxed, and she started massaging him again. He let his head droop. He let his eyes shut.

"From now on," she said in a smooth, soft voice, "let's just keep our distance from any trolls we happen to run into. I don't think we want to be asking them about Gloria. Wouldn't find out anything anyway, not from those people. And we might just blow her cover."

"Okay. That makes sense."

"Besides, they scare me shitless."

That remark was like a rock plopping into the still pond of his lethargy. He lifted his head and smiled, amused by her language but touched by her confession of fear. He put his hands on her sides. "Maybe I'd *better* get that curse removed."

"A *superstitious* macho pig."

"Can't be too careful. We're talking 'squirmy death' here."

She drew Dave's head toward her and kissed him lightly on the mouth. Dave felt her breasts push against him. He wrapped his arms around her, underneath her jacket, and slid his hands up and down her back. She turned her head, taking away the soft moist warmth of her mouth.

"We'd better find Gloria," she whispered, her breath tickling his ear.

"Why don't we just forget about her? Let's get out of this place and—"

"That'd be nice."

"It's her game. She wants to play Ace Reporter, who're we to stop her?"

"Keep talking. Maybe you'll convince yourself."

"Dammit."

"Let's just give it an hour or so," Joan said. "Then we'll go back to my place. Whether we find her or not. We don't have to stop her. We don't even have to warn her. All we have to do is *try*. Give it a fair try."

"She knows the dangers," Dave said.

"But that won't do our consciences a whole lot of good if she gets hurt."

"Okay. We'll give it an hour." He eased himself away from Joan and checked his wristwatch. "It's nine-forty now."

"Funland closes at eleven. Let's give it till then."

"What time is Debbie's party over?"

"She's supposed to be home by midnight."

"This is the pits."

Joan stared into his eyes. "I know. But it's only one night. Then we'll be done with Gloria."

"Yeah. It'll be worth it, I guess, just so we won't have to feel guilty for *not* doing it."

They climbed a flight of concrete stairs at the corner of the pavilion. This end of the boardwalk wasn't crowded. During the past few days, a small crowd had been gathered here for the banjo girl. Dave tried to remember her name. A bird name. Dove? No, Robin. A cute gal. He wondered where she was. This was no place, at night, for a lone girl. Not with crazies around like that bastard they'd just run into. Not with trollers on the prowl some nights, looking for indigents to torment. He hoped she'd taken his advice to stay in motels.

"Should we check in there?" Joan asked, nodding toward the pavilion's doorway.

Dave didn't see any trolls on the boardwalk between this door and the one at the pavilion's far end. "Just a quick walk-through," he said.

They went inside. The big auditorium was brightly lighted and warm. Calliope music accompanied the spinning merry-go-round in the center of the floor. Along the walls were booths where people could buy specialties such as fudge, saltwater taffy, soft pretzels, churros, nachos, straps of beef jerky, and ice cream. At one end was a snack counter for burgers, hot dogs, fries, and pop. There were booths that sold Funland souvenirs: ashtrays, plates, tom-toms, rubber knives, shot glasses, coffee mugs, and pennants. Others offered assortments of seashells. Others sold Funland T-shirts, sweatshirts, caps, and plastic visors.

Dave had often seen the place jammed with people. Tonight it wasn't especially crowded. Quite a few people were wandering around, some sampling food, some browsing for keepsakes, a few snapping photos of their kids on the carousel.

He didn't see any bums.

He didn't see Gloria.

"Hungry?" he asked.

"No. You go ahead and get something, though."

He shook his head.

"We can have a snack when we get to my place."

"Okay." He appreciated the reminder that they would get to Joan's place later.

We could be there right now.

Thanks a heap, Gloria.

They exited at the next door. Stepped out onto the boardwalk right into the path of Jim and Beth.

Beth's head drew back, doubling her chin. Her eyes opened so wide she looked as if her lids might get stuck up there. One side of Jim's face curled up, giving him a cross between a smirk and a snarl.

Thirty seconds, Dave thought. Thirty damn seconds, and we would've missed them.

"Well, I'll be screwed, chewed, and tattooed," Jim said. "Hello, young lovers."

"Don't jump to conclusions," Dave said. He decided that sounded stupid.

"We're looking for Gloria Weston," Joan told them.

"Planning a ménage à trois?"

Jim knew that Dave had been going with Gloria. Hell, *everyone* knew. It had been a source of constant ribbing from most of his fellow officers—the cop and the nosy pinko reporter.

"How about waiting till we're off duty?" Jim suggested. "We'll have a fivesome."

"Try to pull your head out of your butt for a minute," Joan said, "and listen up. Weston's gone undercover to get a lice-eye view of the life of a troll."

"Figures. What's the big deal?"

"It isn't healthy," Dave said.

"Have you seen her?" Joan asked.

"I don't *look* at those maggots. They put me off my feed."

"Would we recognize her?" Beth asked. "Has she altered her appearance?"

"Mussed up her hair," Joan said, addressing Beth. "She's

wearing a gray sweatshirt, purple skirt, and red tights. They're all pretty filthy and ragged. And she's got grocery bags. Two on her feet, and she's probably carrying the third."

"She's wearing *bags* on her feet?" Beth asked.

"The latest fashion in troll footwear," Joan said.

"She really got into this, didn't she?"

"You haven't see her?"

"I doubt it. I think I would've noticed the bags. What do you want us to do if we find her?"

"We try hauling her in," Jim said, "she'll scream bloody murder—all over the pages of that rag she works for."

"Just keep an eye on her," Dave told him. "We'll be looking around ourselves. We'll check with you before closing time. The thing is, I wouldn't be at all surprised if she isn't planning to spend the night out here someplace. She doesn't do things halfway. She wants to find out what it's like to be a troll, she's going to stick it out."

"You ask me," Jim said, "it's none of our business."

"She could get hurt," Beth said.

"And wouldn't *that* be a pity?" He met Dave's eyes. "Sorry, man. I understand you got something going with her. But whistling Jesus, she crucifies us every time she plants her ass in front of the typewriter. You read that trash on the trollers?"

"I didn't like it any more than you did."

"So she wants to cozy up to those runny sores on the rump of humanity, let her. Spends some time with 'em, she'll change her tune. That's for damn sure. She might start calling for mass executions."

"That's not very likely," Dave said.

"Yeah. 'They were children once, who stayed up all night waiting for Santa.' Last time I saw that kinda shit, it was floating in the toilet bowl."

"You're making me sick," Beth said.

Jim scowled at her. "I know what *you* think of that . . . lady."

Beth looked pretty sheepish all of a sudden. She shrugged and met Dave's eyes. "I still wouldn't want anything to happen to her."

"Gloria doesn't know what she's getting into," Joan said. "We just want to warn her off."

"We'll keep an eye out for her," Beth said.

"Thanks."

"Yeah," Dave added. "We appreciate it."

As he stepped past Jim, the man winked and whispered, "Lucky fuck. My advice, lose Weston."

Dave shook his head and kept walking.

"That wasn't so bad," Joan said.

"We'll see." Just ahead were the stairs leading down to the beach. Dave was suddenly glad they'd run into Jim and Beth. "Maybe we can speed things up some by skipping the rest of the boardwalk. They'll spot Gloria if she's up here."

"Beth might, anyway. I think Jim would like to see her *move in* with the trolls."

"I can see his point," Dave admitted. "But how about it? We leave the boardwalk to them?"

"Sure."

They trotted down the concrete stairs. Joan stopped when she reached the sand. "Where do we start?"

"I don't know." Dave scanned the beach. It was pale with moonlight. There were dark patches, here and there, that appeared to be people on blankets. Most of the people were in pairs. Some were sitting, but many were lying down, embracing.

Dave saw a lone man running along the shore. A dog trotted ahead of him to check out a group of three people coming from the opposite direction. The dog wagged its tail. One of the three, a woman with a ponytail, squatted down to ruffle its fur. Off to the right, a couple was strolling past the front of the lifeguard station.

"Wonder if anyone's getting it on," Joan said.

Obviously she was intrigued by the people on the blankets. "Kind of nippy for that," Dave said.

"Love breeds desperate measures."

"Want to check them out?"

"I'd rather find Gloria."

"That's what I meant."

"I'd be awfully surprised to find her out in the open," Joan said. "She's into the life-styles of the down and dirty. She'll be where she's most likely to meet trolls."

"Around here, that doesn't narrow the field by much."

Joan swept an arm back, thumb pointing behind her as if she were trying to hitch a ride.

"I know," Dave said.

"I know you know."

"You don't want to go under there, do you?"

"Do we have any choice?"

"Sure we do."

"Are we looking for Gloria or just pretending?"

"You and Jiminy Cricket."

Joan took his hand. "Let's check it out before I lose my nerve."

They turned around, walked past the stairs, and entered the darkness beneath the boardwalk. Dave switched on his flashlight. Its strong beam thrust out a shaft of brightness. Shadows from the pilings lurched and swayed as the light swept by.

A yelp of alarm made him flinch, and Joan almost crushed his hand. Someone scuttled from behind a post, was lost in the black, then found again by the flashlight beam. Dave couldn't tell whether it was a man or a woman. But it wore dirty brown pants and an overcoat, so he knew it wasn't Gloria. It scurried toward the rear, whining. Dave turned the light away.

"Holy jumping Judas," Joan muttered.

"You sure you're up to this?"

"I can take it if you can."

"I'm not sure about my hand."

"Sorry." Joan eased her grip.

They stood motionless while Dave played the flashlight over the area ahead. "Looks okay," he whispered.

"Most of them are probably farther back."

He aimed the beam to his left. Saw a woman with a dirty face peering at him from beside a distant post. Saw a few huddled shapes far behind her.

Goose bumps scurried up his back.

He swung the light away fast.

Joan muttered, "Shit."

"Should we check them out?"

"No."

"What happened to Jiminy Cricket?"

"There're limits."

"Glad to hear it."

"Try calling out."

"Gloria?" he shouted. "Gloria? You there?"

Voices, five or six of them, some low and gravelly, others high-pitched, called, "Gloria? Yoo-hoo, Gloria? Glorrrria?"

Dave moaned. He hurried forward, holding on tightly to Joan's hand, dodging the posts that blocked the way. The voices kept asking for Gloria. They sounded *amused*.

To the left, a heap of dark blankets broke open and a gaunt man bolted up. Joan lurched aside, crashed into a piling, and gasped and staggered back against Dave.

"Saaay," the troll piped. "How's about two bits for a poor vet down on his luck?"

Throwing an arm around Joan, Dave rushed her out from under the boardwalk. The moonlight found them. They didn't stop until they were far out onto the beach.

Joan hugged him in a fierce clutch. She was panting, chest rising and falling against him, breath hot on his ear.

"Are you okay?" he asked.

Her cheek rubbed his face as she nodded.

"Did you hurt yourself?"

"Not much. My shoulder a little."

"We shouldn't have gone under there."

"God, those *people*."

"Trolls."

"What if Gloria's there?"

"That's her problem."

"Dammit."

"We're not going back in there," Dave said. "I don't care what you say."

"Let's go."

"No."

"To my place."

"Are you sure?"

"I want to get out of here. Right now."

But she kept herself clenched to Dave, and didn't move.

"Couple of real chickens, aren't we?" she said after a while.

"Kentucky fried."

"It's not as if they could've hurt us or anything. I mean, we're armed."

"And you're Kung Fu City."

"Could've choppy-sockied them all over the place."

"On the other hand, who's to say they don't have weapons of their own?"

"That's a pleasant thought."

"Did you mean it about leaving?" Dave asked.

"I meant it. Let's go."

Twenty-seven

"I'd just as soon get going," Shiner said.

"It's early, it's still early." Jeremy's voice sounded slightly muffled to him, as if his ears were plugged. Can booze do that to you? he wondered.

Shiner squeezed his arm and shook him gently. "Come on. Everybody's polluted. Including you."

"I'm fine," Jeremy said. "Can't we stay a little longer?"

"If you really want to. But just a few more minutes, okay?"

He looked down at the glass in his hand and saw that it was empty. He decided against getting a refill just now. Shiner wouldn't like it. She really didn't seem to be enjoying herself much. She should've been drinking like the rest of them. After her first glass of spiked punch, right after Nate left, she'd switched to Pepsi.

"Wanna dance?" Jeremy asked.

"Not much. I'm all danced out. And they keep playing that crap. I hate that crap."

"It's the Beastie Boys."

"Whoopie."

Only Karen was still dancing. A few minutes ago she'd stripped down to her bra and panties. She was writhing and shaking, her hair flying, her breasts bobbing wildly, as if the bra wasn't even there. Her skin was glossy with moisture. Her eyes were fixed on Tanya.

Tanya didn't seem interested. She was staring at her drink and paying no attention to Karen. She'd been dancing herself a little earlier. But she'd kept her clothes on, and kept a glass of punch in one hand. Now she was slumped on the sofa with her bare feet resting on top of the table in front of her. Randy was stretched out, his head on her lap, one arm hanging down toward the floor. He appeared to be asleep.

Passed out is more like it, Jeremy thought.

Randy'd been guzzling the punch. He'd acted pretty funny for a while, giggling and doing his "famous impressions of dead presidents" such as Chester A. Arthur and Thomas Jefferson, and giggling a lot and wearing his glasses upside down. Then he'd collapsed onto the sofa.

Jeremy wished *he* could be the one on the sofa with Tanya. Only not zonked out. Wide-awake.

He imagined himself with her, but not lying there the way Randy was. Sitting up, Tanya straddling his lap the way Liz was on Cowboy in the recliner across the room. They'd been like that for a long time. Jeremy suspected that Cowboy's hands were up inside her sweater.

"Are you ready to go yet?" Shiner asked.

"What time is it?"

"Ten-fifteen. But you said we could leave early. Nothing's going on anyway."

"Coupla minutes?"

"What're you waiting for? Think Karen's going to take off the rest?"

"I don' even like her," Jeremy protested.

"You sure like looking at her. Personally, I happen to find it repulsive. You do know what she's doing, don't you?"

"Dancing."

"Trying to get Tanya turned on."

"Tanya's no lesbo."

"Oh, you're an expert?"

"She was Nate's girl."

"Yeah, and Nate's out of the picture and she's *really* depressed. Maybe Karen'll get lucky."

"Nah."

"Maybe one of the *guys'll* get lucky." Shiner looked at Jeremy and raised an eyebrow. "Maybe you. Is that what you're hoping for?"

He felt heat rush to his face. "No!"

"Yeah. Sure."

"Honest."

Her eyes narrowed slightly. "Then prove it. Let's leave right now."

Oh, God, Jeremy thought. What'll I do? What if I say no? This could be my big chance.

"Okay," he said. "We can leave."

Shiner's lips formed a narrow line. She gazed into his eyes and nodded. "Good." Her hand found his, and she squeezed it gently.

"I gotta use the john, though."

"Hardly surprising." She smiled. "You'll have to wait for Heather to get out. That'll give you a while longer to ogle Karen."

He pushed himself away from the paneled wall. The bathroom door was shut, all right. Determined not to ogle Karen, he turned his eyes to Shiner.

She really *is* beautiful, he thought.

He wondered what would happen in the car. It was still early. She didn't have to be home until midnight, so they'd have a long time if they parked somewhere.

Heather stepped out of the bathroom. She looked saggy. Her bloated face was pale.

"Did you find him?" Samson asked her.

Heather looked confused. "Huh? Who? Find who?"

"Ralph. I heard you calling for him. 'Ralph! Ralph!'"

"Hardy har har har. You're as funny as a pregnant pole-vaulter."

Samson, a wide dazed smile on his face, staggered to the bathroom, hugged the doorframe, and peered inside. "Ralph? Ralph, you in here?"

Jeremy slumped against the wall and wrinkled his nose at Shiner. "I think she barfed in there."

"I do believe you're right."

"It's gonna stink."

"There's probably a john upstairs."

"I'll ask." He pushed himself off the wall again and headed for Tanya. Tanya would know. Aware that Shiner was probably watching him, he walked very carefully. And he didn't look at Karen. He stepped between the edge of the table and the sofa. He bumped Randy's arm, but the boy didn't wake up.

Tanya raised her head and smiled at him. "Hey, Duke. How's it going?"

"Great," he said. "I was just—"

"Get over here, sit down." She took her feet off the table and set her glass on it. Taking Jeremy's hand, she towed him past her knees and pulled him onto the sofa beside her. "You having a good time?" she asked.

"Yeah. Terrific."

"Good, good." She wrapped an arm across his shoulders. "You're a good fella, Duke. You're a real good fella. Know what I like about you?"

He shook his head. The motion of it made him dizzy.

"You got loyalty. Loyalty and guts." She rubbed his shoulder. Staring into his eyes, she nodded agreement with herself. "I didn't wanta see that guy die. You wanta see that guy die?"

"No."

"'Course not. But I don't hear you whining about it and bugging out. No, sir. You got loyalty and guts."

"Thanks," he said.

"You're a true friend. We're *all* true friends. We're family, you know?"

"Yeah."

"We're gonna wipe out those fuckin' trolls. We're gonna lay 'em waste."

"Damn right."

She turned toward him. Her leg pressed his leg. She pulled him against her chest and kissed him.

Tanya's kissing me, he told himself.

He couldn't believe it.

He wondered if Shiner was watching.

He didn't care.

He'd dreamed of this since the first time he saw her, and now it was happening, really happening.

Her full lips were soft and warm and moist. And open. Her breath was going into his mouth. Her breasts were pushing against his chest. Her hands were rubbing his back. He put his arms around her and hugged her tight. Her tongue thrust into his mouth.

Then her face eased away from him.

It can't be over yet, he told himself. He felt cheated, as if he'd just awakened from a dream—the best dream ever, one that had just started. The loss of it made him ache. At the same time, he felt an intense joy. How could he feel so horrible and so wonderful at the same moment?

Her lips and the skin around them looked wet.

That's my saliva, Jeremy thought. Mine. God.

Looking into his eyes, she squeezed his leg. "Come with me," she said.

Stunned, he rose from the sofa. Tanya scooted over, easing Randy's head onto the cushion, and got up. She led the way to the stairs.

Shiner was no longer standing by the wall. Jeremy looked around. She was gone.

Had she actually left?

Doesn't matter, he thought. Oh, God, where are we going? Away from the others. Someplace where we can be alone. What's going on?

We gonna *do it?*

His mouth was dry, his heart thumping as he climbed the stairs behind Tanya.

I don't even know *how!* What if I mess up and she laughs at me?

At the top of the stairs, she took hold of his hand.

"Where're we going?" he asked, his voice coming out hushed and ragged.

"My room."

Her words seemed to suck out the last of Jeremy's breath. He gasped for air as he walked with her.

"I've got something for you."

His legs trembled as he climbed the broad carpeted stairs to the second floor of the house.

He wondered where her parents were. Shiner had said they

might be upstairs, staying out of the way. But this was Friday, so maybe they'd gone out.

What if they come back and catch us?

Jeremy walked with Tanya down a hallway and entered a room. She flicked a wall switch, and lamps came on. She shut the door.

Jeremy was standing inside the biggest bedroom he'd ever seen. It had an enormous bed with lamps on either side, a bureau, a dressing table with a mirror, a roll-top desk, a television with a VCR, a compact-disk player, a recliner, a sofa, and shelves that were crowded with animal dolls, trophies, framed photographs, and books. It had its own bathroom. From where he stood, he could see the sink.

The bedroom's thick carpet was pale blue; the bedspread and curtains were pink. There was a faint, sweet aroma that reminded him of suntan oil.

Tanya's room.

Where she sleeps. Where she changes clothes. Even where she goes to the toilet, showers, and takes her baths.

And I'm here.

And we're going to *do it*. Right there on her bed.

"You better sit down before you keel over," Tanya said. She guided him to the side of the bed. He sank onto it, and clutched his knees to hold himself steady.

She went to the roll-top desk. She removed something from a drawer, and kept it hidden behind her back as she walked toward Jeremy.

A rubber?

She stopped in front of him. "Put out your hand," she said.

He held his hand out. His fingers were fluttering.

Into his palm she dropped a double-edged razor blade.

Confusion and icy prickles of fear moved in with his breathless excitement.

"Just hold it for now," Tanya said. She knelt on the floor and placed her hands on his thighs. The feel of her hands, so close to his groin, sent waves of heat rushing through him. "Tell me why you joined with us."

"To . . . to hunt trolls."

"Why?"

"Cowboy. He invited me."

"Is that all?"

Jeremy shrugged. "I guess it was partly to make friends. Specially you," he added, and felt a drop of sweat trickle down his side.

"Especially me. I know. Everybody's in it because of me."

Except Shiner, he thought. But Shiner's out of it now.

"The trolls hurt me bad," she said. "We're after them because of that. That's why it started. We go after them for revenge. Last night you joined in the revenge. You joined for my sake."

Jeremy nodded.

She stood up and began to unbutton her big loose shirt.

This can't be happening, Jeremy thought. I don't believe it.

He watched her hands move slowly down the front of bright blue and yellow plaid, unfastening each button along the way. When the last was open, she spread the shirt.

The sight seared Jeremy's mind, slammed his heart, sank his stomach, jammed his penis erect, though his scrotum and anus went cold and tight.

"They did this to me," Tanya said as the shirt dropped to the floor behind her.

She stood before him, wearing only her white shorts. Her skin had a soft tan. Even her breasts. They were big, firm, wonderful. In the glow of the lamplight they looked polished. As if they'd been buffed to a glossy sheen. Their dark nipples jutted out.

The scar began as a slick pink curve alongside her left nipple. It swept across the underside of the breast and streaked downward. It was as wide as a fingertip, pale pink, shiny, a little puffy. It passed the edge of her navel and vanished at the waistband of her shorts.

Tanya opened her shorts. She pushed them down around her thighs.

She was smooth and hairless.

The stark rip skidded over her mound, and under it, and seemed to miss the soft open flesh below by a fraction of an inch.

"A broken wine bottle," Tanya said.

Jeremy nodded. Her words seemed to come from a great distance. He couldn't take his eyes off her. He felt dizzy and sick, stunned by her nakedness, pained by the ugly scar, astonished that she was showing herself to him.

"Three of 'em got me in the lifeguard shack," she said. "Trolls. They'd spent the night there. I tried to kick 'em out, and they jumped me. One of 'em broke a wine bottle on my head. Then they stripped me."

"God," Jeremy murmured.

"One of 'em did this." Her fingertip touched the scar tissue at her groin, and slid slowly higher, tracing the tear up her belly and rib cage and breast. "He slobbered on me while he did it. The other two held me down. Then he raped me. Grunting and slobbering. He smelled like stale wine and sweat and garbage. When he finished, the other two had me. One fucked me in the ass. One came in my mouth. Before they left, they pissed on me. All over me. On my face . . ."

She stepped out of her shorts. With one foot she flicked them aside. On her knees, she reached beneath the bed. She dragged out a heap of brown bath towels. She spread two of them on the carpet at Jeremy's feet and left the others wadded nearby. Stepping onto the double thickness of towels, she said, "Cut your hand."

Jeremy nodded. He felt as if his mind had collapsed while he'd listened to her story.

He switched the razor blade to the trembling fingers of his left hand. He pressed its edge into the palm of his right. Blood welled up, and he cupped his hand to hold it.

Tanya took the razor from him. She slid it against the skin of her mound, and a crimson thread appeared alongside the scar. She lifted Jeremy's bleeding hand. She pressed it tightly against her cut. Blood squeezed, spilling around the sides of his hand, trickling down her legs, dripping onto the towel under her spread feet.

She felt hot through the blood. Beneath her skin there seemed to be a curving ridge of bone. Jeremy kept his hand bent back as far as possible, not daring to touch what was below the ridge. But Tanya pressed his fingers upward. Into slippery folds of flesh.

"Your blood is in me," she whispered. She was breathing hard. She was moving slightly, rubbing herself against his hand. "My blood's in you. You're my . . . lover in blood. Say it."

Jeremy heard himself repeat the words.

She guided his hand upward, keeping it pressed to the scar. The scar felt like a narrow, puffy ribbon. His hand left a red smear as it slid up her belly, up her rib cage to her breast. Her breast was pushed upward and sideways by his moving hand. The nipple bent like springy rubber as his thumb passed over it. She slid his hand higher, and Jeremy rose to his feet. His hard penis felt trapped inside his pants, squeezed and bent.

She lifted his hand to her mouth. She kissed its cut palm. She licked the blood from it. Gazing into his eyes, she took his thumb into her mouth. She sucked and licked it clean, then did the same with each of his fingers.

"Your blood and mine," she whispered. Her lips and chin and cheeks were dappled with it. She lowered his hand. She placed the razor blade in his palm. "Keep this with you to remember."

"I'll never forget."

"I know."

Jeremy took a handkerchief from his pocket, wrapped the blade, and closed his fingers around it, pressing the cloth to his wound.

"Go on home now," Tanya said in a gentle voice. "I'll see you tomorrow."

His throat tightened.

He was supposed to leave?

He was so *turned on*! So was she!

It can't stop now!

He suddenly blurted, "But aren't we gonna—?"

She touched a finger to his lips. "You'll have to prove yourself first."

"How?"

"With time. And loyalty. And courage."

"Not tonight?"

"Not tonight. But soon, maybe."

At the bedroom doorway he stopped and looked back at Tanya. She stood on the towels, facing him, naked and smeared with blood. "I love you," he said.

"And I love you, Jeremy."

He left her there.

When he reached the bottom of the stairs, he heard faint sounds of music and voices and laughter from the trollers below. He wondered if he should go down and rejoin the party.

He didn't want to.

And Tanya had told him to go home. She hadn't told him to go downstairs with the other trollers.

One of them might give him a ride, though.

I can walk, he told himself.

He trotted down the veranda stairs, stepped off the curb, and began to stride along the driveway.

The air smelled of pine trees. The night was not especially cold, but Jeremy shivered as he walked. His throat was tight. He squeezed his arms across his chest. The handkerchief and razor were still in his hand.

He felt so *strange*.

Dazed, confused, disappointed, empty, and weak.

Wrecked.

But, at the same time, elated.

He felt like leaping and shouting with joy. He felt like weeping. And somewhere in Jeremy was an odd desire to get home and hide under the covers of his bed and stay away from Funland and the beach and Tanya and all the trollers forever.

Twenty-eight

Gloria woke up in the backseat of her Volkswagen. She had no idea how long she'd been asleep. When she looked out the window, however, she saw that the parking lot was deserted except for three or four other cars.

So Funland was closed for the night.

With a tremor in her stomach that felt like a mixture of excitement and fear, she lifted her grocery bag. She pushed the seat back forward, opened the door, and climbed out. She locked the door. Then she headed for the main entrance of Funland.

Her day hadn't gone as well as she'd hoped. She had suc-
ceeded in carrying out interviews, of sorts, with only three
subjects: Mosby, Dink, and a woman who refused to reveal her
name. She'd taped the conversations on the Sony micro-
cassette recorder under her sweatshirt. Maybe she'd gotten
something she could use, but she doubted it.

She must've spent an hour talking with Mosby on the steps
in front of Funland, and heard about nothing except dogs.
Dogs were the reincarnations of dead Nazis, carrying out a
plot to destroy mankind by dumping radioactive feces in popu-
lated areas. Mosby, a crusader, fought the peril at every turn
by treating dogs to meals of broken glass concealed in hamburger.

Dink, a scruffy bearded man in his early twenties, claimed
to be a researcher from a planet called Zanthion. The popu-
lation of Zanthion was entirely male. Faced with certain ex-
tinction, they'd sent Dink to investigate the reproductive
system of the female Earthling. The "travel gate" would be
closing in two hours, so he had almost run out of time. If he
failed to learn the mysteries of the "secret source," his species
was doomed. Gloria was his only hope. She'd asked how she
could help. "You gotta let me probe yer source wit' my 'vestigation rod." At that, Gloria told him to stick his 'vestigation rod
up his 'testinal terminus. Then she hurried away.

Gloria had met the third indigent in an alley after dark. This
woman seemed rational, though she refused to tell her name.
"Don' tell nobody my name," she'd said. "They know yer name,
they can tag ya." Gloria decided not to press the issue. Instead,
she walked with her, listening to a lecture on how people "trow
out perfeckly good stuff," while the woman stopped her shopping cart at each trash bin and dug for treasures. Mostly she
collected newspapers, cans, and bottles to redeem for cash at
the recycling center. But she also collected scraps of food—
the litter of half-eaten meals—and stuffed them into her mouth
with grunting relish. Frequently Gloria gagged and turned
away.

So far, things hadn't gone at all the way she'd hoped. But she
was sure to find some fresh subjects on the boardwalk this time

of night. Or on the beach. A homeless person with *appeal*, please. Someone who would capture the hearts of her readers.

At this hour, she might even run into the trollers. She had a stun gun in her grocery bag in case they tried to get rough. But once she identified herself, they might be eager to give their side of the story. That'd certainly be a scoop.

You've got to come up with something, she told herself as she trotted up the stairs to Funland's main entrance. You write it the way it's gone so far today, and you'll sound like a propagandist for Great Big Billy Goat Gruff.

And wouldn't Dave like *that*?

Rotten, two-timing bastard.

Fuck him, she told herself.

She wished she'd had the courage to show herself to Dave. All day she toyed with the idea of going onto the boardwalk and confronting him. He would've been shocked. "Have you lost your mind? Don't you know how dangerous this is?" She would've smirked and said, "I'm sure you care. You've got your golden Amazon bitch pig."

But the golden Amazon bitch pig would've been there with him. Gloria knew it would've hurt too much, seeing them together. So she'd stayed away.

They're probably rutting right now, she thought, and sank onto a bench.

To hell with him.

He'd never had it so good, and he'd thrown it away for that golden-haired slut.

He'll regret it someday. He'll be sorry.

"I give him two weeks," she muttered. "Two weeks, and he'll come to a rude awakening. He'll see just how good he had it, and he'll come begging. And I'll laugh in his face."

Bullshit. I'll throw my arms around him and . . .

"Where're the goddamn trolls?" she asked, raising her head and looking both ways. The boardwalk, moon-washed and splashed with black shadows, looked deserted.

"Let's have some action here!" she yelled. "Bring on the bums! Bring on Great Big Billy Goat Gruff! Bring on *something*, Goddammit! Let's stop wasting my fucking time here!"

A huge patch of blackness broke away from the shadows across the boardwalk.

And ran at her.

Jesus! she thought. *I didn't mean it!*

She sprang to her feet, grocery bag flying from her lap. Her blanket spilled out of it. So did the stun gun. It clattered and skittered across the planking, and she knew she couldn't get to it in time.

The blackness had a white face, a big flapping coat. Its arms were stretched toward her like the arms of some kind of horror-movie geek.

"Leave me alone!" Gloria shrieked. She flung herself to the right, out of its path, and ran as hard as she could. Footfalls pounded behind her.

At once, she regretted bolting in this direction. She should've leapt the railing and dropped to the beach. Or gone to the left, tried to dodge the troll and make it out to the street. But now she was racing south on the boardwalk, deeper into the abandoned fun zone. No way out on her left. No way out on her right without climbing fences that surrounded the rides.

Chance it? she wondered.

The thudding footfalls of the troll didn't seem to be getting closer. She risked a glance over her shoulder. He was about twenty feet back, farther away than he'd been when she bolted from the bench.

He looked like a giant.

But he wasn't *fast.*

He won't win any track races, Gloria thought. But her terror didn't subside at all. Not a bit of it. She heard high whiny noises squeaking out of her as she tried to quicken her pace.

If he gets me, he'll rip me up.

That's absurd, she told herself. I'm not a kid. He's not a homicidal giant. This isn't a fairy tale. This isn't a nightmare.

What's the worst that can happen, really?

He rapes and kills me.

A nasty corner of her mind whispered, *That isn't the worst.*

She glanced back again. Now the troll was even farther behind.

I'm going to make it! If I don't trip. If he doesn't corner me. If there aren't *others* waiting in the dark places up ahead.

God, she wished the trollers were here!

Where *are* you, Billy Goat Gruff?

Maybe *he's* Billy Goat Gruff.

He's a troll. He's a troll. A kid's worst nightmare of what's lurking under the bridge. Jesus!

Just ahead, on the right, was the Tilt-a-Whirl. Gloria wondered if she should try for it. What if she had trouble getting over the fence? Once she stopped running, the troll would be on her in seconds. If she snagged her skirt or . . .

No. She didn't dare.

Keep running, she told herself. Widen your lead. *Then* go for a fence.

Once you're on the beach . . .

Light suddenly spilled out of a doorway on the right. It wasn't at boardwalk level, but at the top of a raised platform.

Dunn's place, she realized.

His Oddities place.

Jasper Dunn's tall, cadaverous figure appeared in the lighted doorway. He was wearing his top hat and tails. He raised his cane high and twirled it. "Over here!" he called to her. "Quickly!"

Gloria raced for him.

She had never thought she would be glad to see Jasper Dunn.

Better him than what's behind me, she thought.

Breathless, she bounded up the wooden stairs.

"Quickly, quickly," Jasper urged her. "You'll be safe here."

He stepped out of the way. Gloria flung herself through the doorway.

When she shrieked and whirled around to flee, he rammed the tip of his cane into her belly. She folded and dropped to her knees.

Behind her, trolls whispered and giggled.

"Shall we have her walk the house?" Jasper asked.

Trolls cheered and clapped and whooped.

The worst that can happen . . . ?

Gloria suddenly knew she was about to find out.

Twenty-nine

Dave shut off the alarm and blinked at the clock, confused for a moment until he remembered why he'd set the alarm to wake him half an hour early; he'd wanted time to check on Gloria before heading in to work.

Pain in the ass.

Not half the pain of last night, though—going out to search for her. Putting Joan through that. The business under the boardwalk had really frightened her. And *hurt* her. Back at her place afterward, she'd opened her blouse enough to slip it off her shoulder, and they'd both taken a look. Her upper arm had a nasty bruise from the collision with the post.

Dave remembered that he'd only glanced at the bruise before turning his eyes to the smooth, unblemished areas, savoring the mellow hue of her tanned skin against the stark white of her bra strap and the way her blouse was pulled crooked and taut over the rise of her breast.

He lay back on the bed, closed his eyes, and let his mind linger on the memories.

The hollow of her throat. The hollow above the curve of her collarbone. The way her head was twisted sideways as she strained to study her injury. "Scarred for life," she'd said.

"You'll just have to keep your shirt on."

"Pity." Raising her arm, she made the blouse fall back onto her shoulder. She didn't bother with the buttons. She placed her hands on Dave's sides and gazed into his eyes. "So," she said. "Here we are."

"Alone at last."

"Not a minute too soon."

He kissed her smile and felt it vanish, and Joan clutched him hard against her—so hard that her ribs pressed his wound and he flinched. She whispered "Sorry" into his mouth. She relaxed her hold on him, but kissed him with even greater urgency.

Urgency. Hunger. She acted as if she'd been unleashed, and Dave felt the same way. They'd been kept apart too long.

Dave yanked the blouse tails out of her jeans. He swept his hands up her back. Squirming against him, she sucked his tongue into her mouth. He undid the catches of her bra. All her back, waist to shoulders, was silken and warm under his hands.

Then came the soft thud of a car door bumping shut.

Joan pulled her mouth away. She stared into his eyes. She stood rigid. "It's Debbie," she whispered.

Moments later a doorknob rattled. A key ratcheted into a lock.

In the time it took for Debbie to enter the kitchen door and reach the living room, Dave and Joan broke apart and sat down at opposite ends of the sofa. Joan had time to wipe her mouth dry. Dave had time to pick up the TV *Guide*.

When the girl walked in, he looked up at her. He was stunned. Though Debbie wasn't identical to Joan, she bore an amazing resemblance. Her body, not so developed, was definitely feminine but had a boyish look about it. Her face still had the look of a girl in early adolescence, a freshness and innocence that would soon be left behind and lost forever. Dave felt a small tug of sorrow. This was much the way Joan must've looked at sixteen, and he regretted that he hadn't known her then.

He rose to his feet as she approached.

"You're home early," Joan said.

"The party was a drag." Her mouth twisted as if it didn't know what to do with itself—whether to smile or sneer or grimace. She pressed her lips into a tight line. She shrugged. She looked at Dave and held out her hand.

"I'm Dave," he said, shaking it.

"Yeah, I figured. Nice to meet you."

"In case you haven't guessed," Joan said, "that's my sister, Debbie."

"Hi, Debbie."

"So, did I interrupt something here?"

"Just having a friendly chat," Joan said.

"Oh, I'll bet."

"It turned out that there *weren't* any boys at the party, huh?"

Something happened to Debbie's face. It looked for a moment as if she were about to smirk and make a quip. Then her eyebrows puckered downward, her eyes filled with tears, her mouth stretched crooked, and her chin trembled.

Joan looked stricken. "Debbie! My God, what's . . . ?"

Shaking her head fiercely, the girl rushed out of the room.

Joan leapt to her feet. She met Dave's eyes. "I'm sorry. Dammit. I'd better see what's wrong."

"I'll make myself scarce."

"You don't have to leave."

"Yeah. I should. Take care of Debbie. I'll see you in the morning."

"Damn."

"Yeah." He pulled her against him, gave her a quick kiss, and released her. She hurried toward the hallway. Her shirttail was draping the seat of her pants.

Dave glanced at the clock on the nightstand.

You're going to waste your whole half-hour, he thought. No, not a waste. Not at all.

He rolled out of bed, gritted his teeth when the morning air wrapped his body, and hurried to put on his robe. He knotted its belt as he headed for the bathroom.

He wondered if Joan had fastened her bra on the way to Debbie's room.

The girl had sure picked a lousy time to come home.

Poor kid, though. She'd been awfully upset. Must've had a rough time at the party.

Whatever the problem, Joan had probably made it better. Wouldn't be easy to stay upset with her comforting you.

Half an hour later, his hair still damp from the shower, Dave hurried out to his car. He tossed his jacket onto the passenger seat—always good to have it along in case the fog should roll in—and backed out of the driveway.

He felt wonderful. Soon he would be with Joan again.

Maybe they could get together tonight and not be interrupted. Ask her over to *his* place, maybe.

And tomorrow was their day off.

Have to think of something . . .

He turned the corner, making a left toward Gloria's house, and a shadow blew in across his good mood.

Just let her be there, he thought.

The last thing he needed was to spend another day worrying about her.

She'll be there, he told himself.

Please. I want it over.

He swung around the next corner, peered up the block, and saw Gloria's Volkswagen in the driveway of her house.

He muttered, "Dumb bitch."

He thought: Thank God.

Torn between relief that she'd made it home and anger that she'd caused such trouble with her stunt, he pulled in behind her car. He leapt out and rushed to her door. He jabbed the doorbell button, heard the ringing inside the house, waited.

Come on, dammit! Move your tail.

He listened for her footsteps. And remembered other times he'd stood here, times when he'd been eager to hear Gloria approaching the door. Those times were not very long ago.

How could everything change so quickly?

A hot wave of guilt spread through him.

She brought it on herself by being such a . . .

Where is she?

Dave pounded on the door, shaking it in its frame.

"Gloria," he called. "Come on, open up. We need to talk."

She didn't open up.

Her house key was in Dave's hand, still clipped to his key case. He fumbled it away from the others, unlocked and opened the door partway. He put his head into the gap. The living room looked deserted. There was a stillness to the house.

He swung the door wide and entered.

"Gloria!" he called again.

She was a very sound sleeper and always locked her bedroom door before retiring for the night, so Dave supposed he might've failed to wake her. He strode down the hallway. The bathroom door stood open. She wasn't inside. He continued on to her bedroom.

Its door wasn't shut. The bed wasn't made.

He took four steps into the room.

The chair beside her closet door was piled with clothes.

On top of the heap was a dirty gray sweatshirt. From where he stood, Dave could see ragged holes in it. A corner of purple fabric drooped off the chair's seat. The legs of red tights hung to the floor. The tights, like the sweatshirt, gaped here and there with holes.

These were the clothes that Joan had described to him yesterday at lunch. *Must've been up half the night snipping away at them.*

Dave walked to the chair. How many times had he thrown his own clothes onto it? Gloria rarely used it for that herself. She must've been really beat when she came in last night, too tired to bother putting them away or tossing them in the hamper.

Maybe left them heaped up on purpose, to improve their rumpled appearance.

Dave picked up the sweatshirt and flung it onto the bed. He lifted the next garment off the chair seat. A grimy white T-shirt. She hadn't been at this with scissors.

He wrinkled his nose at the faint stale odor of sweat and tossed the shirt aside.

She'd sure gotten into the spirit of her masquerade. Even down to the small detail of going without antiperspirant.

He picked up the skirt. Joan was right about it. Gloria hadn't owned a frumpy thing like this; she must've picked it up at the Salvation Army store or someplace else that sold cast-off rags.

It was the kind of skirt that fastened at the side with a button and zipper.

The button was gone.

Not only was the button missing, but so was a small patch of fabric where it must've been sewn to the waistband.

As if Gloria had ripped the skirt open.

Gloria, or someone else.

After flinging the skirt onto the bed, Dave got down on his hands and knees and searched the carpet. He found no button.

That doesn't mean it's not around here someplace.

He looked for the button on Gloria's nightstand, and on top of the bureau.

This is crazy, he thought. Upset about a stupid button. It could be anywhere.

Could be on the boardwalk. On the beach. Where someone yanked her skirt open.

Christ, don't jump to conclusions.

Dave's hands were trembling as he picked up the red tights. They were dirty and torn, but Gloria had undoubtedly made them that way on purpose.

A pair of black panties remained on the chair. He picked them up. He had seen her wearing them, or similiar ones. There was little to them other than a thin elastic waistband and flimsy, sheer fabric a few inches wide at the top that tapered down to almost nothing where it would pass between her legs.

Dave scowled at the panties.

For some reason, he found them as disturbing as the lost button.

Why? They weren't torn.

What's wrong here? Dave wondered.

He dropped the panties onto the chair, stared at them, and knew.

What the hell were they doing at the bottom of the pile? Underneath the tights that had to come off first. They should've been *on top* of the tights, probably on top of the skirt, as well.

For that matter, they should've been on top of the entire heap. She nearly always took her panties off last. Often left them on, and nothing else, while she paraded around the house doing last-minute chores before bed: hanging up clothes, brushing her teeth, turning off lights.

Why were her panties at the bottom of the pile?

Dave could think of only one explanation: her clothes had been removed elsewhere, then carried to the chair.

Hold it, he told himself. Hold it just a second here. Don't get crazy. Gloria probably took them off in the bathroom, had a shower, and brought them in herself.

He hurried to the bathroom and searched for the button. He didn't find it.

Doesn't mean I'm wrong.

Makes a lot more sense than thinking someone else was involved.

He opened the medicine cabinet. Gloria's toothbrush stood upright in a mug. He rubbed its bristles. They felt dry. She hadn't brushed her teeth this morning.

He stepped to the bathtub. The bottom of the tub looked dry. Gloria's washcloth, draped over the shower-curtain rod, wasn't even slightly damp.

Too many things wrong.

She *had* to come back last night. Her car's in the driveway.

Dave left the bathroom. His heart was pounding. He felt tight and sick inside.

He walked the entire house, searching for Gloria.

For her body? No. Come on, you're making too much out of this.

But he looked in every room, in every closet, behind and under furniture where there were spaces large enough to conceal a person.

Along the way—partly, he suspected, to protect himself from the knowledge of what he was *really* looking for—he kept an eye out for any detail that might prove she had returned alive and well last night.

He found Gloria's keys and purse on the dining-room table. The eighty dollars in the billfold convinced him that robbery wasn't a factor. But the presence of the purse told him nothing more. She probably hadn't taken it with her yesterday. Joan said she'd been carrying a grocery bag.

The only grocery bags he found were neatly folded and clipped to a plastic holder on the back of the utility-room door, or being used as liners for her wastebaskets. None of the wastebaskets contained wadded sacks. The one she'd been carrying and the two she'd worn on her feet were missing.

She might've discarded the makeshift booties before heading home. But what about the other? Could've left it in her car.

I'll check the car.

He wondered if it was locked.

And suddenly realized he'd seen her keys on the dining-room table.

Her keys are here. Gloria isn't. And the house was locked.

Too damn much is wrong.

He took the key case with him and hurried outside. He peered into the side windows of the Volkswagen. A grocery bag, stuffed full, was on the floor behind the passenger seat. He opened the driver's door, sat down, swung the seat back forward, and lifted the bag onto his lap.

It contained nothing except the old blanket that Gloria usually kept in the car's trunk.

Where's her cassette recorder? She never went anywhere without that.

He checked inside the glove compartment. No recorder.

Maybe it's in the house, and I missed it.

But something *else* was wrong.

Dave reached out and gripped the steering wheel. He stretched his legs until his feet touched the floor pedals.

The wheel and pedals were the right distance away for him. Too far away for Gloria.

Someone had adjusted the seat's position to give himself leg room.

Someone Dave's height had been the last person to drive Gloria's car last night.

He squeezed his eyes shut, slumped in the seat, and heard himself groan.

Thirty

The telephone jangled, startling Robin awake. She saw the ceiling above her, realized that she was in a bed instead of her sleeping bag, and knew where she was. She also knew who was calling. She rolled onto her stomach. Propping herself up on an elbow, she reached to the nightstand and brought the telephone's handset to her ear. "Hello?"

"This is your wake-up call."

"Hi, boss." Her raised position allowed cool air to come in, so she shoved the pillow under her chest and sank onto it.

As she reached back to cover her bare shoulders, Nate said, "Did you get a good night's sleep?"

"Not very. And it's all your fault."

"My fault?" He sounded perplexed, amused. "How could that be? Bad choice of motels? Was it too noisy? Was the bed lumpy? What? I got you back early. I left right away."

"That's the thing. You stayed."

"Huh?"

Robin shifted her body a little, just to feel the caress of the warm pillow and sheets. "I couldn't get rid of you. You kept me awake half the night."

"Wish I'd been there to enjoy it."

"So do I."

The earpiece went silent except for the empty, distant sound of white noise.

"You still there?" Robin asked.

"Sorry. I was busy punching myself."

"Aw, don't do that."

"Boy, do I feel like a dope."

"You're not a dope. You're a sweetheart."

"Yeah?"

"Yeah."

"I wish I'd known how you felt."

"You knew. Didn't you?"

"Yeah. I guess so. But I just didn't want you thinking the whole idea was so I could . . . stay. I mean, that's how it would've looked. Right? Getting you the room. *Hiring* you. I didn't want it to look like I was just pulling cheap tricks to get you in bed."

"Whereas we understand, of course, that that's precisely the case."

The soft whuff of a laugh came through the phone. Robin could almost feel the breath of it against her ear.

"You're something else," Nate said.

"You too."

"Are we still on for breakfast?" he asked.

"Sure. I'm ready when you are. How fast can you get here?"

"Ten minutes, if I push it."

"So push it."

Robin hung up and scurried out of bed. The chill morning air gave her goose bumps. She shivered as she hurried into the bathroom, used the toilet, and brushed her teeth. A bath would feel wonderful. She didn't have enough time. She knew she could've asked Nate to wait awhile, but the bath didn't matter. All that mattered was being with him again as soon as possible.

When he had left last night, Robin felt as if he'd taken part of her with him. It was peculiar, not to feel quite whole. But it didn't hurt much, because she knew the missing piece would be restored to her when he showed up again.

The missing piece is Nate, she thought as she washed at the sink. Or maybe it's my heart. How about both?

She wondered if there might be a song in the concept of the missing piece.

He borrowed my heart and he walked away, but he'll bring it back when he comes to stay . . . Bring it back on a silver tray? Screw the tray, sounds like John the Baptist.

With my heart in his pocket, he walked off that night. I reckon he'll return it in the morning light. If his dog don't eat it, I'll be all right.

Robin grinned at her wet face in the mirror, then grabbed a towel and dried herself. She left the bathroom. Wanting to look her best for Nate, she decided to wear her new dress. The dress with the Funland emblem would, she thought, also be more appropriate for her new job as an actual employee.

She had just finished knotting the sash at her hip when she heard footsteps on the balcony. There was a knock at the door. "Hold on a minute," she called. Stepping in front of the mirror, she brushed her hair. Then she rushed to the door and opened it.

Nate stepped into the room. And into Robin's arms. She squeezed herself hard against him. Their mouths joined. The part wasn't missing anymore.

She was all together again.

Easing herself backward, she looked up into his eyes and whispered, "I missed you."

"I missed you more."

"No you didn't."

"Yes I did."

"Yes you did."

He laughed. She felt his breath on her lips.

His hands moved gently down Robin's back. They didn't stop at her sash. They curved over her rump, then pressed it, bringing her tight to his body.

Wanting to look at him but reluctant to break the contact, she bent backward from the waist. "I haven't packed my stuff yet."

"You've got plenty of time. Checkout's eleven, and it's only eight now. You might want to relax here for a while after breakfast."

"Ah-ha!"

She saw a bath in her future, after all.

"What time do I have to start earning my keep?"

"When you're ready. Just come to the arcade. I've got a back room where you can leave your things."

"Sounds good."

"Yeah. So. Ready for breakfast?"

"Starving."

"Good."

She kissed him again, then left him for a moment while she got her handbag and room key.

Holding hands, they walked along the balcony. The day was clear, but a cool breeze made Robin shiver until they left the shadows of the motel and started across the parking lot. There, the warmth of the sun took the chill away.

Nate led her to the passenger side of a red Trans Am.

"I guess you weren't kidding when you said you're loaded."

"Nope." He opened the door for her.

"There's a really good place right across the street, you know."

Smiling, Nate threw the door shut. "You're the breakfast expert."

They crossed the street and entered the coffee shop. They sat facing each other at a window booth. A waitress filled their mugs. Robin took a sip of coffee, gazing over the mug's rim at Nate. Steam drifted upward, hot against her nose and eyes.

"I don't know when I've ever felt this good," she said.

"You should stay in motels more often."

"It's not just the motel. It's everything. Most of all, it's you."

Nate blushed. "I'm not all that wonderful."

"You beat up old ladies?"

Though he smiled as he said, "Worse than that," Robin saw a grim look come into his eyes.

"Are you all right?"

"Just hungry." He picked up one of the menus and studied its back.

Robin looked at her menu.

"What do you recommend?" he asked. "Being the breakfast expert that you are."

"Number one. The two eggs, country sausage, and hash browns."

"I should've known. And I bet you like your eggs sunny-side-up."

"Righto."

The waitress came, and they ordered. When she was gone, Nate stared out the window.

"It's a beautiful day," Robin said.

"Yeah." He looked at her. "Too bad we have to waste it working."

"It's all right with me."

"We can quit at five. I've got Hector coming in."

"Hector the doofuss? I thought you didn't trust him to run things?"

"Well, in an emergency . . ."

"What's the emergency?"

"I have to be alone with you. I'm gonna go crazy."

Robin felt a warm, swelling sensation inside. Her throat tightened. She reached across the table and held Nate's hand.

"I thought we might go over to my house," he said. "I'll barbecue a couple of steaks. We can swim in the pool."

"I think I might be able to live with that."

"Great. Great."

"You mentioned something about being alone with me. Where are your parents while all this is going on?"

"Where they are right now. San Francisco. They won't be back till next Wednesday."

"Wednesday?" Robin's heart suddenly began to pound very hard.

"You can stay till then. If you want to. We'd have the run of the place."

She murmured, "God." She was trembling. Along with the terrible excitement and hope, she felt nervous.

It's happening so fast.

"You don't have to," Nate said. "I mean, I don't want to push you into anything. We have a couple of guest rooms. Or if you'd rather stay in a motel until we can find you a place . . ."

"I'm just a little overwhelmed, is all. Jeez."

"Well, don't try to decide right now. About staying over. But you'll come for the steaks, won't you? Then . . . whatever you want. See how you feel when the time comes."

When the time comes.

"Okay. You can count on me for dinner. And . . . we'll see about the rest."

The waitress came with the food. Robin stared at her plate.

"What's wrong?" Nate asked.

"I'm not sure I can eat."

"I'm sorry. Look, if it bothers you about tonight . . ." He shook his head, frowning. "I didn't mean to upset you. I'll go back, when we're done eating, and register you for a couple more nights. I've got tomorrow off. We can spend the day apartment hunting. Okay? You're still planning to stay, aren't you? I haven't . . . scared you off? Me and my damn mouth. I *knew* I shouldn't have tried to get you to . . . Shit, I really blew it this time. It's not like I wanted you to shack up with me. I know that's how it must look, but . . ." He stopped. He looked perplexed. "What's so funny?"

"You."

"Me?"

"All rambling and flustered."

"I don't know what I'm doing anymore."

"If you ask me, you're doing fine."

A corner of his mouth turned up. "Yeah?"

"Yeah."

"I just don't want you to think I'm trying to . . ."

Smiling, Robin raised her hand. "Hush," she said. "Eat."

He shrugged, looked as if he might start to speak again, but stopped himself and began to work on his breakfast.

Robin, too, began to eat. Her heart was slamming. She could hardly swallow, but she washed down the food with water and coffee, and kept shoveling more into her mouth, determined not to let Nate notice her turmoil.

He looked pleased. "You got your appetite back?"

"So it would seem. I think your speech cured me."

"Now that you don't have tonight hanging over your head."

"Guess so."

"Well, I never should've—"

"Eat, okay?"

"Was this motel all right?" he asked, nodding at it through the window. "We could check you into a different one if—"

"This one's just fine."

Nate finished his breakfast in silence. He kept looking at Robin and trying to smile. She could see that he was not only disappointed but also embarrassed.

Robin walked behind him to the front counter. He paid. He held the glass door open for her.

Outside, she took his hand. "Come on, cheer up," she said. "It's not the end of the world."

"I know. I'm sorry."

At the curb, they waited for a break in traffic. Then they rushed across the street.

"There'll be other times," she said.

"Yeah."

"I don't want to spend all day wondering what's going to happen tonight. Can you understand that?"

"Sure."

"I'd get my fingers tangled in my banjo strings and forget how to sing."

They stopped in the parking lot. "I'll go ahead to the office and—"

"Come on up for a minute. I want to give you something."

"Okay."

They climbed the stairs. They walked along the balcony. Robin took the room key from her purse. The point of the key clicked and skidded around the lock hole.

"You're a nervous wreck," Nate said.

"And it's all your fault." Finally the key went in. She turned it and opened the door. Nate followed her into the room. He didn't see Robin hang the Do Not Disturb sign on the outside knob before shutting the door.

He turned around. From the look on his face, Robin could see that he didn't suspect. He was still fighting his disappointment about tonight. But being very brave about it.

Robin wrapped her arms around him. She gazed into his eyes. And saw confusion.

"Those other times?" she said, her voice shaking. "Well, this is the first of them."

"Huh?"

"I'd be wrecked all day, waiting for tonight."

Nate looked shocked. "You're kidding," he whispered.

"Think so?"

His moan seemed more agonized than happy. He pulled Robin hard against him and she found his lips with her mouth.

Thirty-one

"He didn't go for it?" Joan asked when Dave returned from the chief's office.

"He agreed it was peculiar, but thought we'd be jumping the gun to launch an investigation. If Gloria hasn't turned up by tomorrow . . ."

"The old twenty-four-hour crap," Joan said. "Same thing I got when my mother disappeared."

"You didn't come up with anything?"

Shaking her head, Joan took her jacket off the back of her desk chair and slung it over one shoulder. "I made the calls. The people at the paper haven't heard from her since yesterday morning. Nobody fitting her description turned up at the hospital. Or the morgue."

"That's something, anyway."

They walked out to the patrol car. Joan tossed her jacket into the trunk, then slid into the passenger seat. The car was warm. She rolled her window down. Dave got in behind the wheel and drove out of the parking lot.

"It had to be someone who didn't want suspicion directed at Funland or the beach area," Joan said. "If there really was foul play, that's the only thing that makes sense. Otherwise, why bother?"

Dave nodded. "They went to a lot of trouble to make it look like she came home last night."

"That was no easy trick."

"Not too hard. The lot's nearly empty after closing time and they could tell she had a VW by the key. The registration in the glove compartment has her address."

"Had to be somebody pretty sharp," Joan said. "And someone who knows the town. I can't see a bum pulling a gimmick like that. Their heads are too messed up."

"Maybe not all of them."

"All of them *I've* seen. This is way out of their league. It almost had to be the trollers."

"Or a third party we're not even aware of. Could be she ran into a serial killer, something like that. We're about due. Haven't had one here since Gunderson, back in eighty-two."

"Possible," Joan said. "But I'd put my money on Great Big Billy Goat Gruff and the gang. They probably jumped her, thinking they had themselves a troll."

"She would've corrected that impression pretty quick, I think."

"Told them who she is? She's not stupid. If they knew they had Gloria Weston, it'd get pretty nasty."

"It'd get nasty enough if they thought she was a troll. If they figured out she wasn't . . ." Dave shook his head. "Suddenly, they're confronted by a lucid victim. Someone capable of fingering them, testifying against them."

"Kill her? Dave, that's a mighty big step for a bunch of kids who've never really done worse than beat up some bums and . . . leave them in compromising positions."

"If it's that or getting busted . . ."

"Yeah. Jesus. I know."

"They wouldn't have fooled around taking her car and clothes home unless they'd known she wasn't going to be turning up. Ever."

"This is getting awfully damn grim."

"She knew better," Dave said.

"Real consolation."

"Yeah."

Dave slowed the car and swung into the Funland parking lot. "Look," Joan said, "this is just 'worse-case-scenario' stuff. Gloria might be fine. There are other explanations. She could've met someone last night. A guy. Maybe an old friend. Maybe they had a few, somewhere, and he drove her home in the Bug. She changed clothes and went off with him."

"Leaving her keys and purse in the house?"

"You said she's got a spare house key."

"It's a nice theory," Dave said. "I hope you're right. But it's got too many holes in it."

"There could be simple explanations for the holes too."

Dave swung into a parking space and killed the engine. He looked at Joan.

"I know," she muttered.

"Dammit, we tried to warn her."

"Yeah. We did. But we should've tried harder."

"We didn't know something like this would happen."

"I just wish we had it to do over again. We could've stopped her. *I* could've stopped her. I could've gone over to her when I saw her sitting there on the steps in that ridiculous troll costume."

"She would've just told you to go to hell."

"She'd still be alive, Dave. I would've *seen* to it. Shit, I would've kept her handcuffed inside her house last night, if that's what it took."

"We didn't know. We can't blame ourselves. We knew it was dangerous, but . . . life is dangerous. I could get shot on duty today . . ."

Joan felt something shrivel inside her. "Hey, don't say that."

"The point is, I'm taking the risk every time I put my uniform on. Would you blame yourself and think you should've kept me handcuffed at home?"

"I'd blame myself for not blowing away the bastard first."

Dave smiled. "That's different. I might blame you for that myself. The thing is, we didn't know her damn stunt would get her dead. *If* she's dead. We don't even know that, for sure. Come on, we'd better get over to the boardwalk."

They left the car. Joan met him behind it. She wished they were alone, so she could hold him.

"We'll get whoever did it, Dave. We'll nail him—or them. We'll find out what they did to her."

"Really? How do we do that?"

"Come back tonight. After closing time. I'll dress up."

"Use you as bait? No way."

"It's something we have to do. And you know it."

Jeremy sat hunched over the kitchen table, slicing apart his fried eggs, bacon, and toast and forking mixes of them into his mouth.

"You certainly have yourself an appetite for someone at death's door," his mother said.

He nodded and scooped more food into his mouth. He'd never had a hangover before. He'd always heard that people in his condition were repulsed by the mere thought of food, but he felt ravenous.

Of course, he'd barfed on the way home last night. That could account for the maddening hunger.

"I really ought to ground you, you know."

He looked up at her. The movement of his eyes was like a rheostat turning up the pain in his head from dim to bright. "I told you I'm sorry. Geez, what do you want? It wasn't my fault Shiner had a flat."

"And whose fault was it that you came home drunk?"

"I didn't know the punch was spiked."

"I'm sure."

"I didn't. Besides, everyone else was drinking it."

"If everyone else jumped off a—"

"I know, I know. God, I said I was sorry. You don't have to crucify me."

"Don't talk that way."

He leaned back in the chair and closed his eyes. They felt hot and dry under his lids. And too big. As if they'd swollen to twice their size with some kind of terrible, throbbing pressure. "I learned my lesson," he muttered. "I feel like . . . horrible. I promise, I'll never drink again. Just don't ground me. Please? I'm supposed to meet Shiner at the beach."

"That's another thing. Shiner. She certainly had me fooled. I thought she was a perfectly nice young lady."

Jeremy opened his eyes and frowned. "She is."

"I don't call it nice to go to a party and get drunk. Not when she has the responsibility of driving you home afterward. There's no excuse for that. And you should've known better than to get into the car with someone who—"

"Mom, she didn't drink. All she had was Pepsi."

"I'm supposed to believe that?"

"It's the truth. She didn't have any booze."

"So *she* knew the punch was spiked?"

"No. She just doesn't like punch." In spite of the pain pulsing through his head, he came up with an idea. "I remember now. She said she's diabetic. That's why she didn't have any punch. She was drinking sugarless Pepsi."

"Hmmm."

He didn't know whether his mother bought that or not. Then he wondered why he was trying so hard to defend Shiner. Hell, she'd gone off and left him.

With good reason.

Maybe they could make up, though. If he ever saw her again.

But the main thing—Shiner was his excuse for going to the beach this morning. He had to convince Mom of her innocence, or she might keep him home.

If he couldn't go to the beach and see Tanya . . .

"She figured out the punch was spiked," he said, "and warned me. That's when I stopped drinking the stuff."

"Well, I might have been a bit hasty in my assessment of her."

"She liked *you*. She told me she wished her mother was more like you."

"Really?" She raised her eyebrows, looking surprised and pleased.

"Yeah, she thought you were neat."

"Well, that's all very well and good, but I still think you'd better just stay in the house. I can't condone last night's behavior."

"Shiner's *expecting* me. She'll be waiting. She'll think I stood her up."

"Alexander Graham Bell invented a convenient device—"

"I don't know her number, Mom. And she isn't listed. They were getting all these crank calls last year, and . . . Please. It's not fair to Shiner. She was going to make a picnic lunch, she'll have gone to all that trouble, and she'll be waiting there not knowing what happened to me. It just isn't fair."

"You should've thought of that last night."

"Right!" Jeremy snapped. "Fine." He flung his knife and fork down. They crashed against the plate, and his mother flinched as if she'd been slapped. Tears glimmered in her eyes. "I'll stay home. I'll stay home *forever*. Ruin my life, why don't you? The first time in my damn life I make a friend, and all you want to do is wreck it. If you hate me so much, why don't you just shoot me and get it over with!"

He shoved his chair back and raced from the kitchen.

"Jeremy!" she cried out after him.

"To hell with it! To hell with everything!"

He ran to his room and threw himself onto the bed. His head roared with pain. It felt as if daggers were being plunged into his brain. He clamped the pillow down over his ears and lay there sobbing in agony.

A few minutes passed before he heard the footsteps he expected. The mattress tipped slightly as his mother sat down on the edge of the bed. Her hand stroked his back.

"If it's that important to you," she said. Her voice was muffled, but Jeremy could hear it trembling. He loosened his grip on the pillow but kept it over his head. "I don't want to stop you from having a picnic with a pretty girl. I was your age once myself, you know. I understand these things."

"I'm sorry," he said. "I shouldn't have . . . yelled and gone crazy."

"That's right, you shouldn't have. But I suppose I was being a little harsh. You do need to be punished, though. I'll dock your allowance for two weeks—and you wash the dinner dishes."

"For how long?" he muttered.

"The same. Two weeks."

"That's pretty stiff."

He heard her laugh. She gave his rump a gentle swat, and he felt the mattress rise.

He rolled over and sat up as she walked toward the door. She looked back at him. Her eyes were red, her face wet.

"Thanks, Mom," Jeremy said.

"Even if we have our little problems, honey, I still love you. Don't ever think I don't."

"I know. I love you too."

"You'd better get a move on, now. You don't want to keep Shiner waiting."

Nate kissed Robin gently on the mouth. "I wish I could stay," he whispered.

"Me too. But I don't want to make you late."

"We'll have tonight. And tomorrow, and the next day and the next."

"You'll get tired of me."

"I'll never get tired of you." Nate kissed her mouth again and eased himself back, kissing her chin, the side of her neck. His penis slid out of her. The loss of it gave Robin an empty ache, but she still held the feel of it like an afterimage. He kissed each of her nipples, her sternum, her belly. Then he was kneeling over her, looking down with wonder and sadness in his eyes.

Robin folded her hands beneath her head. She raised her knees, and pressed them gently against his sides.

"I've never . . . felt this way about a girl before," he said. He ran his hands slowly down her thighs. "What is it about you, anyway?"

"I'm easy?"

"Are you?"

"No. Just for you."

"I think I'm in love with you. It's not because of . . . what we just did. I was in love with you before."

"I was in love with you before too. I still am, only more."

"Same here." He rested his hands on her knees. "God, I wish I didn't have to go."

"I'll go with you."

"No. Stay and take that bath." He smiled. "Now you *really* need it." He patted her knees, then climbed off the bed.

Robin rolled onto her side. She watched him bend down and pick up his underwear. His body was sleek and muscular, his skin deeply tanned but white where shorts had kept the sun away.

As he stepped into his jeans and fastened them, Robin rose from the bed. She sat on its edge, feet on the carpet, and watched Nate get into his T-shirt, socks, and tennis shoes.

It felt strange, being naked while he was dressed.

It felt just fine.

She stood up, and he came to her. He put his hands on her hips. He gazed into her eyes. "Guess I'll see you in an hour or so," he said. "Just come to the arcade whenever you're ready."

"I'll make it quick. I already miss you." She wrapped her arms around him, hugged him tight, and kissed him.

Jeremy rode his bike close to the curb, going slowly and coasting because the exertion when he had to pedal fueled the pain in his head. He was feeling a lot better now. The clean, fresh breeze seemed to help.

So did the prospect of eating a waffle cone when he reached Funland. Though he'd never had a hangover, he somehow knew that ice cream would smother the flames in his stomach.

He remembered hurling the remains of his waffle cone at Tanya, wiping the mess from her leg, going up inside her shorts, and then his thoughts slipped to last night in her bedroom and the memories of that set his heart racing, pounding hot pain into his head.

Don't think about it, he told himself.

But now that his mind had entered her room, he couldn't tear it away.

The images whirled and tumbled, took Jeremy's breath

away, made his heart slam until he thought his head might explode. He squeezed his eyes shut. Felt the bike lurch sideways. Snapped his eyes open and saw that he'd swerved out into the middle of the lane. A car horn blared. Without looking back, he twisted the handlebars to the right. The car sped by. Someone yelled, "Asshole!" Jeremy's front tire rubbed the curb, and he put his foot on the pavement to hold himself up.

He shut his eyes tight and clutched his head. The images of Tanya kept staggering through his mind, jumbled and twisted. Instead of erotic, they seemed nightmarish and sickening. But he couldn't get rid of them. For a long while he thought he might vomit or pass out.

The beach, he told himself. I've got to get to the beach.

He saw himself flopping onto the hot sand.

That would be good. Just lie there and not move and not think.

Imagining himself sprawled on the beach, he felt the pain begin to subside. He thought about the peaceful sounds of the surf and sea gulls.

Finally, no longer crushed by the pain, he took a bottle of aspirin out of his shirt pocket. He popped the cap off and dry-swallowed three tablets.

They seemed to get stuck somewhere in the middle of his chest.

A drink. Need something to drink.

He looked around and saw a soft-drink vending machine beside the office of the motel just ahead. He climbed slowly off his bike. He lifted it onto the sidewalk and rolled it toward the office.

Movement on the second-story balcony caught his eye.

Just a guy leaving one of the rooms.

Something familiar . . .

The guy's back was turned. He was lingering in the doorway, apparently speaking to someone inside. He raised a hand in farewell, pulled the door shut, and started walking along the balcony.

With the side view, Jeremy recognized him.

Nate.

Forgetting his need for a drink, Jeremy turned his bike

around and rolled it toward the corner. He walked it across the street. At the other side, he glanced back and saw Nate climb into a red sports car. He walked a little farther, listening. He heard the engine thunder to life. When the sound began to fade, he looked again and saw the car moving away.

He pushed his bike back to the corner.

He peered at the closed door of the motel room.

What the hell had Nate been doing in there?

A motel room. Ten o'clock on a Saturday morning.

He must've been with a girl. Jeremy could think of no other explanation.

Tanya? Was Tanya in there?

It didn't make sense.

He spotted a coffee shop directly across the street from the motel. If he got a window seat, he would be able to watch the door and see who came out.

And he could get himself a drink to wash down the aspirin that seemed to be burning a hole in his chest.

Keeping an eye on the door, he walked his bike to the coffee shop.

Thirty-two

The Pepsi made the aspirin ache fade, though not quite vanish entirely.

Nobody had come out of the motel room by the time Jeremy finished his drink.

He was beginning to feel pretty good. The soda helped his stomach, and he supposed the aspirin was working on the pain in his head. It also helped, just sitting there.

For a while he sipped the water of the melting ice cubes up through his straw.

The coffee shop had plenty of vacant tables and stools at the counter, but he felt guilty about lingering with his glass empty. He caught the eye of the waitress and asked for a hot-fudge sundae.

He'd planned on a waffle cone at Funland. He supposed he could still buy one later on if he felt like it. But for now he needed something in front of him so he wouldn't look as if he were loitering.

The sundae came, and he ate so slowly that the ice cream was soupy by the time he spooned the last of it into his mouth.

Still nobody had come out of the motel room.

Nate *couldn't* have been alone in there. He'd stood in the doorway for a few moments before leaving, obviously talking to someone.

It had to be a girl, didn't it?

A girl, but not Tanya. It couldn't be Tanya. They'd both been so angry at each other last night when Nate left the party.

What if they had made up?

Jeremy was tired of wondering about such things. The same thoughts must've gone through his mind at least once every five minutes.

The girl *might* be Tanya. But he didn't believe it, wouldn't believe it. If they'd made up and gone to a motel, it ruined everything. Tanya had to stay mad at Nate. She had to. Otherwise, Jeremy wouldn't stand a chance.

Who's in there, dammit?

What if she doesn't come out? I can't sit here all day.

Jeremy wondered if he should order something else. Maybe another Pepsi. He looked for his waitress. She was clearing a table near the door, her back to him.

He glanced out the window again.

The door of the motel room swung open. A girl stepped onto the balcony. A slim girl wearing a powder-blue dress that looked like a jersey. Her bright blond hair was nearly as short as his own. Though she was too far away for Jeremy to make out the features of her face, the hair gave her away. So did the slender build. And the backpack and instrument case.

The banjo girl!

The bitch who had snapped at him Wednesday night on the boardwalk, just before Cowboy showed up. The bitch he'd found the next day singing that sick nuclear-war song about a weenie roast. The bitch he'd imagined himself taking on, wrestling, pinning down.

He watched her stride along the balcony. There was a bounce in her stride, as if she were happy about something.

Yeah, he thought. Happy. She got screwed by Nate.

Wait till Tanya hears about this!

He stared at her slender tanned legs, at the way the dress clung to her small rump. The backpack bounced as she trotted down the stairs.

Jeremy dug out his wallet. He slapped a dollar onto the table for a tip, snatched up his bill, and hurried to the counter. Nobody was there. Fidgeting, he looked back and saw her enter the motel office. Probably to drop off the room key or register herself for another night.

At last his waitress stepped behind the cash register. He paid, and rushed out the door. Unchaining his bike, he saw the girl leave the office. She started walking in the direction of Funland. Of course.

He waited for a break in the traffic, then walked his bike across the street. When he reached the other side, the girl was half a block ahead of him. He mounted his bike and followed.

Incredible, he thought. Tanya's going to blow her stack. She'll *never* make up with Nate, not after she hears about this. Nate screwing the banjo girl. Man, the bitch was only one step away from being a goddamn *troll.*

Explains why Nate turned against everyone at the party. Not because he felt guilty about the fat old guy taking a header off the Ferris wheel. Just wanted us to think that was why. The real reason, he'd fallen for one of the enemy. No wonder he wanted the trolling to stop.

No wonder he sounded off and split.

He had someplace to go.

The motel.

So he could screw his troll.

"Wow," Jeremy said. "Holy shit."

Staying half a block behind the girl, he followed her to Funland. While she hurried up the main stairs, he chained his bike to the rack. He lost sight of her when she passed through the entryway.

On the boardwalk, he scanned the milling crowd. This was Saturday. He'd never seen the place this packed. He wandered through the jam of people, searching for her. Then he gave up.

It didn't matter.

He was sure he would be able to find her later, if he wanted to. Before long, she would probably start playing her banjo. He could simply follow the sound of the music.

The main thing was to tell Tanya what he'd seen.

Blow Nate out of the water.

And score points with Tanya. *You'll have to prove yourself,* she'd said. *With loyalty.* Well, this sure ought to show his loyalty.

Maybe this would be enough.

He went down the steps to the sand.

Stopped.

His head turned to the left as if pulled by a magnet. Kept turning until his neck would allow it to move no farther.

He stared at the Ferris wheel.

Brightly spinning. Then dark, shrouded by fog. He heard the old man's scream rake the night, heard the ringing thuds as he pounded the struts, saw him tumbling down.

Jeremy grinned.

One down, a hundred to go.

They've *all* gotta pay.

Me and Tanya, we'll wipe them out.

Still grinning, he turned away from the Ferris wheel and began to walk across the sand.

Like the boardwalk, the beach was overflowing with people. He made his way carefully around their blankets, towels, canvas chairs, and even passed a few umbrellas. Wet kids were running by, their laughter and shouts mixing with the manic voices of DJ's and rock from radios that seemed to be everywhere. People read, slept, ate and drank, talked to friends or lovers, rubbed suntan lotion on skin that was white or pink or richly tanned.

Jeremy didn't pay much attention to the men.

But he studied the women as he walked past them.

Soon he was dry-mouthed and breathless, hard, achy. His throbbing heartbeat pounded blood into his head, awakening the pain that had nearly disappeared.

He tried to stop looking at the sprawled, exposed bodies.

Then he saw a blond girl in a backless black suit. Shiner? His heart bucked. His head roared.

What'll I do?

Talk to her. Apologize. Maybe it's not too late.

Her head lifted and he saw her face. Tiny eyes, a sharp nose, thin lips, a sunken chin. Not Shiner, after all.

Thank God, he thought.

He felt spared. He felt disappointed.

You didn't *want* it to be Shiner, he told himself.

I'll have Tanya soon. Tanya's almost mine.

He looked up and squinted toward the lifeguard station. On the platform stood a man in red trunks.

"Shit!"

Jeremy pounded fists against the sides of his legs. She'd had yesterday off. She must have today off too.

I've gotta tell her about Nate!

Head spinning with pain, he dropped to his knees. He took off his shirt, spread it in front of him, and lay down. He folded his arms under his face.

I'll go home, he thought. I'll go home and phone her.

Wait. No. There are pay phones on the boardwalk.

He thought about getting up, but he didn't want to move. The hot sand felt good beneath him. The sun's heat weighed him down. A mild breeze ruffled his hair and caressed his back.

Later. I'll do it later.

"Well, durn me if it ain't the Duker."

The voice seemed to come from far away.

Something soft whupped against Jeremy's back. Moaning, he rolled onto his side and looked up at Cowboy. "Hi," he said. Though he felt groggy and leaden, his headache was gone.

He wondered how long he'd been asleep.

Cowboy spread a towel on the sand and sat down cross-legged, facing Jeremy. He wore his old Stetson and a tight bikini-style swimsuit. He looked as if he had an earmuff taped to the side of his head. Otherwise, he wasn't bandaged. Jeremy didn't count, but he guessed there were six or eight cuts on his arms, chest, and belly. Some had stitches. All the wounds looked brown and gooey, and a little red around the edges.

"Don't you believe in bandages?"

"Sun'll do 'em good. How you doing, old hoss?"

"Okay, I guess."

"Me, I'm as hung-over as a dead whore on a fencepost."

"Me too. It's getting better, though."

"How come you didn't stick around last night?"

"It was Shiner," he said, wondering if anyone knew she had left without him. "She had to get home early."

"You didn't tell her about the treatment, did you?"

Jeremy felt heat rush to his face. "The treatment?"

"Your blood pact."

Cowboy *knew* about that? Trying not to sound shocked, he said, "No. I didn't tell Shiner."

"Good thing. It's only between Tanya and the guys. And Karen, since she's a lezzie. The rest of the gals, they ain't in on it."

"She's done that with *all* the guys?" Jeremy asked.

"Sure. And Karen, like I said."

He nodded slowly. He felt cheated, robbed. He had thought Tanya did the ritual because she considered him special. He had thought he'd been singled out. Maybe there's some mistake, he told himself. Maybe Cowboy's talking about something different.

"You had the blood pact," he said. "How'd it go?"

"Man, freaked the needles right offa my cactus."

"I mean, what did she do?"

Cowboy blew his pursed lips. "It was *weird*, man. You aren't gonna believe this."

"I'll believe it."

"I'm home alone, right? This is a Saturday night last summer, and my folks are off at a party, and I haven't met up with Liz yet, which accounts for my being alone. I was down in the den watching *Evil Dead II* on the VCR. You ever seen that?"

"Yeah. It's cool."

"How about when the guy's hand gets possessed and he starts bashing himself over the head—?"

"What about Tanya?" Jeremy asked.

"Okay, I'm all by myself and watching this sucker in the dark, so I'm pretty spooked anyway. This is only like a month after Tanya got out of the hospital. We'd been sneaking out and trying to find the actual shits that done the job on her. It was just her, Nate, me, and Samson. We knew some bums had laid her open with a busted bottle. That was no big secret. Was even in the papers. But we didn't know *everything* they'd done to her. Maybe Nate did, but he never let on. Anyway, we ran into plenty of bums, but not the right ones. We pounded a few of 'em anyway, and took 'em on rides outta town. Then we quit."

"You quit?" Jeremy sat up. The skin of his back felt very hot and stiff. He knew he had probably burned. He picked up his shirt, shook the sand off it, and draped it across his shoulders.

"Quitting was Nate's idea. He didn't see much point in going on with it, seeing as how we couldn't find the creeps that slashed Tanya. We all figured they must've hustled their sorry butts outta town."

Jeremy nodded. "So you were watching *Evil Dead*, and then what happened?"

"Well, I had to take a leak, so I stopped the movie and went into the john. We've got one downstairs, you know, just outside the den. It's got a shower. No bathtub, just a shower stall. So I'm standing there with my back to it, and I finish up and tuck ol' Sneaky Pete back inside my pajamas and I'm reaching out to flush and all of a sudden I hear the shower curtain whip open. Screaming Judas, woulda scared the piss outta me, only I'd just gone. I spin around, and there's Tanya. Man, she's standing there in the shower stall, buck naked and holding a butcher knife."

"A butcher knife?"

"Fuck, man. I figured: This is it. Figured she'd flipped out and I was gonna be a carved goose."

"Christ," Jeremy muttered.

"Only she doesn't come at me. She doesn't say shit. Just looks me in the eyes and starts sliding the point of that knife down her scar." Cowboy shook his head slowly from side to side. His eyes were fixed on Jeremy, but they looked as if they were seeing Tanya instead. "Just touching it, you know? Not hard enough to cut herself. And real slow. All the way from her tit down to her pussy. God damn. Weirdest thing I ever saw. And that bod." His eyes seemed to come into focus. "How'd you like that bod, Duke? You ever seen anything like it?"

"No."

"Tanned all over, and—"

"Well, what happened? Come on."

"Yeah, okay, so she done this thing with the knife. And finally she says, 'This is what they did to me, Cowboy. But they did worse." Then she tells me the whole story. All the stuff they did to her."

"Yeah, she told me."

"Then she says, 'They have to pay. Will you help me make them pay?' I start to remind her how we couldn't find the guys, and she puts the knife to her mouth to shush me. 'Trolls are all the same,' she says. 'If it hadn't been those three, it would've been three others. It could've been any of them. They're all evil. They have to pay.'

"I guess it made some sense. I don't know. I was pretty shook-up. Bet you were too."

Jeremy nodded.

"So I told her I'd go hunting trolls with her from now till doomsday, if that's what she wanted. When I said that, she took holda my hand and got me into the shower stall with her. I figured ol' Sneaky Pete was about to have the time of his life, but what she does is take the butcher knife to my hand." Raising his right hand, he pointed out a small pale scar on his palm.

Jeremy raised his own hand so Cowboy could see the tiny mark left by the razor blade.

"Not much of a cut," Cowboy remarked. "Can't hardly see it."

"Sure bled, though."

"Mine too. So then she cut herself."

"Down there?"

"Fuckin'-A right, down there."

"And made you hold it."

"You betcha. Held my hand right against her twat and she says, 'Your blood's in me, my blood's in you. We're blood lovers.'

Not blood brothers, like that Injun thing you hear about, but blood lovers."

"Said the same thing to me. Pretty much. So then what? Did you make it with her?"

Cowboy's eyes widened. "Did you?"

"No."

He looked relieved. "Me either. But she kinda hinted it might go that way if I stuck with her and kept on going after trolls. Don't know if she really meant it. Hasn't happened yet."

"You don't think it was just a lie, do you?"

"Who knows? I keep waiting. Maybe I just haven't proved myself enough."

"Has she done it with any of the other guys?"

"Nate. But I guess they were doing it before, so it didn't have nothing to do with the pact. If she's put out for any of the other guys, I haven't heard about it. But I know she did the 'blood-lover' thing with 'em."

"Maybe she wouldn't do it because of Nate."

Cowboy grinned. "Now, that's a dandy thought. Hope you're right. Maybe our turn's coming up."

"Now that Nate's out of the way."

"Guy must have rocks in his head, dumping her like that. We're all itching to put it to her, and he's got it made, and he throws it all away. Just 'cause he's got his shorts in a knot over killing a damn troll."

"Yeah," Jeremy said.

He thought: That's not why at all. But hell if I'm going to spill it.

The truth was his secret, his edge, and his alone.

Nobody gets to tell Tanya about the banjo girl but me.

"Are we meeting tonight?" he asked.

"Yup. Sure as shootin', Duke. Same time, same place."

That's too long to wait, he thought. Much too long. I have to tell her *now*.

Thirty-three

"Look who we've got here," Joan said. She didn't sound very happy to see the boys.

Dave stayed at her side as they crossed the boardwalk toward the pair. Both kids had corn dogs and were munching and talking while they strolled along. Joan stepped in front of them. They looked startled at first, then came up with nervous smiles.

"How are you fellows doing?" she asked.

"Reckon I'm all in one piece," said the kid in the cowboy hat. The side of his head was bandaged. He wore a skimpy swimsuit and no shirt, as if he were showing off the wounds on his torso. The cuts looked a little raw, and a lot like the one Dave had seen that morning in the mirror. "I sure want to thank you," the kid told Joan. He glanced at Dave. "You too. I was about two steps short of the ol' stewpot."

"Glad we could help," Joan said.

"How's the ear?" Dave asked, trying to remember the guy's name.

"Well, he's stitched on good and tight."

"You really took care of that guy," the other kid said. Wayne. Something Wayne. He looked in pretty good shape except for the faint shadow of a bruise on his forehead. "No kidding. The way you got him in the chin, looked like you were going for a field goal."

Joan's face went red. Dave knew it wasn't a glow of embarrassed pride. "I'm just glad things worked out," she said.

"So, what's the story on Chingachgook and his pal?" asked the one whose ear had been taken off. "They cooling their heels in the hoosegow?"

"They're both in custody,." Dave said. "One's still in the hospital."

"Hope it's the one tried to gobble my ear."

"It is," Dave said.

"Man, I just bet," Wayne said, looking at Joan with awe in his eyes. "I thought he was a goner, the way you nailed him. That was *really* cool."

"There was nothing cool about it." She turned to the other kid and glared at him. "I'm glad you weren't hurt any worse than you were, but you were asking for trouble and you got it. And you got a lot of people hurt, including an innocent by-stander and my partner. So you'd better watch your step, buddy. You cause any more trouble around here, I'll be on you like wet on rain."

"Yes, ma'am," he said, looking stunned and guilty. Dave suspected that the look was a sham. "I'm sorry."

She glanced at Dave. "Let's go."

He stayed beside her as she hurried away.

"Couple of shitheads," she muttered.

"Well, they got hurt pretty good for their trouble."

"I think the Wayne kid enjoyed it. He stripped the shirt right off that one gal. Probably got in some feelies."

"Two against one, and they were both bigger than him."

Joan smiled. "You on his side?"

"He had to defend himself. Even if they were girls. Some are tough."

"Yeah? Think so?"

"I know of one, for sure."

"She's bigger than you too. But you've got prettier legs."

Dave looked down to compare. "I'd say it's even."

She patted his rump.

"Watch it, partner. None of that."

"Forgot myself."

"Not that I don't appreciate it. When you get to my place, you can do it to your heart's desire."

"What time do you want me?"

"How's six?"

"How about seven? I'll need some time to take a bath and get my costume together."

The costume. They hadn't discussed her plan since early morning. Dave had been hoping the whole idea might just evaporate, but he supposed he had known, all along, there wasn't much chance of that. Once Joan had made her mind up about something . . .

You wouldn't want it any other way, he told himself. Suppose she had been happy to wash her hands of Gloria? Said the bitch got what she deserved, it's none of our business, forget about her and let's have a ball? You'd think she was a heartless jerk.

It's her heart making her do this.

Making her take such a risk.

She sure doesn't *want* to come back here after the place closes. She's probably more scared than me. But she isn't going to back out.

Heart *and* guts.

"Let's wear vests," he said.

Joan gave him an amused frown. "Who's going to be shooting at us?"

"I'm serious."

"So am I. Those things cramp my style, and we've got no reason to think the trollers go around with guns."

"I'd wager they carry knives, at least. I'd rather catch the next blade in Kevlar."

She met his eyes. And nodded. "I'd rather you did too. Okay, we'll go with the vests."

"How about the rest of your ensemble?" he asked.

"Violins, a clarinet . . ."

"No brass," he added. "You've got too much of that already. But have you decided what you'll wear?"

"In addition to the vest? I don't know."

"You haven't got a closet full of filthy rags?"

"Maybe we could roll a bag lady."

"I could stop by Gloria's and pick up her stuff for you."

The cheerful, mischievous look vanished from her face. "Wouldn't fit."

"The tights might be a little snug . . ."

"God, I'm not gonna wear Gloria's tights. Or anything else. They're hers. And they've been pawed by the creep who . . . took them off her."

Joan's words jammed images into Dave's head of Gloria on

her back, struggling and screaming as rough hands ripped at the clothes.

"Besides," Joan said, "if I wore her stuff, it might destroy evidence."

"Yeah."

Evidence. The hairs of a stranger. Maybe blood. Maybe semen. Dave hadn't noticed anything like that, but the crime-scene guys were experts. The smallest trace . . .

"Are you all right?"

"Thinking about evidence."

"I'm sorry. I should't have mentioned it."

"No, you're right. I made a mistake touching her stuff in the first place."

"That's how you figured out . . ."

"Yeah. That too. Exactly. Just like I said, a mistake. If I'd kept my hands off her things, we wouldn't be any the wiser. We wouldn't be doing this tonight."

"Shame I can't get her in stereo," Cowboy said, cupping a hand behind his bandaged ear.

"She's pretty good, isn't she?"

The banjo girl was standing near the long line in front of the Hurricane, tapping her foot as she pounded out "The Rock Island Line." Wearing what she was, she didn't look like a bum anymore. Jeremy liked her dress. It was short, showing off her slender legs, and the weight of the banjo pulled it tight against her breasts.

She's still no Tanya, Jeremy thought.

How could a guy like Nate go for her, when he already had Tanya? It didn't make sense.

Unless it might be something about the way she seemed kind of innocent and mysterious.

Innocent. Sure. Jeremy remembered how she'd snapped at him Wednesday night. She's a bitch, he thought. And tough as nails. Probably about as innocent as a whore.

I've gotta tell Tanya about her!

Why did Cowboy have to show up and get in the way?

Jeremy felt as if time were running out, as if his chance would be lost forever if he didn't get in touch with Tanya soon.

The banjo went silent. Cowboy clapped, as did several people waiting in the line for the roller coaster, and others who had stopped on the boardwalk to listen.

"Reckon I wouldn't mind plucking *her* strings."

You'd have to stand in line behind Nate, Jeremy thought. "I wouldn't kick her out of bed either," he said.

She strummed a lively tune on the banjo and started to sing.

I had me a guy and he lived in the bog
With an old .44 and a one-eyed dog.
The dog was mean, and so was he,
But they weren't near half as mean as me.

Jeremy felt a hand clutch his shoulder. "Hang on, buddy," Cowboy said. "I've gotta take me a whiz."

"See you later."

He watched Cowboy push slowly through the crowd. Then he hurried in the opposite direction.

Finally!

By the time he reached the pay phone near the main entrance, he figured Cowboy had probably finished in the john.

Won't know where to find me, though. Might not even bother to look.

Trembling, he swung the directory toward him on its chain. He flicked through the pages. Ashland. Only three Ashlands. Two were Ronald Ashland, D.C. He remembered that Shiner had said Tanya's father was a chiropractor. One entry was for the father's office on Grove, but the other showed a street address on Avion.

Muttering the phone number that went with the Avion listing, Jeremy picked up the handset, dropped a quarter into the slot, and dialed.

The ringing sounded faint, muffled by the noises of the crowd and rides and calliope music. He pressed the phone hard against his right ear and jammed a finger into his other.

That helped.

He heard the ringing more clearly.

God, he thought, I'm actually calling Tanya. The beat of his heart quickened, and he could feel it awakening his headache. The plastic handset felt wet and slippery.

Maybe she's not home.

He almost hoped she wasn't.

What am I doing?

Lovers in blood. Loyalty. You've gotta prove yourself. You want her, don't you?

Yes!

"Hello?" A female voice.

"Hi. Tanya?"

"Just a moment, I'll call her to the phone."

Must've been her mother. Went to get her. She's home!

Jeremy looked around and scanned the crowd. So far, no Cowboy.

Come on, Tanya. Come on!

"She'll be right along," said the mother's voice.

"I've got it, Mom." Tanya's voice. Jeremy heard the other phone click down.

"Hi," he said. His heart pounded. His head pulsed with pain. "It's Jeremy. Duke."

"How are you doing? Have you heard we'll be meeting tonight?"

"Yeah. Cowboy told me."

"You'll be there, won't you?"

"Sure! The thing is, I've gotta tell you something. It's about Nate."

"Rotten bastard."

"Yeah, he sure is. But the thing is, I saw him this morning. He was at a motel. With a girl."

Tanya said nothing.

"I'm sorry," Jeremy said after a few moments of listening to the silence. "I just thought I oughta tell you."

Tanya mumbled something.

"What? I didn't hear that."

"Who was she?"

"I don't know her name. She's that girl who's been playing banjo on the boardwalk. Maybe you've seen her. She's sort of skinny. Real short blond hair like a guy's. She's eighteen or twenty, I guess. She plays for money. People toss it into her banjo case. She's here right now, over by the Hurricane."

"I've seen her around."

"Well, Nate was in a motel room with her. I don't know if they spent the night, but he came out at around ten this morning. I just happened to be walking by when I saw him. He didn't see me, though. So anyway, I waited around in a restaurant for about an hour and kept my eye on the room to find out who he'd been with. I mean, after last night, I didn't think it was you, you know? And it was that girl who plays the banjo. She finally came out and I followed her over here to Funland. So anyway, maybe she's why he . . . you know, acted weird and split last night."

"Had her stashed in a motel."

"Yeah."

"The dirty prick."

"He sure is," Jeremy said. "Man, he must be crazy, dumping you for a goddamn troll. She's not even close to being as pretty as you. Nobody is."

"Thanks. You're a good guy."

His heart seemed to swell. In spite of his raging headache, he felt a glow of pride and hope. "I just thought you oughta know about it. I mean, after last night . . . we're lovers in blood."

"That's right. And you did the right thing, telling me about this. I owe you." She went silent again.

She owes me. Does this mean I proved myself? Yeah. Probably. God!

"Is Cowboy with you?" she asked.

"Not right now. I got away from him to call you."

"Does he know about any of this?"

"No. I kept it quiet. I didn't tell anyone. I figured nobody oughta know except you. I mean, it's sort of a personal thing, and . . ."

"That's good. Don't tell anyone. This is our secret, just you and me. You said she's still there on the boardwalk?"

"Yeah. Singing a bunch of stupid songs."

"Okay. Will you do me a favor?"

"Sure. Anything."

"Keep an eye on her. Follow her if you can. I want to know where we can get our hands on her tonight."

"I don't have a car."

"That's okay. Just do the best you can. And give me a call when you find out something."

"I will."

"Good. Good man. We'll get together later. Just you and me."

Thirty-four

It was a very long afternoon. Robin tried to lose herself in the music, and often went for several minutes without thinking of Nate. The tunes with lyrics were the best for that; she had to focus on the words. But between numbers and when she played those that didn't require singing, her mind lingered on him.

She felt comfortable and full and glowing. And excited and a little nervous when she wondered what would happen next.

There's no reason to worry, she told herself again and again. The Big Thing was already taken care of. It wouldn't be hanging over their heads, making them nervous and awkward. They'd be free to enjoy themselves . . .

If five o'clock ever arrives.

Sometimes she ached to be with him. When the ache got very bad, she took breaks and went into the arcade, and just the sight of Nate was enough to soothe the longing. They talked and she followed him around, enjoying his friendly manner with the customers. Most of the kids treated him like an old pal. He passed out coins, showed newcomers the basics of some of the games, and insisted that Robin play Space Invaders and Jet Assault and Super Mario Brothers. But she never stayed long, for she didn't want him to think she was taking advantage of the situation.

The best time had been their lunch break. They picked up pizza slices and Pepsis at one of the stands, and ate in the back room. "My home away from home," he'd called it, and Robin had commented that it looked more like a sporting-goods store. A desk cluttered with paperwork stood in the center of the small room, but in the corners were volleyballs, running shoes, and a Frisbee. Several swimsuits, towels, a face mask and snorkel, a sweatshirt, and a wet suit hung from hooks. Propped against one wall was a surfboard.

"Will you teach me to surf sometime?" she'd asked.

For just a moment his eyes looked bleak. Robin wondered if he'd had a bad experience surfing. Maybe a friend had drowned or something. But the look passed quickly. He nodded while he chewed his pizza. "Sure thing. I'll turn you into a California girl."

"Like, rad, man."

And when they finished eating, he leaned back against the door to prevent anyone from barging in. Robin leaned against him. They held each other and kissed for a long time.

She wished she were in his arms right now.

It must be almost five, she thought as she played her Beach Boys medley. The last time she'd asked someone the time, it had been four-thirty-five. That *seemed* like an hour ago.

Time may fly when you're having a good time, but it creeps when you're waiting.

She segued from "Surfin' USA" into "California Girls." And smiled at the reaction. Whenever she went into that one, her audience went wild, cheering and clapping. It had been that way since her arrival at Funland. She picked and strummed, thumb plucking the drone string, and saw Nate behind a couple of teenage girls who were mouthing the words, waving their arms, and gyrating.

She finished to cheers and applause. People wandered in from the crowd in front of her, from the Ferris-wheel line behind her, tossing money into her banjo case at her feet, several stopping for a moment to offer compliments. She thanked them all, then announced, "That's it for now, folks." She heard some moans and protests. Then came more applause, and more people stepped forward with kind words and money.

"You were a hit," Nate said.

"Went pretty well," she admitted, crouching down to gather

the money. "Didn't think five o'clock would ever get here, though."

"Yeah. Same here."

She passed coins and bills to Nate, then latched her banjo inside the case. They walked to the arcade. In the back room, they counted the money. It came to $48.50. "Not a bad haul," Nate said. They split it sixty-forty. He gave Robin her portion, then handed her a check.

"What's this?"

"A week's advance on your wages."

"You don't have to do that."

"If you don't want it . . ."

"Well, I didn't say that, exactly."

He laughed and kissed her. "Ready to go?"

"I've been ready for a while. Like maybe just aeons."

Nate held her backpack while she slipped her arms into the straps. He carried her banjo case, and they walked through the noisy arcade.

Jeremy whirled around, grabbed the railing, and stared out at the beach the instant they stepped out of the arcade. He waited a few seconds, then looked around. He couldn't spot them at first, and felt a quick flicker of panic. Then a group of bikers strutted out of the way. He saw Nate and the girl walking along the far side of the crowded boardwalk. Their backs were toward him.

He followed, picking up his pace and closing the gap, afraid he might lose them.

If he lost them after all this . . .

He couldn't believe how long he'd been forced to wait. Hours and hours. After the call to Tanya, he'd returned to the girl's audience. Cowboy should've been there, but wasn't. Maybe he'd gone off looking for Jeremy. But time passed, and he didn't return. Jeremy felt a little miffed at him. What kind of friend goes off and deserts you? He was relieved, though. Keeping an eye on the girl would've been difficult if Cowboy had kept hanging around.

Once he realized that Cowboy wasn't likely to come back, he got away from the girl's audience. As long as he could hear her, he was doing his job. He spent some time sitting on a bench and watching the people go by. He visited nearby game booths and watched people try to win prizes: tossing basketballs at hoops that looked too small for the balls; hammering little contraptions to send rubber frogs flopping head over heels toward a pool where you won if they happened to land on one of the circling lily pads; shooting squirtguns into the open mouths of plastic clown faces in hopes of being the first to fill and explode the balloons on their hats.

Occasionally he wandered over to the food stands. He bought drinks and swallowed aspirin. He ate nacho chips smothered with melted cheese. Later, an ice-cream sandwich. Later still, a corndog on a stick.

About once an hour the girl took a break. Each time, she packed up her banjo and headed straight for the arcade. She hung around with Nate, sometimes played games, then returned to the boardwalk, but not to the same place. She seemed to have three different locations: in front of the arcade, near the line for the Hurricane, and at the Ferris wheel.

She was playing for the Ferris-wheel crowd when Nate showed up. Jeremy watched her from a distance, and thought: This is it. Somehow, he knew that this was not just another break. Maybe because Nate had come to her. Maybe it was the fact that she handed the money to him. Or it might've been a subtle change in the girl—an eagerness about the way she gathered up the money and packed her banjo and walked away with him.

He followed them to the arcade. Entering, he saw them disappear into a back room. Then he took his position at the far side of the boardwalk, near the railing, and waited.

They came out less than ten minutes later, Nate carrying the banjo case, the girl wearing her backpack.

This *is* it, he thought.

Just don't lose them now, he told himself, hurrying to narrow their lead.

He followed them past the main ticket booth. From the top of the stairs he watched them step off the sidewalk, cross the road, and angle across the parking lot. He watched them climb into Nate's red sports car. The car drove slowly out of the lot and headed east.

Jeremy rushed to the pay phone. He dialed Tanya's number. The phone at her end rang only once. "Hello?"

"Tanya, it's me. Jeremy."

"I've been waiting. What's going on?"

"They just left. In Nate's car. A red sports car?"

"The bitch was with him?"

"Yeah. I don't know where they're going, but—"

"I think I know. I'll make sure, though. You did really good, Duke. Really good. Are you going to be home later?"

"Yeah, sure, I think so."

"I'll call you around nine. We'll get together tonight. Just you and me. Before the trolling."

"Okay. Great!"

Tanya hung up.

Jeremy hung up. He stared at the phone. His mouth felt as dry as paper; his heart drummed and he panted for breath.

I did it, he thought. Oh, man, oh, man! *Just you and me.*

Even before they started up the narrow road into the hills, the houses looked big and expensive. Robin knew that higher up— where Nate was taking her—the homes must be fabulous. She didn't find the notion comforting.

Her family hadn't been poor. With both her parents working, they'd gotten by just fine. Then there had been the life-insurance money. But they'd never been rich. Not even close to rich.

"Something the matter?" Nate asked.

"I'm feeling . . . a little bit out of my league."

"I don't get it."

"You live up here in a huge house. You drive a car that must've cost more than my Dad made in a whole year."

"What's that got to do with anything?"

Robin shrugged. "I don't know. Shouldn't you be going with a debutante or something?"

He laughed. "Well, you'll do until a deb comes along."

"What happens if your parents find out about you and me?"

"What do you mean, if?"

"What do *you* mean?"

"They'll find out Wednesday," he said. "No if. I'll introduce you."

"Great. They should be delighted to find out you've taken up with a street musician."

"We'll tell them you're a debutante."

"Right."

"You'll knock them dead, Robin."

"Yeah. I'm sure I will. Cardiac arrest. Their son and the bum."

"You're not a bum. You're an employee. And you weren't a bum before you were an employee. You're an artist, a poet, a musician. They'll love you."

"That I doubt."

Nate swung the car to the side of the road and stopped it. The road was deserted, shadowed by overhanging trees. Ahead on the left was a mailbox and the grated entrance of a driveway, but no homes were in sight.

He switched off the engine and set the emergency brake. He turned to Robin. Reaching out, he curled a hand behind her neck. His hand rubbed her gently while he stared into her eyes. "Just because my family has money," he said, "it doesn't mean we're bad people."

"I know that, but . . ."

"Nobody's going to dump on you. Especially not my parents. All they'll care about is whether you're a decent person, and you are. They'll love you. Same as I do. Well, not *exactly* the same."

"I should hope not."

"We won't announce that you've been staying over. That'd be pushing it. I mean, they're terrific, but they *are* my parents. They'd bounce off the ceilings if they found out about that. Even then, I'd be the one to catch hell and they'd figure you were my innocent victim."

"Yeah?" She smiled. "You know that from experience?"

"Oh, I've been caught a couple of times doing what I shouldn't."

"Caught with girls in the house?"

"Once or twice. None that ever stayed over, though. You'll
be the first. You're the first in a lot of ways."

"How?"

"You're my first banjo picker."

"Creep."

"You're the first I've ever fallen in love with."

Robin's throat tightened. "Really?"

"Really." He drew her toward him by the hand on her neck.
She turned on the seat and leaned closer. As they kissed, his
hand moved up the back of her head. She felt his fingers slide
into her hair. His other hand closed gently over her breast. She
moaned into his mouth.

"I love you so much," she whispered.

"Would you love me more if I were poor?"

"Probably."

"Now who's the creep?"

"I wish we'd met a long time ago," she said, and squirmed as
he rubbed her breast.

"Me too. God, I do wish that. It would've made . . . such a
difference."

"But I almost feel as if I've always known you. Does that
make sense?"

"No."

She laughed into his mouth, and kissed him again. "Yes, it
does," she said.

"If you say so. You're the breakfast expert."

"What does breakfast have to do with anything?"

"Makes sense to me."

"Are you making fun of me?" she asked.

"Yeah." He kissed the tip of her nose. As he stroked her hair,
his other hand slipped away from her breast. "Ready to go?"

"Let's went."

He started the car and steered it back onto the road. Shortly
after they rounded a bend, the road split into a Y. The lane
sloping down from the left had a stop sign. A white Triumph
was waiting there. The girl in its driver's seat was a blonde
wearing sunglasses. Nate glanced toward the car and suddenly
flinched as if he'd been poked in the back. He gunned the

engine, swung the wheel, and they sped up the road's right-hand branch.

"Uh-oh," Robin said.

Nate grimaced at her and shook his head. He checked the rearview mirror.

"Who was that, your girlfriend?"

"Former."

"Does she know that?"

"Yeah. We broke up. It's all over." He looked again at the rearview.

Robin twisted around and peered out the back window. The road behind them was empty. "It's over but it isn't, huh?"

"What do you mean?"

"If you're afraid she might come after us . . ."

"You never know with her. She does crazy things some-times."

"A jilted woman with tendencies toward craziness. Great. I should've ducked."

"Don't worry."

"Why not? You're worried."

Nate glanced at the rearview mirror again, then swept the car across the downhill lane and gunned it up a driveway. He downshifted. The engine thundered as the car climbed the steep slope. The narrow, curving driveway was bordered by trees that kept out all but spots and patches of sunlight. Robin couldn't see any house.

"Did you dump her because of me?" she asked.

"There were other things, but . . . yeah, I guess you entered into it."

"Does she know that?"

"She does now, I suppose."

"Wonderful."

They roared over the crest of the slope. Straight ahead, be-yond a lawn shadowed by several trees, stood a dark wood house that reminded Robin of ski lodges she'd seen during her travels. Not quite as huge as a ski lodge, but big, with steeply slanted roofs, a covered porch, and high balconies.

"Neat," she said. "Makes me want to yodel."

"Feel free."

"I don't want to ruin your ears for you."

The driveway turned, and they followed it alongside the lawn. Nate fumbled with a remote device clipped to the sun visor. Ahead of them, a garage door began to rise. It was one of three, and nearest to the adjoining house. The engine noise swelled as the car entered the garage. Then it sputtered to silence.

Nate pulled the key from the ignition and faced Robin. "Here we are," he said in a hushed voice. He managed a smile, but it looked awfully nervous.

Robin realized she was suddenly trembling. Her heart was thumping hard, and her chest felt tight.

"Guess we might as well go in," Nate said.

"Guess so." She climbed out. Her legs felt weak and shaky. She closed her door and stared over the roof of the car. Nate gave her that nervous smile again, then ducked out of sight to retrieve her banjo and pack. Robin stepped around the rear of the car. "Do you feel right about this?" she asked.

"You mean coming here?" He backed away from the door with his hands full, and kneed it shut. "I'm a little jittery, I guess."

"About your girlfriend seeing us?"

"Former girlfriend. And no, it isn't really that." He set down the banjo case and pushed a button on the wall. As the garage door rumbled shut, he unlocked and opened a door into the house.

Robin picked up the banjo. She followed him inside, and saw that they had entered a large kitchen. He shut the door and set her pack on the red tile floor. She put her banjo down beside it.

She slipped her arms around him. Head back, she gazed into his eyes.

"You're trembling," he said.

"You too. So what have you got to be so jittery about?"

"It's just being here with you, I guess."

"Afraid we'll get caught?"

"No. It's you."

"I make you nervous?" Robin asked.

"Yeah."

"Good. You make me nervous too. That doesn't make sense, does it? I mean, after the motel . . ."

"Maybe we're both afraid of blowing it."

"I think you may be right."

"I care so much about you, Robin. It's like . . . there's so much at stake. If I screw up, somehow, and lose you . . ."

"I love you. If you screw up, I'll still love you. Unless you burn the steaks."

Thirty-five

"What do you think?" Joan asked.

Debbie, sitting at the kitchen table, looked up from half-eaten pizza that Joan had brought home for her supper. She stopped chewing. Her eyes widened.

Joan stepped closer, paused, and turned, posing like a model walking the ramp at a fashion show.

She'd spent the past half-hour in her bedroom preparing the attire: dingy sneakers with holes in the toes that she kept only for working in the garden, faded baggy blue sweatpants, a loose gray sweatshirt, and an old green stocking cap that she'd last worn a year ago when she went deep-sea fishing on a charter boat.

Even before checking herself in the bedroom mirror, she'd known the clothes didn't look scruffy enough. The mirror confirmed it. So she used scissors to start a hole just above the left knee of her sweatpants, dug her fingers into the hole and stretched it wide, ripping the fabric until it gaped like a slack mouth. She made a similar tear in the sweatshirt a few inches below her right breast. Then she touched up the outfit with brown shoe polish, lightly brushing the polish here and there, creating a nice illusion of mottled filth. For no good reason other than that she liked the idea, she knotted a red bandanna around her right knee. Finally she wrapped herself in the tattered brown blanket that used to go along on family outings when she was a kid. She swept a side of it over her head, held it there like a hood, and once again inspected herself in the mirror. Her face was all wrong—too clean and smooth, the eyes too sharp. No wens or whiskers, she thought, and made a grim smile. But the costume itself looked just fine, so she went into the kitchen to show Debbie.

"What's going on?" Debbie asked, her voice muffled by pizza. "Somebody having a masquerade party?"

"Am I fetching?"

"Fetching barf. You look like a *troll*."

"Thank you."

"You're not seriously going *out* looking like that?"

"Don't you think Dave will find me alluring?"

"Gimme a break. What're you doing?"

"Going trolling." She draped the blanket over the back of a kitchen chair, plucked off the stocking cap, and went to the cupboard where she kept her liquor. "I'll be playing the role of bait."

"Are you nuts? What do you mean?" Debbie sounded upset.

Joan crouched and opened the cupboard door. She took out a bottle of bourbon. "It's all right," she said. "Dave will be with me. We'll be heading over to the boardwalk after Funland closes."

"Why?"

"We're going to bust some trollers. We hope." She unscrewed the bottle cap, poured bourbon into her cupped hand, and splashed it onto the front of her sweatshirt. Adding more, she said, "Do you know who Gloria Weston is?"

"No."

"She wrote for the *Standard*. She did that piece on the trollers a few days ago." Joan took a sip of the bourbon, then capped the bottle, put it away, and stood up. "Gloria went undercover as a troll last night to get herself a scoop, and she disappeared."

"Oh, Christ." Debbie looked shocked and sick, as if she'd just spotted half a worm on the pizza slice poised near her mouth.

"We think the trollers got her."

"So you're going out to . . ."

"To see if they'll try for me."

"Joany, you can't!"

Joany. Debbie hadn't called her that in years.

"Hey, it'll be all right." Joan went to her. She stroked the back of Debbie's head. The girl gazed up at her, face red and anguished. "Nothing will happen to me, honey. I promise."

"Sure, you promise. I bet Mom didn't think anything would happen to her either."

Joan sighed. She shouldn't have told Debbie of her plans.

"Dave will be there. If we can't take care of a handful of teenage hoodlums—"

"What about the *trolls?*" she blurted. "What if it wasn't the kids that did something to that reporter? What if it was the trolls, and they come after you? That place is *crawling* with them. What if they get you and . . . ?"

"First, I don't think trolls are the problem."

"They got Mom!"

"You just think they did. We don't *know* what happened to Mom. We'll probably never know. But no trolls are going to get their hands on me. I wouldn't let one get close enough."

"Yeah, sure."

"Dave and I will both be armed. I don't care who—kids, trolls—nobody gets funny with a gun in his face."

"What if you don't have enough bullets?"

"You worry too much." She mussed Debbie's hair. "Hey, we run out of ammo, it's choppy-socky time. I'm deadly weapons from head to toe."

"It's not funny."

Debbie began to cry.

Joan crouched down and caressed her sister's cheek. "Hey, come on, no tears."

"You're all I have."

"I'll be very careful. I can't promise nothing will go wrong. Hell, an airplane could crash into the house right now and wipe us both out. You can't control everything. You just be as careful as you can, but you do what has to be done. I have to go out there tonight."

"Why?"

"It's my fault that Gloria Weston disappeared. She was Dave's girlfriend. She played dress-up and got nailed because of us, because she was upset and wasn't thinking straight."

Debbie sniffed and blinked. "Because Dave dumped her?"

"That's right. So we owe her. Do you understand?"

"No. If she did something dumb, it's her problem."

"It's our problem too. Now, I'd better go take my bath and get ready, or I'll be late to Dave's."

"How would you like it if *I* went to Funland in the middle of the night?"

"I wouldn't, honey. Of course not. And I don't expect you to like it that I'm going. But I'm not in the habit of keeping secrets from you. You wouldn't want that, would you?"

"No, I guess not."

"You just have to be brave about this kind of thing. My job gets dangerous sometimes, but I'm a pretty dangerous gal myself." Smiling, she ruffled Debbie's hair. "You'd better finish your pizza before it gets cold." She stood up, took her cap and blanket off the chair, and headed for her room.

From the living-room window, Dave saw Joan's car stop at the curb. He hurried to the front door and opened it. Joan came up the walkway, a grocery bag in her arms. The last time she'd come to his house, she had also been carrying a grocery bag. Champagne in that bag. He guessed, however, that this one held her troll costume.

He wished it didn't.

The stuffed bag was a sharp reminder of what lay ahead.

Always something bad ahead of us, he thought. Won't we ever get a chance to be together without a sword hanging over our heads?

We've got hours before we have to go, he told himself. Just try not to think about later on. It doesn't have to ruin things.

Coming up the walkway, she saw him and smiled.

What if this is it? What if this is our last time with each other?

The thought shook him. He told himself it was ridiculous, but realized he was taking a mental picture of her. To store this moment in his memory.

She looked wonderful. Her hair was golden and glossy in the evening sunlight, and blowing slightly. She wore her short white dress—the one she'd worn Thursday when she came with her "medication" to perk him up. The sleeves were rolled up her forearms. Her bare legs looked tawny and sleek and strong.

"How's my guy?" she asked, climbing the front stoop.

"Okay, I guess."

"You don't sound very sure."

He stepped backward through the doorway. She entered, and he shut the door. She set the bag down. She put her arms around him. They kissed.

Dave held her tightly. He felt her warmth and her strength and her softness. The pressure made his chest wound sting, but he didn't ease his hold.

I won't lose her, he told himself. No way.

She patted his rump and took her mouth away, and he felt the smoothness of her cheek against the side of his face. Her hair smelled clean and fresh. "Are you all right?" she asked.

"Yeah." He relaxed his arms and held her gently. "I'm just not overjoyed about our little mission."

"That's not for a long time."

"That's what I keep telling myself."

"Five hours. Five whole hours."

"And maybe there'll be a call from the governor."

"You *are* in bad shape." She looked him in the eye. "Did you get the vests?"

"Yeah."

"Then we're protected. Barring, of course, the fulfillment of the 'cursa squirmy death.'"

"Very funny."

"Very hungry."

"Is that a hint?"

"I had to watch Debbie eat pizza. You got any pizza? Huh? Do ya, do ya?"

"How about shish kebabs?"

"Even better."

"And beer," he said.

"I like beer."

"Does it make you a jolly good fella?"

"If it makes me a fella," she said, "we're both in for a big let-down."

Her mouth went to his again. As they kissed, her hands slid up and down his sides. He caressed her back, curled his hands over the firm mounds of her buttocks, slipped her dress a little higher. Her panties felt skimpy and silken. He smoothed the fabric against her rump, then moved his hands above the thin elastic band and stroked the sleek bare curves of her lower back, her sides.

Her stomach growled. She laughed softly into his mouth.

"Is that another hint?" he whispered.

"Are you barbecuing the shish kebabs?"

"Uh-huh."

"Is the fire going yet?"

"Not yet."

She kissed him briefly. "You'd better start that one too."

Joan eased away from him. Looking into his eyes, she rubbed her wet lips with the back of a hand. She straightened her dress. "We can probably get back to this other thing later," she said. "Do you think you can remember your place?"

"I don't know."

"I'll remind you. I've got a memory like an elephant."

"And an appetite to match."

They went into the kitchen. Dave took cans of beer from the refrigerator, popped them open, and gave one to Joan. She followed him outside through the sliding glass door. She sat on a padded lounge and sipped her beer while he dumped charcoal briquettes into the grill, piled them neatly with tongs, squirted fuel over them, and lit the fire.

"It'll be a while," he said.

"Do you need help with anything?"

"Nope. We just have to wait for the fire. Would you like something to nibble on?"

She shook her head. "I've got to start watching my figure."

"Something wrong with it?" he asked, turning a lawn chair toward her and sitting down.

"So far, so good," she said. "But you know how it goes. We start letting ourselves go to pot the minute we hook the right guy."

He felt a glow spread through him. "I'm the right guy?"

"Oh, I think there's a good chance of it."

"And you've hooked me?"

"Oh, I think so." She gave him a smug smile. There was a glimmer of mischief in her eyes. "What do you think?"

"Good chance of it."

"Then again," she said, "maybe I'm the one who's hooked. You're reeling me in." She flipped her sandals off. They dropped to the concrete patio. She slid her bare feet up the cushion and rested the beer can atop her raised right knee. "Stupid analogy, huh? Makes us sound like a couple of bass."

"Hope you don't turn out to be the big one that got away," Dave said.

"Consider me landed."

"So now what, I beat you on the head with a club? Clean you and throw you on the skillet?"

"Hell, no. I'm a trophy. You mount me."

"I like that idea."

"Me too."

She lifted her beer, shutting her eyes as sunlight caught the top of the can. The reflection lit her face briefly with a bright disk. Dave watched her throat move as she swallowed. She set the can on a tray beside the lounge. She stretched, and her raising arms drew the front of her dress upward, molding it against the undersides of her breasts. She folded her hands behind her head and straightened out her legs.

"This is very nice," she murmured.

"What is?"

"Just lying here. The sunlight, the beer, the smell of the fire. You. And knowing that nobody will barge in and ruin things."

"We've had a run of bad luck that way."

"I'm glad you had a chance to meet Debbie, though."

"She's a beautiful young lady."

"She likes you."

"We barely met."

"She's a quick study. And supercritical about the guys I go with. You seem to be the first to pass inspection."

"Good taste on her part."

"She's got a keen eye for losers. Not me. I'm more like our mother. She always fell for weak guys with sad eyes. She must've been a basset hound in a previous life." Joan opened her eyes and frowned at Dave. "I guess it's an overdeveloped mothering instinct. It can screw you up, get you involved with guys who are . . . I don't know, more like children than men. That's no

good, and I know it. I saw what it did to my mother. She wanted
a knight in shining armor, but when it came right down to it,
she always wound up with a lackey. I don't want that happening to me. But it *was* happening to me. Time after time. It
seems like I'm always getting attracted to guys who can't stand
on their own two feet. In my previous life, I guess I was a
crutch."

"I wouldn't mind leaning on you," Dave said. He meant it.
From the look in Joan's eyes, he could see that she knew he
meant it.

"Anytime," she said. "Shining armor, that's heavy stuff."

"So you think I'm a knight, do you?"

She smiled. "Close enough."

"Are you a damsel in distress?"

"Frequently."

"You're pretty tough for a damsel."

"I'm not so tough," she said, and a soft, pleading look filled
her eyes. It was the look he'd seen when she spoke of destroy-
ing Woodrow Abernathy with a kick. It was the look of a little
girl who needed to be hugged and assured that everything
would be all right.

Dave rose from his chair. He straddled the lounge, and Joan
scooted toward him, wrapped her legs around him, pressed
herself against him. "It's all right to be tough," he whispered,
brushing her lips with his mouth. "I like you when you're tough.
But I like you when you're not, too. I like everything about you.
Almost everything."

She drew her head back. The vulnerable look was gone from
her eyes. Their mischief was back. "Uh-oh. You mean I'm not
perfect?"

"Well, there's one little thing . . ."

"I know, I'm taller than you. I'll always wear flats. I'll buy
you lift shoes."

"Don't bother. I like it that you're tall. Your body is perfect
just the way it is. Every inch of you."

"You haven't seen every inch."

"I will."

"That all depends. What's wrong with me?"

"You won't get mad, will you?"

"I might get even." He saw a shadow of worry in her eyes. "What is it, Dave?"

"I wouldn't want you to be a coward. But . . . sometimes . . . like the way you went climbing up the damn Hurricane to help the guy they put up there. Like the way you went rushing off ahead of me to break up the fight. Like the way you're so determined to go out on the boardwalk tonight. I don't want to lose you. I don't want to ever lose you."

"You're saying I got more guts than brains?"

"I don't want to knock your brains. But less guts might be an improvement."

"That's sweet," she said.

"I couldn't stand it if something happened to you. I love you."

"You love me?" she asked.

"Yeah."

"I love you too."

"Heroes don't last long, Joan. And I want you to last. I want you to be with me till we're old and doddering."

"So we can lean on each other," she whispered.

"Right."

"I'd like that."

Thirty-six

When the telephone rang, Jeremy leapt from the sofa, saying, "I'll get it."

His mother looked up from her book only long enough to nod, then resumed reading.

He knew it was early for Tanya's call. Without even looking at his wristwatch, he knew. He'd been horribly aware of the slow passage of time all afternoon, all evening. The minutes had crept by while he waited on the boardwalk for the banjo girl to join Nate. After his second call to Tanya and her promise to phone him at nine—and *meet* him later . . . *just you and me*—time had crawled at an even slower pace.

The call was half an hour early.

But it saved him an endless half-hour of agony.

He snatched up the handset of the wall phone in the kitchen. Though he was sure that his mother could hear nothing over the sounds of the television in the living room, he spoke softly. "Hi. Tanya?"

"Terrific."

It wasn't Tanya's voice.

"Shiner?"

"Sorry to disappoint you."

"No, that's okay." His face felt burning. "It's just . . . Tanya said she'd phone me about tonight. You know, the trolling."

Shiner was silent for a few moments. "Is it on for tonight?"

"Well, I don't know. That's what she'll be calling about."

"I suppose you're planning to go."

"I haven't decided yet." He realized that it hurt somewhere deep inside, lying to her.

"Really?"

"What about you?" he asked.

"No way. I told you, I'm done with it. And I think you should quit too."

"I've thought about it."

"It's going to hit the fan. It really is. Nate was right to quit when he did. I think we all should, but nobody's going to listen to me. Except you, maybe. Do you still care about me, Jeremy?"

"Sure. Of course I do."

"Honest?"

"Yeah."

And that, he knew, was not a lie.

"What about Tanya?" she asked. He heard the pain in her voice.

"There's nothing going on."

"I saw her kiss you."

"Well, she was drunk. So was I. It didn't mean anything. She was kissing *everybody* last night after you left. I guess she was just grateful that we hadn't quit on her, like Nate."

"Don't tell me you didn't like it."

"I wish it had been you."

More silence. Then she said, "I'm sure."

"I mean it. She's not . . . my type. You know? She's weird."

"I could've told you that."

"I wanted to be with *you* after the party."

"I wanted to be with you too. Until you kissed her."

"She kissed *me*. It wasn't my fault."

"It really hurt. It hurt a lot. I mean, I know she's gorgeous and she's got every guy in the world drooling over her—not to mention Karen, for Godsake. But I thought . . . I thought you and I had something going, you know?"

"We did. We do. I really like you. When I figured out you'd left the party, it really messed me up. I left right away, myself. It took all the fun out. I couldn't stay without you there. I felt so out of place. And, like, lonely all of a sudden."

"I'm sorry," she murmured.

"No, I'm the one who's sorry. I messed up so bad."

"How did you get home?"

"I walked."

"Oh, no. You walked? That's miles. I figured somebody'd give you a lift."

"After you left, I didn't want anything to do with the rest of them."

"It must've taken you all night."

"Just a couple of hours."

"God, I'm so sorry. I knew I shouldn't have gone off that way. I felt rotten about it. But I had to, you know? I was awfully upset."

"Can we see each other again sometime?"

"Why do you think I called you, doufuss?"

He could almost see her smile when she said that. Her beaming Shiner smile.

"My mom's out on a date," she said. "I'm all alone here. She won't be back for hours. I thought maybe you'd like to come over."

"That'd be great!"

Tanya.

Tanya would be calling soon.

He'd forgotten. He couldn't believe that he'd forgotten. The promise of her call, of their later meeting, had been his sole focus, his obsession, all evening.

"Great," Shiner said. "I'll give you the address. Do you have a pencil and—?"

"Wait. I can't. I can't come over. It'd be great, but my mom's here and there's no way I can sneak out."

"You don't have to sneak out. Just tell her you're going for a bike ride or something. It's not all that late. I'd really like to see you."

Jeremy sighed.

She's alone, he thought. Jeez. We could do stuff, make out. She *wants* to make out, or she wouldn't be asking me over with her mother gone. She wouldn't risk it. She must really want me bad.

But Tanya.

"I just can't," he said. "Mom won't let me out of the house. She grounded me because of last night. I got in late, and also she knew I'd been drinking. I really caught it. So she isn't about to let me leave."

"You won't come over here, but you'll go trolling."

"Mom'll be asleep by then. Besides, I only said I *might* go trolling, I didn't say I would."

"Did they go out last night after the party?" Shiner asked.

"I don't think so. I went right home. Why?"

"Nothing," she muttered. She was silent for a moment. "Look, if you can sneak out later for the trolling, you could come here instead. I'm sure my mom's going to be gone most of the night. We'd have lots of time together. How about it?"

Shit! He could miss the trolling. He wouldn't mind that. But the meeting with Tanya beforehand . . .

How do I get out of this? he wondered.

"Think up a good one," Shiner said.

"Hey, come on."

"If you'd rather be with Tanya, why don't you just admit it?"

"It isn't that."

"No. I'm sure."

"I'll look like a chicken if I don't show up."

"I'm not going to beg, Jeremy. It's your choice. Who is it going to be, me or Tanya?"

"That's not fair!"

"Okay. Well, I guess that pretty much answers it. Good-bye."

"Shiner!"

She hung up.

"Shit!" Jeremy jammed the phone down. He hurried into the bathroom, locked the door, and leaned against it. Baring his teeth, he pounded his fists against his legs. He slid down the door until the floor stopped him. He hugged his knees.

The bitch! he thought. Damn her! It's not fair!

Fuck her anyway, she wants to be like that.

He clamped his teeth on his knees and bit hard enough to feel pain. The taste of his corduroy trouser leg was dry in his mouth.

I could've gone to her house, he thought.

He pictured himself on a sofa with Shiner in a dimly lighted room. He could feel her in his arms, feel her mouth against his. She was all soft and smooth, and she smelled of suntan oil.

His teeth loosened their grip. He closed his mouth and pressed his lips against the moist corduroy.

It would've been so wonderful.

So right.

It's not too late, he thought. If I call her back . . .

Then I'd miss out on Tanya.

He saw himself in Tanya's room last night, saw her standing before him naked and glossy, felt her skin under the slick layer of blood. Heat spread through the pit of his stomach. He felt the stirrings of arousal. He began to tremble, aching for her but afraid of her.

She's *bad*, he thought. She's probably crazy. I shouldn't want her. I should stay away from her. What's wrong with me? God!

So call Shiner. How? I don't know her phone number. Not even her real name.

Jeremy heard footsteps in the hallway. Then came a knocking on the door.

"Honey? There's a call for you."

His heart lurched.

He crawled away from the door before answering, "I'll be right out."

He scurried the rest of the way to the toilet, flushed it, then got to his feet and hurried back to the door. He opened it. His mother looked at him, frowning slightly. "Is everything all right?"

"Yeah. Fine. Who's on the phone. Shiner?"

"She didn't say."

"Must be. She told me she'd call back."

As he hurried away, his mother said, "Now, don't make any plans without checking with me first. You're still in trouble around here, young man."

"Yeah, I know." Before entering the kitchen, he glanced back and saw her step into the living room. He picked up the phone.

Let it be Shiner, he thought. Please.

"Hello?"

"It's me."

Tanya.

He felt a quick pull of disappointment and loss. Then heat rushed into the empty place. His heart quickened. "Just a second," he said.

"Have you got it?" His mother's voice on the extension.

"Yeah. Thanks."

She hung up.

"Okay," he said. "She's off."

"Can you get away later?" Tanya asked. "Around midnight?"

"Midnight?"

"It'll be just you and me. We'll meet the others later."

He felt as if his breath had been sucked out. He managed to say, "Yeah."

"We'll take my car. I'll park across the street from your house."

"Okay."

"Are you all right? You sound funny."

"Just excited," he said.

"So am I. I can hardly wait. Midnight."

"Yeah."

"See you then, Duke."

"See you." He hung up the phone, turned around, and stared at the wall clock. Ten till nine. Three hours and ten minutes to go. Forever.

Not forever.

Midnight would get here. He knew that. And somehow he suspected that it might arrive too soon.

He was hot and sweaty, but shivering anyway. He clenched his teeth to hold his jaw still. He wrapped his arms tightly around his chest.

Felt like his *lungs* were shaking.

I'll take a shower, he thought. A hot shower. It'll make the shivers stop. And it'll help pass the time. Besides, I want to be clean for her.

He walked unsteadily toward the bathroom, images twisting through his mind of Tanya's scar, her bare breasts, Shiner's smile, the razor blade sliding on Tanya's flesh, the comfortable, exciting feel of Shiner's hand in his, the suck of Tanya's mouth taking the blood off his fingers. Spreading suntan oil on Shiner's back. Spreading blood up Tanya's belly and breast.

Thirty-seven

Robin sat cross-legged on the sofa, a folded towel beneath her to protect the upholstery from the dampness of her bikini pants. She played her banjo and sang for Nate.

He sat on the floor in front of her, a dreamy faraway look on his face as he gazed at her. His hair was mussed from the swimming. It shimmered golden in the light from the fireplace at his back. The fluttering light burnished his bare shoulders and thighs. The wine in the glass that rested on his knee gleamed like a ruby. He didn't sip the wine while she sang.

Ending a piece, Robin said, "It's getting a little warm in here."

"I could turn the fireplace off."

"No, don't. It's lovely."

"It makes you glow," he said.

She drew a forearm across her wet face and looked down at herself. Her chest gleamed in the ruddy firelight as if it were slicked with oil. Her bikini top was no longer damp from the pool, but its edges were darkened with moisture. "That's sweat," she proclaimed.

"Your sweat's beautiful."

Beads of it dribbled down her sides. She lowered her arms and smeared them to stop the tickling. "Beautiful or not," she said, "I'm gonna warp my banjo." She lifted it away from her belly, slipped the strap off her head, and used a loose corner of her towel to dry its back. She laid the banjo on the sofa beside her.

"That's all?" Nate asked.

"I don't want to bore you."

"I could listen to you forever."

"Maybe I'll write a song just for you."

"I'd like that. What would it say?"

"Oh, I don't know." She reached to the table, picked up her wineglass, and took a sip. "A lot of stuff rhymes with 'Nate.' 'Great,' 'first-rate' . . . 'fate.'"

"'Mate,'" he added.

"Yeah. 'Mate.' that's a loaded one, isn't it?"

"Says a lot."

"Nautical, too. Nautical's good on the banjo." She picked up the instrument again, played a few bars of "Blow the Man Down," and began to sing:

I've got a first-mate
And his name it is Nate.

   Yo-ho, I think he's just great!

He's sweet and he's sexy
From his toes to his pate—

   And oh how I love to mate with my Nate!

Laughing, he shook his head, set his wineglass on the carpet, and clapped. "Fantastic. What's a pate?"

"That's the top of your head."

He put a hand up there and ruffled his hair. "Sexy, huh? And my toes too?" He wiggled them.

"You making fun of my song?"

"I love your song."

"I know it's sort of silly," she said. "Most of my stuff is. The banjo's not meant for serious stuff. It's bright and plucky."

"Like you."

"Is that how you see me?" she asked.

"Only part of the time. I see you a lot of different ways. Serious, sad, innocent, full of hope, afraid . . . but brave too. You must be damned brave, going on the road the way you did."

"That was just plain desperation."

"I feel like there's so much I don't know about you, Robin. I want to know everything."

"I'm just a simple gal who likes the banjo, big breakfasts, and hot baths."

"Hot baths, huh?" Smiling, he finished his wine. "I bet you'd love the spa."

"Hey, that'd be terrific."

"It'll take a while for the water to heat up," he said, getting to his feet. "You want to wait here while I turn it on?"

"I could use some fresh air."

He picked up the wine bottle and watched as Robin stood, took her towel off the sofa, and mopped the sweat from her face and body. She draped the towel over her shoulders. Then she picked up her wineglass and followed him to the sliding door. His back was shiny in the firelight. The seat of his tight blue swimsuit gleamed. The fabric was dark in the center, dampened by sweat in a narrowing triangle between his buttocks.

She put a hand low on his back and rubbed the slippery wetness of his skin as he tugged the door.

He smiled over his shoulder at her.

"Yo-ho," she said.

Then the chilly air got her. "Yo-*yikes!*" she blurted, suddenly shuddering.

"Get in the pool quick! Save yourself!" He reached for the wineglass, and Robin gave it to him.

Hunched over and hugging herself, she abandoned Nate and trotted over the concrete toward the deep end of the pool. She tossed the towel behind her. She leapt, hit the water, and felt it rush up her body, cool but warmer than the night air. Her feet touched the bottom. She rose slowly to the surface and swam until she again found the pool's floor. Though it slanted down steeply behind her, it was just right. Standing on tiptoe, she was covered to her chin.

She saw Nate in the darkness near the fence, bending over a unit of boxy equipment and pipes, turning nobs.

"How can you stand it?" she called in a shaky voice.

"Willpower."

"Get your willpower into the pool before it freezes and breaks off."

He finished and walked slowly toward the pool's shallow end.

"What a he-man," Robin said.

He curled his arms up like a body builder showing off his biceps.

"Mr. Universe," Robin said.

"Want me to turn on the pool lights?" he asked.

"Yeah. All the better to see your magnificent body."

He wandered off again, and flicked a switch near the door. The patio remained dark, but the pool suddenly filled with light. He came back to the edge. Pale blue reflections shimmered on his skin as he crouched and dived. He darted out low over the water, knifed in with barely a splash, and glided straight and smooth to the far wall. There he stood and turned to Robin. He waded toward her, standing tall, though he must've been freezing from the chest up. Below the surface, his body wavered and rippled.

"You look like something in a funhouse mirror," Robin said. Her chin shook as she spoke.

"The kind that makes you ten feet tall?"

"The kind that make you wobbly."

The water rose around him. When it almost reached his shoulders, he was near enough. Robin drew herself against him.

"You're shivering," he said.

"How come you're not?"

"Man of iron. Are you nervous, or just cold?"

"Just freezing. I'm over being nervous. That was a life ago."

"We didn't blow it," he said.

"You didn't burn the steaks."

"Lucky me."

Where their bodies were pressed together, a warmth grew. The warmth spread through Robin, calming her tremors but not making them vanish entirely. Where she wasn't tight against Nate, the water rubbed her like an October breeze.

"We could've waited in the house," he said.

"I'm all right now. Sort of."

"Just think of all that hot water pumping into the spa."

"How long will it take?"

"It's probably a little warmer right now."

"Then what the hell are we doing in the pool?"

"Kissing."

"No we're not."

"Yes we are." He pressed his open mouth against Robin's. His wet lips were chilly at first. But his tongue was warm. His arms tightened their hold, and he began to step backward. Robin hugged him with her arms and thighs. She felt the water slipping over her, sliding down, baring her to the cold air.

Finally he turned and lifted her onto the tile wall of the spa. "Thanks for the ride," she said.

"I'll go turn the bubbles on."

He stepped away from Robin, breaking the warm bond. The cold stole her breath away, but only for a moment while she swiveled around. Then she sank into the mild, soothing water of the spa. It wasn't hot. It wasn't even warm. But it wasn't chilly either. It was wonderful. Sighing, she settled onto a smooth benchlike ledge, and the water covered her to the shoulders. She stretched out her legs, let them drift upward. Something that felt like a summer wind blew against the side of her left thigh. She put her hand there, moved it against the pressure, and found a hole low down in the wall—a hole that gushed hot water. She went to it and sat in front of it. The heat pushed against the small of her back and spread out against her. She moaned with pleasure.

Suddenly a rushing sound filled her ears. All the water in the spa began to froth and bubble. It seemed to throb, pulsing against her skin.

Nate came out of the darkness. He had the wineglasses, the bottle, and the towels. He set them near the edge of the spa, filled the glasses, then climbed down. He handed a glass to Robin. She took a drink. The wine was cool in her mouth, but once swallowed, it seemed to glow inside her, radiating warmth.

Nate sat across from her, only his head and glass-bearing hand above the surface. His body, reddish in the murky crimson light from the bottom of the spa, was visible but blurred through the roiling water. His face was smudged with shadows. Distorted and unfamiliar.

"You look like the bogeyman," she said.

"Thanks a bunch. You look kind of like an evil queen yourself."

She cackled. "Who's the fairest of them all, ducky?"

One of his feet stroked her skin. "The fairest is Robin. Cock Robin."

Cockless Robin.

Poppinsack.

"A bum called me that," she said. The water was very warm now. Cozy. Steam drifted off the churning surface, a pink mist that was shredded and scattered by the breeze. She drank more wine. "Cock Robin," she said. "He also called me Cockless Robin."

"Bastard," Nate muttered.

"He was a funny guy. I actually liked him at first. Poppinsack. He really had a way with words. He reminded me of those medicine-show guys you see in old cowboy movies. Hawking a cure-all from the back of a wagon. You should've seen him, all decked out in a buckskin jacket with fringe, feathers in his derby hat." Nate's foot dropped away from her shin. "A real character. I liked the guy, and then he robbed me."

"Robbed you?"

"Yeah. While I was sleeping on the beach. *Before* I even met him and he acted so friendly and gave me tea. All the time he was being nice to me, he knew what he'd done."

Nate shook his head slowly from side to side.

The theft had been buried inside Robin like a secret shame. Sharing it with Nate felt good and right. She needed to tell him the rest.

"My money? I kept it in my underwear." She expected a hot rush of embarrassment, but it didn't come. "I was asleep and he stole it out of my underwear. God knows what else he did . . . his hands in there. Then he goes and calls me 'Cockless Robin.'"

Nate muttered something that was lost in the gurgling sounds of the water.

"What?"

"Nothing."

"I wanted to kill the creep."

"I did."

"What?" Robin asked, certain that she hadn't heard him correctly.

"I killed him."

She gazed at Nate, stunned. She set her wineglass down and went to him. She knelt between his legs in the swirling hot water and put her hands on his thighs.

"An old guy with a walrus mustache," he said.

"Yeah."

"I killed him Thursday night."

"I don't believe it," Robin said. But she *did* believe it. Nate was too grim to be joking. "How?" she asked.

"You know about the trollers."

"You're a troller?"

"I was. Not anymore. After what happened to the old man, I lost my stomach for it. It was awful. And it was my fault. They couldn't have started the Ferris wheel without me. I had the key. We didn't know he'd fall, but . . ."

"How did it happen?"

"We cuffed him to the safety bar of one of the gondolas and took him up. The bar wouldn't hold him. He fell. He fell from the top, screaming. Then I took his body out on my surfboard. I took him way out, belted to it, and dumped him."

"God," she muttered.

"It was the night I met you."

She remembered waiting for Poppinsack that night. Waiting in the fog with her knife, then getting spooked and hurrying away to find safety under the house beyond the public beach. "I was going to take him," she said. "I was going to get my money back. I was waiting for him in the dunes."

"Well, we killed him."

"I might've, if he'd shown up. I had my knife out. I wanted to hurt him. I wanted to make him pay."

"At least . . . it helps some, knowing what he did to you.

Maybe he deserved it. Still makes me sick to think about it, though."

"I know," Robin murmured. "I'm sorry."

"So how do you like it? You've been making love with a murderer."

She gently rubbed his legs. Her throat was tight with sorrow for him. "It sounds like it was an accident."

"Well, it *was* an accident. He was too heavy for the safety bar. But we set it up, you know? He was up there because of us. Everybody wants to say it was an accident, but we did it to the guy. He was a troll, and we nailed him. Most of the others seemed pretty happy that he fell. I'm sure Tanya was overjoyed. She's been out for their blood ever since we got into this Billy Goat Gruff thing. And she's been getting a lot worse lately."

"The girl at the stop sign?" Robin asked.

"Yeah. She's been losing it, you know? I can't really blame her. Some trolls messed her up really bad—cut her up, raped her, all kinds of stuff. So, you know, it's not surprising that she hates trolls. I do too, for what they did to her. She used to be . . . innocent, happy. She was never mean to anyone."

"You loved her, didn't you?" Robin asked.

He hesitated. He put his hands on her shoulders. "I used to love Tanya. Before the trolls got her. They killed the part of Tanya that I loved."

"I'm sorry," Robin whispered.

"Now she's just full of hate. All she cares about is nailing trolls." He shook his head. "We got *so much* revenge for her. She's had a feast of it, but she keeps wanting more. Her appetite's been getting worse and worse. Now that she's actually killed one . . . I hate to think what they'll do to the next troll they catch. But at least I won't be part of it. I only wish I'd quit sooner. Before it came to killing. But I didn't. Now I'm a murderer." His hands moved up and gently caressed the sides of Robin's head. "I have to live with it," he said. "And I guess I had to tell you. Better to lose you now than later."

"You haven't lost me," she said.

"Weren't you listening? I'm—"

"I killed a man once."

"No." Nate's fingers tightened on the sides of her head.

"Yes. I think I did, anyway. I try to tell myself he might've lived. Every day, I try to tell myself that. But I don't really believe it. My knife's big, and I shoved it right into the middle of his chest. Maybe he didn't die. He probably did, though."

Groaning, Nate drew her forward. Robin climbed onto him and straddled his lap. He slipped his arms around her and held her tightly. "Aw, Jesus," he murmured close to her ear. "Robin, Robin."

"He attacked me," she said. Voice cracking, she added, "Doesn't make it any better, though."

"Aw . . . aw. God, I'm sorry. I'm so sorry."

"We're a hell of a pair, huh?"

His body began to shake against her. He was crying. Holding her tight and jerking with sobs, his breath hitching. Robin cried too.

Caressed by the hot throbbing water, they hugged one another and wept.

Thirty-eight

At eleven o'clock Jeremy's mother set her book aside and started to watch the television news.

"I guess I'll go on to bed," Jeremy said.

She looked surprised. "What about *Saturday Night Live?*"

"Not on," he reminded her. "And its summer replacement stinks. Besides, I'm really tired."

She arched her eyebrow. "I can't imagine why, getting home in the middle of the night."

"Yeah." He kissed her, told her good night, and went to his bedroom. With his door shut, he gathered the clothes he would wear later. He slipped his Swiss Army knife into a front pocket of his corduroy pants. From the bottom drawer of his desk he took Tanya's razor blade. *Keep this with you to remember,* she'd said. It was still wrapped in his handkerchief. The white cloth was smeared and blotched with dried brown blood.

He unwrapped the blade and looked at it. Memories of last night rushed in, seizing him with fear and desire.

Who needs the razor as a reminder? he thought. Who's going to forget *that?*

But Tanya had asked him to keep the razor with him.

He wound the handkerchief around the blade and tucked it into a pocket of his cords.

Then he rolled up his clothes and pushed the bundle under his bed. He tossed his robe over the back of a chair. He turned off the light and got into bed.

The glowing face of the clock on his nightstand showed eleven-fifteen. Half an hour before time to get dressed and sneak out.

The minutes crawled by.

His mind seethed with fevered images. Tanya and Shiner. Their faces, their bodies, their smells, their voices. Shiner and Tanya. And detours into memories of the troll falling from the Ferris wheel, Tanya straightening his broken legs, Jeremy earlier snapping the guy's finger to pay him back for striking Shiner. Detours into Jasper's Oddities, Cowboy shaking the jar of the fetus, the huge awful spider, the leathery remains of the mummy, Cowboy's wisecracks, the chase and the fight and jerking the shirt off the wild girl and feeling her breasts. A detour to Karen dancing at the party, sweaty in her transparent bra and panties. A detour to the dry, amused voice of the troll calling *Tha's a fack* from the darkness under the boardwalk. Every detour led him back, soon, to Tanya. To Shiner. The thoughts of Shiner hurt him with guilt and loss. The thoughts of Tanya strained him with hard desire. He wanted her, he ached for her. He felt dirty for choosing her instead of Shiner. And afraid.

The sound of footfalls in the hallway released Jeremy from the dark turmoil of his thoughts. He heard a door close, running water, the flush of the toilet, and finally his mother's footsteps passing his door as she went to her bedroom.

Eleven-thirty-five.

He waited for the minutes to pass, his mind occupied now with thoughts of sneaking out, but sometimes slipping into fearful wonder about what might happen in his rendezvous with Tanya.

At a quarter to twelve he rolled silently out of bed. He stuffed his pajamas and robe under the covers. Naked and shaking, he knelt beside the bed and reached beneath it for his clothes. He sat on the carpet and put them on.

Then he crept to his door. He eased it open. The hallway was dark, even in front of his mother's room. But he suspected she hadn't fallen asleep. Holding his breath, pulse pounding in his head, he trailed his fingertips along the wall to help guide him, and made his way forward, the rubber soles of his shoes silent on the floor.

At the front door he slipped the guard chain off its runner and lowered it gently. He turned the latch. The tongue of the dead bolt made a quiet thump. He turned the knob, swung the door slowly open, stepped onto the porch, and closed the door behind him.

Beyond the porch screens, the street was bright with lamp-light. A few cars were parked along the curbs. One of them might be Tanya's. He knew he was early, though. Maybe she hadn't arrived yet.

Maybe she wouldn't come.

The thought filled him with hope, ripped him with agony.

He shut the screen door carefully and stepped down the stairs.

If she doesn't come, he told himself, I could walk over to Shiner's.

Look, I changed my mind. Can I come in?

Hell, I don't even know her address.

Across the street, the headlights of a parked car shot bright beams and then went dark.

Jeremy's heart jumped.

He quickened his pace. At the sidewalk he glanced back at his house, half-hoping to see lights bloom in the windows, the door fly open, his mother rush out yelling, *And just what do you think you're doing, young man?*

The house was dark. He'd made a clean escape.

He stepped into the street. An arm waved to him from the open driver's window of the car that had flashed its lights. He returned the wave. He rushed around the car's front, noting that it was an old Ford LTD. The passenger door swung open as he approached it, but the interior remained dark. The dome light was either out of order or Tanya had disconnected it on purpose.

Stopping beside the door, he crouched and peered in. Tanya was shrouded in shadow, her features masked and blurred, but familiar enough to wrench Jeremy's breath away. He dropped onto the passenger seat. He tugged the door shut.

"Here," Tanya said.

He scooted toward her. The engine was running, but not smoothly. He could feel the car vibrating under him. Though the windows were rolled down, unpleasant odors of gasoline and stale cigarette smoke lingered in the air. And there was another scent, musky and humid, strange to him but somehow making him think of jungle nights and savages. It came from Tanya.

She turned to face him. She wore a dark sweatshirt and sweatpants. She took hold of Jeremy's hand—the one he had cut with the razor—and pressed it to her lips. With her other hand she pulled the loose front of her sweatshirt away from her body. She guided Jeremy's hand under the shirt, up her hot bare skin to her breast. Leaving it there, she put her arms around him and leaned toward him and kissed him. Her mouth seemed to engulf him. She moaned as he fondled her breast. It was so incredibly smooth, its nipple big and jutting and springy. He rubbed his hand all over it while her tongue swirled into his mouth. He squeezed it. He fingered the slick scar below the nipple and traced it downward, stopping only when he reached the drawstring of her pants, wanting to follow the scar lower but not daring. He glided his hand up again, felt the whistle tumble beneath it, and swept his hand toward her other breast. Suddenly he didn't dare touch it. He clutched the whistle.

Tanya's mouth went away.

"We have to get going," she whispered. "Later. We'll have time later. For everything."

Jeremy nodded. He took his hand out of her sweatshirt.

She kissed him gently, her lips slick against him. Then she took something out of the pouchlike pocket at her belly. "These are for you," she said.

Jeremy held the flimsy packet up to the windshield.

"Surgical gloves," Tanya explained. "We don't want to leave fingerprints." She took another packet out of her pouch, opened it, and put the gloves on.

"We have to wear them now?" Jeremy asked. He didn't want his hands covered. He wanted them bare and feeling Tanya.

"The car's hot," she said.

"Oh," he muttered. His stomach seemed to tighten. He could feel his penis start to shrink. "You mean you stole it?" he asked.

"Of course."

He squinted at the ignition. There was no key in it, but the car was running.

"Jeez," he said.

She turned to the front, released the emergency brake, tugged down the shift lever, and swung the car away from the curb. "We'll be leaving it at Funland," she said. "Don't worry, the owners will get it back. But we can't take a car they might trace to me."

"What're we going to do?" Jeremy asked.

"Get us a troll," she said. "I know right where to find the perfect troll for tonight."

"Really? Where?"

"Nate's house."

Robin, braced up with an elbow against the mattress, gazed at Nate. He looked as peaceful as a child. His arms and legs were spread out, just as they'd been when he fell asleep beneath her a while ago. His chest rose and fell slowly with long breaths. Robin rested a hand on his chest. Though his skin looked golden and warm in the wavering candlelight, it was cool to the touch.

She rolled cautiously away from him and left the bed. At the foot of it she picked up the sheet and covers that had been kicked to the floor while they made love. She spread them over him. He didn't move.

Robin smiled.

The poor guy is wiped out, she thought.

Who isn't?

She felt weak all over, herself. Her muscles were warm and shaky, as if they'd been turned into pudding. The area around her mouth felt puffy and tingling from the ceaseless kissing. Her cheeks burned slightly from the chafe of his whiskers. So did her shoulders, and the sides of her neck, and her breasts. Her nipples were tender and achy. She felt mushy and a little raw inside.

Maybe we overdid it just a little bit, she thought, and smiled again.

She walked toward the dresser, watching her slow progress in the mirror. The way she held herself and hobbled, she looked as if she expected any quick movement to jostle something loose. When she reached the dresser, she bent over and puffed out each of the candles. Then she made her way to the nightstand on Nate's side of the bed and blew out that candle. She was tempted to crawl over him, but she didn't want to disturb his sleep. So she forced her weary, aching body to circle the bed. Before snuffing the last candle, she bent over and carefully eased Nate's arm down against his side.

At last she blew out the candle and slipped under the covers. She rolled toward Nate in the darkness, squirmed closer until she felt the heat of his skin, and rested her arm gently on his chest. She listened to his breathing. She kissed his shoulder.

He made a quiet whimpery sound.

Dreaming a bad dream.

Robin rubbed his chest, hoping to distract him from whatever bad images had seized his sleeping mind. The sound of his breathing didn't change. He still slept. Robin listened, ready to wake him if he should whimper again.

Was he dreaming of Poppinsack's fall?

She wished she could make it go away for him. Kiss him and make him well.

If love could only cure him . . .

But he was doomed to live with the guilt. He had his burden, and Robin had hers.

Thank God we told each other, she thought.

She had loved him before, but the sharing of their awful secrets had been like a fire that fused their souls to one another.

She remembered herself in the spa with him, clutching his racked body tight against her while she sobbed, their tears mingling, and how she had felt as if they were one person, and how they had kept crying while they kissed.

As her mind lingered on the memories, she slipped into sleep.

Tanya shut off the headlights. Darkness collapsed over the road ahead. She swung onto a narrow driveway that rose in front of the car like a dim gray path through the woods. She shifted to a lower gear, but didn't accelerate, apparently to prevent a swell of engine noise that might warn of their approach.

"Are you sure they're here?" Jeremy whispered.

"They're here," Tanya said. "It was supposed to be me."

"Huh?"

"We had it all planned. His folks are gone till Wednesday. I was going to stay with him."

"Gosh."

"The rotten shit."

"He must be crazy, dumping you for that girl."

"Bad mistake. He's gonna find out how bad."

They came to the top of the slope. The house beyond the clearing was a vague shape of steep roofs. All its lights were out. Moonlight gleamed on some of the windows. It looked gloomy and abandoned.

Jeremy hoped it *was* abandoned.

He felt sick with dread.

He had to stand by Tanya, no matter what, but it would be so wonderful if they got into the house and nobody was there.

He rubbed his sweaty hands on the legs of his corduroys, but they were encased in the gloves and stayed wet.

It'll be all right, he told himself.

She'd said she would take care of Nate. Jeremy only had to worry about the girl. That shouldn't be a problem. He'd taken on two of them in front of the Oddities—and loved it. Here was his chance to fight the banjo girl.

So strange. After his first encounter with her on the boardwalk, he'd imagined how it would be.

Tanya seemed to be breathing life into his wildest dreams, making them real with her dark magic.

I don't want to fight that girl, he thought. I don't want it real.

He trembled with fear, trembled with a sharp ache of desire. *Please, let nobody be home.*

The car glided to a stop in front of the house's porch. Tanya shifted to Park and set the emergency brake. The engine rumbled quietly as she opened her door and climbed out. Jeremy almost reminded her to turn it off, but realized she had no key.

He got out. He moved on shaky legs to the front of the car while Tanya removed something from the backseat. She came toward him carrying a paper sack at her side.

"What's in that?" he whispered.

"Stuff," she said. "You'll see."

He followed her up the porch stairs to the front door. With a key from her sweatshirt pocket, she unlocked it.

At least we don't have to break in, Jeremy thought.

Tanya swung the door open. Inside was darkness.

They entered the foyer, and she shut the door without making a sound.

Jeremy heard only the drumming of his heart. It pounded so hard he thought he could feel the blood surging through his vessels.

Tanya squatted down. She set the bag on the floor. When she reached into it, there came a quiet metallic rattle. Jeremy recognized the sound and thought of the old bum. In the faint light from the windows he saw Tanya's arm come out and lift toward him. He saw the dangling bracelet of a handcuff. She gave the cuffs to him and slipped a second pair into her sweatshirt pouch.

She pulled a hammer out of the bag and handed it to Jeremy.

He felt his breath squeeze out. His stomach knotted. Icy fingers seemed to clench his scrotum.

She took out a hatchet for herself and stood up, leaving the bag on the floor.

Jeremy whispered in a choked voice, "We aren't going to kill them, are we?"

"What's the fun of that?"

"What're we gonna do?"

"The girl comes with us. Nate doesn't. Come on."

Shivering and weak, he followed Tanya to a stairway. They climbed slowly toward the second floor. Each time a stair creaked, Jeremy flinched. Somehow, the mad thud of his heart was causing a dry clicking noise in his throat. He swallowed hard, and the sound stopped.

The stairway seemed endless.

I could've been at Shiner's right now, Jeremy thought. God, why didn't I go there instead?

Handcuffs. A hammer. A hatchet.

It was worse than he could've imagined.

He pictured himself whirling around and racing down the stairs—running from the house and from Tanya and from whatever form of madness waited for him in the minutes ahead.

Then he remembered his hand inside her sweatshirt.

We'll have time later. For everything.

She was three stairs above him, barely visible in the darkness. He knew that she was naked under the sweatclothes.

He knew that he wouldn't run.

She waited for him at the top of the stairway. "Don't do anything till I say so," she whispered.

Jeremy nodded. He pushed the handcuffs into a pocket of his jacket.

Side by side, they walked down the hall. Tanya stopped at the open door of a bedroom. She peered inside. For a long time she didn't move. Then she pressed the head of the hatchet against Jeremy's back and nudged him forward. He entered the room. In the dim moonlight from the windows, he saw a bed. The covers were mounded.

It's them.

Tanya was right. They're here.

What if she lied about killing them?

What am I doing here?

She closed the door. She nudged Jeremy's left forearm with the hatchet, then put it into his hand. Why wasn't she keeping it for herself?

She wants both hands free, Jeremy realized as he watched her sneak across the room, not toward the bed but toward a dresser by the wall. At the end of the dresser was a straight-backed chair. She picked it up and started to return.

If I don't let her have the hatchet . . .

She set the chair down silently on the carpet in front of the door, tipped it backward, and eased its backpiece under the knob.

The chair would prevent anyone from entering the room, but Jeremy knew it had a different purpose. It was there to stop a quick escape.

She took hold of the hatchet. Jeremy made no attempt to keep it from her. She switched it to her left hand, gripped his wrist, and guided him to the foot of the bed. From here he could hear the breathing of the people beneath the covers.

Tanya glided along the left side of the bed. She bent low over the sleeping form. Her right hand took the hatchet.

Jeremy saw the hatchet rise.

Chop down.

No!

The thud flashed pain through his own head. He cringed and felt his legs go rubbery, but he heard a harsh gasp, and the covers on the other side of the bed suddenly flew up. "Get her!" Tanya snapped.

The girl was naked and dusky against the white sheets, one hand thrusting the blankets aside as she squirmed to free her legs and sit up.

He dived onto her, smashing her down. The mattress bounced her against him. She twisted and writhed. He pinned one hand, but the other was free and he couldn't catch it because of the hammer. Her nails ripped streaks of fire down his cheek. He let the hammer fall. As it pounded the floor, he grabbed her wrist.

Now I've got you!

She bucked, hurling him sideways. He fell. His back slammed the carpeted floor. The hammer jabbed his shoulder blade. She came down on top of him, whimpering and snarling. She bit his chin and he cried out, released her wrists, and punched her in the face. The blow ripped her teeth from his flesh. In a frenzy of pain, Jeremy grabbed the short hair over her ears and twisted her head, rolling with her as he forced her sprawling onto the floor beside him.

She drove a knee into his stomach. His breath blasted out. He doubled up, hugging his belly.

"What the fuck's going on!" Tanya's voice.

Sucking for air, Jeremy saw the girl push herself up and get to her feet.

The room filled with light.

The girl seemed to freeze in position, hunched over and ready to run, head turned, looking over her shoulder toward the other side of the bed.

"Don't move a muscle," Tanya warned.

Jeremy struggled to sit up. Panting and clutching his chin, he saw Tanya glaring at the girl. She was bent over Nate's motionless body, the hatchet poised for another strike. In the light from the lamp beside her, he saw that Nate's face was bathed with blood that spilled out of a gash on his forehead. No huge, gaping wound, though. Tanya hadn't chopped him with the hatchet's sharp edge. But it was the sharp edge, now, that hovered above him.

"Get her clothes for her, Duke. She's gotta look right."

Nodding, he picked up his hammer and stood. He stepped closer to the girl. She hadn't moved since Tanya turned the lamp on. She didn't look back at Jeremy.

"Put your hands on your head," he gasped.

Her body straightened. She raised her arms and interlaced her fingers on top of her head.

Jeremy stared at her back, her smooth tanned skin, the pale mounds of her buttocks, her slender legs.

He took his hand away from his chin. The rubber glove was slick with blood.

He raked the claws of the hammer down the middle of the girl's back. She made a hissing sound, and flinched rigid as the claws gouged twin furrows in her skin. Blood began to well from the rips.

He glanced at Tanya.

Tanya nodded. She wore a tight smile.

Jeremy stepped to the front of the girl. Her eyes fixed on him. They looked frightened and hurt, but they were filled with loathing, as if she longed to destroy him.

He smeared his blood onto her chin and cheeks. He slapped her face, rocking her head sideways. But she faced him again. She bared her teeth and kept glaring at him, but didn't resist as his hand moved over her, caressing, squeezing, pinching. When he rammed the hammer head into her belly, she folded and dropped to her knees, wheezing for air. His knee crashed her mouth shut, snapped her head backward, and she tumbled sprawling onto the floor.

"That's enough," Tanya said. "We're running low on time."

While he searched for the girl's clothes, Tanya cuffed one of Nate's hands to the bed frame. Jeremy found the backpack inside the closet. He took jeans and a faded blue work shirt from the pack. He tossed them onto the girl and watched her slow, pained struggle to put them on. Before she could button the shirt, he snatched her by the hair, hauled her up, and cuffed her hands behind her back.

He took off his belt, slipped one end through the buckle, and dropped the loop over the girl's head.

Tanya grabbed Nate's keys off the top of the dresser. She stuffed them into her pouch, then turned off the light.

"Okay," she said. "When we get outside, I'll bust a window to make it look like a break-in. Don't let me forget."

"Right," Jeremy said.

Pulling his belt like a leash, he led the girl into the dark hallway.

Thirty-nine

The bed wobbled slightly, stirring Dave from sleep. Through his closed eyelids he saw light. Is it morning? he wondered. Joan had made him set the alarm clock for midnight, but maybe he'd turned it off in his sleep or something. He hoped so. He hoped it was morning.

A bare bottom sat down on him. He squirmed under the pleasant weight and opened his eyes. With a tug of disappointment and fear, he saw that the light came from the bedside lamp. Joan was straddling him, hands against the mattress near his shoulders. She smiled gently and lowered herself. Her nipples touched his chest, and she rocked herself to make them move, stroking him. Then he felt the solid warm heaviness of her breasts. They pushed against him. Her mouth covered his.

He ran his hands slowly up and down her back.

She lifted her mouth away from him. "Time to shine, honey."

"Time to *rise* and shine," he said.

He saw the familiar mischief in her eyes.

"Oh," he said. "I get it."

She kissed him again, then said, "We have to go."

"I was afraid of that. What time is it?"

"Twelve-thirty."

"What happened to the alarm?"

"I shut it off. I was awake anyway."

"Couldn't sleep?" Dave asked.

"Didn't want to. It seemed like such a waste of time. It was so much nicer, staying awake and looking at you."

"Voyeur."

"You got it, pal."

"You should've woken me."

"Didn't want to. You've had a hard night. You needed your sleep. That's why I didn't wake you up sooner." She kissed him once more. "Okay, now, at 'em."

She climbed off Dave, taking away her weight and smoothness and heat. He sat up and pulled the blanket to his waist. He watched Joan step into her panties, watched her pull a T-shirt down over her head. When her face reappeared, she said, "Show's over. You can get dressed now."

Dave scooted to the edge of the bed. He lowered his feet to the floor, but didn't stand up.

Instead, he watched Joan slide into one of the dark blue vests he had picked up at the station that afternoon. She fastened it shut around her torso with Velcro straps. "You look like you're ready to go water-skiing," he said.

"Wishful thinking." Squatting beside the grocery bag, she took out a shoulder harness. She slipped into it, and tucked her S&W .38 into the holster below her left armpit. A smaller holster went around her right ankle. She filled it with a chrome-plated semiauto. Still another harness came out of her sack. Dave shook his head as she got into it. She straightened the leather sheath against the right side of her rib cage and slid a long double-edged knife into it.

"God Almighty," Dave said. "Where do you get your stuff, from *Soldier of Fortune* magazine?"

"How'd you guess?"

"Anything else? Have you got an Uzi in there?"

"This about does it." When she reached into the sack again, she came out with a pair of gray sweatpants that looked as if they'd been dabbed with shoe polish.

Dave got up from the bed. He took fresh underwear and socks from his dresser and put them on while Joan covered the top part of her arsenal with a baggy sweatshirt. The shirt had rips in it that showed the blue of her Kevlar vest. The tears in her pants showed bare leg.

"My sexy Rambo," Dave said. Like Joan, he put on a T-shirt to keep the vest away from his skin. Then he got into his jeans and vest and running shoes. He went to the closet for his own weapons: a snub-nosed .38 with a clip-on holster that he fastened to his belt on the right, and a 9mm Beretta with a shoulder harness.

"You don't travel exactly light yourself," Joan said, nodding at the Beretta.

"We oughta be able to take on an army," Dave said.

"Debbie thinks we may have to."

"You told her, huh?" Dave slipped into a heavy plaid shirt and watched Joan knot a red bandanna around her thigh. "What's that for?"

"Style. Yeah, I told her. Probably should've kept it to myself, but I don't like to do that. She was not pleased, to say the least. She's afraid I won't come back."

Joan's words made a cold knot in Dave's belly. "I don't blame her," he said.

"She's more worried about trolls than the teenagers. Still

thinks they had something to do with Mom." Joan carried her socks and a ratty old pair of running shoes to the bed, sat on its edge, and tried to hunch over to put them on. "Damn," she muttered, having trouble because of her vest and harnesses.

"Allow me," Dave said.

"My knight. So chivalrous."

Kneeling in front of her, he started to put the socks on her feet.

"You're pretty good at this," she said, ruffling his hair. "You can be the official sock-putter-onner for our kids."

He smiled up at her. "Our kids?"

"Or don't you want any?"

"Of course I do."

"How many?"

"As many as you want," he said, and suddenly wished she hadn't mentioned kids, hadn't touched him with dreams of the future. A future that might not be there. The night ahead loomed in front of Dave like a black wall, and he feared there might be nothing beyond it.

That's ridiculous, he told himself.

But they got Gloria.

Gloria was alone. She wasn't armed. This is a whole different ball game.

He finished tying the shoes, and rubbed Joan's thighs through the soft fabric of the sweatpants. He slipped a hand inside one of the rips. "Maybe we should check Gloria's place on the way over," he said.

"What's the point? She won't be there, we both know that."

"Couldn't hurt to check one more time. It'll only take a few minutes."

Her eyes darkened. "I don't want to go in there again."

"You can wait in the car," Dave said. They'd driven over after dinner. Joan had gone in with him, and the experience had obviously upset her. She'd walked stiffly through the house, clutching Dave's hand, a grim look on her face. He couldn't blame her. It was the home of his former lover, a woman who had probably been murdered last night, whose ruined body had likely been discarded in some lonely place where the killers hoped she would never be found.

When Dave started showing Gloria's cast-off clothes to her, she'd shaken her head sharply, blurted, "I don't want to see that stuff," and nearly dragged him out of the house.

It was no wonder she didn't want to go there again.

"I'll make a phone call instead," Dave told her.

"If you want."

He went to the telephone on the nightstand and dialed Gloria's number. After three rings the line opened. "Hello. This is Gloria."

Dave's heart jumped.

"Gloria?" he asked. He saw Joan's head snap toward him, stunned surprise on her face.

"I'm not home right now, but if you'd like to leave a message . . ."

"Shit," he muttered. "It's her answering machine." He'd probably left messages on the damn thing a hundred times. How could he have let it fool him, lift his hopes?

Joan's face was slack with disappointment.

". . . I'll get back to you as soon as possible."

Right, he thought. Sure you will.

Dead. She's dead, and talking to me just as if nothing is wrong.

Her machine beeped, signaling him to leave his message.

He remembered how she used to complain about hang-ups.

He remembered how she often talked to him, home after all, once he'd identified himself.

"It's Dave," he said.

Joan's lips curled. She looked sick.

"If you're there, for Godsake pick up the phone."

He listened to distant, empty sounds.

"Gloria? It's Dave. Are you there?"

I'm talking to a dead woman.

He hung up.

Joan came to him and put her arms around him.

"We might as well get it over with," he muttered. He hugged her tightly, feeling her stiff vest, the gun and knife, but also feeling the warmth of her legs, the softness of her cheek. He kissed her. "If I lose you because of this . . ."

"We owe God a death," she said.

"Just what I wanted to hear."

"'Tis not due yet." She gently swatted his rump and stepped away from him.

He watched her reach into the paper bag, pull out a stocking cap, and drag it down over her head until only a fringe of blond hair showed around its edges.

She raised her eyebrows. "Am I devastating yet?"

"Gorgeous."

She picked up the bag, which still had something in it.

"You *do* have an Uzi."

"Just an old blanket," she said.

"What's that for?"

"More style."

In the living room Dave waited while she opened her purse. She took her badge out of its leather case. "Can't forget this," she said. "Have you got yours?"

He patted his wallet.

Joan lifted her sweatshirt and pinned the shield to a strap of her shoulder harness. Then she picked up her bag again, and they left the house.

Dave locked the door with his house key, found the ignition key, and walked beside Joan toward the driveway, where his car waited.

Waited on flat tires.

"What the hell?" he muttered.

He walked around the car. All four tires were mashed against the pavement by the weight of the car. Joan, he saw, was heading for the street.

She looked back at him. "Mine too," she said.

"You're kidding." He caught up with her. Joan's car, parked at the curb, rested on four flat tires. "I'll be damned."

"Looks like somebody decided to sabotage our mission," she said.

"That's crazy. It was probably just some kids."

"One kid in particular. My sister."

"Debbie? You think she did this?"

"She must've. It can't be just some weird coincidence. God, she must be a lot more upset than I thought."

"Does she know where I live?"

"You're in the book, partner. She just looked you up, hiked over here, and had at 'em."

"Well, good for her!"

"The little beast. Wait'll I get my hands on her."

Dave tried to force the smile off his face, but didn't succeed. "She's a spunky kid. Must run in the family."

"I'm gonna strangle her."

"She just did it because she loves you."

"Yeah, I know. I'm gonna draw and quarter her, the rat." Dave laughed.

"Yeah, yuck it up. Right." Turning away from him, she crouched beside the front tire.

"It isn't slashed, I hope."

"Debbie wouldn't go that far. I'm sure she just let the air out." Joan rubbed her hands on the side of the tire. Standing up, she rubbed her face, then lowered her hands. Her brow, cheeks, and chin were smudged with grime that looked gray and smoky in the streetlights.

"I know," Dave said. "Style. Does this mean we're still planning to go?"

"I am."

"Great," he muttered. "Should I go in and call a cab?"

"Let's just walk. It's not that far."

"All right. Hang on a minute, though. I want to get my flashlight." He walked toward his car, feeling strangely cheerful. Nothing was about to stop Joan, but the flat tires would certainly slow her down. A hike to the beach should take the better part of half an hour.

A reprieve.

Thank you, Debbie. Thank you very much. I owe you for this.

I'll buy her an ice-cream cone, he thought, and grinned.

He unlocked his car, took the flashlight out from under the driver's seat, then ambled back toward Joan. "Let's take it slow and easy," he said. "God forbid one of us should turn an ankle."

Forty

"How's it going back there?" Tanya asked, glancing over her shoulder.

"Fine," Jeremy said. His own voice sounded strange to him—a little whiny, but mean. "Just fine."

The girl was stretched across the backseat, pinned down by his weight on her belly. He bounced on her, and heard a gush of breath that pleased him.

They passed a streetlamp. Its light swept briefly across the girl's bare chest. He took off his gloves. He pinched her again, and felt her flinch.

It made him feel good to hurt her, but it didn't turn him on. He felt cheated.

Could've been great, back here sitting on the bitch. Her hands were cuffed behind her back. Her shirt was open. She was *at his fucking mercy*.

She might as well have been a guy, for all the lust he felt.

He slapped her. She winced. He slapped her again. "You ruined me, you cunt!"

"Hope so," she muttered.

He made her cry out.

"Take it easy," Tanya said.

"What'm I gonna do?" he asked. "You see what she did to me? How'm I gonna go home with my face like this? What'm I gonna tell my mom?"

"Don't worry about it."

"God, I can't go home." Gingerly he fingered the torn flesh of his chin. Touching the wound brought fresh tears to his eyes.

"We'll think of something," Tanya told him.

"Everybody's gonna know I was in on this. All they gotta do is look at me."

"I'll take care of you," Tanya said. "There's nothing to worry about."

"Easy for you to say. It's not your face."

"It's my ass. We're in this together, Duke. It's all right. I'll take you home in the morning and tell your mother that a dog attacked you on the beach. I'm a lifeguard. She'll believe me."

Yeah! That might work. He felt a little better. He'd have to come up with a story to explain why he'd left the house without telling her, but that shouldn't be too hard.

"What about Nate?" he asked.

"He's deader than shit."

A horrible keening noise burst from the girl. She began to writhe and buck under Jeremy. He rammed his fist down, smashing her just below the rib cage. The blow made her sit halfway up as her breath exploded out. Then she slumped down again, wheezing loudly.

"She won't be in any shape to talk either," Tanya said. "We'll make sure of that."

"*I'll* make sure of that." Jeremy twisted sideways and worked on her. She flopped and jerked, shuddering with pain, and he knew she'd be screaming if she had any air.

"Not yet, for Godsake. Everybody gets a crack at her. We don't want to cheat the others out of their fun."

"I'm not killing her." He glared down at the girl. Her head was flying from side to side, lips peeled back as if stretched by fingers trying to rip her mouth wider. "Am I killing you?" he asked her. "Huh? Naw. Maybe just hurting you a little bit. Maybe just a little bit. How's *this* feel, huh? And this?"

He felt the car stop.

"Okay," Tanya said. "We're here."

She climbed out and opened the passenger door beyond the girl's head. Reaching in, she grabbed her under the armpits. Jeremy lifted himself up, and watched Tanya drag her from the car. He crawled out after her.

He shut the door quietly. The girl was on her back, Tanya straddling her and fastening the buttons of her shirt. "Get her legs," Tanya said.

The girl thrashed, trying to kick him, but he got her legs apart and hugged them tightly against his sides. Tanya raised her shoulders. Together they lifted her and carried her up the stairs. They passed beneath the grinning moonlit face of the clown. In the entryway, shadows closed over them.

Something pale stepped out from behind the ticket booth.

Jeremy sucked a quick breath and froze. He felt the girl's legs pull in his grip as Tanya took one more step. Then Tanya halted too.

"It's just me."

No!

Guilt rushed through him, hot and sickening.

Shiner, standing in the darkness, wore white clothes that almost seemed to glow. Her arms were folded across her chest. The ocean breeze stirred her hair.

She doesn't know what I've done, Jeremy told himself. But her presence was like a brilliant light, and he saw his deeds in that light as sordid and horrible.

What have I done?

Oh, God, what have I done?

"The others here yet?" Tanya asked.

Shiner shook her head.

"We've already got ourselves the troll for tonight's festivities," Tanya said.

"So I see. Jeremy, let go of her and come with me."

"What's this shit?" Tanya snapped.

"Stay out of it," Shiner said. She came toward Jeremy. "You're going to get in real trouble if you stay."

"If you don't like it," Tanya said, "get out of here."

"Shut up. Jeremy." She put a hand on his shoulder. It suddenly tightened. "What happened to your face?"

"We had some trouble with this one," he muttered.

"Jesus."

He released the girl's legs. She started to thrash. Tanya wrestled her away, flung her facedown onto the floor of the boardwalk, and planted a foot on her back to keep her still.

"Does it hurt?" Shiner asked.

"Yeah. A lot."

"I'm sorry. But it wouldn't have happened if you'd come to me tonight. I know I'm not as . . . exciting as Tanya. I know you want her. Hell, you're a guy. Who wouldn't? The thing is, she's going to ruin you. Look what happened to you."

"Tell her to get the fuck out of here," Tanya said.

"She's right," Jeremy said. "Go away."

"I'm not going anywhere. Not unless you come with me."

"I'm not leaving," he said.

"Yo!" Cowboy called. "All set to kick some troll ass?"

"Got one here," Tanya said.

Cowboy and Liz walked over to her. "Hey, hot damn!"

"A trollette," Liz said.

"We've also got a traitor."

"Yeah?"

"Shiner."

"Naw. What gives, Shiner babes? You're not quitting on us, are you?"

"Turned chicken?" Liz asked.

Cowboy came closer. Shiner let go of Jeremy's shoulder and faced him.

My pal, Jeremy thought. He felt a wonderful sense of relief and gratitude. It was like the time that Cowboy had chased the begging troll away from him.

"Tell me it ain't so," he said, sounding concerned.

"I'm done with trolling," she told him.

"You're joshing me, right? These're the low-life scum suckers that did your sister."

"Greetings, gang." Randy. "Hey, you got one already?"

"Shiner wants to bail out," Liz said, disgust in her voice.

"Really?"

"What's that car doing in front?" Samson had arrived.

"Duke and I brought the troll in it," Tanya said.

"You left it running."

"Doesn't matter."

"Say, what we got here? A gal? All *right!*"

"We'll get to her in a minute. Duke has to *make the god-damn traitor go away.*"

"She ain't no traitor," Cowboy said. "She's just riled up." To Shiner he said, "What's the story? You upset 'cause of the one that bit the dust?"

"That's one thing. It's all gotten out of hand, Cowboy. Look what this one did to Jeremy."

Cowboy peered at him. "Holy heifer shit. That bitch do this?"

"She bit me," Jeremy said, his voice shaking. "And scratched me."

"Well, she's durn sure gonna wish she hadn't."

Liz and Randy came over to look at him. Samson didn't. He was kneeling beside the girl, turning her over.

Randy pushed his glasses higher on his nose, squinted at Jeremy's face, and muttered, "Gosh."

Liz said, "She's gonna die."

Their sympathy for his injuries made Jeremy's throat tighten. These are my friends, he thought.

I didn't do anything to the girl that they wouldn't have done. They're on my side, even if Shiner isn't.

The hell with Shiner, anyway. Who needs her?

Heather was suddenly there, nudging Randy aside. Her pale, bloated face came very close, and Jeremy smelled her onion breath. "Poor Dukey," she said. She put her arms around him. Her breasts and belly felt like swollen bags of jelly. She pushed her hands into the back pockets of his corduroys and rubbed his rump.

Shiner pulled her away.

"We're leaving," she said. "Come on, Jeremy."

"No." His voice came out strong. His friends were here now. So many friends. They were on his side. "I'm not going. If you don't like it, lump it."

She tugged the shoulder of his jacket.

Then someone hooked an arm around Shiner's throat and yanked her backward. Her arm flew up. She clutched the head of her attacker, twisted, and ducked. The body flew up behind her, legs kicking, and slammed the boards at Shiner's feet. She lurched backward a few steps and raised her open hands, ready to defend herself.

Nobody else went for her.

Karen, gasping, lay sprawled on the boardwalk where Shiner had thrown her.

"Everybody just stand still and listen to me," Shiner said. "Nate was right. It's gone too far. But I'm not here to stop you from going after trolls. I hate them as much as any of you. I still do. They took my mother from me."

"Sister," Cowboy corrected her.

"No, my mother. I don't have a mother, thanks to the trolls. But I have a sister, and some of you know her. My real name is

Deborah Delaney. My sister is Joan Delaney, the cop who's been patrolling Funland the past few weeks."

Cowboy lifted a hand to the bandaged side of his head.

"Yeah," Shiner said. "She's the one who saved your ear for you."

"I'll be hog-tied."

"Your sister's a *cop*?" Tanya blurted.

"I knew you wouldn't let me troll if I told you about her. But I'm not trolling anymore. I came here to warn you. Joan's coming here tonight, dressed like a bum. She and her partner. They'll be coming to bust you guys. I let the air out of their tires, but I don't think that'll stop them. For all I know, they might get here any second. You're my friends. You, especially, Jeremy, but the rest of you too. I don't want Joan to arrest any of you. And I don't want her getting hurt trying. So, please, call it off. At least for tonight. Call it off and get out of here before it's too late."

She stood there, breathing heavily, her head turning slowly as she looked at each of them.

Tanya stepped toward her.

Shiner stiffened. She raised her hands again.

Karen, on her knees, muttered, "Nail her."

"Shut up," Tanya said. She held out a hand to Shiner. "Thanks for the warning, Debbie. You're all right. Even if your sister *is* a cop."

Shiner took the offered hand. Tanya drew the girl closer, released her hand, and put her arms around her.

They hugged each other.

Jeremy couldn't believe his eyes.

He half-expected Tanya to knee her in the guts.

They parted, and Tanya turned to Jeremy. "Go with her if you want. Nobody'll hold it against you—against either of you."

"I can't," he said.

Not after what we've done, he thought. Not with my face like this.

It's way too late.

"I'll stick with you," he told Tanya.

"Good man. All right, trollers! You heard what Debbie said.

Cops are on the way. We've gotta make it quick. Randy, you stand watch. You see anyone coming, blow your whistle like crazy and run for it. Let's do it!"

She squeezed Shiner's arm, then hurried toward the cuffed girl. The others went to join in.

Shiner stepped up to Jeremy.

"I'm sorry," he said.

"Me too. What the hell, I guess I'd be after Tanya too if I was a guy. Still friends?"

"Sure. If you want me for a friend," he added in a trembling voice.

"I do."

"Great. And thanks for . . . warning us."

"Hey, what're friends for?"

He wanted to embrace her, but he kept his arms at his sides. He knew that he could never hold her again.

He had removed himself from the part of the world where teenage boys and girls dated, hugged and kissed, made out in innocent questing passion. That was the world where he and Shiner might have dwelled. But it was lost now forever.

"Go for it, hoss!"

Some others cheered.

Jeremy looked away from Shiner and watched Samson lift the handcuffed girl. He hoisted her off the boardwalk by the front of her shirt and the crotch of her jeans, swung her up, and raised her over his head as if she were a living barbell. He led the way. The others followed, except for Randy.

"I guess you don't want to miss out," Shiner said.

Jeremy shook his head.

"Let's go, then."

"Aren't you leaving?"

"I told you before. I'm not leaving without you. You stay, I stay. Somebody's got to look out for you."

They hurried to catch up with the group.

The procession moved quickly down the moonlit board-walk. Tanya, taking the lead, rushed to the gate of the fence that surrounded the Ferris wheel. She opened it for Samson, and climbed the wooden platform.

At the top, Samson lowered the girl. He held her standing

while Tanya stepped behind her. Jeremy heard a quiet click and realized that Tanya was unlocking one of the cuffs.

"How're you gonna get the thing running?" Samson asked.

"I've got Nate's key."

"Hot damn," Cowboy said.

"Let go of her." Samson released his grip on the girl's shirt-front. As she sagged backward, Tanya braced her up, reached around her, ripped open the shirt, and yanked it off.

"All *right*," Samson said.

"Get her pants."

Samson tugged the jeans down her legs. Tanya, arms around the girl's chest, hoisted her up. Samson pulled the jeans off her feet and tossed them aside.

"Who wants some fun?"

"What about the cops?" Samson asked.

"Forget the cops. Who wants to fuck her?"

"I don't know," Samson said. He caressed the girl's breasts. "I wouldn't mind, but she's a troll, you know? Wouldn't want to catch something."

"Well, I reckon . . ."

Liz jabbed Cowboy's arm.

"Reckon not," he muttered.

"Jeremy?"

His heart pounded.

Not with Shiner watching.

He just couldn't.

Besides, Tanya had made promises about later.

"Not me," he said.

"Bunch of candy asses." She drove a knee up. The girl jerked as it smashed against her rump. The blow lifted her feet off the boards. Tanya hurled her down. The platform shook as she slammed against it. Dropping to her knees, Tanya pinned the girl's hands. "Come on, somebody!"

Karen scurried forward and crawled over the girl, moaning as she delved, caressed, squeezed, licked, and sucked.

"You don't want to be in on this," Shiner whispered.

I want to be *doing* it, Jeremy thought, feeling guilty and hating Shiner for being here to shame him.

The girl bit the top of Karen's head.

Yelping, she clutched her scalp. Then she battered the girl's face with her fists until Samson pulled her off.

"Let's run her up there and haul on out," he said. "Those cops are gonna show up."

"Yeah, yeah, okay."

Tanya and Samson dragged the girl to the bottom gondola. Tanya propped her against the seat, rump on the footrest. She swung the safety bar down, hooked the connecting chain of the handcuffs over it, and closed the empty bracelet around the girl's wrist.

"If she falls too . . ." Shiner muttered.

"One more good troll," Liz said. "Give her a ride!"

"Hang her high!" from Cowboy.

Tanya pulled a calling card from the pocket of her sweat-shirt. "Greetings from Great Big Billy Goat Gruff," she said. She took a small plastic case from her pocket, opened it, and held up a straight pin for everyone to see. She poked the pin through the middle of the card. The girl winced and her legs flinched as Tanya stuck it into her, just above the left breast.

"God," Shiner muttered.

Liz laughed. "Looks like a name tag at a nudist convention."

Tanya hurried over to the machinery. Moments later, the mo-tor rumbled, sending vibrations through the platform. The wheel began to move, dragging the girl's bare heels over the boards as she was swept backward.

The gondola tipped out from under her. She let out a sharp gasp as her weight was borne by her cuffed wrists.

The wheel picked up speed, carrying the moonlit girl quickly to the top. Just as she swept over the crest, Tanya stopped the wheel. The girl snapped rigid. She shrieked. She looked as if she might be torn loose. Jeremy half-expected her arms to be wrenched from their sockets, and he pictured her naked, arm-less torso falling through the night. But nothing gave. After the harsh tug, she seemed to be flung upward. She dropped straight again and dangled there, her pale body suspended in front of the swinging gondola.

All the trollers on the platform stared up at her.

"Holy jumping Judas," Cowboy muttered.

"Well, shit," Liz said. "Isn't she gonna fall?"

The motor went silent.

Jeremy, suddenly alarmed, hurried over to Tanya. "She's alive," he whispered. "We can't leave her alive. Christ, she'll tell—"

"Don't worry, huh? The cuffs are loose. Real loose. I'm surprised she hasn't already fallen. That stop should've done it. She must be keeping her hands fisted."

"What if she *doesn't* fall?"

"She will. I don't give her ten minutes."

"You sure?"

"I told you, it's my ass too. She'll be taking a big dive." Tanya stepped past Jeremy. He followed her, and they joined the others. All their heads were tilted back.

The gondola had stopped rocking. The girl dangled straight down, her rump against the edge of the footrest. She looked limp.

Is she passed out? Jeremy wondered. If she's out cold, why hasn't she fallen yet? Maybe the cuffs aren't as loose as Tanya thought.

"Okay," Tanya said. "Let's get out of here."

They hurried down the stairs and out the gate. Standing in the middle of the boardwalk, Jeremy again looked up. From here he had a very good view of the girl. She was incredibly high. A fall would kill her for sure. She wasn't moving at all. Her head hung. But he couldn't see whether or not her fists were clenched to keep the cuffs on.

A brilliant burst of light suddenly hit his eyes.

Heather blurted, "Shit!"

Jeremy snapped his head around. No more than thirty feet away stood a giant troll with a camera at his face. Its flash blinked again.

"Get him!" Tanya yelled.

They charged the troll. He whirled away, camera swinging at his side by its strap, and vaulted the railing. He dropped toward the beach and vanished.

"Get him!" Tanya shouted again. She was first to reach the railing. She hurled herself over it. Samson rolled over the top bar, turned around, and leapt. Cowboy cleared the railing and held on to his hat as he plummeted. Karen and Liz climbed

the railing while Heather squirmed under it. Jeremy started to
climb. Shiner grabbed the back of his jacket.

"Don't," she said.

"The guy *took a picture!*"

"They'll take care of him."

He knocked her hand away and straddled the bar.

"Please. Dammit, *please!*"

He shook his head, climbed down onto the edge of the boardwalk, and jumped. The beach pounded his feet. His legs folded,
and he rolled over the sand. As he pushed himself up, Shiner
landed beside him.

"Leave me alone!" he snapped.

"I'm coming with you."

"I don't *need* you."

But she stayed at his side as he rushed after the others into
the darkness beneath the boardwalk.

"Where is he?" Tanya's voice.

"Oh, God, we can't lose him." Karen.

"We'll get him." Cowboy. "We'll nail his sorry ass."

"Dance on his face." Liz.

"Christ, it's dark down here." Samson.

"Everybody shut up," Tanya said. "Maybe we can hear him."

Off to the left, a patch of ruddy, shimmering light appeared
in the blackness.

"There! There!"

"Judas priest, a fucking door."

The huge form of the troll was silhouetted against it as he
crouched and entered. Then he was gone, but the light remained.

They rushed toward it, dodging the thick pilings that sup-
ported the boardwalk.

The next shape Jeremy saw silhouetted against the light was
Tanya. She didn't hesitate for an instant. She lunged inside.
The others followed.

As Jeremy stepped through the opening, he heard the faint,
distant shrill of a whistle.

"That was Randy," Shiner whispered behind him. "Joan's
here."

Jeremy thought she would rush off to join her sister. But she
put a hand on his back and entered.

"The cops are here," Jeremy announced. "Randy just blew his whistle."

"They won't find us," Tanya said. "Close the door."

Shiner pulled it shut.

They were crowded into a small room lighted by candles on wall holders. The door at their backs was tight against a concrete wall. Another door on the left. Ahead of them was a staircase.

Cowboy tried the second door. "Locked," he said.

"Where the hell are we?" Heather asked, her voice low and whiny.

"Looks like a basement," Samson said.

"Brilliant deduction," Liz muttered.

"Tha's a fack," came a dry, ancient voice from above. "Welcome t' Jasper's Funhouse."

Tanya pulled a folding knife out of the pouch of her sweatshirt. She pried its blade out.

Jeremy dug into a pocket for his Swiss Army knife.

He saw Samson, Karen, and Cowboy produce knives of their own.

"Everybody ready?" Tanya whispered. She scanned the group, her eyes glinting and fierce in the candlelight, then turned around and began to climb the stairs.

Forty-one

Robin's eyes were squeezed shut in pain and fear, but she opened them just a crack when she heard sudden shouts. The shapes of the trollers, far below, started running up the boardwalk.

Her stomach seemed to take a sudden drop.

God, she was so *high*!

A blink of light flicked a quick white glare over the tiny figures. It came from a big man ahead of them, who suddenly ran to the railing, leapt over it, and rushed out of sight under the boardwalk.

The kids, in pursuit, started throwing themselves over the railing.

Are they leaving me up here? she wondered.

Are they done hurting me?

No. No, they aren't done. They'll come back. They have to kill me. I'm a witness.

Oh, God, Nate.

Deader than shit.

They murdered him. Tanya did.

But why did she cuff him to the bed? Maybe she lied to that kid. Duke, she'd called him Duke. She wouldn't have cuffed Nate if he was dead, would she?

Maybe.

Maybe he's alive.

I can get help for him if I get down from here.

If I don't get down, they'll come back and kill me. Tanya or Duke will. Maybe they won't do it in front of the others, though.

All they had to do was start the wheel going again, make it stop once more, and she'd probably go flying.

The last stop had almost torn her loose.

It was like being yanked downward by a mighty giant. The steel edges of the bracelets tore at her, and she'd thought her hands might rip off. Her fists had been clenched all the way up and over the top. If they hadn't been, she was sure she would've been jerked out of the cuffs.

The end of Robin.

Even now, her fists were all that kept her from falling.

Open your hands, she thought, and it's all over.

Out of your misery.

Just one big pain, and that's it. All the pain gone.

I don't want to fall!

A numbness was starting to replace the pain in her hands. She felt blood trickling down her arms and sides. The breeze off the ocean turned the blood cold. It also chilled the long raw wounds on her back, but those didn't seem to be bleeding now.

The hands get numb enough, she thought, or you lose enough blood to pass out, and it's all over.

She knew that her nose and lips had bled, but that had stopped. So there was just her wrists and hands, and a single dribble of blood working its way down her left breast from the damn pin hole.

Like to pull the pin out and stick it in Tanya's fucking eye!

Robin tucked her head down, thinking it might be possible to pluck out the pin with her teeth. But she couldn't quite reach it. Her chin was in the way.

Worried about a pin.

Gonna fall to my death any second, and I'm worried about a goddamn pin.

Her chin brushed a corner of the card. She winced as its slight movement jostled the pin under her skin.

Then she saw, far below her, three dim figures shambling over the boardwalk. They came from three different directions, as if each, on its own, had spied the morsel suspended from the Ferris wheel.

One halted directly below her. His bald pate gleamed in the moonlight. When he looked up, Robin saw that one eye was covered by a patch. His mouth drooped open.

Gooseflesh rushed up her skin. She pressed her legs together.

While the one-eyed troll gazed at her, another shuffled through the gate. The third followed him into the fenced area beneath the wheel.

Robin heard a quiet whimper escape from her throat. She heard the rush of the surf. And she heard the far-off blast of a whistle.

"What was that?" Dave asked.

"Sounded like a police whistle," Joan said.

"Did it come from the boardwalk?"

Joan shook her head. "I don't know. It seemed to come from that direction."

"Maybe whoever belongs to that car . . ."

She frowned at him. "Somebody might be in trouble," she said, and started to run.

Dave broke into a sprint and caught up with her.

They raced up the sidewalk alongside the Funland parking lot.

If someone *is* in trouble, he thought, it might be over before we get there.

He suddenly regretted that their cars had been disabled, and wished he hadn't taken such delight in their brief reprieve.

Jeremy stepped onto a landing. We must be at the ground floor, he thought. A door was there. Tanya tried to turn its knob, shook her head, and started up the next flight of stairs. Samson climbed them at her side. Karen went next, followed by Cowboy and Liz.

"I don't like this," Heather whispered. She was behind Jeremy, holding on to the bottom of his jacket.

"I think we were *supposed* to come in after that guy," Shiner said.

Jeremy's grimace made the wounds on his face stretch and sting. He wished Shiner hadn't said that. It was bad enough, being inside the Funhouse, without having to worry about the possibility that they'd been *lured* into it. He thought about how gloomy the boarded old place looked from the boardwalk. And it was right beside Jasper's Oddities. His mind lingered on what he'd seen in there—the Gallery of the Weird and those monstrous displays. Jasper's Oddities was part of the same damned building. It might even open into here.

At the next landing, the stairway ended. Those ahead of Jeremy halted. He climbed the final step. Looking past them, he saw a dark hallway.

"Wish we had some flashlights," Samson whispered.

Tanya stepped to the wall and lifted the single candle out of its wrought-iron holder. She started slowly forward, and the others followed. Shiner, clutching Jeremy's left arm, pressed herself against his side and matched his small strides.

Tanya gasped, "Jesus!" and lurched away from the wall as a hand darted out at her.

"Two bits, ducky?"

From the other wall, a hand snatched the hat off Cowboy's head. Blurting "Shit!" he grabbed it back and stumbled against Liz.

"Oh, jeez!" Liz cried out. "Jeez!"

Jeremy felt his guts shrivel. In front of him, trolls were *inside the walls*, faces pressed to barred openings, arms stretched out, hands grabbing for the kids as they hurried along. The trolls laughed, jeered, squealed with delight, and yelled.

"Two bits! Gimme two bits!"

"Suck me, sweets!"

"How's about a buck!"

"Fun 'n games, fun 'n games!"

"Ours now!"

"Whee, yes!"

"Fuck me, fuck me!"

"Dead meat! You're all dead meat!"

Heather shrieked. Jeremy whirled around. A toothless crone, both arms outside the bars, had Heather by the sleeve of her jumpsuit. Jeremy slashed one of the hands. The old woman yelped and let go. Heather, still screaming, stumbled away and ran for the stairs. She bounded down the stairway and out of sight.

"Let's go with her!" Shiner shouted close to his ear.

"No!" he gasped. "You go if you want. I'm sticking with Tanya."

"Idiot!"

He went after the others. In the glow of Tanya's candle he saw them hurrying single file down the middle of the hallway, troll arms straining to reach them through the bars. A hand grabbed his shoulder, and he sucked a harsh breath before he realized it was only Shiner.

The hallway went dark.

Tanya's candle had gone out.

"A door!" he heard her yell over the frenzied voices of the trolls.

Reaching into the black, Jeremy touched cloth. Cowboy's denim jacket? He blurted, "It's me," and held on.

"Everybody in!" Tanya called. "Quick, quick!"

"Jumping Judas!"

Jeremy lost his grip on Cowboy's jacket. His shoulder bumped something. A door frame? He stepped forward. His feet sank into a soft, springy substance.

"What is this?" Samson's voice.

"Foam-rubber floor," Liz said. "It's a funhouse thing."

"Some fun."

"I want to get out of here!" Karen whined.

"Last one in, shut the door!" Tanya ordered.

He felt Shiner's hand release him. "I've got it," she said. He heard a door thump shut and latch, and the wild voices of the trolls faded to a dull murmur.

"Okay." From Tanya. "Everyone here?"

"Heather ran off," Jeremy said.

"Reckon she's the smart one," Cowboy said.

"Let's get out of here," Karen pleaded.

"It's like they were waiting for us," Samson said. "I say we scram."

"Yeah," Liz agreed.

"We have to get the camera from that guy."

"What for?" Samson asked. "So he's got pictures. Kids on the boardwalk. Big deal. They don't prove nothing. This is bad shit here."

"Ain't worth it," Cowboy said.

There was silence for a moment. Jeremy heard only his heartbeat, and the breathing of himself and others all around him.

All around him.

Shiner was at his side, and he thought the rest of them were ahead of him. But quiet sounds of breathing seemed to come from everywhere. The hot, stuffy air smelled foul.

"Okay," Tanya said. "We'll go back the way we came and get the hell out of here."

Shiner held on to Jeremy's arm and stepped behind his back. He heard a harsh metallic rattle. Her ringers tightened their grip. "The door's locked," she whispered.

"Oh, shit."

"I don't think we're alone," Liz said, the pitch of her voice climbing with panic.

Something soft and wet lapped the back of Jeremy's hand. His right hand. The one that held the knife flat against his leg.

Something licking it like a dog.

"Yaaah!" He jerked his hand up.

The black room erupted with gasps of alarm, yelps and shrieks and curses.

Shiner's hand flew away from his arm.

He wheeled around to find her. His leg was clutched, hugged tight to a body. He staggered, trying to stay up, but his feet sank into the deep rubber and he fell.

The assailant scurried up his legs. A stench of rotten garbage filled his nostrils. His shirt was torn open. Hair tickled his belly. A face pushed against him, and he felt its nose and whiskers, its dry lips, its quick wet tongue. He grabbed a handful of greasy hair, tugged the face away from him, and rammed his knife down. The blade punched in deep—somewhere near the middle of the back, Jeremy thought. The attacker cried out, jerked rigid, and twisted away, rolling off Jeremy but wrenching the knife from his grip.

He sat up fast and stared at the blackness in front of him. He blinked to make sure his eyes were open.

All around him were sounds of struggle.

Off the floor, he thought. It's the worst place to be.

He got to his knees. Someone tumbled against his back, knocking him forward. He scrambled, kicking at the body, freeing his legs. Gasped as his face met skin. He lurched backward. A hand clamped his raw chin and tried to shove him away. As pain streaked from his wound, a voice in front of him said, "Jeremy?"

The hand flew from his chin to his shoulder and pulled him closer. Shiner flung her arms around him.

Holding each other, they struggled to their feet. They took a few staggering steps and bumped the rubber of a wall.

Off to the side, a vertical band of light appeared. Faint yellowish light. Suddenly the band spread wide.

"A door!" Shiner whispered.

Beyond it, a hallway glowed with candlelight.

Someone lurched through the doorway, escaping.

"Let's go!" Jeremy gasped.

Hanging on to each other, they rushed for the door. The way ahead of them was cluttered with the faint silhouettes of bodies struggling on the floor, others kneeling, some up and staggering. They dodged, leapt. Hands grabbed at them, and they kicked and twisted their way free. Someone lunged in from Shiner's side. Her elbow sent the troll hurling backward.

A dark shape blocked the doorway.

Jeremy threw himself at it.

Hands clutched his jacket, yanked him forward, and flung him into the lighted corridor. Tanya caught him. Turning away from her, he saw Samson tug Shiner out of the black room.

Cowboy was leaning against a wall, Liz sobbing against his chest.

The door slammed shut.

Samson tried the knob, then hit the door with his shoulder. It didn't give. He rammed it again.

"For Godsake, don't!" Tanya blurted.

"Karen's not out." He shot his foot forward, smashing it against the door just beside the knob. Still the door stayed shut.

Samson turned around and leaned against the door frame, shaking his head. His face was twisted with an expression of horror.

Shiner put a hand over her mouth. She stared at Jeremy. Her eyes looked wide and dazed. She was breathing hard. Her white blouse was open to her belly, twisted and hanging off her left shoulder. Her shoulder was streaked with scratches. She had a bloody handprint on the white cup of her bra.

Jeremy went to her. Gently he lifted the blouse onto her shoulder and drew the front shut. He put his arms around her. She was panting for air, trembling.

"It's all right," he said. "It's all right."

Vaguely he wondered why he had gone to Shiner instead of Tanya.

It felt good, though.

"Poor Karen," she whispered.

"Let's worry about us," Tanya said from somewhere behind Jeremy.

Shiner squeezed herself tightly against him.

Then they separated. Shiner took hold of his hand.

Cowboy and Liz were still embracing. He had lost his hat. He still had his knife, though. It was a folding buck knife with a wicked-looking blade. The blade was slick with blood. So was the hand that held it flat against the small of Liz's back while his other hand stroked her hair.

A rear pocket of her jeans hung like a flap below her rump. She had lost one of her sneakers.

Except for his mussed hair, Samson looked as if he hadn't been touched. But his arms were wrapped tightly around his chest, and Jeremy could see that he was shaking. If he still had his knife, it didn't show.

Tanya's knife was at her side, clenched in her right hand. The sleeve of her sweatshirt was drenched in blood to her elbow. The front of her sweatshirt, dark and sodden, clung to her breasts and belly. Her pants, too, looked drenched in blood from her waist to her knees.

A corner of her mouth turned up. "Don't worry, Duke. It's not mine. Just this," she added, and touched a knuckle to a torn crescent of skin over her left cheekbone. That side of her face was sheathed with blood. Trickles spilled off her jaw and ran down her neck.

He went to her, pulling the wadded handkerchief out of his pocket. He took the razor blade from it, dropped the blade into his shirt pocket, and gave the handkerchief to her.

"Thanks," she muttered, pressing it to her wound. "Guess what, Duke? Now you've got a good excuse for your face. You can tell your mom the trolls nailed you."

"If I ever see her again," he said.

"Don't worry, you will." Looking toward the others, Tanya said, "We'll all get out of here. Right?"

Only Samson answered. He said, "Yeah, sure."

"Let's get to it." Tanya waited while the others gathered in close to her. Shiner took Jeremy's hand again. Her mouth twitched as she tried to smile. There was dread in her eyes.

Tanya took the lead.

This section of hallway had no barred openings in its walls. There was no sign of trolls.

Not until Jeremy's shoes scraped a metal grating on the floor and he looked down and saw the blur of a face. He sprang off the grille. "They're under us!" he blurted.

Samson, standing on a similar panel just ahead of him, leapt forward.

Jeremy looked back. Cowboy swooped Liz up. Cradling her

in his arms, he stepped onto the grate. He danced on it, stomping it with his boots.

Jeremy and Shiner continued through the hallway. Beneath the next grille were two faces. The trolls watched in silence as they took long strides and cleared the grate without stepping on it.

Jeremy heard Cowboy, still back there, prancing on the first grate. "I'll be durned if I'm not starting to—"

A deafening clap pounded Jeremy's ears. Even as he whirled around, he knew he would see Cowboy dropping through the floor, Liz in his arms.

But he was wrong.

Cowboy still stood on the grate. Liz was falling. He was bringing up his knife as something swept down at him.

A man. A naked burly man with a hairy back and a bald head. Swinging down headfirst like a live pendulum from the trapdoor in the ceiling. Ropes around his ankles. A meat cleaver in each hand.

He yelled, "Wheeeee!" as he flew toward Cowboy.

Cowboy hopped backward. The cleavers flashed, trying for Liz. But she was flat on the floor. The blades chopped the air above her, missing by inches. The man began his upward arc, going for Cowboy with the cleavers.

Cowboy lunged at him and leapt backward again. The body jerked, twisted on its ropes like a swing knocked crooked, and crashed against the wall. One of the cleavers sank into the wall. The other dropped to the floor.

Cowboy snatched that one up as the man swung downward. Swung over Liz, showering her. Swung toward Jeremy and Shiner, spinning. The handle of Cowboy's knife jutted from his throat. He spouted blood and urine.

Cowboy jumped over Liz and threw himself against the man. Slammed him against the wall. Went at him with the cleaver. Shiner twisted her head away as Cowboy hacked him. The blow split him down the middle. Intestines slopped out like coils of wet snakes.

Jeremy doubled over, retching.

His vomit cascaded onto the grate at his feet.

Someone below him gasped, "Ugh!"

When he finished and straightened up, Cowboy was helping Liz to her feet. The body hung in the middle of the hallway, swaying and turning. Jeremy didn't let himself focus on it. Instead, he watched Cowboy and Liz step past it.

Cowboy had a cleaver in one hand, his knife in the other. Liz held the second cleaver.

As she stepped past the body, she gave it a whack in the chest. The blow severed a small section of hanging guts, which fell past the man's face and hit the floor with a soft wet smack.

Jeremy gagged and covered his mouth. This time, he didn't throw up.

Cowboy grinned. His eyes and teeth were white. The rest of him was red. He looked as if a tub of gore had been dumped over his head. Jeremy could *smell* it. "Weak stomach, Duke?"

"You sure creamed him."

"Massacred the son of a whore, huh? No quarter."

"Thought you were goners," Samson said.

"Are you both all right?" Tanya asked. Her voice came from close behind Jeremy.

"I reckon I could use a bath," Cowboy said.

Liz laughed and slapped his chest. Blood flew off his shirt like red dust.

"Okay," Tanya said. "Let's keep going. Everybody look sharp. God knows what we're gonna run into next."

They started to walk. Jeremy stepped on gratings without any hesitation. They all stepped on the grates. As if the weird attack and Cowboy's slaughter of the swinging man had numbed them to such matters as trolls lurking below their feet.

They watched the ceiling. They watched the walls.

They came to the end of the hall.

On the right was a closed door. On the left was a dark opening.

Tanya pulled a candle from its holder, knelt in front of the opening, and leaned forward. The candle and her head vanished for a moment. Then she stood up. "I don't know," she said.

"What is it?"

"A slide."

"A slide?" Samson asked.

"This is a fucking *funhouse,*" Liz reminded him.

"Where does it go?"

"It goes down," Tanya said. "I couldn't see much of it. But it should take us down to the ground floor."

"Yeah," Samson said. "And whatever's waiting for us there."

"Better than being up here."

"Why don't we try that door?" Shiner asked.

"Good thought," Liz said. "*You* try it,"

"No, don't," Jeremy warned.

"I'll try the slide," Tanya said.

"Don't," Jeremy told her.

"What're we supposed to do, stay here? Let me borrow that chopper of yours, Cowboy."

He held it out. Samson took it from him. "I'll go down first," he said. "You guys wait up here till you hear from me."

Tanya kissed his mouth.

Jeremy expected to feel a pang of jealousy, but he didn't. The guy deserves a kiss, he thought. Better him than me.

"Good man," Tanya said. "This is one I owe you."

He made a sick-looking smile. Turning away, he sat on the floor. He scooted into the opening. Tanya gave him the candle. "It'll probably blow out anyway," he said, but he kept it. He clutched the cleaver against his chest, hunched forward, and dropped out of sight.

Tanya knelt and peered in after him.

"Get ready to go fast," she said. "He'll need us."

Suddenly a shriek welled out of the opening. Not a shriek of fright, but a high ragged cry of agony.

"Samson!" Tanya yelled.

"Oh, sweet Jesus!" Samson wailed. "Oh, mother of . . . Ahhhh! Ahhhh!"

"What is it?" Tanya called.

"I'm . . . I'm . . . God, *it hurts!*"

"Should we come down?"

"No! *No!* For Godsake!"

"Maybe the door," Shiner said. She squeezed Jeremy's arm, then rushed across the hallway.

"Wait!" he yelled.

She yanked the door open and lurched back fast.

She whirled around, gasping, as the troll sprang out. A gawky gray-faced man with a wild black beard. He grabbed the back of Shiner's blouse and yanked her off her feet. Jeremy leapt to save her. She was falling backward, eyes bulging, hands reaching out for him. A cleaver, apparently thrown by Liz, flipped end over end and flashed past the man's head, just missing him, and vanished into the dark room at his back. Jeremy's fingers grazed Shiner's fingers. They flew away from him. He cried out, "No!" as she was hurled into the room. The door struck his upper arm, knocking him sideways, and slammed shut.

An instant before he threw himself against the door, Jeremy heard the clack of a sliding bolt. He clutched the knob, twisted it, tugged at it, crying "No! Let her out! Let her out, you bastard!"

He pounded the door, smashed at it with his shoulder, kicked at it.

The door stayed shut.

He sank to his knees, weeping.

Forty-two

Seconds after hearing the faint sound of the whistle, Robin saw a kid run out onto the boardwalk. He was the one, she guessed, who'd been left behind by the others to stand watch for the cops.

That's what the whistle meant.

The cops are coming.

I just have to last, she thought. They'll get me down.

If they know I'm here.

The kid was *so* far away.

He stopped in the middle of the boardwalk. There he turned around in circles, probably wondering where his friends had gone. He looked like a little kid lost in a supermarket, trying to find his mom.

If he was calling, Robin couldn't hear him.

His head swung around as he glanced over his shoulder toward the Funland entrance. Then he ran straight ahead. Robin saw him start down the beach stairs. After that, her left arm blocked her view.

She looked down again.

No sign of the three trolls. But she knew where they had to be. Behind her. Probably on the Ferris wheel's platform. Probably trying to start the thing going.

She wished she could see what was happening back there.

A handcuff suddenly slipped up her left hand, scraping over the knuckle of her thumb. Her stomach seemed to drop out from under her. Gasping, she willed her fist to clench.

Her fingers tingled with the effort.

The cuff slipped up her hand.

Christ!

Her fingers hooked the curved rim of the bracelet, and she held on, heart suddenly thundering, feet kicking.

Now! her mind shouted. *Now or never! Christ!*

Right hand balled in a tight fist, left hand clinging to the cuff, she bent her arms at the elbows and drew herself upward. Higher, higher. The edge of the footrest rubbed against her rump, then against the backs of her thighs. Her muscles ached. The cuffs felt like knife blades pressing into her fingers and fist. She whimpered and groaned, pumped her legs as if trying to climb the rungs of a ladder that wasn't there. The gondola rocked, its footrest nudging her forward and easing away, swinging her.

Slowly she rose until her bleeding left wrist was in front of her eyes. Then she came to her fingers squeezed tight over the curved steel of the bracelet, her other hand pinched inside the right cuff. She forced herself higher. Her eyes were inches from the connecting chain. Higher. Up to the safety bar. Higher, until the bar was even with her chin.

Now what? she wondered.

Her arm muscles burned. She gritted her teeth. Sweat stung her eyes. Sweat or blood trickled down her sides and was turned cold by the ocean breeze.

Go for it!

Robin gripped the safety bar with her right hand, released the cuff, and grabbed hold with her left hand. She thrust her head forward, catching the bar under her chin.

Her sudden motions set the gondola rocking. Its footrest shoved at the backs of her knees.

Swinging by the bar, she jerked her legs up. When the footrest swept forward again, it brushed the bottoms of her feet. She flung herself away from the bar, thrusting her body backward, and tumbled onto the seat. The gondola pitched madly, as if it wanted to toss her out. She spread-eagled herself, jamming her heels against the metal lip of its floor, shoving herself hard against the seat back, grabbing the sides.

Soon the gondola slowed to a gentle sway.

Robin brought her arms down, slid her legs together. She sat there for a few moments, shuddering and gasping for breath.

I made it, she thought.

My God, I made it!

With the thumb and forefinger of her right hand, she pinched the head of the pin and gave it a quick pull. The pin slid out of her chest. The breeze lifted the card free and sent it tumbling away into the night. Robin tossed the pin after it. The hole felt sore and itchy. In a way, it seemed more irritating than her other wounds. They were serious hurts, but this one was pesky. She rubbed it with the heel of her hand.

When it felt better, she lowered the hand onto her lap and pulled the cuff off. She dropped the cuffs onto the seat. She flexed her hands. Though they still felt a little numb, blood was beginning to circulate better. Her fingers tingled as if they'd been asleep.

A chilly gust buffeted her. Gritting her teeth, she folded her arms across her chest, cupped a breast in the warmth of each hand, and squeezed her legs together.

Now all I've got to worry about, she thought, is dying of exposure.

She suddenly remembered the three trolls somewhere below.

Icy fear spread through the pit of her stomach.

They can't get me, she told herself.

If they could start the wheel going, they would've done it before now.

Maybe they're just lying low until the cops . . .

The cops!

Robin leaned slowly forward and gripped the safety bar. She peered past the side of the gondola. The area near Funland's main entrance was deserted. She scanned the entire length of the boardwalk. The moon-washed planking looked as gray as driftwood. The shadows were black smudges.

Maybe the kid's whistle had been a false alarm.

Maybe he had seen cops, but they were on the way to some other destination.

Give them time, she told herself.

Though it seemed like forever since the kid had blown his whistle, it was probably no more than two or three minutes ago.

They might still show up.

The thought no sooner passed through her mind than a dark figure stepped out of the entryway's shadows. Robin caught her breath. Then let it out, sighing with frustration.

This wasn't a cop, it was a goddamn troll. She shuffled along, hunched over like an old witch, wrapped in a blanket that covered her head.

Wait!

That girl who'd warned the others—she'd said her sister the cop would be coming dressed as a troll.

That's her!

Robin scooted across the seat, leaned out as far as she dared over the safety bar, thrust an arm out, waved, and shouted.

In the middle of the boardwalk, Joan slowly turned around.

No one.

Where the hell are they? she wondered.

Somebody *had* to be here. There'd been the whistle. There was the car parked in front, its engine running.

Shouldn't have wasted time at the car, she thought. That had eaten up a minute or two.

The car might be all we'll get, she told herself. It had been hot-wired, obviously stolen. Maybe by the same people who nailed Gloria.

But where are they now?

And where's their victim?

Somebody in the backseat had bled.

They must be around here.

At least they won't be driving off on us, she thought.

While Dave was copying the license number, Joan had cut the ignition wires with her knife, then rolled up the windows and locked the doors.

They aren't going anywhere. Not in that car.

She turned around and shook her head. "The place looks deserted," she said.

A silhouette, backlighted by the glow from the parking lot, appeared in the darkness beside the ticket booth. "What do you want to do?" Dave asked.

"They've gotta be somewhere."

"Do you want me out there with you?"

"It'd blow the cover."

"If they've already got someone, they might not try for you anyway."

That was true enough. And the whistle might've been blown by a sentry, warning his friends that intruders were on the way. They might have fled up the beach, or scattered and hidden themselves somewhere among the rides or buildings of Funland.

"Just stay close enough to keep an eye on me," Joan said. "I'll head on down the boardwalk, see if I can draw them—"

"Behind you!"

She whirled around.

Two pale figures rushing up the stairs from the beach.

Their hands were empty.

A boy and a girl.

No threat from these two, Joan thought.

The guy had a slight build, and wore glasses that gleamed in the moonlight. A chrome whistle hung from a chain around his neck. The huffing girl beside him had a face as round as a bowling ball. She was dressed in a jumpsuit that bulged over bouncing piles of fat.

Could these be trollers?

A wimp and a blimp.

But they might have friends nearby, watching, waiting to pounce.

Joan released the grips of her .38 and took her hand out from under her sweatshirt. She held the hand toward them, palm up.

Might as well play it to the hilt, she thought.

Hope they didn't hear Dave.

Still a few strides away from her, the two kids halted. They glanced at each other. They were both out of breath.

"How's about a coupla bits?" Joan croaked. "Ain't had me a bite t'eat in—"

"I think we need help, Officer," the boy said.

Officer?

"Something awful's happening," the girl suddenly blurted. "I got away. I got out and I don't know what's going on, but I think it's awfully bad. The trolls. Trolls in the walls. You gotta come."

"Dave!" Joan called over her shoulder.

He hurried forward. He had his Beretta out, barrel raised beside his head.

"They've made me. They say there's some kind of trouble."

"Pat 'em down," Dave said. "Hands on your heads, kids, and interlace your fingers."

"We haven't done anything," the boy protested, but he followed instructions. So did the girl.

"What're you doing out here?"

"Nothing."

"We'd better let them talk," Joan said. Flinging her blanket off, she stepped behind the boy and started to frisk him. "Something's going down."

"The others . . ." the girl said. "We went in a . . . a basement . . . and . . ."

"Let's hear about last night," Dave said. "Tell us about the troll you got last night."

Joan felt a long hard bulge in the boy's right-front pocket. "Got something here."

"We didn't do anything last night," the boy said. "If you waste time giving us the third degree about some stupid—!"

Joan stuffed her hand into his pocket.

"Hey! You don't have a search warrant. I've got my rights!"

"You've got the right to shut up," Joan said.

"Please!" the girl whined. "Our friends!"

"Your friends are trollers," Dave said. "If they've gotten into a mess, too damn bad. Let's go back to last night."

Joan pulled a knife from the boy's pocket. She thumbed a button on its handle. The blade sprang out and locked. "Switchblade," she said. She closed it and tossed it underhand to Dave. He glanced at it, then pushed it into a pocket of his jeans.

"You kids are in deep shit," he said. "Now, I want to hear everything you know about a woman you and your friends nailed here last night."

Done frisking the boy, Joan stepped behind the girl and started to pat her down. Her flesh felt loose and soft under the velour jumpsuit.

"We weren't here last night," the boy said. "I don't know what you're talking about."

The girl began to sob. "They're gonna be killed! They're *all* gonna be killed! I just know it!"

"She's clean," Joan said.

"Okay. Well, we've got this one on a weapons charge."

Joan stepped in front of them. "Where are the others?"

"They want to *bust* me. Don't tell them."

"I have to! It was so bad! You weren't there, you don't know how bad it was."

The boy's face twisted with indecision.

"They aren't gonna bust you, Randy. They can't. If they bust you, they've gotta bust her sister, and—"

Joan's heart lurched. "Whose sister?"

"Yours," the boy said.

"Shiner," the girl said. "Betty."

"Debbie," the boy corrected her.

Joan went cold and rigid.

"Jesus Christ," Dave muttered.

Debbie. A troller. No, that was impossible.

Trolls in the walls.

They're gonna be killed! They're all *gonna be killed!*

"Show us where they are," Joan said.

"No." The kid grabbed the girl's sleeve and glared at Joan. "First you have to promise you won't—"

Joan's open hand hit his face. His head snapped sideways. His glasses flew off and skidded across the boards.

"Move it!" she yelled in the girl's face.

The girl swung around and trotted toward the stairs, Joan close behind her.

"It'll be all right," Dave said.

"No!" Robin shouted. "Come back!"

But they didn't hear her. They'd heard none of her yells. They'd never even glanced in her direction.

She was just too far away, too great a distance down the boardwalk, and too high up for her voice to reach them through the sounds of the wind and surf.

Clinging to the side of the gondola, she watched the fat girl rush down the stairs to the beach, followed by the woman and man. The kid bent down. He picked up his glasses and put them on, stood there for a few moments as if he didn't know what to do, then ran to catch up with the others.

All four of them disappeared beneath the boardwalk.

Robin groaned.

She leaned further out over the side of the gondola and peered down.

The platform beside the Ferris wheel was deserted.

Where had the trolls gone?

Twisting her head around, she saw them.

On the wheel. Climbing its struts and spokes. Coming for her.

Forty-three

"You won't do Shiner any good crying about it," Tanya said. She pulled Jeremy to his feet. Through his tears, he saw Cowboy step to the door, jerk its knob, shake his head. "We've gotta keep going," Tanya said. Her open hands rubbed his chest.

"She was just here 'cause of me."

"She was a troller like the rest of us. She took her chances, month after month, before you even came along."

"Can't we do something?"

"She's likely dead as monkey shit by now," Cowboy said.

"You've gotta be brave," Tanya said. "For me. You're my soldier. You're my lover." She pulled him gently toward her. She lifted the bloody front of her sweatshirt. Though Cowboy and Liz were right there, probably watching, neither of them said a word. Tanya rubbed her breasts against him. They felt a little sticky from the blood that had soaked through her sweatshirt, but they were smooth and soft.

This is wrong, Jeremy thought. Wrong for her to do this . . . everything that's happened . . . Shiner . . . Shiner's gone . . . I couldn't save her . . . Shouldn't be doing this to me . . .

Even as tears rolled down his cheeks and his breath hitched with sobs, he felt heat spreading low inside him.

"You're my brave lover," Tanya said.

Jeremy took one of her breasts in his hand and caressed it.

"Yes," she said. "Yes, feel me. I'm alive. I'm yours." She squeezed him gently through the front of his pants. "When we're out of here, you'll have me."

He sniffed and nodded.

"That's in case savin' your own hide ain't incentive enough," Cowboy said.

Tanya backed away from Jeremy. She pulled her sweatshirt down and turned to the opening low in the wall. She squatted. "Samson?"

No answer.

Jeremy hadn't noticed any sounds from Samson since the moment Shiner opened the door and . . .

He saw it all again in his mind—the horrible troll, the stunned, pleading look on Shiner's face, the cleaver flying by, the door slamming. To be locked in a room with that monster . . . Oh, God!

She'd told him once that her greatest fear was to be caught by trolls. Now it had happened.

Jeremy hoped she *was* dead. Hoped that she had died quickly. So much better than to be alive while that hideous troll *did things* to her.

I'm sorry, he thought. God, Shiner, I'm so sorry. It's my fault. If only I'd gone to your house tonight . . .

"Samson must've bit it," Cowboy said.

"This is our only way out," Tanya said

"I'll go down," Jeremy said. He sniffed and wiped his eyes. "I'll go first."

Tanya nodded. "Okay. Good man."

"Let's try to lower him down," Liz said. "You know, hang on to him."

"Good," Tanya said. "Go down headfirst, I'll hang on to your feet and go down after you. Liz, you take my feet."

"I'll be the anchor," Cowboy said.

Tanya gave her knife to Jeremy. She took a candle off the wall and gave it to him.

Holding the knife and candle out ahead of him, Jeremy lay on the floor and squirmed forward, thrusting himself along with his elbows and knees. The metal sheet of the slide below his face shimmered golden in the candlelight. There were wooden walls on both sides, a wooden ceiling about three feet above the ramp. Not far down the slide, darkness swallowed the meager light. He squinted, but saw nothing in that darkness.

"Can you see him?" Tanya asked.

"No. I can't see much." He scooted forward, bending at the waist. First his elbows and chest, then his belly met the cool slick surface. He felt Tanya's hands wrap around his ankles. They held him, pushed him, and in seconds the entire length of his body was stretched flat against the slide.

For a few moments he didn't move. Then he started downward again. He pictured Tanya above him, being lowered as he'd been.

"See anything?" Tanya asked.

"Not yet."

"Here I come," Liz said.

Jeremy slid lower, lower.

At the dim border of his candle's glow, he saw the head and shoulders of Samson. "I see him! Samson? Samson?" The boy neither answered nor moved. "It's like he's stopped here."

"Is he dead?" Tanya asked.

"I don't know. I guess so."

"Can you tell what happened to him?"

"Huh-uh."

He stretched his arms out. His fists pushed against the tops of Samson's shoulders. He shoved at the body. It shook slightly but didn't slide away. "He's stuck," Jeremy said.

"Can you get past him?"

"I don't know. Maybe you'd better let go of my feet." He felt Tanya release him. He raised his head. Samson's eyes and mouth were wide open. The arms were raised from the elbows, fingers hooked down, as if he had died clawing at the darkness.

"Do something," Tanya said.

"Yeah. Okay." He lifted his fists and slid until his throat pushed against the top of Samson's head and his elbows met the dead boy's shoulders.

There, with the candle high, he gazed down the length of the body. He saw no wounds. But Samson's legs were spread, and below them the slide gleamed with blood.

Not far beyond Samson's feet was the end of the slide.

"I see the bottom," Jeremy announced.

"What happened with Samson?"

"I think there must be knives or something under him. I think they're in the slide."

"Jesus," Tanya muttered.

"Okay, I'm going over him."

Jeremy pushed himself up, clamped Tanya's knife in his teeth to free his right hand, and began to move forward, squirming, lifting himself onto the body. The head turned sideways under his chest. He felt the tickle of Samson's hair, the bristle of his whiskers. He had a sudden fear of the clawed hands, so he pushed Samson's arms down before squirming further. The body wobbled under him. It slipped a few inches, and he heard wet ripping sounds as he rode it. When the body halted, Jeremy studied the bloody slide to make sure there were no blades waiting for him, then scurried over the rest of Samson, wanting off him fast, no matter what might be in the darkness below. He felt the head press against his groin. He felt the cool damp of Samson's jeans against his chest, then the slippery metal of the slide. He grabbed the boy's leg as if it were a banister, using it to ease him along, to slow his descent and prevent the candle from blowing out.

Holding on to Samson's shoe, he glided to the lip of the slide. He listened. He heard nothing except his thudding heart, his gasping breath, and sounds of movement on the slide behind him.

If trolls were waiting for him, they were being very quiet.

Candle in front of him, he dragged himself forward. The floor was a yard below his face. He raised his head and swung it from side to side. In the light of the candle he saw a section of hallway.

He saw no trolls.

He scurried off the slide and stood up. He scanned the darkness beyond the candle's glow. Then he turned to the slide. "I'm down," he called, his voice rasping and shaky. "I don't see anyone. It looks okay."

"I'm on my way," Tanya said.

"Hurry."

"There," the girl said. She pointed. Dave swept his flashlight past a piling. It lit the concrete wall of a building's foundation. The wall was scribbled with graffiti. "More to the right," the girl said. He moved the light. The pale disk of its beam found a patch of boards. "It's a door. It opens up. They went in there. It's the Funhouse. We were chasing some guy."

Dave stepped past Joan and rushed to the wall. He clamped the flashlight under his arm and pulled at the edge of the boards. They swung outward. He leaned into the opening. A small enclosure. Lighted candles on the walls. A staircase leading upward. He looked over his shoulder but couldn't see anyone back there. "They went up the stairs?" he asked.

"Yeah," came the girl's voice. "We all did. But I chickened out and ran. All those trolls."

"All right," Joan said. "You two get out of here. Go home."

"Aren't you arresting me?" the boy asked.

"No. Go home."

"Jeez. Thanks."

"Sorry I hit you, kid. Now, go!"

Seconds later, Dave saw the dim shape of Joan rushing toward him. She came into the faint light from the candles, reached under her sweatshirt, and pulled out her revolver. Her face, smeared with grime from the tire of her car, was intended to make her resemble a troll. Instead, she looked like a commando camouflaged for a night raid. Dave saw fear in her eyes. And outrage.

"We'll get her," he said.

"Bet your ass we will," Joan said, and rushed past him.

"Hold it!" he snapped.

She stopped and looked around.

"I go first. Stay with me. Stay *glued* to me, dammit."

Joan nodded.

Flashlight in one hand, pistol in the other, Dave bounded up the stairs, taking them three at a time. At the first landing he covered Joan while she tried the door. It was locked. They raced up the stairway to the second floor.

In front of Dave was a dark hallway. He swept it with his flashlight. Nobody ahead. But his blood seemed to freeze when he saw barred windowlike openings along the walls.

Trolls in the walls.

He saw no trolls, though.

He flinched as something nudged him. Just Joan. Pressing against his back.

"Don't stop," she whispered.

He started forward, shining his light from wall to wall. Faces rose behind the bars. The dirty, leering faces of men and women. A small whimper came from Joan.

All along the corridor ahead, arms reached out, flopping and waving like the tentacles of a beast that lived in the walls.

Dave rushed forward, Joan at his back.

The trolls in the walls laughed and jeered, begged for coins, tittered, snapped obscenities and threats. Fingertips brushed Dave's arms, plucked at his sleeves. Someone yelped, but it was the outcry of an injured man, and Dave guessed that Joan had struck one of the reaching hands.

At least she's not blowing the bastards away, he thought.

He was tempted, himself, but he kept his finger off the trigger.

He batted a hand away with the barrel of his flashlight.

As the beam of his flashlight skittered through the dark, it lit a door in front of him.

Robin knelt on the seat of the gondola, clutching its back. She gazed down through the maze of wires, unlighted bulbs, struts, and spokes at the three trolls who were slowly climbing the Ferris wheel.

"Pritty, pritty," called the nearest one. He was about twenty feet away, climbing a spoke that would lead him to the highest gondola. Once there, he would be able to come at her along the outer wheel, which had only a gradual slant before it met the side of Robin's carriage.

He was lean, gray-faced, bald except for a fringe of hair around his ears. He wore a dark suit coat and slacks that looked as if they'd been made to fit a much larger man. The wind fluttered his clothes, and he was near enough for Robin to hear their quiet flapping. "Gonna getcha!" he squealed. "Yessir. Don' go nowhere, pritty!" He wheezed out a laugh, as if he thought that was a great joke.

"I get her first, you piece of shit," snapped the man below him. The one with the patch on his eye.

His voice was strong. He didn't sound crazy or loaded.

The third troll was lower than the other two, apparently climbing with more caution. He seemed like a distant threat.

These creeps will get to me long before he does, Robin thought.

The one in the oversize suit grabbed the side of the uppermost gondola. He turned his face to her and grinned. "Ooooo, yer all mi—"

He shrieked as the one-eyed troll tugged a cuff of his trousers, yanking him downward. He kicked and squirmed for a moment, then lost his hold and tumbled away. Robin caught her own breath as she watched him fall, twisting through the moonlight. He landed headfirst on the platform. The Ferris wheel shook with his impact.

The one-eyed troll climbed to the side of the upper gondola. Instead of getting into it, he pulled himself onto the narrow steel beam of the outer wheel. Straddling the beam, he began to work his way toward Robin.

On the floor at the foot of the slide, Jeremy found another candle. He supposed Samson had dropped it. He used his candle to ignite its wick. The light seemed to double around him. He spotted the meat cleaver. It must've flown off the end of the slide, for it lay in the middle of the hallway.

Holding both candles in his left hand, he squatted and snatched up the cleaver and hurried back to the slide.

He watched Tanya crawl out. She pulled herself forward, walking her hands over the floor. Her sweatpants hung around her knees. Her bare rump and the backs of her legs looked wonderful in the soft glow of the candles.

She dropped onto the floor, rolled onto her back, and lay there gasping.

Jeremy felt as if his breath were being sucked out.

"Looky there," someone whispered.

"Yummmmy, yum yum yum."

"Poke her, young fella," urged the raspy voice of a woman.

Jeremy's stomach clenched. Tanya gasped, jerked the sweatpants to her waist, and bolted up.

"Awww."

"Havin' fun yet, kiddies?"

Raising his candles high, Jeremy looked up.

Grates on the ceiling. Faces pressed to the strips of metal.

"Fucking trolls!" Tanya snapped.

A string of drool spilled onto her forehead. She wiped it off with a bloody sleeve, grabbed Jeremy's arm, and pulled him close to the wall so they no longer stood beneath any of the grates.

"I'd like to kill 'em all," he whispered.

His remark brought laughter and jeers down from the ceiling.

As they waited, he handed Tanya's knife back and gave her one of the candles.

Liz crawled out of the opening, stood up, and joined them.

"Another girlie."

"More the merrier."

"Hurry it up, Cowboy!" Liz called.

"Cowboy?" A troll giggled. "They got 'em a cowboy."

"Strip down, gals. Gimme a peek. C'mon, be nice."

"Eat shit," Liz snapped.

"Lemme eat you!"

Finally Cowboy came out. But not headfirst, like the others. His boots appeared. He crawled backward, dragging Samson after him. The huge body tumbled off the slide, smashing Cowboy to the floor.

The back of Samson's jeans were ripped and bloody. A slab of flesh from his inner thigh hung out. One blade had done that. A second had split his inseam. The sight made a cold ache in Jeremy's groin.

Cowboy crawled clear, and Tanya crouched beside Samson.

"Two big knife blades sticking up right outta the slide," Cowboy said. He spoke loudly to be heard over the laughter, squeals of delight, and remarks from the trolls in the ceiling. "Fuckin' A. All I could do to get him off the things. One of 'em got him right in the nuts."

"One must've clipped his femoral," Tanya said. "That's why he died so fast. You don't last a minute when that gets hit."

"Must've been one bad sucker of a minute," Cowboy said.

Tanya patted Samson's back. Then she stood up. "Okay, let's get going."

"I ain't gonna leave him here," Cowboy said.

"That's crazy," Liz said.

"He's too big for us to carry," Tanya said. "We'll be lucky to get out of this hellhole ourselves—we sure can't make it hauling around a stiff."

"No way I'm leaving Samuel here. He was my friend. What do you suppose these fuckin' trolls'll do to him when we're gone?"

"He's dead," Liz said. "He isn't gonna care."

"Well, I reckon I care."

He rolled the body over, took hold of its hand, and pulled it to a sitting position. Jeremy crouched at Samson's back and lifted. Then Tanya joined in.

They raised Samson off the floor. Cowboy ducked and hoisted the body in a fireman's carry.

Just the way Samson carried that fat old troll to the Ferris wheel, Jeremy thought. Only Cowboy was a lot smaller than Samson.

"You got him okay?" Tanya asked.

"Yeah."

Liz stayed at his side, and Jeremy walked with Tanya.

He kept the cleaver in his right hand and held the candle ahead of him, squinting, trying to see beyond its glow as they made their slow way through the corridor. The trolls went silent behind them. There didn't seem to be any openings in the floor, walls, or ceiling along this section of the hall. That was a relief, but Jeremy half-expected an attack at any moment, and he knew it might come from anywhere.

It's up to me, he thought.

With Samson dead and Cowboy burdened under the big guy, Jeremy felt as if he had become the group's main protector.

I'll take care of them, he told himself. Me. Duke. I'm the main man now.

He felt a small flicker of pride.

Just ahead of him the hallway suddenly looked *round*.

"I'll check it out," he whispered, and took quick strides past Tanya.

He stopped at the edge of a contraption that looked like an enormous barrel lying on its side. A wooden barrel. Its inside walls bristled with spikes that gleamed in the light of his candle.

He nudged the rim with his foot.

His touch started the barrel into a slow spin.

Tanya brushed against his side. "Real cute," she muttered.

"We can't go this way," Jeremy said.

Liz appeared at his other side and peered at the turning cylinder. "Shit. They sure rigged this damn place. How're we gonna get through there? It'll tear us to pieces."

"We'll get through," Tanya said. "Cowboy, haul Samuel on over here."

Forty-four

Dave swung the door open. He probed the room with his flashlight, and what he saw made him want to run from the Funhouse. But he knew they couldn't leave without Debbie. He stepped inside. "Police officers!" he snapped. "Drop your weapons! Up against the wall!"

Joan entered. "Oh, dear God," she muttered. The door bumped shut.

Shoulder to shoulder, they swept their handguns back and forth as the powerful beam of Dave's flashlight moved through the darkness.

The trolls climbed off each other. They climbed off sprawled, motionless bodies. They shambled to the right side of the room, a couple of them tossing knives to the soft rubber floor, and pressed their backs against the wall. About a dozen of them. Most wore little or nothing. All were drenched with blood.

Four bodies remained on the floor.

Two males, two females.

Naked and mauled. Dave saw caved-in faces, eyeless sockets, slashed throats, a severed arm, a man whose chest had been stripped of skin. He saw worse, and jerked his flashlight away from the carnage. He stared at the trolls lined up against the walls.

"What *are* you?" he whispered.

A wizened old crone cackled, raised a hand from her side, and said, "What're you? What're you?" As she spoke, her hand worked, moving the "mouth" of the bloody sock it wore.

Dave aimed his pistol at her face.

"Bullet in the bean," her sock puppet chanted. "Slug in the noodle. Bad for the brain-pan, that."

"Shut up!"

Joan stepped forward. She stood over one of the female corpses. Dave lit it for her.

It was young and slender. The legs stuck straight out to the sides, as if a couple of trolls had played tug of war with them. Not much was left of the breasts. Nothing was left of the face.

"It's not Debbie," Joan muttered.

How could she tell?

Dave couldn't bring himself to ask.

He saw for himself that the other mutilated female wasn't Joan's sister. This corpse was fat.

Joan stepped over the body. Turning around, she walked backward toward the door at the other end of the room. "Let's go," she said.

Dave swept his light over the trolls at the wall. "What about these . . . things?"

"I don't care. Let's just leave 'em."

"After what they've done?"

"I don't care. I want Debbie."

Dave started across the room, shining his light on the bodies, stepping around them, his shoes sinking into the soft rubber mat, sliding on the blood. He aimed the beam forward to light Joan's way. He shone it on the trolls along the wall.

Joan waited until he was close to her, then opened the door.

"Anybody comes out after us is dead," he warned. Then he followed Joan through the doorway. He pulled the door shut and tried its knob. The door was locked. But just from this side, probably.

He backed away from it, pistol ready in case it should fly open, half-hoping the trolls would make a try for them.

Jeremy, crouching, put his cleaver on the floor and gripped one of the steel spikes to hold the barrel as steady as possible while Tanya crawled through. In the light from her candle, he could see Liz and Cowboy at the other end, also gripping spikes. Their efforts weren't enough to keep the barrel from rocking slightly from side to side while Tanya made her way over Samson.

It sickened him to think they were using the boy this way. But none of them could've gotten through alive if they hadn't dropped the body across the bottom of the barrel. Samson was tall enough to stretch most of the way from one end to the other, and thick enough to absorb the full length of the four-inch spikes.

Must have twenty or thirty in him, Jeremy thought.

Samson can't feel them.

If he knew what was going on, he might even be happy about it. He was like a bridge that might get his friends out of here. And he would probably like the idea of Tanya squirming over him like that.

Tanya was almost out now. She stopped, sank down against Samson, kissed his lips, and whispered, "Thank you, Samuel."

They're all calling him Samuel now, Jeremy realized. As if it's not right to use his nickname anymore.

Tanya raised herself. Kneeling on Samson's chest, high up near his shoulders, she reached out. Jeremy set his candle on the floor. He grabbed her wrists and pulled as she sprang forward.

They stumbled together away from the barrel.

When they crouched down to hold it for Liz, it was rocking slowly, lifting Samson's body from one side to the other. In spite of the motion, he didn't slip or slide at all. He might have been glued to the thing. But he wasn't.

Robin pressed her shuddering body tight against the back of the seat and watched the troll scoot slowly along the Ferris wheel's rim.

He was almost near enough to reach her.

She prayed that he would fall.

Though he moved cautiously, he didn't seem afraid of that. His legs were hugging the narrow beam, his hands sliding forward, gripping it, pulling himself closer to her. He never looked down at his hands. His single eye stayed on Robin.

She had thought about trying to get away. She had even turned from him for just a few moments, peered over the front of the gondola, and weighed her chances of reaching the safety of the next car down.

It was about eight to ten feet below her, but farther out. Too far out to attempt a leap into its seat. More than likely, she would miss and fall behind it. She might be able to shinny down one of the outer wheels that slanted down from the side of her gondola, but even that seemed like too great a risk.

Face it, she'd thought, you're a chicken.

She'd spent too long out there dangling in midair.

Besides, getting to a lower gondola would be no more than a temporary solution.

It would put her closer to the other troll, who was still a good distance below.

Unless she was ready to try climbing all the way down . . .

No way.

I'll make my stand right here, thank you.

Now, with the one-eyed troll no more than an arm's length away, she wondered if she had made the right choice.

"Don't come any closer," she said. "I'll knock you down, dammit!"

A grin slid up his face.

Robin reached down to the seat. The cuffs lay there beside her right knee. She curled her fingers inside one of the bracelets.

"I'm warning you," she said.

"I'm trembling."

Hanging on to the seat back, she thrust herself away as the troll's left hand dropped onto its edge. He leaned toward her, the gondola rocking under his weight. Before he could lurch forward and pounce in beside her, she grabbed his wrist. She tore his fingers from the seat, shot her other hand up from beside her leg, and swung at him. The loose cuff, flying at the end of its short chain, lashed his cheek. The impact knocked his head sideways. His mouth jerked open in pain. Robin twisted on her knees, yanking his clutched wrist across her body, tearing him off the beam, and letting go.

The troll yelped with alarm.

His right hand caught the back of the gondola. His left hand batted the air. Before it could find a hold—while he hung by only his right hand, twisting and kicking—Robin clawed his fingers off the edge.

He dropped straight down, yelling, *"Noooooo!"*

* * *

Joan had felt stunned and disgusted by the carnage in the dark room, nearly numb with worry about Debbie, but only a little frightened.

This spooked her.

A man hanging by his feet in the middle of the hallway. Waiting for them.

She felt as if an icy snake were squirming through her bowels. A chill climbed her back. Goose bumps swept up her legs and arms, prickled her face and the nape of her neck. Her nipples went achy and hard. Under her tight stocking cap, her scalp seemed to crawl.

She halted and stared at the man.

What's he doing there?

He didn't move.

Just waited, hanging in shadows not quite reached by the light of the few candles glowing along the walls of the corridor. Something about his indistinct shape made Joan suspect he was naked. And something about his shape was wrong.

She raised her revolver, aimed at him, and started walking closer.

"How does it look ahead?" Dave asked.

She glanced around at him. He was still walking backward, keeping his eyes on the door of the dark room. "See for yourself," she said.

He turned. "Jesus!"

He swung his flashlight forward. Its beam found the hanging man.

He groaned.

Joan felt an odd mixture of revulsion and relief. The guy looked sickening, his guts drooping out like that, but this wasn't any worse than what she had seen in the room. She was glad to know that he was dead. He wasn't so scary anymore.

Dave turned the flashlight away from him.

Joan waited for Dave to come up beside her, then quickened her pace. When they neared the body, he hurried ahead. He kept his flashlight off it. He turned sideways, back to the wall, and stepped past it. Joan did the same.

Then she ran behind him. A couple of times she heard metal gratings ring under her shoes.

She recalled the stories of how Jasper Dunn used to lurk in the Funhouse and peer up skirts. This must be where he'd done it, she thought.

The next time she came to one, she glanced down and saw the faint, pale blur of a face. She gasped.

Dave's head snapped around.

"Nothing," she said. "Keep going."

She saw more faces beneath the slatted panels.

A goddamn audience.

Dave halted. He had come to the end of the hallway. On the right was a closed door. On the left was an opening low in the wall.

He went to the opening, knelt down, and shone his light inside. "Christ," he muttered.

"What?"

"It's a slide."

Joan crouched behind him and looked over his shoulder. The slide gleamed like silver. Three-quarters of the way down, twin blades stood upright, as if hunting knives had been plunged in through the back of the metal ramp. The blades and the lower portion of the slide were smeared with blood.

"Somebody went down it," Dave whispered.

Joan squeezed his shoulders.

Not Debbie, she thought. *It wasn't Debbie. Please.*

"The others must've gone a different way," she said.

"I don't know. After the first kid, the rest of them might've gotten past the knives okay."

"Crawling over him?" *Or her.*

"Yeah."

"God."

"Let's see about that door," Dave said.

He gave the flashlight to Joan. She stood in the center of the hallway, left hand at her hip, shining the light on the door, right arm extended, aiming, finger ready on the trigger of her Smith & Wesson. She knew by the door's hinges that it would swing outward when it opened.

Dave positioned himself to the right of the door, his weapon raised, its muzzle close to the frame. Reaching across his body with his left hand, he turned the knob and tugged.

The door stayed shut.

He looked at Joan and shook his head.

"Why don't we shoot it open?" she said.

"If it's locked, the kids didn't go this way."

"Maybe it locked behind them."

"I think they took the slide."

"Well, we can't."

A bolt snicked.

Dave flinched. Joan's heart lurched.

He threw the door wide.

"Freeze!" Joan snapped.

The bloody thing on its knees in the doorway smiled. "Don't shoot, Joanie."

"We couldn't get him out of there if we wanted to," Tanya said.

"And we don't want to," Liz added.

"I sure hate to just leave him for the trolls," Cowboy said.

"We left Shiner," Jeremy reminded him.

"And Karen," Tanya added. "Don't worry, we'll figure a way to get them out. We'll put in a call to the cops or something. But first we've gotta get ourselves out of here in one piece."

"Yeah, I reckon."

"You want this back?" Jeremy asked, offering the cleaver.

"You keep it. I've got my toad-sticker." Cowboy turned around and said, "Adios, there, Samuel."

They started walking down the hallway, Tanya and Jeremy in the lead, Cowboy and Liz close behind them.

They stopped at a set of double doors.

Jeremy's stomach knotted.

Tanya muttered, "Shit."

Jeremy kicked one of the doors. It flew open, and he lurched backward as he glimpsed someone in the candlelit room ahead of him—a skinny kid, red with blood, holding a candle. As the door swept back at him, he realized that the kid was himself.

He pushed the door wide and held it open.

Saw himself holding it open.

The room, about three times the width of the hallway, was paneled with mirrors. The candles standing upright on its floor reminded Jeremy of the spikes in the barrel. The surrounding mirrors multiplied their number and filled the room with tongues of brilliant fire.

No mirrors on the ceiling. Up there were grates. For the spectators.

The mirrors in front of Jeremy showed only him and candles—no waiting trolls. He stepped through the door.

As the others came in, he wandered beneath the nearest grate and saw a dirty bearded face above him. "Hiya, kid. How come y'ain't dead yet?"

"Fuck you," he said.

"Scrappy little pisser, ain't ya?"

Jeremy raised his candle high, stretching upward, rising on tiptoe. Its flame licked up between the metal slats. The troll cried out as his beard caught fire.

"Ha!" Jeremy blurted.

"Good going, Duke!"

Jeremy watched the screaming troll shove himself up. Kneeling in the crawl space above the ceiling, he slapped at his fiery beard, but the flames swept up his face, caught his wild tangle of hair. In seconds his head was a ball of fire.

"How you like it, bitch?" Cowboy yelled.

Jeremy lowered his gaze to the mirrors in front of him. Cowboy, Liz, and Tanya all held candles high, were reaching toward other grates, jumping, shoving fire at the faces of the trolls above them. Liz laughed as she did it. Cowboy snapped curses, let out wild war whoops, called out, "Remember Sam!" Tanya did it in silence, rushing about the floor, dancing among the upright candles, stabbing her flame into the grates. Her sweatshirt flew up as she leapt, baring her tawny scarred belly.

Trolls gasped and shouted. At least a few of them, caught by surprise, squealed as fire found them.

"It's all right," Joan murmured. "It's all right now." She was on her knees hugging her sister, crying. Debbie clung to her and wept.

Dave's throat was tight, and he had tears in his own eyes as he watched their reunion.

We did it, he thought. We got to her in time. Though God knows what she's gone through.

Dave stepped to the other side of Joan, crouched, and picked up the flashlight. Slipping behind Debbie's back, he entered the room. It was the size of a large closet. It seemed to have no way out except for the single door.

A dead man lay sprawled in the middle of the floor. Beside his leg was the sodden red rag of Debbie's blouse. Her bra was clutched in his right hand.

Dave shone his light on the man's face.

Though the bushy beard and hair were matted with blood, Dave recognized him.

The troll who'd put the curse of squirmy death on them.

The troll with Charlie Manson eyes.

Now he had no eyes at all—just empty wet sockets.

His lower lip, probably torn by Debbie's teeth, hung by one corner. It looked like a slug lying dead on his bearded chin.

His head was resting against his right shoulder. The left side of his neck gaped open, split wide by the blade of a meat cleaver that stood upright in the wound.

His overcoat and shirt were spread open. The shiny red skin of his chest was furrowed with rows of scratches.

Dave turned around. Joan's face was pressed to the girl's cheek, her eyes shut. He wondered if she'd seen the carnage yet.

Debbie's back and buttocks had been raked by fingernails. Her underpants, one side torn away, hung at her knees. Her jeans were down, gathered around her ankles.

Dave stepped past the two hugging, weeping women. He leaned against a wall and shut his eyes.

God, the savagery of the fight that must've gone on inside that dark locked room! It seemed incredible that Debbie had prevailed.

Maybe not so incredible, he thought. Hell, she's Joan's sister.

What a kid!

She must've gone at the guy hand-to-hand before she was able to finish him off with the cleaver.

"We . . . we've gotta help the others," Debbie said.

"The hell with the others."

"They're my friends."

Dave looked at them. Joan was helping the girl up. He turned his eyes away when Debbie bent down and tore at the remains of her underwear. He heard the ripping cloth.

"Where did he hurt you?" Joan asked.

"Doesn't matter."

"Did he . . . ?"

"He didn't screw me." She sniffed. "Can't believe I'm alive."

"Neither can I," Joan said.

"When I heard you guys talking . . ." Her voice cracked.

"It's all right," Joan told her.

"Dave, is that guy dead in there?"

"You didn't see him?" he asked, looking at her. She was pulling her sweatshirt off.

"He's dead," Debbie gasped through her sobs. "He better be." She wiped the tears from her eyes with bloody hands. She had pulled her jeans up and fastened them. Parts of the jeans were still white.

Though her torso was smeared with blood, Dave saw no wounds.

Joan removed her shoulder holster and the knife rig. She took off her bullet-proof vest

Her T-shirt looked glued to her skin. It was white. Its whiteness struck Dave as strange and comforting. He'd seen so much blood in the past few minutes that he'd begun to feel as if scarlet was the natural color of things.

Joan put the vest on her sister and fastened its Velcro straps. She gave her sweatshirt to Debbie. The girl wiped her face with it, then pulled it down over her head while Joan quickly slipped into the harnesses again.

Bending down, Joan removed the small semiauto from her ankle holster. She gave it to Debbie.

Debbie stepped past her, heading for the slide.

"Wait!"

"I know. Something wrong with it."

As Dave stepped close to Joan, she took hold of his left wrist and swung it sideways, aiming his flashlight into the room. "Jesus Christ," she muttered.

They both flinched as someone cried out in agony and alarm. In seconds, the air was full of shouts, laughter, and screams,

some faint, others loud. They seemed to come from somewhere down the hallway. Dave snapped his head in that direction. He saw smoke drift up through one of the floor gratings.
Smoke, and the shimmery light of fire.

"What the hell's going on?" Joan said.

"We'd better get out of here fast," Dave said.

Debbie took hold of Joan's hand.

Dave rushed past them, dropped to his knees, and shone his
light down the slide.

"Let's go back the way we came," Joan said.

"We can't!" Debbie blurted. "My friends are down there!
We've gotta save them!"

"I think we can make it down the slide," Dave said.

Forty-five

"That oughta show 'em," Tanya gasped.

"Hope the place burns to the ground," Liz said.

"Not till we get our tails outta here," Cowboy said. Candle
in one hand, knife in the other, he started into the mirror
maze. Liz rushed after him.

Jeremy, staying close to Tanya's side, headed for the opening
in the wall of mirrors. Someone above the ceiling was still
screaming. He heard others whimpering and sobbing up there.

We hurt them, he thought. Maybe even killed one or two.

Like to kill them all.

Like to burn the fucking place to the ground, barbecue
every damn one of the trolls.

But he doubted that setting some hair on fire had been
enough to do the job.

Just as well. The idea of burning up Shiner appalled him.
Samson and Karen would be cremated too. They deserved better than to have their bodies go up in smoke with the trolls
who had murdered them.

He saw Liz vanish among the mirrors. But she reappeared,
along with Cowboy, when Jeremy entered a gap in the front

panels. They were over to the left. He thought. It was hard to tell exactly where they were. With mirrors on both sides and in front of them, reflections were everywhere. A multitude of bloody kids with candles, knives, and meat cleavers. Images within images, receding and diminishing. Jeremy couldn't tell the real Cowboy and Liz from their glass doubles. Then they disappeared, and Jeremy was surrounded by images of only himself and Tanya. He probed ahead with the cleaver. Walked toward himself and Tanya, duplicates matching them on both sides. A corner of the heavy blade tapped glass. He reached to the right and met no resistance, so he turned that way just in time to see Cowboy and Liz—or their reflections—vanish around a corner.

"Hold up," Tanya said. "Let's not lose each other."

Jeremy hurried forward, keeping his shoulder against Tanya, rubbing the knuckles of his left hand along the glass to guide him.

"Well, I'll be hog-tied."

His knuckles lost the glass. He stepped forward, reached sideways, and nudged Liz's back.

"Hey, watch it with the candle," she warned, flinching away from him.

"Sorry."

"Look what I've found," Cowboy said.

Jeremy stepped sideways to see past Liz's head. Cowboy was in front of him—or somewhere—bending down. He stood up and turned around. His knife was clenched in his teeth. His candle was in one hand. In the other was a camera with a flash attachment.

"Fantastic," Tanya said.

"She's a beaut, too," he said around the knife. "A Minolta."

"Who gives a shit?" Liz said. "Take the film out."

"I'm just gonna keep the whole thing." He slung the strap over his head, wincing slightly as his hand brushed against his bandaged ear.

"Keep it if you want," Tanya told him. "But get the film out of it right now. We can't take a chance on losing it."

"Okay, you say so." He lowered his head and squinted at the camera, trying to figure it out. "I'm not real sure—"

"Behind you!" Tanya shouted.

Liz screamed.

Cowboy jumped with surprise and whirled around, snatching the knife from his mouth as a giant of a troll loomed out of the mirrors and swung an ax down. Ten giants. Fifty of them. Countless monstrous trolls chopping, splitting Cowboy's head down the middle. Gore sprayed the air. The halves of his head dropped toward his shoulders. His legs shot forward. His rump pounded the floor. The troll ripped his ax free and started to raise it.

Liz, still screaming, lurched toward Cowboy. She crouched at his back, slipped her hands under the sides of his head, and lifted them as if she thought she could put him back together.

"No!" Tanya yelled.

The troll took one long stride toward Liz.

Jeremy hurled his cleaver. It flashed in the candlelight as it flipped end over end. Its blade thudded into the troll's chest. He bellowed. But he didn't go down. The cleaver stayed buried in him as he swung his ax sideways.

Jeremy heard a wet smack.

Liz's head flew from her neck, tumbling, streaming hair and blood. The ax didn't stop. It swept past her and crashed the mirror on her right. Liz's head hit the mirror, bounced to the floor, and rolled.

Her headless body was still crouched behind Cowboy. Blood spouted from the stump of her neck like water from a thick hose. Beyond the bodies, the troll was turned sideways. He twisted, swinging his ax away from the smashed mirror. As he raised it toward his shoulder, Tanya dashed to Liz's back and leapt through the geyser of blood. She slammed against him. It must've been like hitting a tree. The troll didn't budge. She bounced off his chest and was thrown backward onto the bodies. The cleaver, knocked crooked by Tanya's impact, stayed in the troll's chest for a moment, then fell and hit the floor with a clatter.

He stood above her, ax raised over his shoulder.

Jeremy saw the handle of Tanya's knife protruding from his throat.

He stood tall and motionless, then toppled backward. The

head of the ax shattered the mirror behind him. He fell through the disintegrating glass, his back breaking through the bottom of the panel as shards rained down on him.

All the candles were out except Jeremy's.

But its single tongue of flame was multiplied by the mirrors, filling the scene with a fluttery orange glow.

He watched Tanya climb off the bodies of Cowboy and Liz.

She crawled onto the felled troll, reached beyond his head, then scurried off him, dragging the ax.

Standing astride his hips, she raised the ax. Jeremy saw it swing down, heard the wet thud as it struck.

Bending over, Tanya pulled her knife from the troll's throat. Then she stepped off the body. "Come here and get the ax," she said, her voice husky and breathless. "We can use it."

Jeremy nodded. He moved forward, glanced at Liz and Cowboy, turned his eyes away from them, and looked at the dead troll. Tanya had left the ax in his face.

Good, Jeremy thought.

And slipped on the blood-slick floor. Yelping, he flapped his arms.

Shook his candle out.

Darkness dropped like a black cloak over his eyes.

He fell onto the bodies of his dead friends.

At the top of the slide, Dave wrapped his Kevlar vest around his shoes. "Here goes," he muttered.

Joan squeezed his shoulder.

He pushed off and sped down the slide, sitting upright, legs tight together in front of him, flashlight aimed at the twin upright blades. His feet struck the blades, stopping him with a jolt. Through the vest and soles of his shoes, the edges felt no sharper than a couple of steel rods.

He clamped the flashlight between his thighs, pointing its beam at his shrouded feet. He lay back, stretched his arms overhead, and called out, "All set."

Debbie came down on her belly, hands first. Dave caught them, halting her glide. He drew her down to his face. "Take the flashlight with you," he said. "Be careful going over the knives. And have your pistol ready when you get to the bottom."

Straddling him, she squirmed down his body. She took the flashlight, scooted lower, and rose to her hands and knees to crawl over his upright feet and the blades. "Made it," she whispered.

She hunkered at the end of the slide, shining the light around. Then she climbed off.

"Okay, Joan."

Joan came down. As she struggled onto him, the side of one breast rubbed his cheek. Dave felt its softness through the thin damp fabric of her T-shirt. Its touch was like a memory of the real world.

There *is* a real world out there, he thought.

He lifted his hands. He caressed her back as she worked her way down his body. He caressed her buttocks, the backs of her legs.

"You pick odd times to get fresh," she whispered.

He laughed softly.

"There's a real world out there," he told her. "Believe it or not."

"I'm glad you reminded me." She squeezed his knee. "We're doing okay so far, huh?"

"Doing just fine."

Then she crawled over his feet, skidded to the end of the slide, and Debbie helped her off. She took the flashlight and aimed it at his feet.

Dave sat up. He bent his knees until he could reach the vest with his hands. Pressing it against the blades, he freed his feet and stretched his legs down until he was astride the covered knives.

"Seemed like a good idea at the time," he muttered.

Joan passed the light to Debbie, then climbed onto the end of the slide. She shoved her knees against the bottoms of his feet and reached up.

"Ah-ha," Dave said.

"Ah-ha," she repeated.

As she clutched his wrists, Dave leaned forward. She tugged. His rump lifted off the slide. The inner sides of his thighs rubbed the padded blades. The back of his head scraped along the top of the enclosure. Joan suddenly gave him such a pull that he nearly folded in half. His knees buckled. He hit the ramp, and tumbled with Joan until the slide was no longer under them. They hit the floor.

After untangling himself, he retrieved the vest. He held it toward Joan. She shook her head. "It's yours. Put it on."

"I want you to wear it," Dave said.

"Well, *I* want *you* to wear it."

"I don't want you wearin' nuffin'," came a voice from the ceiling. "C'mon, sweet stuff, lemme see—"

"Bastard!" Debbie snapped. She shoved her arm straight up, aimed her pistol at the grate, but didn't fire. Shaking her head, she lowered the pistol.

"Hey, sweet stuff," the troll said.

"Babes babes babes," said another.

"Tasty bits."

"Where are the others?" Debbie yelled at the ceiling. "Where are my friends?"

Trolls laughed.

"Oh, they been by, they been by."

"Bound fer hell."

"Let's go," Joan said. She swept the walls with the flashlight, probed the darkness of the hallway to the left, and jogged in that direction.

"Bye-bye, sweets."

"Say hi to Webster!"

Dave nudged Debbie's back, and she started to run.

He hurried after her. He slipped his arms into the vest as he ran. Though he wanted Joan to wear it, he saw no point in wasting time on argument.

Joan and Debbie crouched at the edge of a barrel that filled the hallway. Dave stepped up behind them as Debbie muttered, "Oh, jeez, no."

A dead kid was stretched out inside the barrel. All around him, the wooden staves bristled with spikes.

"One of your friends?" Joan asked.

"Samson."

"Looks like they used him for a bridge," Dave said.

"I guess we do too," Joan said.

Debbie curled her left hand against the side of her mouth

and shouted through the barrel, "Hello! Jeremy! Hey, you guys, it's Shiner! Can you hear me?"

No answer came.

"Jeremy? Tanya? Cowboy? Liz? It's Shiner. We've got guns! Wait up! Or come back! You'll be all right! We've got guns!"

Still no answer.

"Dammit," she muttered.

"I'll go first," Dave said. He stepped around them. He swept the edge of his shoe against one of the spikes. The barrel rocked from side to side. "Christ," he said.

Joan and Debbie grabbed spikes near the rim of the barrel to hold it steady.

Dave knelt on the dead boy's shins. They felt steady under him. Of course they do, he thought. They're nailed down.

Leaning forward, he gripped the boy's thighs and started to crawl.

Robin, kneeling on the seat and clutching its back, watched the troll climb onto the beam that led straight to her gondola.

The same route the other had used.

Well, she'd taken care of that one.

Two down, one to go.

This guy was bigger than the last troll. He had a round face, hardly any neck at all, and shoulders the size of hams. His eyes were small and close together. Pig eyes, Robin thought. A squat, upturned nose. A tiny slit of a mouth, lips tight.

He really looks like a pig, she thought.

But he also looked, somehow, like a little boy in a body that had bloated out of control.

He wore a ball cap with its bill turned up. The skin around its sides was hairless.

"Go back," she said. "I don't want to kill you."

As she spoke those words, she saw herself in the steaming spa with Nate, holding him tightly, both of them weeping for the deaths they had caused.

She saw Nate sprawled on the sheet. His bloody head.

She felt her throat tighten.

Oh, God, Nate.

Had he deserved it? she wondered. Was all this some kind of rough justice at work?

"I really don't want to kill you," she pleaded, her voice sliding to a higher pitch. "I don't want to kill anyone."

The troll straddled the beam and stared at her.

"Just go away," she begged. "Please."

The troll lowered his head. Looking down at the dead ones? He hunched himself over and hugged the beam.

He's afraid, Robin thought. He doesn't want to fall.

"If I knock you off here," she said, "you'll be broken to pieces."

He began to make soft whimpery sounds.

Oh, no, Jeremy thought. We forgot the camera.

It was back there somewhere, hanging around Cowboy's neck, the incriminating film still in it.

He decided not to tell Tanya.

She might insist they return for it. They'd come a long distance, winding their way through the total darkness, bumping into mirrors, often backtracking when they found themselves at dead ends. To go back now . . .

To be in the same place with those bodies again . . .

Jeremy shivered as he remembered falling onto Liz and Cowboy. Trying to get up, he'd pushed a hand into something sodden and mushy.

Besides, he told himself, the film doesn't matter. Most of the kids in the pictures are already dead.

There're just the two of us. And Heather. Lucky Heather. She'd fled down the stairs before it got bad.

We should've gone too.

If only I'd listened to Shiner.

I got Shiner killed.

It seemed like ages ago, and the pain and guilt of it were muffled by all that had happened since.

It was probably fifteen minutes ago, he thought.

The head of his ax bumped glass. He swung it slowly to the left, met no resistance, and turned in that direction. Tanya followed, her hand tight on his shoulder.

If we had a candle, he thought, we'd be out of this thing by now.

We could've smashed straight through with the ax, fuck the maze.

But doing that without light would've been disastrous. They'd discussed it, and both agreed that they'd be cut to pieces if they tried.

This was taking forever, but at least they might get through with their skin intact. If they didn't get jumped by more trolls.

Jeremy turned, and turned again.

And saw a glimmer of light.

"All *right*," Tanya whispered.

The faint glow ahead of them turned out to be a reflection. The ax thudded the mirror. Jeremy turned, and the light was stronger.

Instead of a mirror, there was suddenly a hallway to his left. Candles on the walls. He stumbled free of the maze and took a deep breath.

"Made it," Tanya whispered. She hugged herself against his back, then stepped around beside him.

Along the left side of the hallway were barred windows like those they'd passed in the corridor above. Jeremy saw no trolls behind the bars.

"So where the hell's our audience?" Tanya said.

"Maybe they all cleared out. Maybe the fire scared them off."

"I wouldn't bet on it."

Midway down the hall, on the right, was a door. Another door waited at the end. "What'll we do?" Jeremy asked.

Tanya said nothing. She looked from one door to the other and frowned.

"The one at the end," Jeremy said, nodding toward the far door. "It might be the one at the stairway."

"If it is, you can bet they've got a nasty surprise waiting for us."

"Yeah. They aren't gonna let us just walk away from this."

"Fuck the doors," Tanya said. "Let's chop our way out."

"Yeah!"

"No more playing by their rules. We've got the ax, we can play the game our own way." She took a few strides forward, turned to the right, and tapped the wall with the point of her knife. "There's probably some kind of a room through there. All we've gotta do is bust in, then we can knock a hole in the wall and maybe step right out onto the boardwalk."

"Sure hope so."

Tanya moved aside. Jeremy raised the ax overhead and swung with all his strength. Its heavy blade bit into the wall. As he tore it loose, a thick splinter of wood split away and dropped to the floor. He put his eye to the narrow gap.

Darkness on the other side.

Stepping back, he chopped again. The entire head of the ax broke through the wall.

"It's going to work!" he blurted.

"Damn right!"

As he struggled to free the trapped ax head, a sudden sharp tug yanked the haft from his hands.

In the instant it took him to realize what was happening, the entire length of the handle vanished into the hole.

"Oh, Jesus," he gasped.

"We'd better get . . ."

They both jumped as a chunk of the wall flew at them. Jeremy glimpsed an inch of the ax blade before it withdrew.

Now they've got it. And they're coming for us.

Jeremy heard maniacal laughter.

It came from him.

Tanya tugged his arm, and they ran down the hallway.

Ran until the floor dropped out from under their feet.

Then, side by side, they dropped into the black chasm of the Funhouse basement.

Forty-six

Whirling away from the three corpses in the mirror maze, Debbie hunched over and vomited. Joan rubbed her back while she heaved.

The poor kid had been through hell. And it wasn't over yet.

The worst is over, Joan told herself. The worst had to be in that closet upstairs, alone and fighting for her life. Debbie was damn lucky to have survived. With her mind in one piece, too. A lot of people might've flipped out, having to deal with something like that.

She was holding up pretty well.

Losing her dinner was probably a good sign. Showed she was still in touch with reality.

"This one must've come down a goddamn beanstalk," Dave said. His trembling voice sounded astonished and disgusted.

Debbie finished. She straightened up, sobbing, and wiped her mouth with the front of her sweatshirt.

"Two of them are kids," Dave said. "One's a girl. The other's the guy from the fight."

"Our fight?" Joan asked.

"The one with the ear."

"Oh, no."

She'd saved his ear for this. So he could get his head split open in this mad perversion of a funhouse.

Debbie turned around. She sniffed and rubbed her eyes. "That's Cowboy," she said. "And Liz. God!" She slapped a hand to her mouth and squeezed her eyes shut.

"Is anybody left?" Joan asked her.

She nodded. "Jeremy," she said through her hand. "And Tanya. Only them." She took her hand away, pressed her face to Joan's shoulder, and hugged her tightly. "Jeremy's my friend, Joanie. I tried to stop him. I don't want him to die."

"Okay," Dave said. "We're going through this thing the fast way." He drew his pistol. He shouted, "Anybody can hear me better hit the deck! Hit the floor! Bullets are coming!"

Standing at the feet of the giant dead troll, he clamped the flashlight between his legs, aimed at the mirror in front of him, and fired.

Debbie jumped as the shot blasted the silence. She stuck her fingers into her ears.

Joan covered her own ears.

Dave kept firing, the Beretta roaring, jerking in his hand, walls of mirror exploding in front of him as the 9mm slugs smashed through them. Disintegrating glass flashed in the beam of his flashlight. He swept the muzzle just a bit from side to side, blasting a corridor straight through the maze.

Some forty feet ahead, a glow of candlelight appeared. The size of the lighted area grew as Dave kept firing, knocking apart more mirrors.

After thirteen shots he dropped the magazine into his palm. He shoved a fresh one up the pistol's handle and jacked a cartridge into the chamber.

Joan and Debbie stepped carefully around the bodies. They stopped beside Dave. Looking past him, Joan saw the dark rubble of shattered glass, then a lighted hallway.

And bodies sprawled on its floor.

Dave rubbed a trembling hand across his mouth. "God," he muttered. "I warned 'em to duck."

"Then they should've ducked," Joan said.

"Maybe they couldn't hear me."

"Let's go." She pulled the flashlight from between Dave's legs, ducked under jagged teeth of glass, and started walking through the litter of demolished mirrors. The glass crunched under her shoes. "Be careful back there," she said.

She proceeded slowly.

Sometimes, before stepping through a panel, she knocked hanging shards out of the way with the barrel of her revolver. She heard Debbie and Dave close behind her, glass tinkling and popping under their shoes.

Ahead, some of the people in the hallway began to move.

Roll over, crawl, stand up.

At least three bodies stayed down.

Those Joan saw rising were not kids.

Nor did they look like trolls.

She felt a chill squirm through her. Her skin began to crawl.

She remembered that Jasper Dunn used to be the proprietor of a freak show. He'd been forced to close it down after some of his freaks got loose and attacked people in the Funhouse.

He'd closed the show.

Obviously, he'd kept his freaks.

Made a home for them in the Funhouse.

Behind Joan, Dave groaned.

A hand clawed at the back of her T-shirt, peeled the wet cloth away from her skin, tried to pull her backward. In a low, shaky voice, Debbie said, "I wanta go back. Please, Joanie. Can't we just go back?"

As Jeremy dropped into darkness, he expected his descent to be stopped with a bone-jarring crash. Instead, he landed on something springy. A net? It sank under his back, then lifted him. The taut lines quivered as he tried to untangle his arms and legs from them.

They felt gluey.

They stuck to him.

He heard Tanya gasping. To his right, and not far away. Her struggles shook the netting.

"You okay?" he whispered.

"What *is* this shit?"

In front of Jeremy and off to his left, a door opened.

That's the other door, Jeremy realized. The one at the foot of the stairway.

The way out is right there.

Someone entered, carrying a kerosene lantern. Jeremy squinted as the harsh glare from the lamp's twin mantles stabbed his eyes.

He saw that the tall cadaverous man wore a top hat and tails. Jasper Dunn.

Trolls poured through the doorway behind Dunn, crowding the small balcony on which he stood. They were oddly silent.

As Jeremy's eyes adjusted to the light, he saw more.

He saw too much.

He felt as if he were collapsing inside, shriveling into a black ruin.

The sticky cords that held him trapped were the strands of a web spread across the Funhouse basement. A spiderweb. Hanging in it, suspended several feet above the sand, were the crushed husks of people wrapped in transparent gray silk.

Tanya shrieked.

He twisted his head toward her.

Saw her writhing and bucking.

Saw the *spider* scurrying over the top of the web, rushing in from a corner of the basement.

A spider like the one he'd seen in Jasper's Oddities.

But bigger. Much bigger.

Jasper's Giganticus. Jeremy heard Cowboy's voice deep inside the abyss of his mind. *Discovered in the jungles of New Zealand.*

The one in the display might've been this spider's baby.

"No!" Tanya yelled. *"No!"*

The web swayed and bounced under the weight of the rushing black beast.

Its eyes were yellow. Its mouth looked like a huge open sore. Its fangs dripped.

The bloated black thing danced over the web.

And onto Tanya.

Her shriek ripped his ears.

The spider's mouth muffled her scream. Jeremy saw its fangs sink into her face.

Her tangled body flinched rigid, jerked with spasms.

Jeremy twisted sideways, freeing his right arm from the trapped sleeve of his jacket. He reached to his shirt pocket. For the razor blade he'd put there after giving the handkerchief to Tanya.

A quick slash across the throat.

Maybe he could die before the spider came for him.

The pocket of his shirt was empty.

He'd lost the razor blade. Maybe while going down the slide. When didn't matter.

It was gone.

Jeremy heard gunfire as the legs of the spider wrapped around Tanya, squeezing her like a monstrous lover.

Robin heard the faint hard claps of gunshots. She looked over her shoulder. Saw nothing except the deserted moonlit boardwalk. The muffled tone of the shots made her wonder if they came from under the boardwalk, or maybe from inside one of Funland's buildings.

After a few seconds they stopped. The only sounds she heard

were her heartbeat, the rushing wind, the wash of a comber hurling itself at the beach, and the troll whimpering quietly behind her.

She turned her head forward again.

The troll was still four or five feet away, hugging the steel beam.

He'd frozen there.

He'd come this close, and lost his nerve.

Obviously the height had suddenly gotten to him.

Robin remembered her own experiences with climbing. Shinnying up trees when she was a kid, once in a while working her way up bluffs and mountainsides during her travels. You could go along just fine for a while. Then, sometimes, it just hit you. Stark, paralyzing fear. You knew you were going to die. All you could do was hang on, waiting to fall.

Until something broke the spell.

Killed the curse.

And you were suddenly able to function.

This guy, she thought, will either fall or come to his senses.

If he comes to his senses, I'll be fair game again.

But she didn't want him to fall.

The troll raised his head when Robin began to sing.

I climbed a mountain peak last night
To see what I could see,
To take a peek at the moon so bright
And the stars in the midnight sea.

He sat up and stared at her.

On his way through the broken mirrors, Dave saw enough of those in the hallway ahead to know they were the remnants of Jasper Dunn's freak show.

He'd heard stories about them, seen their photographs a number of times in the Gallery of the Weird.

Supposedly they had scattered and left town after the show was shut down.

Six years ago. Shortly before he arrived from Los Angeles.

All that time, they'd been living here in the Funhouse?

Those who hadn't been hit by his bullets were standing in the hallway only a few yards beyond the last shattered mirror. Standing motionless, watching.

Dave didn't want Joan to be first out of the maze.

First to face this crowd of deformities.

He hurried past her.

Without Joan's back blocking the way, he had a clear view.

On the floor, her throat torn open by a slug, lay Donna the Dog Woman. Sprawled beside her, writhing in pain, was a shirtless man with a withered brown arm in the middle of his chest. Julian, the Three-Armed Man. His little brown hand was clutching the bullet wound near his left shoulder. Wonderful Wilma lay near him, naked except for leopardskin bikini pants. One hand was clamped to her bleeding thigh. Her other arm pressed in modesty across her two normal breasts, the third mound uncovered, pale and sweaty below her wrist.

Only Donna was dead, Dave thought. Could've been worse.

But, God, he wished he hadn't hit any of them.

Stepping through the last shattered mirror, he aimed his pistol at Snake-Tongue Antonio. "Drop the ax," he said.

The man's tongue slid out of his mouth. As he glared at Dave, the pink slab of his tongue slithered from one side of his face to the other, licking tears from under his eyes.

"I don't want to shoot you," Dave said.

"Drop it," Joan snapped, coming up beside him, also taking aim at Antonio.

The two-headed woman, who had a name for each head, but which Dave couldn't recall, turned both faces toward the man. She reached out a hand and patted his shoulder. He glanced at her, retracted his tongue, and made grunting sounds.

One head nodded at him. The other's face smiled gently.

He dropped the ax to the floor.

"I'm sorry," Dave said. "I'm sorry about the shooting. I didn't mean for anyone to get hit."

"We didn't know you were here," Joan said. She holstered her revolver and gave the flashlight to Dave. Bending down, she started to untie the red bandanna knotted around her leg.

Dave lowered his pistol but kept it in his hand. He doubted

that these people would try anything. They seemed wary, confused, sad. And he saw something like hope in the eyes of a few.

"We're trying to find my friends," Debbie said. "Did you see them? Do you know where . . . ?" Her voice faltered. "Their throats," she whispered.

Some of the people nodded. Others grunted. Jim or Tim, one of the Siamese twins, touched a finger to the scar on his throat and mouthed a breathy, voiceless noise. "Haaaspaaa."

"Jasper?" Dave asked. "Jasper Dunn?"

Nods, more grunts.

"He cut your vocal cords?" Joan blurted.

"Hyesss, hyesss, haaaspaaa."

"Jesus," Debbie muttered.

"He was keeping you prisoners here?" Dave asked.

The two-headed woman pointed at a door-size opening someone had chopped into the corridor wall.

"We're gonna get you out of here," Joan said. Dropping to her knees, she wrapped the bandanna around Wilma's leg wound and knotted it tight.

"What about Jeremy?" Debbie asked, her voice high and pleading. "We have to find him!"

"We will, don't worry." Joan looked at the others. "Two kids," she said. "A boy and a girl. Did you see them? Do you know where they are?"

The crowd parted, turned. A few hands pointed down the hallway.

Dave saw a door on the right, another at the far end.

But between here and the hallway's end was a square of darkness where the floor should have been.

A trapdoor?

Debbie bolted. She leapt the body of Donna the Dog Woman and dashed through the break in the group.

"*No!*" Joan shouted.

Dave rushed after her.

Debbie was nearly clear of Jasper's freaks when a hand darted out and grabbed her ankle. She yelped, crashed to the floor, and skidded.

Dave pounced and gripped the back of her neck, holding her down as she struggled to rise.

He looked back. A bald man lifted his head and made a grim smile. He had no legs. But he had two muscular arms, and the hand of one was wrapped tightly around Debbie's ankle. Andy the Amazing Torso Man.

"Thanks," Dave said.

He winked.

Joan patted his shoulder, stepped over him, and crouched on the other side of Debbie. "Dumb kid," she muttered. "Just stick with us and don't—"

Debbie gasped and flinched rigid.

Squeals and grunts erupted behind them.

Dave snapped his head around. Jasper's freaks were going wild, some pointing down the hallway, others rushing toward the ragged hole in the wall, some racing for the ruins of the mirror maze.

"Dave."

Joan's voice. A mere whisper.

"Dave?"

He looked at her.

Joan's wide, stunned eyes met his for an instant, then looked away.

Toward the other end of the hallway.

Dave followed their lead.

And saw black arachnoid legs waving in the candlelight. They hooked over the edge of the floor. Claws clicking and scraping on the wood, a huge spider clambered up from the darkness below the trapdoor.

On its back rode Jasper Dunn, top hat perched rakishly atop his head, a revolver in each hand.

Can't be.

Dave felt as if he'd been clubbed in the belly.

He gaped at the spectacle—the monstrous spider scurrying toward him, Jasper mounted up there like a crazed cowpoke brandishing six-shooters.

Can't be happening.

Dave rose on numb, shaky legs, pulling Debbie up with him

by the back of her neck. "Go," he said. His voice sounded far away. "Run."

She stood beside him, frozen.

Joan rose to her feet, going for her .38 in slow motion as Dave raised his Beretta and Jasper brought down both barrels in their direction. Gunfire roared through the hallway. Bullets snapped past Dave's face. The hat sailed off Jasper's head. Debbie, hit, flew backward. An eye of the beast exploded in a red mist. A slug smashed through Jasper's right wrist, and his revolver tumbled away. At the same moment, one caught him in the face. It snapped his head sideways and tore off half his chin. But he stayed on the spider, blasting at them with his remaining gun.

The beast was less than six feet away. It would be on them in seconds.

Dave concentrated his firepower on it. A bullet slashed the side of his arm, but he stood steady, squeezing the trigger. One of the spider's front legs broke. As his bullets pounded holes in its squat, bristly head, he saw Joan rush forward.

"No!" he yelled.

The spider seemed to stumble. Its abdomen dragged the floor, but it still scuttled closer, palpi coming at Dave like pincers.

The last shot from his Beretta exploded another of its eyes.

Reaching for his .38, he saw Joan, knife in hand, jump over two of the spider's thrashing legs. She no longer had her revolver. Must've emptied it.

Jasper aimed at her face. He wouldn't miss. A point-blank shot.

Dave drew his .38.

But raising it seemed to take so long . . . so long.

He heard Jasper's hammer snap down.

A quick hard clack.

No blast.

It had fallen on a spent cartridge!

Now Dave's gun was up, leveled at Jasper, but he held fire. Afraid of hitting Joan as she hurled herself against the bloated side of the spider, just behind Jasper. She vaulted onto the beast. Jasper, twisting, rammed an elbow into her. She hooked an arm beneath his ruined chin, jerked him backward, and her right arm swept in around him and plunged the knife into his chest. She pulled the knife out, rammed it in again, then flung him sideways. He toppled from his mount, sliding, falling headfirst among the spider's legs.

As its pincers caught Dave.

They clamped him just below the knees.

How could it still be alive?

He fired, jerking the trigger fast, pumping round after round into its head as the beast squeezed his legs together and Dave toppled backward. He was hammering at spent shells when he heard Joan screaming. His back slammed the floor.

What's she screaming about? Dave wondered.

Shoving himself up with his elbows, he saw Joan still on top of the spider. Shrieking like a banshee as she thrust her knife into the hump of its back.

She's screaming about me.

As he twisted and tried to kick free, the pincers began to pull him. He slid over the floor toward the spider.

It raised its head.

What was left of its head. A hideous oblong thing shattered by bullets, caved in, cracked and split, red and yellow fluids gushing from its wounds.

The fucking thing's dead in its tracks! Dave's mind screamed. *Why's it doing this to me?*

It dragged him.

Squealing, he rammed his right foot against its single dripping fang. He shoved at it, trying to keep himself back.

Antonio leapt past him, swung the ax down with both hands, and split the spider's head in half. The pincers loosened their grip. Dave tore his legs free and scrambled backward as the man chopped again.

He rolled onto his side.

Face-to-face with Debbie.

As they stared into each other's eyes, the wet crunching sounds of the chopping went on.

She scooted closer to Dave.

He put an arm around her back, pulled her against him, and felt the girl's face press the side of his neck.

"The bullet hit your vest?" he whispered.

He felt her nod.

Robin kept singing as the troll inched closer. Then she stopped, and reached out to him. He gripped her hand. She held it tightly as he climbed onto the seat.

Gasping and shuddering from the ordeal, he sat down beside her. With one hand he clutched the side of the gondola. The other held Robin's hand against his leg.

She pressed her legs together, wondering if she'd been crazy to let this troll in with her. She used her free arm to cover her breasts. "It's okay," she said. "You're safe now."

He flinched as gunfire erupted again.

Robin looked away from him. The shots sounded as if they might be coming from inside Jasper's Oddities or the Funhouse, which were on the far side of the boardwalk, about halfway between the Ferris wheel and the main entrance. The last time, the shots had sounded like rapid fire from a single gun. Now it seemed that several weapons of different calibers were firing at once.

The troll released her hand. He slid an arm across her shoulders and drew Robin against the side of his quaking body.

It's all right, she told herself. He's just scared.

She realized that the gunfire had stopped. Then came a quick series of blasts, and the shooting ended again.

Slowly the troll relaxed. She could feel his shudders fade. He began to caress her arm from shoulder to elbow. His touch made her skin crawl.

She faced him. "That was the police," she said. "They'll be coming out soon."

I hope, she thought.

God, what if the cops had *lost* that shoot-out?

"When they come out," she said, "they'll get us down from here. So you'd better not try anything, you understand?"

He turned toward her, a knee pushing against the side of her leg. Though his eyes were hooded with shadow, she could feel their gaze roaming her body. "Denny likes you," he said. His voice wasn't high and childish, as Robin had expected from this man who looked like an overgrown boy. It was low, raspy.

Holding her shoulder, he slid his other hand up her thigh.

"Soft," he said.

Robin grabbed his wrist. "Don't," she whispered. "Please."

"Denny likes you," he said again.

"Then don't."

He took his hand off her leg, and she released it. His other hand left her shoulder. He fumbled with the buttons of his filthy, ragged trench coat.

"Denny, no."

He opened the coat. He wore a sleeveless undershirt and baggy trousers. The tight shirt bulged over massive muscles.

I won't stand a chance.

He'll only hurt me worse if I struggle.

Dammit, I'm not gonna let him rape me!

This is what I get for helping him.

Denny pulled the coat off his arms and tugged its tail out from under his rump.

He draped it over Robin's shoulders.

Her throat tightened. As she slipped her arms into the sleeves, the man cupped a hand gently over her right breast. "Soft," he said. Then he took his hand away, drew the coat shut, and began to button it.

When he finished, Robin leaned against him.

"Thank you, Denny," she said. "Robin likes you."

He put an arm across her shoulders.

"Sing?" he asked

"Sure."

Forty-seven

She was singing "Amazing Grace," Denny holding her and slowly rocking their perch high above the boardwalk. The song took Robin back to her father's funeral. Her dad's old buddy, Charlie MacFerson, had played the bagpipes at her side while she stood by the grave with her banjo, strumming the tune and singing the melancholy words.

This time, the song was for Nate.

Her voice trembled. Tears streamed down her cheeks.

Denny looked at her and cocked his head. Then he pulled off his ball cap. He put it on Robin. It was way too big for her. It slipped down, covering her eyes. She kept singing as he slid it back on her head and turned it sideways.

Over the tremor of her voice, Robin heard a quiet thud. A chunking sound. A chopping sound.

She went silent.

Off to the left, a slat of wood flew off the front wall of Jasper's Funhouse and clapped the boardwalk. The pale beam of a flashlight probed through the narrow gap.

The chopping went on. Wood flew and clattered down.

Soon the opening was the size of a doorway.

People began to emerge from the Funhouse.

Denny pointed. He began to laugh.

Robin could hardly believe what she saw. A woman down there seemed to have *two* heads. A man clutching his shoulder had a growth on his chest that looked like a small arm. A man— one of the cops she'd seen earlier—stepped through the break in the wall, carrying a man who had no legs.

Denny slapped his leg and pointed as a tall lean man helped a woman through the opening. The woman, clad only in bikini pants, seemed to have three breasts.

A man, or two men, sidestepped through the gap. They looked as if their hips were glued together.

A girl with a flashlight came out, turned to the opening, and shone her light on it while a woman ducked through, carrying a limp body.

Robin's stomach clenched as she gazed at the boy cradled in the woman's arms. She was too far away to make out the features of his face, but she knew him. She knew him by his size and dark hair and clothes, by the raw wound on his chin— made by her teeth.

That bastard Duke.

Dead?

Where's Tanya? she wondered. Where are all the others?

Did they get away?

The woman crouched. She set Duke's body down on the boardwalk in front of the Funhouse. As she started to rise, the kid suddenly grabbed the front of her T-shirt and tried to pull himself up. The woman fell to her knees. Duke screamed in her face.

Denny yelped with alarm and flinched.

Robin, patting his leg to soothe him, watched the woman twist Duke's hands from her shirt and pin them to the boardwalk. Still screaming, he writhed and bucked and thrashed his legs.

The girl gave her flashlight to the male cop, squatted, caught Duke's kicking feet, and helped to hold him down.

Robin took off the ball cap. She put it on Denny's head and tipped the bill up the way he liked it. "Time we let them know we're here," she said.

"Denny likes it here."

"I guess there are worse places to be," she told him.

The gondola rocked back as she leaned forward and gripped the safety bar.

It tipped wildly when Denny did the same.

She shouted, "Help! Up here!"

Denny shouted, "Help! Up here!" He grinned at her.

Down on the boardwalk, heads turned.

Forty-eight

"Are you ready for my big finale?" called Maxwell the Somewhat Magnificent.

The crowd in the stands yelled and cheered.

"I'll require a courageous and beautiful volunteer from the audience. No men need apply." Even as arms went up, he pointed at someone in the third row. "You. I think you'll do just fine."

As the young woman rose from her seat and started making her way forward, men in the audience whooped and whistled their approval.

Joan said, "Oh, my God."

"It's Debs!" Kerry blurted, and bounced on Dave's lap. "What's she going to do?"

"Watch and find out," Dave told her.

"Doesn't Steve get to go up too?"

"Boyfriends probably get in Maxwell's way," Dave said.

"But he's all alone."

"They wanted to sit by themselves," Joan explained to the four-year-old.

"Can't imagine why," Dave said.

"'Cause you're old farts," Kerry said.

Dave gently cuffed the side of her head. "Watch your language, young lady."

She laughed.

Then laughter erupted from the crowd as Maxwell the Somewhat Magnificent tried to mount his unicycle, clinging to Debbie, pretending to lose his balance as the wheel rolled and twisted under him. He fell against her, hugging her, squeezing her rump through the seat of her white jeans. Finally, perched unsteadily on the high seat, he lurched away. He careened around the stage, spinning and jerking as if out of control.

At last he seemed to find a semblance of balance. He mopped his brow with a red bandanna.

Debbie turned to leave, but he said, "Wait, wait! You don't get off that easy!"

Maxwell's assistant appeared with three flaming torches. He gave one of them to Debbie.

"Dear thing," Maxwell said, "she's carrying a torch for me."

He kept up the banter, telling Debbie, "You really light my fire," making nervous queries about her throwing arm, then instructing her to toss the torch to him. "*To* me, not *at* me. I'm gentle, but I'm not tinder."

The audience didn't respond to the pun, so he swept an open hand above his hair. Dave knew what the gesture meant— that the joke had gone over the heads of the crowd. He'd seen a lot of performers make the same sign during the years he'd been bringing his family to the Funland Amphitheater. He always found it annoying.

It didn't go over our heads, he wanted to yell. It just wasn't funny.

Debbie tossed each of the three torches to Maxwell the Somewhat Magnificent. The third went high. Maxwell swept backward on his unicycle and made a catch that Dave considered Truly Magnificent.

While he juggled the torches, he thanked Debbie and suggested that she meet him after the show to help him "put the fires out."

Her long blond hair flew from side to side as she shook her head. Still shaking her head, she turned around and waved to the cheering audience. Then she rushed down the stairs as if eager to escape Maxwell's further remarks.

Kerry leaned sideways and tugged the sleeve of Joan's sweatshirt. "Mommy, why don't *you* go up?"

"No, thanks, honey."

"Come on, it'd be fun."

"I don't think Maxwell needs another dupe just now," Joan told her.

"What's a dupe?"

"Somebody to poke fun at."

"Besides," Dave said, "Mommy's already done it. She went onstage once with Fred the Magician. So did you, kiddo."

"Me?"

"You were in Mommy's tummy."

"God, don't remind me," Joan said. "The worst experience of my life."

"Were you a dope?"

"I sure felt like one, honey."

"You've gotta admit," Dave said, "the guy had an amazing assortment of bun jokes."

"He was pregnant with quips," Joan added.

Maxwell finished his routine, leapt from his unicycle, and bowed. Then he did an encore. Blindfolded by his assistant, he juggled the torches. He ended by dropping onto one knee, reaching under his leg, and catching the last torch before it hit the floor of the stage.

Putting his arms around Kerry, Dave clapped in front of her stomach. She grabbed his wrists and helped.

Maxwell the Somewhat Magnificent left the stage after many elaborate bows.

The lights went out. The audience fell silent. Dave heard the faint sounds of calliope music, voices, and laughter from the boardwalk. He heard the distant roar of the Hurricane.

"Is it time for Robin?" Kerry whispered.

"I imagine so," Dave said.

"Is she going to sing 'The Land of Purr'?"

"She promised you she would."

"Hope she doesn't forget."

In the darkness, a voice boomed over the loudspeaker. "Ladies and gentlemen, the Funland Amphitheater is proud to present a very special attraction. Our next performer has just returned from her most recent engagement at the Grand Ole Opry."

Dave heard eager murmurs from the audience.

"You may have heard her songs on the radio. You may have seen her on the Dolly Parton special last month."

Let's get *on* with it, Dave thought.

"Our own Boleta Bay songbird, Funland's Banjo Queen, *Miss Robin Travis!*"

The audience went wild. Joan's shoulder pressed against Dave. Her breath tickled his ear as she said, "Nate sure laid it on pretty thick."

"What do you expect?"

The crowd roared as brilliant lights hit the stage. Robin stood motionless in front of her band, smiling.

She wore an outfit that Dave hadn't seen before: a buckskin jacket with fringe swaying in the breeze, a shiny white blouse, and a short leather skirt that left her slim legs bare to the tops of her white boots.

She glanced back at her band. Drums began to pound through the noise of the cheering crowd. Robin faced forward. Her right boot tapped the stage in time with the drum. With the first notes of her banjo, a hush descended on the audience. A quick, twangy tune filled the night. A roar came up again as those in the stands recognized the intro to "Gypsy Girl."

I am the gypsy banjo girl.
I've wandered far and near.

I am the gypsy banjo girl
With a song for you to hear.

It's a mountain song,
It's a desert song,
It's a song of the windblown sea.
It's a prairie song
And a woodland song—
It belongs to you and me.

Kerry bounced on Dave's lap, and he heard her soft voice as she sang along. Joan leaned against him and slipped a warm arm around his back.

"My next number is very special to me," Robin announced midway through the show. "I sang it for a fellow named Nate the night we met. He must've liked it, 'cause he married me. So this one's for you, Nate, and for another special friend, Kerry Carson, the daughter of my two favorite cops."

Then she began to sing:

Kelly and Kerry went off one day
For the Land of Purr where the kitty-cats play.
They packed their pockets with nacho chips,
Bubble gum, jelly, and chocolate lips . . .

Kerry twisted around on Dave's lap. "It's *me!*" she blurted. "*I'm* in it!"

After Robin's final song and the standing ovation, she played and sang three encore numbers. Then the stage went dark. Seconds later, when the amphitheater lights came on, she and the band were gone.

Dave, Kerry, and Joan waited. When the crowd had diminished, Joan folded the old brown blanket she'd used to cover the bleacher seats. Dave took hold of Kerry's hand, and they started down.

Debbie and Steve met them just outside the amphitheater's entrance. The rides and attractions had already closed for the night. The bright carnival lights were dark, but lamps near the boardwalk railing still glowed to illuminate the way for the departing concertgoers. Funland seemed strangely quiet.

"You going to let me have your autograph?" Debbie asked Kerry.

"Huh?"

"Well, you're a big celebrity now, you know."

"Both of you," Joan said.

"God, don't remind me. I've never been so embarrassed in my life. I wanted to curl up and die when he was grabbing me that way."

"He never could've gotten onto the unicycle without your valuable assistance," Dave told her.

Debbie bared her teeth and punched his shoulder.

"Now, now, children," Joan said.

Debbie took hold of Steve's hand. "Anyway, we'll see you guys later, okay?"

"Where are you off to?" Joan asked.

"Pete's Pizza. Since Steve has to go home tomorrow and everything, we thought we'd . . . you know, make the most of it."

"Can I go too?" Kerry asked.

"No, you may not," Joan told her.

"Whyyyy?"

"Because it's late, young lady. You should've been home in bed hours ago."

"I'm not sleepy."

"You'd cramp their style, kid," Dave explained.

"No I won't."

"It's fine with me if she wants to come along," Steve said.

"Sure," Debbie said, rubbing the girl's hair. "This is a big night for her. Wouldn't want to spoil it now."

Dave and Joan looked at each other. Joan shrugged. "It's okay with me. If you're sure."

"We'll have her home in an hour or so," Steve said.

"Maybe we should *all* go to Pete's," Dave suggested.

Kerry looked up at him and shook her head. "You'd crump our style."

"Besides," Joan said, "I want to take a stroll on the beach."

Dave caught the look in her eyes. "Me too."

They stood together and watched their daughter walk away with Debbie and Steve.

"Two lovebirds and a duck," Joan said.

"She'll have fun."

"They sure won't get much smooching done with her around. Speaking of which . . ."

She faced Dave.

He looked up and down the boardwalk. It appeared deserted.

He put his arms around her, pulled her close, and kissed her mouth. While they embraced, the lamps went dark.

"Let's go down to the beach," she whispered against his lips.

They strolled along the boardwalk, Joan cuddling against his side. At the bottom of the stairs they stopped while Joan shook open her blanket. The beach was pale with moonlight. Beyond it, the ocean looked black except for the white froth of combers rolling toward shore.

"Want to share?" she asked.

"You bet."

They draped the blanket over their shoulders and pulled it closed in front. "Nice and snuggly," Joan said.

"And private," Dave added, slipping a hand under her sweatshirt. He caressed the sleek skin of her back.

"Privacy from whom?"

"You never know."

Joan looked over her shoulder. Toward the darkness under the boardwalk. Dave felt her back stiffen.

He snapped his head around.

He saw no one.

"Now you've got us both spooked," Joan said. Smiling, she slipped a hand into the seat pocket of his corduroys. "Creep." She gave his rump a squeeze.

"Come on." He led her forward, anxious to put some distance between themselves and the black area that stretched under Funland.

Probably *are* some derelicts under there, Dave thought. Boleta Bay still had its share of them. Not many, though. Not nearly as many as there'd been before that night so long ago.

Trolls had fled from the Funhouse even before the police

swept through it in the early-morning hours. By noon there was not a troll to be found near the boardwalk or beach. Many were spotted on roads leading out of town.

Some who didn't flee fell victim to outraged citizens. They were beaten, taken for rides to the city limits, even murdered. In the weeks that followed, the bodies of fourteen trolls were discovered: in alleys, dumpsters, under the boardwalk, in the woods outside town. All but three of the corpses had been left with hand-printed cards or signs that read, "Greetings from Great Big Billy Goat Gruff and Friends."

The killers were never apprehended.

Soon, not a troll could be found within miles of Boleta Bay.

Jasper's Funhouse and Oddities were demolished that winter. The first event to take place in the amphitheater erected in their place was the June wedding of Nate and Robin.

To Dave the wedding had seemed like an exorcism—a holy ceremony that banished all remnants of evil from the place where so much horror had been.

That summer, a few drifters and beggars began to appear. They met no harm at the hands of the townspeople. Indeed, they seemed different from those who had haunted the area in the days of Jasper's Funhouse. Somehow, they seemed less threatening.

Less threatening, but the sight of one never failed to remind Dave of the night in the Funhouse, never failed to send chills crawling over his skin. Joan, he knew, had the same reaction.

When they reached the shore, she glanced back again, as if to make certain they hadn't been followed.

"Is the coast clear?" Dave asked.

"Looks okay."

She opened her side of the blanket as Dave eased against her. He lifted her sweatshirt above her breasts. He caressed them. Her skin was pebbled with goose bumps, her nipples standing erect. She moaned softly. "Let's find a place to spread the blanket," she whispered.

"Right out here in the open?"

She looked up and down the beach, then pointed at the lifeguard station a hundred yards or so to the north. "It's dark under there," she said.

Dave kissed her breasts, then drew the sweatshirt down. With the blanket wrapped around themselves, they walked over the hard-packed sand toward the patch of black shadow.

"It's going to be cold," Dave said.

"It's your job to keep me hot, fella."

"Well, I'll sure try."

"And I'll return the fav—"

A dark shape rose like a hump on the deck in front of the elevated lifeguard shack. Joan pressed herself hard against Dave's side. Her hand tightened on his hip.

The moonlit form dropped to the sand, stumbled, went down on its knees, then stood and began to shamble toward them.

"Oh, shit," Joan muttered.

It was a man. A troll. His wild tangle of hair and beard shone like snow under the pale moon. He wore a dark overcoat that looked many sizes too large for his skinny frame. The cuffs of his baggy trousers were rolled up. His white ankles were bare. One of his ragged sneakers had no laces, and flopped under his foot as he staggered closer.

He held out a hand.

"Let's get out of here," Dave said.

"Gimme a quarter?" The voice was harsh and whiny. It sounded too young to be coming from a white-haired troll. "Jes' a quarter? How's 'bout it, folks?"

"Give him something, Dave."

Dave's hand trembled as he took out his wallet. He felt sick, frightened, and angry that this damn intruder had ruined things. But he felt a little sorry for the guy too. He took out a five-dollar bill and gave it to the troll, being careful not to let the scrawny hand touch him.

"God bless ya! God bless bote a ya!"

He whirled away and scampered up the wooden stairs of the lifeguard station.

Dave and Joan hurried over the sand toward the distant stairway to the boardwalk. He could feel her shaking against him. "It would've been nice," he said.

"*Will* be nice. In our own bed."

"We can spread this old blanket on it and pretend we're on the beach."

"Leave the windows open."

"Let's take some sand along and make it authentic."

"Let's not."

Five whole bucks. Five smackaroonies.

God bless 'em.

He wondered who they were. They'd looked a little familiar. Maybe he'd seen them around someplace.

Could be, the gal'd been one of his nurses at the funny farm. He tried to picture her dressed in white, smiling and giving him pills.

Maybe that was it.

He shoved the bill into his shirt pocket. Dropping to his knees, he squinted at the boards of the platform.

He knew the spiders were there. He just couldn't see them.

Too dark, even with the moonlight.

From a deep pocket of his coat he took a can of insect spray. The white mist hissed from its nozzle. He crawled along, sweeping it back and forth, trying not to miss an inch of the deck.

"That'll getcha," he muttered. "Yeah! No way y'gonna get ol' Duke."

When he was sure it was safe, he slipped the can into his pocket. He took out a bottle of red wine. Holding it up to the moon, he shook it.

Still a few good swallows in there.

He popped the cork and began to drink.

Made in the USA
Monee, IL
15 April 2024

56612531R00233